Cary J. Lenehan is a former trades assistant, soldier, public servant, cab driver, truck driver, game designer, fishmonger, horticulturalist and university tutor — among other things. His hobbies include collecting and reading books (the non-fiction are Dewey decimalised), Tasmanian native plants (particularly the edible ones), medieval re-creation and gaming. Over the years he has taught people how to use everything from shortswords to rocket launchers.

He met his wife at an SF Convention while cosplaying and they have not looked back. He was born in Sydney before marrying and moving to the Snowy Mountains where they started their family. They moved to Tasmania for the warmer winters and are not likely to ever leave it. Looking out of the window beside Cary's computer is a sweeping view of Mount Wellington/Kunanyi and its range.

T0165051

Warriors of Vhast Series
published by
IFWG Publishing Australia

Intimations of Evil (Book 1)
Engaging Evil (Book 2)
Clearing the Web (Book 3)
Scouring the Land (Book 4)
Gathering the Strands (Book 5)

Warriors of Vhast Book 5

Gathering the Strands

by
Cary J Lenehan

This is a work of fiction. The events and characters portrayed herein are imaginary and are not intended to refer to specific places, events or living persons. The opinions expressed in this manuscript are solely the opinions of the author and do not necessarily represent the opinions of the publisher.

Gathering the Strands

Book 5, Warriors of Vhast

All Rights Reserved

ISBN-13: 978-1-925956-79-5

Copyright ©2021 Cary J Lenehan

This book may not be reproduced, transmitted, or stored in whole or in part by any means, including graphic, electronic, or mechanical without the express written consent of the publisher except in the case of brief quotations embodied in critical articles and reviews.

Printed in Times and LHF Essendine font types.

IFWG Publishing International
Gold Coast

www.ifwgpublishing.com

Foreword

Five books and we are nearly there as far as the main story is concerned. Now, with the shorter stories on Patreon going back thousands of years into the past, the chance of another series is looking more and more remote as it is, to my mind, unnecessary. Of course the stories will still need to be collected to put the rest of the story together, but we can hope.

The story this time is spread out and goes all over The Land. Those who have been looking at the maps in Patreon will be able to follow along in detail as people go through the places mentioned. It is my goal to get every place mapped, along with all the plants drawn and animals described. Hopefully, one day, these will get collected along with the recipes, the plants and animals, and the Tarot deck

I reiterate that the books only talk about one part of The Land and the areas around it. The Land is one of the seven continents of Vhast, and it is also the smallest of them. The Patreon stories also provide back story and historical context to the books, with tales running back over 10,000 years into the past to the creation of the world.

I thank you for reading my books and I hope that I continue to entertain you with my stories. If you have enjoyed what you have read, please keep going, share my world with your friends, and (please) post reviews. You would not believe how important these are to a writer, even a short one of a couple of lines. I also am happy to answer questions if you contact me via my website or writer page on Facebook.

Cary J. Lenehan
Hobart

A cast list and glossary of terms used in this novel can be found from page 353.

How do you thank someone for forty years of support and belief? Once again I show gratitude to my wife, Marjorie, for everything.

Sorry I cannot give much more than this, but at least you get to see the thanks that are due to my friend and beta reader Pip Woodfield for the help that she has also given me. She may know some parts of Vhast better than I do.

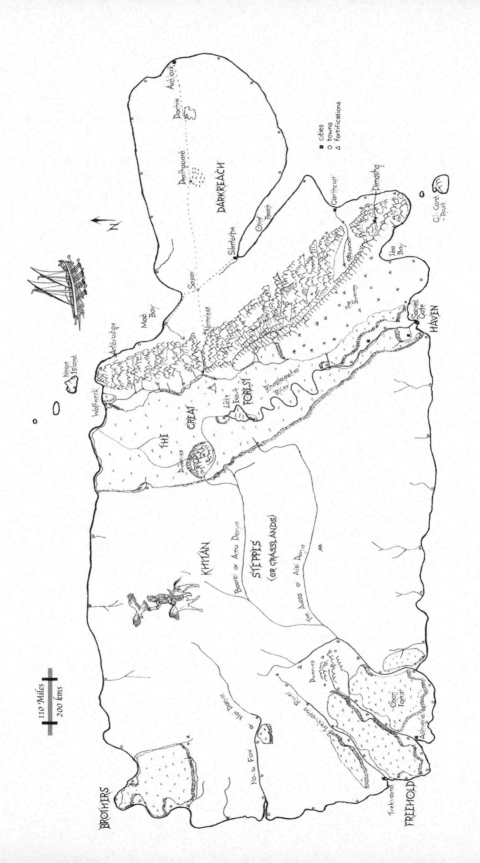

Tengeriin Sünsnüüd bidniig doosh ni tavidag
Bükhel büten bayalog övs deer. Tiim shüü
Emeel amidarch baigaa khümüüs ünegüi güideg
Muu yoryn sünsnüüdiig esergüütsekh
Sky spirits put us down
On all-encompassing rich grassland, yes
The Khitan[1] run free
Resist evil great spirits
Bid dairakh yostoi. Bid dairakh yostoi. Bid dairakh yostoi. Tiim shüü.
Tiim shüü
We must attack. We must attack. We must attack. Yes. Yes.
Khoyor umard arga khemjee avakhyg khüsdeg
Ovgiin arav no khajuu tiishee zogsoj baiv
Khoyor tangarag örgödög khümüüs unana
Bindii ner töriig doromjlokh bolno
Two totems want action
Ten of the clans stand aside
The two oath-keepers fall
Our honour is tainted
Bid dairakh yostoi. Bid dairakh yostoi. Bid dairakh yostoi. Tiim shüü.
Tiim shüü
We must attack. We must attack. We must attack. Yes. Yes.
Odoo suns bidniig dakhin duuddag
Bidnii övög deedsee bid getelgekh yostoi
Dakhiad Mori irne, nögöö ni nuugdmal kheveer baina
Mori dagaj, bid negdej, ajil khayakh yostoi
Now spirits again call on us all
We must redeem our ancestors
Again comes Horse, the other stays hidden
Following the Horse, we must join and strike
Bid dairakh yostoi. Bid dairakh yostoi. Bid dairakh yostoi. Tiim shüü.
Tiim shüü
We must attack. We must attack. We must attack. Yes. Yes.

---

1 Literally "people who live in the saddle"

Bison Clan

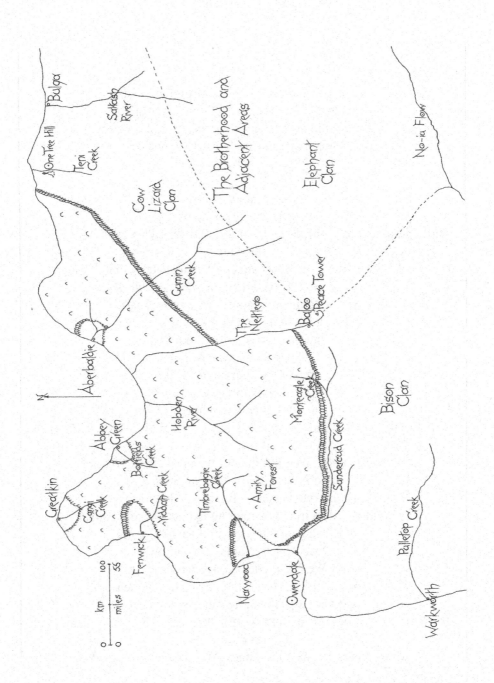

Daisagnalyg khoish tavij, bindii üüreg yum
Ert deer üyed Moritnuud sünsig aldav
Martakh ni bindii zovlong khöngövchildög
Bindii sanaj bui ichgüürtei tulgarson. Tiim shüü
Put aside feuds, take up our duty
In the past, Riders[2] failed the spirits
Forgetting eases our pain
Faced with shame we remember. Yes
Bid dairakh yostoi. Bid dairakh yostoi. Bid dairakh yostoi. Tiim shüü.
Tiim shüü
We must attack. We must attack. We must attack. Yes. Yes.
Sogtuu üyedee shiid. Dakhiad ukhaalag shiid
Tangarag örgöj, zogsokh esval unakh
Üzen Yadaltaag Düürgen baikh kheregtai
Üsleg düü narynkhaa khölnii dor butalsan
Decide when drunk. Decide again sober.
Take an oath, stand or fall
The Hate-Filled[3] need to be brought low
Crushed under the feet of fur siblings[4]
Bid dairakh yostoi. Bid dairakh yostoi. Bid dairakh yostoi. Tiim shüü.
Tiim shüü
We must attack. We must attack. We must attack. Yes. Yes.

Part of a song composed and sung often by Qorchi Narjee Khadagin,
a böö (shamanka) and ban (bard) on the way to the battle of One-
Tree Hill. It was first sung with her playing a Yoochin and with the
audience pounding the beat.

---

2 "Riders" is one of many names the Khitan call themselves
3 "Hate-filled" is the Khitan name for the Brotherhood
4 "Fur siblings" are the totem animals of a clan

The Lands of the Khitan

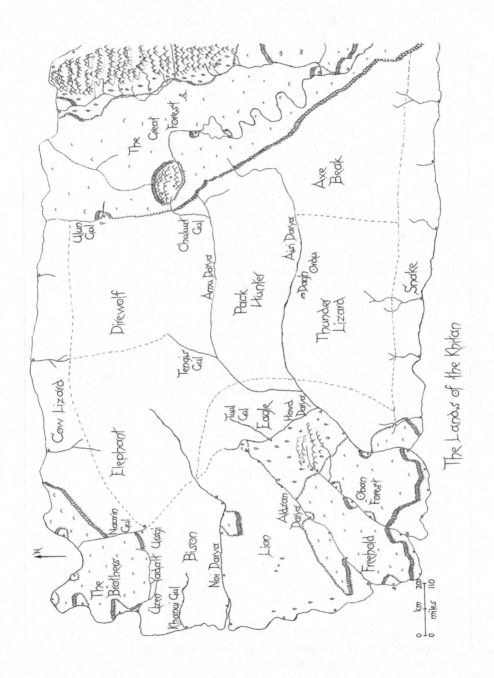

Chapter 1

Rani
21st Secundus, the Year of the Water Horse

*N*ow *that we have returned from our voyage south, it is time to once again view my cards for guidance as to what we Mice should do next. I am fairly sure that I know which way I want us to move next, but I am skilled in foretelling, and having some confirmation of what I think I know is always good, even if only for my own peace of mind.*

The question for me is: should I do this openly, performing my scrying before the whole village of Mousehole? No, it is not necessary. The others seem to be willing to follow what I ask of them without too many questions and this time I really do not want new information. I only want some clarification of my own thoughts.

Rani lit some incense, to help focus on the need for information; she took out her deck and shuffled the cards well, thinking carefully about what they should do subsequently as a group. Once she was comfortable, she began laying out the four cards on her table as she kept her thoughts focussed. Inhaling the perfume of camphor, she turned the cards over one by one and looked at them.

The first card showed a woman dressed in robes and seated on a stone chair. At her feet were piles made of sacks and mounds of produce. Some of the sacks had coins spilling from them. Behind her was a scene of a marketplace and in the top corners were two figures of robed women offering sheaves of corn.

The second card had come up before in dealings for the Mice. It showed a robed and blindfolded woman holding in one hand a jeweller's scale and in the other a sword with no tip. Above and behind her flew a huge grey owl.

The third card showed a sheaf of six swords while above them was an armsman striding out. He was arrayed for both war, with his weapons, and for travel. On his back he wore a pack and it had equipment hanging off it as if he would be camping in the wilds. There were words written in the corners of the card in Old Speech.

The last card showed a bearded Khitan man seated on a rearing horse, holding a sword in his hand. Behind him, standing on each side of him, were a lion and a representation of an elephant-headed man riding on a huge mouse.

That is an unusual set of cards that face me. The Queen of Talents usually denotes security and richness and a rich place for new growth, and she stands in the position of the environment that we are in. However, she is also, with the connotations of harvest, the ruler of the season of autumn.

The Mice can be said to be in a secure place. We are certainly rich, and the sound of children and working coming into my study from the village outside shows that new growth is around me, but I also have a strong feeling that the approaching season is a major part of the environment that we are acting within.

The reading of the Tarot is not like magic. It is not exact and predictable. Like all other ways of foretelling, it merely serves as a focus for the reader's thoughts; otherwise a novice with a book would be as accurate as a person who has been doing it for many years. It takes time to learn to listen to one's inner feelings.

Justice is in the place of the enquirer. Usually the card means that right will prevail over wrong and evil will be vanquished and feel retribution, but here it could only mean that we are simply the tools of Justice and not just acting for ourselves. Within me I feel that there is no other possible interpretation.

Her fingers lingered over the third card. *The six of swords lies in the position of the way ahead. It is possibly the most predicable card that I could have seen. The words in the corners say "courage" and "travel". It has the obvious meanings of long and often difficult travel, and being of the suit of swords, it will also mean that there is warfare at the end of the travel.*

Changing her gaze to the Knight of Swords, sitting in its place as the answer, brought a smile to her lips. *The card is an injunction to act quickly and boldly. Behind the young man are the lion of courage and a depiction of Ganesh, the remover of obstacles, riding on his fabled mount, the mouse. Could it be any clearer? We, the Mice are surely a part of the answer.*

For me there is now no doubt to be seen here. Although in our valley we are safe from the world, and comfortable and growing steadily, we cannot allow ourselves to just rest. As the agents of a personified Justice we must sally forth again and act boldly and decisively. Whatever we have to do must be done before autumn is finished.

She stopped in her musings. *I am being called from somewhere else in the house. I hear that it is time for us to have dinner. I will have to do the rest of my planning tomorrow. But now at least I am very sure within myself that the way is clear.*

Rani
22nd Secundus

The next day Rani sat relaxing and thinking in her study, listening to the normal sounds of the village outside. *Between what was said in Wolfneck and what I saw yesterday in my readings, it is obvious that we have a time limit bearing on our activities.*

We must get to Neron Island before winter arrives in order to try and save those who had fled the priests of these so-called Old Gods and to get their help against those holding the island. This gives us a little under five months. I will talk to Olympias and find out how long it will take to get the River Dragon *around to the north, and how many crew she will need with her to safely sail it there.*

I have now seen the boats that they use in Wolfneck, and despite how Astrid claims they sail safely in them even through the ice to the Northern Waste, I am not going to trust my people to them in the northern seas. As far as I am concerned, they are far too frail-looking and uncomfortable.

I had been going to keep it to myself, but I really do need to let this reading become more widely known in the village. The others need to realise just why we are acting as we are. I must stop just ordering people about. The more they know, the better they can give me advice. Damn that Astrid. She keeps saying that.

However, we have to wait for as long as we can. Before we go out to the edge of everything, we must think about cutting off the patterns in Freehold and destroying the centre of the disease of evil in the Brotherhood. Both lie at the centre of power in The Land and can easily strike at our friends or us.

Thinking of the Six of Swords, both also represent travel and battle in their own right. It will do no good for us to send people away from the valley to the northern ocean if we were to fail at either of these hurdles. Each of them presents a unique problem and will be difficult. Either of them are tasks that could kill us.

We have survived and succeeded so far by acting on our strengths and avoiding our weaknesses. In the next set of conflicts, we will have the advantage of speed of manoeuvre, but we will suffer greatly from a lack of numbers. We need to look at what we can do to avoid a full-on confrontation until we can correct that.

For Freehold we will possibly face greater mages than ourselves, and certainly stronger priests. And if any of our priests are caught, they will be killed as heretics. Any of our people from the Swamp who have kept their religion will die as Infidels… It is even possible that, if caught, my Theo-dear and I will be killed by the ignorant just for the sake of our 'unnatural' relationship.

Still we must somehow get to the places that are called Khmel and Topudle. I am quite sure that Astrid is right again and that these are Camelback and Toppuddle. We will have to travel a long way to get to either of them. I have looked up these places in our books.

The village of Camelback is named after a long rocky island that lies across a wide channel. It has the shape of a sleeping camel. At least now that I have been to Darkreach I know what a camel looks like. It seems that the island stretches from a lumpy head along a long neck into two peaks and then has a short tail.

If what I have is right, the village has no real dock but the island, which had no one living on it, is often used as a shelter from storms and strong winds and it even shelters the beach, the only sea access for the village, from storms that come from off the ocean. The island makes it a well-used and safe harbour even though it is really only a shallow bay.

The village is located right near the southwest tip of The Land. It is nearly as far from Mousehole as it is possible to be. It is a centre for harvesting timber and a lot of the masts and spars used in Freehold come from there, being shipped by land or over the beach. It has nothing else to commend it.

She was trying to work out why there was a pattern there when she realised the reason. *The important thing is the rock itself and not the village. The rock exists in the very centre of the sea trade around the west coast. Any boat that is going from Trekvarna to Ashvaria, the two cities of Freehold, must pass straight by it.*

Not only does any ship going around the coast have to pass it by, but a vessel could even come there easily from a western land. No vessel goes the long way past Darkreach, so they all travel that way past Freehold. Any ship passing by could stop there without question simply by faking a rigging problem, or to buy a spar. A boat could even fish in near the island and put ashore for water or just to cook. It is ideal as a nexus.

That isolation will, however, work against them for our enemy. There probably will not be a guard set on the pattern. It will be hard for them to protect something covertly in a spot like that without being seen. I am sure that they will just rely upon its isolation, and perhaps some sense of fear of the location that they have instilled.

Although we cannot risk the River Dragon *near so many Freehold ships and mages—and even without asking Olympias, I am sure that it will take too* long to get it there and back—we can come in from the sea with the saddles and check the island first. If the pattern is there we can simply wait and get rid of it the next day.

If it is in or near the village itself the issue is nearly as simple. From everything we have available in the way of information, it seems that the place is possibly as small a village as Wolfneck. If we strike fast and hard, then we can seize and hold it for long enough to do what we must and then fly out.

The only problem is getting there in the first place. It is a very long way from our home and, even with the saddles; it will take us several days of travel in order to reach it. We will be tired and stiff and will probably need to rest before doing anything if it is in the village, although we can use the island for that.

Toppuddle is a very different problem for us. It is on a very different scale. Instead of being a small village, it is a major town in Freehold. It sits near the South-West Mountains on the Oban River and is upstream of Ashvaria. From what we know it has many thousands of people living in it. It will be hard to intimidate or take over such a large place.

We have no real local knowledge, not like we have in Haven, and there is sure to be an Inquisition into our faith if we are caught. It will not matter how good a case we make for what we are doing, we will all still be reluctantly condemned for other "offences". Large towns have lots of soldiers, many mages, and large numbers of priests.

Between Toppuddle and Camelback lies what the Freeholders call the Great Forest. I was taught to call it the Oban Forest. From our maps it actually covers less land than Mousehole claims an interest in as a village, even if it does cover a sizeable part of Freehold, but the people of that realm are still arrogant enough to call it the Great Forest.

We can probably fly over it with a degree of impunity if we move both fast and high. Mages usually only fly if they have cause to, and if we move at night it is likely that no one will see or sense us and come to find out what we are doing. That will solve the problem of travel.

I think that finding somewhere to hide while we search for and then destroy the pattern is a problem we just have to face when it arrives. We cannot plan for something we know so little about. The Knight of Swords tells us to be bold, and that is just what we must be.

We will have to leave the carpet behind. It is far too slow. Even with the saddles, which travelled a little faster than a dragon, it will take three long days or nights of travel. Taking the carpet with us will more than double that flight time.

That will increase our risk of discovery, and if we are fleeing after being detected, cut us back to a speed where many mages—and more importantly all *of the powerful ones who fly—will be able to catch us.*

We can stay at Glengate and then, especially if we take Thord along (and he is probably wanting to get away from Dwarvenholme for a while anyway) we can then stay with the Dwarves in the southwest on the second night. The Dwarves know what we Mice are fighting for. They should give us a safe place to stay and rest at least.

For the third stage we can travel at night down the Oban Forest and sleep during the day somewhere near the coast in the woods. The next night we can cross the coast and then sweep up to find what is at this Camel Island.

If we reverse that process when we return then, if we need, we can lie up in the South-West Mountains and come down from there each night to locate and then eventually destroy the pattern near Toppuddle.

She thought about who should go and kept coming back to the original questers. *They have all been in it since the start and, although there are more challenges ahead, they deserve to see this hopefully penultimate clearing in The Land through to completion. This time all the babies can be left behind and if anyone is pregnant again, I don't know about it yet.*

She sighed. *While I am doing this, I might get time to think about how we are going to tackle the problem of this Brotherhood of All Believers. What an arrogant name. Just how does a tiny and remote village declare war on a whole religion? Not only is it that, but attacking this religion is the same thing as taking on a heavily armed nation.*

We are going to have to somehow attack this place with the aim of destroying what are possibly its holiest and best-guarded sites. Oh Kartikeya, of all your teaching, why did I miss the class on how to go about this, when it was held as a part of my training? I am sure that I must have just slept through the clear instruction on such a case

Theodora

In her study, Theodora was pondering her failures so far. *Wolfneck and the Swamp were easy. We struck hard and fast and there had been little magical interference. In the Swamp, our pursuers were just arrogant and stupid. Haven was another issue. We lost Ayesha and only a super-human effort on the part of Father Christopher had brought her back.*

We might even have lost them both and it is because my husband and I failed. We were just there to take on any mage that fled. We were not able to protect our people. I need to invest in some protective spells for my people. I am not only the ruler of the village, and in many ways its mother, but I am also its senior mage. It is thus doubly, or even triply my job.

We will soon be going places where, unlike Wolfneck, we will not necessarily be the strongest casters around and where we will definitely be outnumbered. I am sure that my husband will still try and work out a way to get us to strike unexpectedly, but this may not always be possible—nor will surprise always be enough to protect us.

It didn't take her very long to work out what had to be done, despite every aspect of the two spells that were going to be needed against her favoured realms. *From the signs involved, it would be easier for my beauty to make them, but she lacks both the power and the time. I have both. I just need to work out how to make it easier.*

In our last three adventures outside we used up far too many wands and arrows and now we must replace them for the next time that we go. It is always a problem when you give a magical item to someone who is not a mage to use. They will happily bring it into play without too much thought for its replacement. But, in most cases they were needed.

Now it seems that whenever we are at home there is always a lot more casting to be done. The nights when we both go to bed without having used up all the mana that we have are rare already and they are likely to get even rarer.

From what I have heard many village mages will only cast a spell or two a week. I can do several each day. It is tiring, but it is paying off for my mental strength, even if we are sometimes left too tired to enjoy each other's bodies as much as we would like. I will be glad when our apprentices are stronger and can render more help, and indeed, make their own magic.

Rani
23rd Secundus

Next day Rani took the carpet and some saddles up to Dwarvenholme with Harald along as an attendant, and with Verily and Aziz and some of the school children. *For my plans for the school to succeed, the children have to learn to meet the neighbours and to get used to all of the different cultures around them. Most have never even seen one Dwarf.*

The girls from Gil-Gand-Rask, the new children from the Swamp, the three Bear children and Menas from Darkreach were taken along with Tiffany—*she is included, seeing that she is from Evilhalt and so speaks Dwarven.* This would be the first visit outside for any of the children, apart from Fear.

I would take them all if I could, but we need to fit Thord on the carpet to come back. *We need to get Ruth to begin using the carpet, and taking the children to each of the neighbours and even out on the* River Dragon. *If they are going to learn about all the cultures of The Land, they have to see them at home as well as hear about them.*

As I thought, Thord is glad to get away for a while. He had gone back to exploring the mountains and tracing out the aqueducts and tunnels and all the other places that were attached to Dwarvenholme, but he was more than ready to go back to having some real adventure. *I think it best to take Mayor Thorgrim into my confidence.*

He equipped her with letters, both to carry to the Dwarves for his own purposes, and another asking for their co-operation in the task. Although traditionally the Dwarves interfered little in the ways of men, and expected the reverse to be true in return, any matter that involved the Masters and their patterns they deemed to be one that very closely concerned them.

Seeing that the Masters have once taken over Dwarvenholme, if they have time they might be able to do it again. So, it seems that every single trace of them and their work needs to be eliminated from the world for the long-term safety of the Dwarves.

"If'n need be," said Thorgrim, "you a' should be able to call on all t' Dwarves t'ere to attack Toppuddle in order to destroy t' pattern and to have 'em obey you."

I am surprised. I have obviously grossly underestimated the strength of feeling that they have over this issue. Such an attack could result in their towns being destroyed, and yet the Mayor thinks that they will be ready to risk it. It is a pity that I cannot use them to help against the Brotherhood.

Rani was suddenly struck by a thought. *If the Dwarves feel this strongly, how will the Khitan feel about the matter? It is not only the Dwarves who hold their honour as being important. I should have realised, from what I have seen in the village…even now from Bianca…that the Khitan might have the same ideas.*

If the Dwarves can be launched at Freehold, maybe I can send the Khitan against the Brothers. The Masters have long been laying the blame of their banditry on the Khitan and trespassing on the land they think of as theirs, and the Brotherhood is on the verge of pushing out of their enclave and trying to take control of more of the plains.

Was what the Masters have done in their name a serious enough blot on their honour to get them to help us Mice? I will have to ask Hulagu about this when I return home from here. That may be the solution that we need. We use one culture to destroy another.

From the point of view of the children, the visit was a huge success. None of them had seen anything like the vast caverns, which were now just starting to return to the light and noise that they should have. The noise was increased greatly with only nine exuberant human, or at least part-human, young even if the halls still echoed emptily. *It will be many centuries before they are full, but it is apparent that they are starting to see life once more.*

Mayor Thorgrim Baldursson

*W*hat these Mice are doing is very important to us, and not just for getting rid of these so-called Masters and returning lost Dwarvenholme to us. Watching and listening to these children from several lands chattering in their polyglot way shows me the way ahead. It may be time for us to take more of a role in the wider world instead of just focussing on ourselves.*

Even the Crown-finder shows us that, damn him. He may be an annoying fool in many ways, but we need more like him if we are to come out of our caves and take our rightful place in the world. There are very few who are like Thord to lead us down this new path. We need to look at changing how we meet and deal with the outside races.

If I look around carefully, I might find one or two young and promising Dwarves to send to this school that they are setting up. When they grow up to lead us, it will not be like we were in the past. We will not be left behind to stagnate and be ignored as the world around us changes. I think that I need to get serious and think about bargaining on the subject of price.

Verily I Rejoice in the Lord Tiller
that night

*G*uk has arrived at Dwarvenholme on one of his trips. It is good for Aziz to see and talk with another Hob. It turns out that he is still the only trader operating between the Hobs and the Dwarves, and he and his family only stop a night at each end on their trips between the two. It seems that they have no time for longer stays.*

He is already getting very wealthy and now has a string of horses, people working for him and a home at each end of his trip. There are always some of his children at each home and others on the road with him. He even now has a junior wife in Dwarvenholme as well as his first (and now senior) wife in Dhargev. He has two wives? This is the first that I have heard of this custom.

He is very pleased with the report that Rani gave him on his daughter

Ząmrat and is even more delighted to see that his daughter now has people from many lands as fellow students. He will talk about this and his status will grow. He is glowing. The isolation of the Hobs from all the other people of the world is ending, and he is a part of it.

Guk proudly showed Verily and Aziz his new silver crucifix that he wore to show that he was one of the converts that the missionaries had made. *He has predicted that almost all the Hobs of the tribe will be Christian within a year. He said that many were waiting for the first Hob priest to come back from Greensin and then the Hobs were thinking of going to go back to the Hobs of the north to try and convert them.*

At least he admits that the priests want them to wait longer, until they have enough military support to protect them from the larger tribe. He dismisses this as being a minor concern. I do have to admit that my husband's people never seem to lack courage, even if it does often land them in trouble. I suppose that is one reason they do not have their own Kingdom.

Aziz

*M*y *yųmųkimşe seems to have missed that Hobs can have more than one wife. I have had to be very quick to point out to her I have not been hiding this from her. I have not raised the matter, as it has not seemed to be of any importance to me. I pointed out that any warrior society, where it is mainly the men who die, must have a chance for all of the women to have children when there is more often going to be many more women than there are men.*

Even we Mice do the same. I had to point out that I, personally, have no interest in having a second wife and besides, the man usually has little say in the matter. The decision lies with the senior wife. At least Guk confirmed this to her. It may not have helped that he went on to suggest that my status would be higher if I had a second wife as well.

I had to hurriedly point out that I can make a suggestion, if I want to, but that is just a suggestion. It is up to the senior wife to decide if she wants another set of hands to help her. I am not sure if Verily is actually angry with me or whether she is just teasing me, but it is best for me to be sure about these things.

Theodora
in Mousehole 23rd Secundus

With the help of Eleanor, Theodora produced the first of a series of broaches that were made of tin and garnets. It depicted a tiny mouse holding a shield and would, several times each day, protect the wearer from a fairly strong spell.

I regret that it is not a perfect solution to the problem, but it will certainly help if the wearers are only in a raid and not actually in a full-blown battle. Even in a battle it will help if there are not too many spells cast at the people who wear them.

Before we go on to Skrice I will try and work on something better. For now, it was easier to make this first one than I thought it should have been. I am sure that I can now make one of them every second day and not every third as I first thought. Perhaps, after so long back in Ardlark without change, I have grown again. I feel that I have.

This first one is for Father Christopher. Above all else I need to keep our best healer alive. The second one goes to my husband. She should not rely on her natural protection and she will be the one who will be the biggest target for another mage. Eleanor will have to work on starting the rest while we are away in Freehold, and I will finish making as many of them as I can before we leave to attack the Brotherhood.

Chapter II

Rani
24th Secundus, in Mousehole

*N*ow *that we have returned from Dwarvenholme with Thord we can start preparing to go out to Freehold. My wife says that Twelfth Night is nearly upon us. I think that we will stay here until then and leave the next morning. I could do with some bed-time with her before we have enforced abstinence again.*

Armour was seen to, weapons were sharpened, magic prepared, potions and other needed equipment were made ready. Once it was known what was afoot, there were a series of complaints brought to Rani from those who were not going.

Some have not been on any raids at all and are feeling left out, while others, usually wrongly, feel that they can be more useful than some who are going. I have tried pointing out that most of those who will be staying are needed, either on the River Dragon or in Mousehole working on the rebuilding. It does not seem to have noticeably cut down on the grumbling. I wonder if other rulers have these problems.

Basil Tornikes
25th Secundus, the Feast of Twelfth Night

*F*ather Christopher has expressed several concerns to me in a letter. He does not realise that Metropolitan Cosmas and I are already in discussion as to when there should be a new Suffragan Bishop created, a junior position responsible for the Mountains, and whether it was too soon for such a move yet.

I have sent a note through the Gap to Metropolitan Tarasios in Ardlark, and to the far south to Metropolitan Demetrios in Bridgecap asking their opinions. Cosmas and I are both also curious, now that the faith is reconstituting itself, and might be seen as being able to push back against the schismatics to the west, whether it is time for us to actually meet in person and perhaps for one of us to be appointed overall Patriarch.

Conceivably the time is propitious. Not only do we have missionaries with the tribe of the Cenubarkincilari, but maybe we also have a real chance coming up of saving the people of the Brotherhood from their heresy. Demetrios has already answered.

Tarasios

*M*y *reply to this Basil Tornikes is now on its way back with a delegate and an escort and I have proposed a meeting. Hrothnog has shared with me Theodora's comments on the state of the west, and with Hrothnog's permission, the escort are all retired soldiers. They are men who will, I am sure, cause quite a panic in Evilhalt as they pass through.*

They are all volunteers who are going west to add themselves to the numbers of the Basilica Anthropoi to defend the Faith. There are enough retired men without any ties who were keen to go west, or at least who are curious enough, to add another four files to the ranks. With all that I have sent they can double the numbers that are in the field.

With some fortune I may be able to get more to follow these. Almost all so far are kataphractoi, heavy cavalry of long experience and of good behaviour, and they brought their own monk-priests with them. The rest are kynigoi and now they can have their own scouts with them without people taking the armour of their horses. If what I hear is right, they might be needed in the months ahead.

It was good to send those retired men. I have not told the other prelates, but I am glad to be about to follow them up with another three younger men towards the Mice. I suspect that I have a lot more people available that I can convince to move about than the other two do. I also have more girls whom I wish to send, but I think it more diplomatic to send some men first.

With the Mice having the saddles, I am not sure how many they still need, but good cavalry are always useful, even if they end up having to find their own brides. Hrothnog has told me about sending Olympias to the village. She is a start, but he is not used to thinking on such scales.

From what I know, these Mice will have too few people to man the ship for a protracted period, even with an experienced captain, so I am sending three couples of Insakharl with the cavalry as well. They all understood that they are intended to be a part of the village and no longer a part of Darkreach, even if it is to be the ship part of the village.

Although they are young, they are all experienced sailors used to working the coastal trade of Darkreach, even if they are not now from the navy. He thought over his plans. *Yes, that will do for now. Next summer I will see about sending more girls. There are always girls who can do with rescuing…and even some men.*

Theodora
26th Secundus

I hate early morning starts. Our horses are getting neglected. The same ten are setting out now that left Evilhalt over a year before, but in many ways, we are a very different group of people. For a start there is the matter of our partners.

Thord is the only one of us who now lacks a companion, and even he has his mother, whichever one of the two that is (I have met them both but am still not sure) searching for the right one for him. Stefan has two wives waving him off and Hulagu has one woman with him and two waving him farewell…and yet he is married to none of them.

I am married, and that is a surprise. About the only predictable relationship when we set out might have been Astrid and Basil, and that had only just begun. Second, we are all riding, even though we are riding through the air. Even Astrid flies now instead of walking.

We are leaving behind a number of babies in the care of fosterers, and then there were all of the other changes. I am on better terms with my granther than I have ever been in my life. Astrid has killed the man she had fled from in fear and loathing and feels free enough to kiss an Emperor in public. Bianca has taken her revenge on the bandits, and Christopher has joined the world instead of having just left a monastery. Ayesha seems to have abandoned some of her vows at least, although I never can be sure about her.

Basil is about the only one of us that is, in essence, unchanged. He still stays in the background quietly, only now he uses his wife as cover so that he is, in many ways, even more invisible than when I first saw him. As for Rani, well…However far my husband thinks that she has come, her journey is really only beginning. Theodora smiled to herself and unconsciously rubbed her stomach.

Chapter III

Astrid
27th Secundus

*G*lengate lies in a large clearing near the edge of the Great Forest with *assarts hidden around its edges…that is, it lies inside the edges of the real Great Forest, not the area that the Freeholders give the same name to, but which everyone else calls the Oban Forest, or even the Little Forest. I have looked at maps and can be sure of this.*

For us in the rest of The Land, the Great Forest is the wooded area that runs from the north at my old home in Wolfneck right across the land to Haven in the south, changing from pines and firs to deciduous or eucalypt, and lastly to wet broadleaf evergreen forests and jungles as it rolls south in its uninterrupted path.

Travelling here I got to put into practice the navigation that I have learnt. Glengate lies just inside the edge of the forest at a ford on the Aissa River on one of the most usual paths from Erave Town to Freehold across the plains that ends at Frosthill in the west. The northern route goes direct to Evilhalt, but the more southern one ends at Glengate before continuing on.

There is a second set of tolls on this southern route, but also a far shorter transit across the plains. Traders tend to balance the two. According to what I have learnt, the people of Glengate crowd within its strong inner stone walls, and it has a second outer set of lighter walls enclosing campsites for trade caravans and stock.

The people living there do not place too much trust in either their neighbours, the Khitan, or in the caravans that provide much of their income. Many farm in the cleared area around the village while others go to hidden assarts in the forest and even mine amber nearby, but most retire secure inside their village at night.

That we are flying is a cause of great excitement to the villagers. It looks like a nest of ants that someone has kicked. Flying is rarely seen, and when it was it was only with a rare carpet or a broom or with individual mages travelling for short distances on their own. The last is all I ever saw until I left home.

I am sure that some rumours about flying warriors who treat the air as the Khitan treat the plains have come to the village from Greensin to the north and the villages of Lake Erave to the east, and have been dismissed as confabulation, but seeing us in the sky above their own village is another thing altogether, and they cannot easily put it aside.

People are not slow to realise that a flying army, even such a small one as this, renders their walls useless. As far as our other exploits are concerned, Thord says that the routes of the Dwarves from both the northwest and southwest tend to avoid the village, and so few people will believe the rumours about Dwarvenholme. They will regard them as mere tales as well.

Rani said that we should treat this as a private trip, and so headed us straight for the Sparrow and Bull, the best tavern in the village. However, given the fuss when we arrived, I knew that it would be only a few minutes after we put the saddles away before we had an "invitation" to visit the Mayor of Glengate. I was right as usual. She still does not understand villages.

Astrid
soon after

*A*imee Tate, the Mayor of Glengate, is an older woman. From what I found out in the tavern, a retired and successful trader, and one who is experienced and capable of dealing with the usual run of visitors to the town. I don't think, however, that we count as the usual run of visitors.

We are travelling in full battle array as we are not sure what lies ahead of us, and so Rani, Theodora and Ayesha are fully accoutred, even if they might later doff their armour when they actually come to do anything. The only people who are not wearing at least mail are Basil, Hulagu and Bianca, and if any persons know how to tell apart such a rare type of leather, they are all wearing different thicknesses of dragon-hide. At any rate it has an exotic appearance.

In Hulagu's case it is the solid lamellar of a heavy cavalryman, and my husband's and Bianca's jerkins are of thinner leather and more tailored as jerkins and trews. For Bianca, the profusion of blades she always carries, and the Khitan cut of what she wears, makes it unlikely that she is just a trader.

For Basil it just looks…severe and official…even if exactly what officialdom it represents is not clear. It looks sexy on him though.

As we all follow the messenger the villagers stand aside in the street. I don't even have to smile. Even Father Christopher looks more martial than theological. One bystander looks sharply at us as we pass, but even I can tell that he is a mage anyway. He is just reacting to the feel of the magic passing him by.

Most people who can afford to own at least a single magical item of some sort. A few wealthy ones might have two or three. Some of those passing him have six or more items on them, even counting a quiver of arrows, or a pouch full of wands as only one item. The mage has probably not felt so much magic in one place in his life.

Unlike Evilhalt or Erave Town, Glengate lacks an office for its Mayor. It seems that she does town business where she can, as is done in Wolfneck. In this case it is in the school of the church of Saint Menna. No children are in the school, even though Twelfth Night is past. Unlike in Mousehole, where school goes for most of the day in one form or another, it is probably too late in the afternoon for this more normal village school. They often only run for the morning.

The Mice were shown into a room where the Mayor was attended by two guards. *They are obviously professionals from the way they stand. She seems surprised that we have all arrived. Her outnumbered guards each stand there nervously without their weapons being drawn, but with a hand on the pommels.*

With her are a priest and a pair of other people, who are probably standing with her for support or to give advice. One, a woman, has a long rectangular pouch on her belt that is similar to those that both Rani and Theodora have at theirs and that look to be about the right size for holding some wands. She is probably a mage, but the other, a man with a sword at his side, has no obvious profession, although his clothes betray a certain sense of style and colour that the others lack, and he holds himself confidently as he watches us coming in.

"I had asked for your leader to come and see me," the Mayor said in Hindi. *She is looking from one to the other…but mainly at me.* "Whom should I talk to and what language do you use". *Although the armour of the mages is the most elaborate, I am in the lead. With my size and build, a set of mail on my body and a helm on my head with my braids descending from under it and armed the way I am with just a spear, I make an impressive front person, especially when I smile. She is confused about us. Thord, Hulagu and Rani may have a clear origin, the rest of us do not.*

"We have reason to be cautious when we do not know where we are. So, we all decided to come." Astrid moved aside as she spoke. "This tongue is only native to one of us, but we can all speak it and it is fine for us to talk in, if you are happy with it. I am Astrid the Cat."

"Let me introduce the Princesses Rani and Theodora," she continued. "They are both potent mages and have the honour to be our rulers in the village of Mousehole in the Southern Mountains. We happen to be passing through your village on a quest, and we are just seeking a peaceful passage and a night's rest."

"I have never heard of you or of your village," said the Mayor. "Who are you really and what do you want?"

"We are who Astrid says we are," said Theodora. "You may not have heard of us and our village, but that is because its former rulers tried very hard for you not to know. We have seized the village from them only a bit over a year ago and we have, for reasons of our own, not been loud in letting this be known."

There is an increase in the awareness of the two guards. It looks like Theodora noticed as well as she is hurrying on. "I am sure that you were aware of the problems with caravans disappearing that existed up to a year or so ago." *She has paused until there were some nods of acknowledgment from her listeners.*

"They were caused by the people we defeated," continued Theodora. "You might ask your local Khitan tribe, the Pack Hunters. They, along with the Dire Wolves, helped us wipe them out by defeating most of their warriors just north of here."

"The Dire Wolves are not local to this area and we have not heard of this tale from any visiting Pack Hunters," said the Mayor.

"Perhaps you didn't ask them. We do not always hear all of what happens all the time either, but you will remember how caravans were not arriving and now, by the look of your outer bailey, they are doing so again. The Khitan regard such matters as private to themselves unless you need to know about them."

The Mayor is looking at our Khitan. Both Hulagu and Bianca are nodding. "I noticed that there were a small group of Khitan among those in the outer area. I am not sure of their totem...but you could go and ask them. Tell them that Hulagu of the Dire Wolves and Bianca—"

"—of the Horse" interjected Hulagu.

"—are with us," finished Theodora without pause. "As for the rest of us... we are from all over this land and are on a destined mission. It may sound a little strange to you, but there has been a battle going on for some time that most of The Land know nothing of." She waved her hand.

"You can send to Metropolitan Basil in Greensin for more details if you wish. He is aware of this battle and we consult with him regularly. We must eliminate the Masters of the bandits. They are a form of undead and yet also powerful mages. They hold many men in thrall as their willing servants and these men do evil in return for power and wealth."

Theodora is looking at those in front of her; I think to gauge their reaction. None of them look too believing. What I can see of the village power in front of me provides scarce challenge to us, although the villagers probably do not realise that. I could possibly defeat them all on my own, including the mage if I move fast.

Theodora continued. "We destroyed the first of them when we found Dwarvenholme and we cleansed it for the Dwarves. You may not have heard of it here, but the Dwarves are returning to their ancient seat now."

The man behind the Mayor leaned forward and touched her sleeve. She turned her head to him as he spoke. "I have heard of this from a Dwarf. He was more than a little merry at the time and I thought him imagining things when he told me the tale." He looked now at Thord. "If it is true, he gave me a name. What is your name, if you are the one he named Crown-Finder?"

"I am the Crown-Finder and my name is Thord," was the proud reply.

The man nodded, and he turned again to the Mayor. "It agrees with what I was told. I thought that he was drunk or crazed. I guess that I should have paid more attention to his tale. I will now have to get someone else to teach it to me."

"I will do that tonight," said Thord proudly.

The Mayor grunted as if perhaps half convinced by what they said, but only half. "Do you have any other proof?" she asked.

Rani

"**P**roof is not something we are usually asked for. That we are powerful mages should be obvious." She waved in the direction of the village priest. "Your priest should have a good idea by now if we are good or evil. He may question Father Christopher if he wishes. It is almost time for the Hesperinos service anyway and most of us wish to attend it."

"We had hoped for something to eat before we went, but we will not have time for that now. Perhaps if you care to join us in the Sparrow and Bull after the service, we will get one of our bards to tell you the full tale. You may find it convincing."

"One of your bards?" interrupted the man who had spoken earlier, somewhat surprised. *Even I know that out in the general world bards, by the nature of their finding work, are often solitary people and rarely travel in packs.*

Rani nodded and waved in the direction of her wife and then Ayesha. "We only have two of them with us at present that are really professional, although our village has many more entertainers than that."

"Neil, stop interrupting," said the Mayor. "Neil is the only permanent bard in the village," she explained. "I will agree to accept that invitation and we will see you later."

"Do you go to Hesperinos often?" asked the priest pointedly as they started to leave.

"Most days we go to that and to Orthros as well. Frequently many of us go to Apodeipnon before retiring. When you rely on the prayers of a priest as much as we have to when we are on our quests, it is sensible to pay attention to what he says at other times."

"Although I was married in a Christian fashion, I am not a Christian, but I still attend the services. My wife…" *That provoked a shocked expression on several faces… It is time to change tack and wave off his questions.* "Just wait until tonight. Be assured that the Metropolitan Basil knows what we do and has given his approval of our union and of our deeds. So do the Metropolitans Cosmas and Tarasios."

She received a blank look on mentioning the second name and sighed. *We do have to start right at the very beginning with the explanations, don't we?* "Please wait until tonight," Rani said patiently. "There is a lot that we have to tell you. I assure you that it will all become clear once we are finished with it."

Rani
that night

When Rani came downstairs it was obvious that rumours of what was happening that night had spread through the village, and the best tavern in Glengate was packed. *Not only are all the Mice there, and the Mayor and her advisors, but also Hulagu has brought a group of Khitan into the tavern. He and Bianca are sitting with them as old friends, and there are others as well.*

When she approached, she was told that the group was headed by Kāhina's cousin, Malik, who also happened to be in the village selling furs, and that Tzachaz and Uzun were with them.

Good, I will leave them alone in their corner. From what I have heard we have at least one set of reliable messengers, people who know of our story, and will believe our tale and will carry it for us. There is at least one source who can tell the Clans of our attack on the Brotherhood. We may yet have allies there. She realised then what she wanted the people of Glengate to do for them.

As well as the Khitan there were some traders and perhaps their guards present. *The origin of most is clear from their dress. Whether we like it or not, the story will now make its way to Freehold. Every available piece of space between these groups is filled with villagers, and it looks like several of the locals have been drafted to work the night in the tavern and to help serve the influx of customers.*

Astrid, with her flair for drama, will take charge of the night. If we want to achieve anything, we need to make a big impression and Astrid can be relied upon to do that. We are all in a tavern and yet she still has kept her spear in her hand and has not taken her mail off either. The mail does very little to disguise the swell of her breasts under it.

Astrid moved to the centre of the floor—between some tables, the only clear spot in the room—and stood there with her two long blonde braids hanging down her sides, striking the floor three times with the butt of her spear before calling for silence.

The martial effect is spoiled somewhat by the large tankard she is holding in the other hand, but it must have been fairly empty. She waves it around as she speaks without spilling anything. By Saraswati, if anything, it makes Astrid look even more a warrior woman. Perhaps it is a deliberate look that Astrid has taken after all.

When she had everyone's attention, Astrid looked around the room and spoke. "I am Astrid the Cat. I was born in Wolfneck in the far north, but I now live in the village of Mousehole in the Mountains. Tonight, you are going to hear how that came to be. You will hear the story as a tale but remember as you listen that this is not a story from the past. Remember that the people that are in the story are sitting here before you and that the story is still happening."

As she spoke, she waved her spear around in one hand to point the people out so that the watchers could see who they were. *In such a crowd the point of the long and wicked spear casually sweeping around the room past their noses causes some consternation, but Astrid is ignoring its effect as she speaks.*

"The bards who will tell this tale to you tonight are: Theodora do Hrothnog, our Princess and granddaughter of the Emperor of Darkreach himself. She is a most puissant mage. And Ayesha bint Hāritha, who is a daughter of the Sheik of Yāqūsa in the Caliphate up in the Mountains."

There is a pause between each introduction to give the onlookers a chance to see the person named and take them in. Both have changed into their Caliphate dancing costumes and murmurs accompany the revelation that these are not just dancing girls.

"So that you know who we are when the story mentions us, I will tell you

of the rest of our people. The Dwarf sitting there is Thord. If later on you talk
to a Dwarf about what you hear they may refer to him as the Crown-Finder,
and he is very famous among his kind."

"Over there with the People of the Plains are our Hulagu and Bianca.
Hulagu is from the Dire Wolves. Bianca was born in Freehold, but she is now
both fully Khitan and yet she is also a Presbytera of the True Church." *I can
see the Freehold traders looking intently at Bianca and taking in both her hair
and her knives.*

"Our other Princess is Rani Rai and she sits beside me there. She was a
Havenite Battle Mage." *I am dressed in a sari and sitting beside my wife. I was
trying to look demure and inoffensive, but I do have my belt pouches for wands
on and more than a few rings. I suppose I was never going to have anonymity
tonight anyway.*

"Our Father Christopher is with your priests over there. By the Grace of
God he has brought someone all of the way back from the dead and I have seen
it happen." *Murmurs accompany this, and it is obvious that Christopher has
not told the local priests about that as he is waving his hands deprecatingly
as he whispers to them.*

"Stefan over there is about as local as you can find. He is from Evilhalt. If
any of the ladies here have taken a shine to him, change your mind quickly.
He already has two wives and they are both fierce hunters. He also struck the
blow that killed the Dragon of the Mountains." *Stefan looks embarrassed and
Christopher is back into explanation mode with the local priests.*

"My husband Basil is sitting on my other side. He is a high officer from
Darkreach and greatly in Hrothnog's favour. So am I, although I am not from
that land." *She is smiling and showing off her teeth. They always have quite an
effect on anyone, even when she is not making the most of them as she is now.*

"Now you will find out how we got together, and how we have changed
the world, and how much we still have to do. You may even find that, as time
goes by, you have a small part to play in this story. Do not be surprised. When
I left home fleeing a bad marriage, I had no expectations of being part of a
saga either."

"Now make yourselves comfortable and make sure that the servers can fit
between you to bring the drink out. You will need it, as we have a long story
and we are making it get a little bit longer with every day that passes." *She is
looking around...ahh, for a server.* "Girl... I want more beer already," she said
and drained what was left in her tankard before propping her spear against a
wall and sitting.

*It is a very late night before Theo-dear and Ayesha, taking it in turns to
speak, are finished with the main story. They allowed Astrid to tell of the
Imperial wedding in the middle as they rested, but beyond saying that we are*

out to destroy the Masters, none reveal what we are going to do next. For all we know, a spy for the Masters might be in the room.

It is, however, unlikely, as Father Christopher has managed to station himself and the other priests right beside the door to check everyone as they go in and out. It seems that the local priests questioned why this was necessary at first, but as the story unfolded, I am sure that they soon realised why.

None of the priests are showing special reactions to those that pass them by, so I am sure that they only feel the normal venalities. Unless someone is listening in from outside the building, it is likely that there are no spies around, unless the listener does not know who they are passing information to.

Rani
pre-dawn of the 28th of Secundus

By the time we leave, very early and still sleepy in the pre-dawn, the Mayor has a group of riders already preparing to head towards Greensin with a message for the Metropolitan, and Malik and his group have a series of written messages to pass to the Tar-Khans and the Kha-Khan. It was obvious they had gotten drunk last night and are working on being coldly sobre now.

Having made their own decisions, they are apparently already bearing the marks of messengers. With luck all the clans will be roused, but it is almost certain that at least some of them will be. Whether they can get into a position to help is another matter.

Indeed, seeing that the most likely clans who will want to help us are the Pack Hunters and the Dire Wolves, and the lands of neither of them border onto the Brotherhood, we will have to hope that the clans they will hopefully rally will not have to fight their way through other clans in order to give us aid.

Astrid
a few hours later

During the flight to the Mountains in the southwest I am keeping us very high, and it is just as well that we have the cloaks of warmth with us. Despite it being summer, it is always very cold that high up in the sky. Even the Princesses cannot tell me why. We should be warmer. We are closer to the sun after all. We are not so high that it is hard to breathe, and that is another mystery as to why that should happen.

Still, the flight is uneventful and we, lacking sleep, must keep talking, or rather calling to each other, to stay awake. Beneath us on the plains I can occasionally see some of the herds, and here and there are clusters of Khitan tents and herds that are just tiny dots beneath. Nothing I see gives a single sign that we have been observed.

Gradually, some bumps appeared on the horizon, which grew steadily until they had become the South-West Mountains. *These are more like large hills than mountains to someone who is used to the real mountains that run north and south across The Land. There are only three larger peaks that I can see, and a steep-sided hilly plateau connects them and none of the peaks are really any higher than the foothills around Mousehole.*

I am sure that if it accidentally snows on them it will only be a light fall and will not last on the ground more than a day or so. They are all about the same height as the Darkreach fort of Forest Watch north of Mousehole, but they are all more rounded and weathered than it. You would not climb them so much as stroll up to the top.

Beneath them as they flew were the Baerami River and the Freehold town of Brickshield on its southwest bank. *There is even a caravan visible coming up to the ferry across the river and some boats can be seen as tiny dots on the river. This is where some of the traders who heard our tale last night will end up in a few weeks. It will be one of the first parts of Freehold to hear our story.*

Hopefully we will be well on our way to what we must do in the Brotherhood before then and before the Dominican Brothers, with their zeal at keeping their faith unsullied, realise that an Orthodox priest and people whose lifestyle is anathema to them have been in the area.

Astrid
late that afternoon

We *have arrived at Oldike as dusk is fast creeping across the sky, not having stopped all day. It seems that Oldike is one of the rare Dwarven settlements that is built entirely above ground, although the Dwarves compensate for this as much as they can by building their homes and workshops into the slopes of the hills that surround it, and where this is not possible, piling earth over the buildings so that there are a series of long mounds with doors lining the streets.*

It is almost like Wolfneck only more neighbourly. There are watchtowers and small fortifications in the passes leading into the valley, but Oldike is otherwise unfortified. Unlike Kharlsbane they have no ridge of hard rock to burrow into. Coming in to land it also seems to be largely deserted.

Of all the areas of the Dwarves, Thord has said that the southwest has sent more of its people to Dwarvenholme. Apparently, if it had not been for the rich iron mine of Ironcone, and the supply of diamonds to be found in the blue clay outside Oldike, the area might have been completely abandoned by the Dwarven race.

Once it is known who we are, the Dwarves greet us warmly. Having Thord with us we are taken straight to see the local Baron. Hrolfr Strongarm has been to Dwarvenholme and has now returned to supervise the migration of most of his people.

It is a hard task for him. He must watch his power decrease, while still making sure that the resources of the area are not taken by Freehold, who would love to gain control of both the diamonds, and more particularly, the iron of his neighbouring Baron in Ironcone.

Consequently, it seems that the less obvious settlement of Oldike has lost more people than the other, and a greater amount of its resources are devoted to keeping up an appearance of strength and size. Despite his loss, the Baron is a jovial and happy Dwarf who is more than glad to see us.

It seems that whatever we need of him, he will do. It is soon evident that the Dwarves here have responded to the change in circumstances in other ways, and this now small village shows more evidence of Dwarven young than I have seen at any previous settlement we have been to, even more than Dwarvenholme. Rani has made sure that the Baron knows about the school.

Rani and I get to spend time peering over a vellum map of Freehold, which has many notes attached to it. Given the isolation and small size of the Dwarf settlements, and the fact that their hills are entirely surrounded by the territory of Freehold, the Shepherds here keep the knowledge of their potential nemesis as current as they can. It is good to take advantage of that.

I am memorising what markers I can for our destinations. It is an easy path to follow the Warialda River from its source near Oldike down to the Oban River which we will cross, and then fly down the centre of the forest. It is a far shorter flight than we faced from Glengate, given that we will be transiting out to the sea.

Rani has decided to leave later in the day so that we can approach this Camel Island around the time of dusk. This way we will still have some light to work with, but will not be silhouetted against the horizon as easily when we fly in. By the look of it, I shall have no difficulty finding it. It is the only island that is more than just a rock.

At least we will get more sleep than we did last night, as almost all the Dwarves, with a couple of rare exceptions among the younger members of the audience, lost interest in the tale we have to tell once it reached its peak with the finding of Dwarvenholme.

While they are happy to give any support that is needed to prevent the return of the Masters, the insular mindset of most of them means that, unless the story directly touches their interests as Dwarves, it is not important to them at all. Thord is a very unusual Dwarf indeed in that he shows more curiosity about the world that lies outside the Dwarven enclaves than the whole of this village put together.

Chapter IV

Astrid
29th Secundus

I *have us spiralling up over Oldike to gain altitude before we come off the plateau and follow the course that I have laid out.* They peeled off and crossed the Oban. *I can see Toppuddle to the left. We will be returning here, and now I have a good view of the approaches. Like Wolfneck, the assarts are clustered on just one side of the river along with what looks like a couple of abbeys.*

In this case everything is on the eastern side of the river, where the town is. The forest itself has very few clearings in it, and they may just be those where wildfires have been or where charcoal cutters work. With luck it might be possible for us to approach from, and then hide in, the forest on the western side. From a place in hiding there we can perhaps seek our target more safely.

Astrid
later that afternoon

C *amel Rock is now well in sight in the distance.* Astrid brought them down into a clearing in the forest. *I can see no one nearby. I think that we will settle down and wait here for the light to go. We can set some sentries to watch out and the rest of us can have some food and an hour's sleep in shifts.*

Astrid
a few hours later

I am glad I did that. We are all feeling more rested. I am keeping us flying low and spread out as we head out to sea and eventually turn north along the coast. We need to keep a watch below and around for any boat that might be at sea to see us. So far there is nothing except for a couple of very small craft close against the shore.

The swell beneath us is low, and a light wind barely moves the clouds that keep obscuring the rising moons and cover half of the sky. It is pleasant fishing weather. Even the seabirds think so. Eventually the rise of the Camel could be seen against the shore and Astrid turned them towards it. *It does look a bit like the animal.*

Once they came close to the island, she halted the Mice well out of bowshot, going on with just Hulagu and Ayesha, each of whom flew with their bow in hand and with an arrow nocked. *I am going to land and check if anything is visible on the island or if it is occupied.*

She headed for the saddle between the humps. *It stands several hundred paces above the sea and is half the height of the humps.* She looked for the other two. *They are doing as they are supposed to, heading directly towards each of the humps, skimming up the flanks of them to avoid being silhouetted against the sky.*

Astrid landed, and spear in hand, began to look around her. The saddle between the humps was an artificially flattened and cleared space fifty paces square. The rocks that had been shifted from the clearing were piled along the sides in a loose parapet around a pace-and-a-half high with a small gap in the centre on each of the seaward sides.

The rocks at the bottom of the wall have been here a long time and they are worn and weathered. Some others have been placed there more recently. There has been something built here long ago in the past, but other people have been here lately doing things as well.

It did not take much looking for her to see two things. Firstly, there was no one guarding the Pattern, and secondly, they would not have to get Father Christopher to waste a spell looking for it. *Even in the light that is available I can see that a Pattern lies at my feet on one side of the saddle. What is more, there is a second one on the other side of the flat area.*

I am not a mage, but the second one does not look complete. It is much larger than the first, and the first looks far older. It is far more elaborate in its design than the first. It is carved into a recently levelled patch of stone and there is no paint or blood in the grooves that I can see. They are still fresh, naked rock. I am no miner either, to tell the age of workings, but that all looks to have only been cut within the last few weeks.

She was soon intent on trying to make out if there were any tracks that would indicate when they were last used, but was having little success in the low and uncertain light. She was still looking at this when she sensed that Ayesha, who had gone up the northern hump, was fast coming down it towards her.

"We need to bring the others in," she said. "There is a ship approaching the outside of the island from the north. Unlike the others that I can see, it is travelling well out to sea. It is as if it does not want to be seen from the shore."

"We have the Patterns." Astrid pointed. "Bring our people here. Keep low if there is a chance of being seen." Ayesha left, and Astrid looked around. *Hulagu is coming down from his hump. He is not travelling quickly and is obviously looking around as he flies.*

"There is no one there now, but there is a lookout point on top and a path leads up there," he said when he arrived. "Where has Ayesha gone?" Astrid explained and got him to fly up the northern peak to see in more detail what was happening, as the view from the saddle was very confined.

All that can be seen from here is a small cove with a beach on each side of the island and the coast immediately around each cove. Still it cuts both ways. It is hard for others to see us here. She kept looking seaward. *I can just make out Ayesha moving as a darker patch returning with the others. She is keeping them low until they are all in the cove and then, as they fly up to here, still skimming the ground as they come.*

As Christopher and the mages looked at the Patterns, the others settled into making a camp and getting ready to defend it if they needed to. The mages, after conferring, affirmed that the second Pattern was not charged and was still inactive. On hearing that, Christopher declared that he would then eliminate the active one tonight. He was starting to prepare to do this when Hulagu arrived back from on top of the northern hump.

"The boat is smaller than the *River Dragon*," he said, "and it is not sailing past. It is definitely coming here, and although the wind is coming fresh from the sea, it is coming to the outside of the island and I am sure Olympias said that it was not a good idea to do that… Unlike on the plains, when you are at sea you want to be downwind…in the lee," he amended, "of an obstacle that you can be wrecked on. I don't think that it wants to be seen from the shore."

"That makes it even more important that I get rid of this Pattern tonight," said Father Christopher. "It is past time for Hesperinos and well on Apodeipnon, so we will have both services before I perform the dispelling. You may all be seated." With Astrid, who had the best eyes, sitting on the low wall and keeping watch, the others obediently took seats around the priest.

35

Rani

*A*gain, *I wonder why I am stubbornly refusing to consider conversion to my wife's faith. I have no priest of my own and have not even seen one since I first left Haven. I have already thoroughly broken caste and almost every rule of my natal religion.*

If what I was brought up with turns out to be right after all, and I am to be reborn, then it will be as a very much lower animal anyway and I will be many lifetimes away from a higher incarnation than that. What is it that keeps me away from converting? Am I scared of opening my thoughts to the priests in confession? Is the symbolic cannibalism too much for me?

Simeon has said that for a Catholic it is not just a symbolic act, but due to what he said the Pope had called the Miracle of Transubstantiation, is an actual act of cannibalism even if it does not count as such. As a person who had been trying to leave his lycanthropy behind, he had always found that hard to swallow and too close to the bone, as he had put it with a smile.

She pulled her thoughts back to the present and to the priest talking in the dark to them all and to his God. *I can think about those things when we are safe back in Mousehole. Now is not the time for the consolations of philosophy.*

Theodora

*C*hristopher finished his services and went straight into his attack on the enchantments built into the Pattern in front of him. *We are getting used to this performance of a miracle, and Christopher has now built responses from us into what he says to make it more effective. Most of us can now say these without any prompting.*

Even as I respond, I am musing about the differences between the work of a cleric and the enchantments of a mage. Both might refer to how much mana a person can direct, but we are so different in what we mean by the term and how it is used. Our spells and their miracles may in theory be built similarly, but there it ends.

You cannot rely on a priest to snap cast anything useful in a battle, but give them time to sit and prepare or a safe place behind the front lines, especially if they are in a church, and they can literally work miracles far beyond what a mage might dream of undertaking. I have seen that time and time again from Christopher.

Eventually, Father Christopher concluded and this time the Pattern gave up its contained mana in a soundless shriek as a greyish blob of freed mana streamed off straight up into the sky. *I am sure that, if I had done this enchantment the freed mana would have attacked me at least once. What the priest does is far more efficacious and safer.*

Having finished the disenchantment, Father Christopher gave a benediction and they prepared for some food, taking watches and their turn at sleep.

Astrid
a little later

I think that it is time to take the mages out and to look at what we face. They flew low and kept moving as if large leatherwings looking for fish.

The ship is a caravel, and smaller than the River Dragon *even if it has one more mast. It has a square-rigged main mast and a large triangular lateen sail on a second large mast and yet another on a much smaller quarter mast. I saw a few of them when we were sailing along the northern coast in my father's craft.*

It is partway between the simple rigging of the North and the more complex, and better handling, sails of the River Dragon. *From what little I have seen of them; it may even be a Brotherhood vessel. As far as I know they only have a couple of these, or maybe even only this one. I have seen all that I can, and the mages do not know what to look for. Now we can go back.*

Astrid then pointed out to Hulagu where the boat was going to be anchoring and made sure that the first watch kept a constant gaze on the ship, using the telescope when they needed to. *I don't want anyone from it landing without us knowing everything about the event. If anyone comes up to the saddle from it, I want us to have the element of surprise and to be able to ambush the climbers, not the other way around.*

Astrid
30th Secundus, the Feast Day of Saint Junia

The night passed quietly. Once it had anchored, the boat had shown a small light all night. *It is not bright; it is just enough for them to be sure of their distance from the shore. Someone on board is an experienced enough sailor to take this precaution. They don't want their anchors dragging with their vessel pressed against a lee shore.*

Astrid
in the early light

*N*ow *that there is light enough to see, there is a person examining the area where we are with a glass.* Astrid kept everyone out of sight while she, in turn and wearing her ring and cloakpin, watched what she saw, passing back details. *That was a tingle of someone trying to scry for someone up here. My caution is justified.*

Astrid
an hour later

*W*e *are preparing, and so are they. We are celebrating Orthos and saying our Confessions. Christopher can make much of today's Saint in his preaching. They are moving people to the shore. They only have two very small rowboats, so it will take a while.*

One party, by their actions, and what they are carrying, are going along the beach to get water for the ship. There must be a source there that cannot be seen from up here. At the same time another group is assembling on the beach. It looks like we will need our element of surprise. Without it we are well outnumbered.

Although three of the group are women, with bound hands, at least two, from their dress, are mages, clumsy with the swords that they both wear. They both make Rani look skilled in the field. At least three, and maybe up to six, are possibly priests. Christopher has noted the prisoners and I can hear him saying prayers to Saint Junia for them.

They headed up the hill towards the Mice. There are two scouts who come first and fifty paces ahead of the rest. "There are two in front who I will bet knew Vengeance well," she said.

There are also ten men at arms, but six of them are carrying things with them in their hands or strapped to packs on their backs. Some of the items in their hands are definitely tools, probably to complete the unfinished Pattern. Except for the first of the two scouts, presumably the most experienced man, the rest mainly look at the slope that is ahead of them, where their feet will go.

It is a normal thing to do and almost everyone does it. It takes a lot of training to actually get a person to look above their eye height when they are walking, and all that is at eye height while climbing a steep slope is the rock a few paces from your face.

I suppose that is because most threats come from ground level. Few things will attack a person from above, and numbers will intimidate most of those, so people in numbers naturally just look at where their feet are going and what is near their feet. Still, having people climbing towards us makes for a perfect ambush opportunity, one that we can take advantage of.

"The two scouts do have the Flail on their breasts. The next two after the scouts may be priests…and it is one of them who seems to be giving the orders. Then there are the mages and then another who may also be a priest. After him are all of their soldiers, and right at the back are the other three who may be priests, or they may just be servants."

She kept describing what she saw. "Each one of the last priests leads a woman with a rope that is attached to their bound wrists. That, combined with them having those silly dresses that Make wears, is making it difficult for them to climb and they look very afraid. I think the women walk as if they are in pain and they may have an idea that something bad is going to happen to them."

Astrid paused and thought about what she was seeing. "I would say that the men are not expecting opposition, and except for the first man, they are all very casual. None of them except for the first two actually have weapons in their hands. Both have a bow in their hand without an arrow nocked."

By now she was whispering. "I will be quiet now as they may soon be close enough to hear me. Ayesha, it is time for you to go out for your man." Astrid felt a brief pat on her rear in acknowledgement and she then took her place in the gap where the path entered. She still kept mostly out of sight behind the rocks, with just her eyes and hair showing. *I must not rely on being invisible.*

Ayesha

*E*veryone is keeping low with a missile weapon in their hands except Astrid *and me. I have my ring on, and will kill the second scout once I see Astrid make a move on the first. I am trying to stay hidden from the mages as I move, but neither is even casually glancing in my direction yet. They are just making sure that they do not trip on the steep climb. Allah, the Just, please keep it just like that.*

I will not see Astrid killing her man, but I should hear him die and the northern woman will call out if he doesn't. His death will be the signal for everyone to rise from behind the wall and concentrate their fire, firstly on the mages, and then on the priests. Every arrow that they use for the casters will, or course, be enhanced. Hopefully, they don't miss as I will be unseen, and in the same direction as their targets.

Astrid

*T*he first man is nervously looking all around him. He senses an ambush, *and he has now placed an arrow in his bow, but his leaders have not confirmed what his senses are telling him. I can see where he is looking, and he can see nothing at all in any of the likely ambush spots.*

He is mainly looking up the flanks of the humps and to his sides, but he is also keeping up a nervous scanning of the top of the parapet. The scout kept stopping briefly and looking around. *He has made his companion more alert as well and the second man is now looking around in the same way, and now he also has an arrow nocked.*

Their leader obviously does not share their concern and he is yelling at them. I bet that he wants them to hurry on up here, from the way he is waving his hands. I cannot understand his words, but I think that is Sowonja he is using.

Behind them, people are talking to each other. It all sounds like Latin, only it is Latin spoken with a heavy and hard accent and with unfamiliar sounds in it. Every now and then I can make a guess at a word, which may, or may not, be a correct one. The mages are intent on where their feet go and show no sign of looking up more than briefly. They have little chance of seeing Ayesha and myself, invisible, but still fairly exposed, on the slope ahead of them. All too soon the first scout came to where he would shortly be able to see the people crouched behind the parapet.

Astrid left it another pace until she saw his eyes widen and his mouth open to yell, and then stood and drove her spear, in a hard thrust, up to its crosspiece in his chest, slanting it so that it would hopefully go through his ribs and straight into his heart. Whatever he had been about to say came out as a gurgle as he dropped his bow and clutched at his chest.

She withdrew the blade and thrust it at him again. *This time I aim at the base of his throat above the collarbone. This time I can see his eyes start to glaze as he slumps. I sense the movement around me as the Mice rise as one and fire.* She withdrew her blade from the body and moved to put it aside.

There is already the start of absolute carnage below me. The second scout is lying on the rocks coughing his life out through an almost completely severed neck. Another stream of blood comes from his back. The first supposed mage is hit by a flurry of explosions, and the second by one, and then by another shaft.

The first priest was close to being only twenty paces from the scout, and was paying the price of his impatience as he clawed at one of Basil's iron martobulli that had sprouted from his throat. As Astrid reached for where she had put her bow, another appeared in his head above his nose. *Whatever damage the first dart would have caused, that one will be fatal as the weight of sharp iron will shatter his skull and go straight into his brain.*

As she picked up her bow, more explosions could be heard. She looked up. *The mages are both down, as is the first priest. The second priest has been hit, but is starting to try to cast something, as is the supposed third priest.* She left them to the ones already firing. *The soldiers are still in the disorder and panic of an ambush and only one is taking cover and starting to get a weapon out.*

He is likely a leader. Astrid sent a shaft at him. At a range of thirty paces it is hard to miss a target as large as a man and, with the strength of Astrid's bow the shaft was nearly inside him before it exploded. She was firing from above, and the shaft entered his body on his shoulder near the junction of his neck, where there was no armour. The explosion caused his head to fly to the side. As she nocked and drew again, she noticed the rearmost priest receive a shaft. *That will be Ayesha then.*

The three bound women are screaming and trying to huddle together. One of their keepers is drawing a sword, and seems more likely to hit the poor bloody women rather than to, more bravely, charge up the hill. Fuck him. She sent a shaft at the man.

It seems that Ayesha has the same idea. He was hit by two shafts enhanced for killing the dragon. The remains of his body fell upon the women, covering them in gore. *Their screams have redoubled, and they have fallen in a heap clutching at each other with bound hands. At least that is the safest place for them to be.*

Once the mages and the lead clerics were eliminated the archers shifted to using normal shafts for their bows... *although Bianca and Christopher are probably still using enhanced bullets in their slings. It is hard to tell with an earth blow such as Christopher uses in his enhancements.*

Basil is already bounding down the slope, keeping away from the path so as to not block anyone's shot. The soldiers have no chance. They have very little cover, and as soon as one looks as if they are ready to stop panicking and actually do something, he becomes the next target and dies. The last cleric has turned and is trying to flee.

Astrid and Ayesha put a stop to that. It was not long before a degree of silence returned to the crown of the island. *Only the three bound girls are left alive, and they are understandably loud in their terror and cries, for what I presume is mercy.*

Looking down, Astrid could see that Basil had reached the women and was checking them. *They are talking to him, and he back to them, but it is obvious that neither is understood. He has one shortsword drawn, and the women are cowering from it until he grabs one of the women's wrists and starts to slice the ropes. They get the idea.* The other two held their hands up, even while their eyes were looking at the ground.

Moving her gaze further afield she could see that the ship was making hurried preparations to try and leave. *It is obvious that, in their panic, the crew of the caravel have forgotten the offshore wind. Maybe the captain of the ship is on the shore. There are still some people there on the land and in the rowboats frantically trying to get to the ship.*

It is only a gentle breeze, but they have cut their seaward cable before they have the sweeps out and are actually ready to go. The ship is now swinging around on its bow cable and drifting towards the shore. Some of the crew are getting the sweeps into the water, but it is going to be close. Astrid drew Rani's attention to the ship. "What do we do? Is it a good idea to let them go?"

"No," said Rani, calling out. "Basil, you are best at throwing things. Take some molotails and ensure that the ship is destroyed. Stay above them until we are sure that there is no one with a bow left, and then Hulagu and Ayesha can despatch the survivors. Use your judgement on whether to give quarter. We don't want any word of our presence getting out."

Leaving the women, Basil came leaping back up the path and onto his saddle. Quickly, it catapulted into the sky, with the rider still fastening himself to it as he flew headlong down the slope.

Soon a gout of flame from the ship showed that the first bomb had hit nearly amidships, and in the centre of the men using the sweeps, splattering them with fire. The second hit further to the rear and the third nearer the bow.

Men are jumping in the sea and screams can be heard, as the water does not put out the clinging flame very well, if at all. The ship is now drifting more determinedly towards the shore as the column of flame grows from it. It is increasing as the flammable stores that are always found on ships add to the conflagration. No one is trying to attack except one who is on the shore.

Others have flown down on their saddles. The man on the shore is soon full of arrows. All the rest are just trying to escape. None were given the chance and soon the bay was filled with bodies as archers went to glean any shafts that were still usable and regain the heads of the rest. The ship soon came to rest, nudging against some rocks a little way out from the shore as it continued to burn.

Bianca

"**Y**ou from Brothers?" Bianca asked in broken Sowonja. *There are three girls sitting meekly in front of me. I am the only one of the Mice who speaks any at all and that is at the same level that I originally had of Khitan. Now, to make it worse, I am out of practice.* All three nodded.

From what I can see of their hair escaping from under their headscarves one is blond, one has brown hair and one has black. It looks as if the servants of the Masters are again only using beautiful women for their sacrifices, even if these three show bruises from ill-treatment. I wonder if they keep the plain ones at home to do the work.

The one with black hair, the shortest, has green eyes while the blond and the brunette, both tall girls, have blue and brown eyes respectively. She sighed. *Just when it looked like we were getting Make to behave in a human fashion, we now have three more to deal with. I suppose that I should find out what they know and think. They just sit there waiting to be told what to do.*

She indicated the bodies lying around. "They tell you what here for?" The three cast glances at each other. *None wants to set herself apart by speaking.* "Me not hurt you. We set you free." Again, they just looked at each other. Bianca waited in silence. Finally, the brunette sighed and spoke. *I am only catching a part of it.*

She repeated back what she heard. "… that what they say?" All three nodded. It was Bianca's turn to sigh. "We know them here to kill you." She pointed at the Patterns. "We see them do before. Them serve evil demons." *Again, the three are looking at each other, but none are raising a protest. At least that is better with them than with Make. They make no protest at what I say.*

"You all slave?" The girls all nodded. "Did them…" she made a motion putting a finger on one hand in and out of the joined thumb and forefinger on the other and moving it back and forward. The three shared a look between them before nodding.

The brunette spoke, this time she spoke simply and slowly: "All the time. Last night all of them." She pointed down at her groin, up to her mouth and then behind her. She shrugged. *That seems to be the lot for a girl born as a slave among the more brutal of the Brothers and the girls do not seem to expect anything else.*

Bianca's face hardened. *It seems that the Master's servants keep using sex as if it is a weapon. It has to be a sign of something wrong among them…some sort of weakness…a consciousness of impotence…a lack of power perhaps.*

The girls drew back from her a bit. *I must be looking too fierce for them. Any news of rape has that effect on me.*

She worked on her face to try and soften it. "You want healer?" The girls blushed and shook their heads vigorously. *What else should I do? This time, as a questioner, I am a total failure. I suppose that I can try starting again to win their trust.* "Me Bianca. Me wife of priest," she pointed, "Father Christopher."

All three had started to raise their eyes a little, but now all are furiously studying the ground in front of them. The wife of a priest must be a powerful person in their land. "You free now. You can look me. Who you?"

After a delay of exchanged glances and mistakes, many repetitions and misunderstandings, some that would not be fixed until they came back to Mousehole to speak to Make, it turned out that they had *It Shall Come To Pass*, the blonde, *There Shall Be Lemons*, the black-haired girl and the brunette *Turn Away My Eyes From Beholding Vanity*.

Somehow I cannot imagine someone being called "There shall be lemons", but we will have to wait to get home to clear that up.

Almost as an afterthought an increasingly exasperated Bianca asked: "Where you from?" *The three are back to looking at each other.*

"Owendale," said the brunette Vanity. *I am excited. This is exactly what I need to hear.*

"These," she pointed at the bodies, "from there too?" *There is a chorus of nods.* She pointed at one body "Mage?" *More nods.* "Priest?" *Even more nods as I go around the rest. It turns out that the guesses were correct.* "All from Owendale? Ship too?" *Still more nods.*

They are happy to nod and answer guesses. I hope that they really do understood what is being asked and are being honest, not just trying to keep me, the priest's wife, happy. "More ships?" she asked. *This time there is a shaking of heads.*

One of them, the one with black hair, and I am still not sure as to the name... It cannot be Lemons, that is a fruit. Anyway she is holding up two fingers a little way apart. She may have been making a comment on her captor's manhood, but I know what she means. "Only little ones?" *They are back to nodding.*

She thought for a moment before waving her hand at the other bodies. "Soldiers," she declared. "Many in Owendale?" *There is some chatter between the three, far too fast for me to follow.* Eventually, the black-haired girl pointed at the dead soldiers and held up one finger.

The girl then pointed north and held up her hand with the thumb and all five fingers extended and then deliberately folded her thumb down. *It is now my turn to nod. By this time, Rani is beside me and wondering what is going on.* Bianca turned to explain what she had found out.

She concluded with saying: "There used to be six times this many soldiers in Owendale, but I think that we have killed one sixth of them. We are lucky that we are killing people now that we would have had to fight later."

The girls are agitated, and were trying to say something while I spoke to Rani, but I do not understand what it was. Eventually, two of the girls got down on hands and knees while the brunette Vanity stood behind them and made a motion of a person with reins. "Chariots!" She thought for a moment and reverted to Latin "Carroccio" as she moved her hands in a vertical circle on each side of her near the ground.

The three have started nodding again and the black-haired one is opening and closing both her hands twice before holding up four fingers on each hand. Bianca turned to Rani "Well, I think that we have thirty-two of their chariots as well. We will have to hope that some of that force is drawn off… I wonder…"

She turned back to the girls: "More mages?" This led to another discussion between the girls before three fingers were held up. "More priests?" *This time nine fingers are quickly raised. They pay more attention to priests.*

"We have a long way to go with the priests," Bianca said to Rani "and they will be at home. It will be too much to hope that we took out all of their most powerful ones, but the first three could have been, as would the mages. Unless they get reinforcements soon, that should help us, and they won't even suspect that something is wrong for a week or two."

She turned again to the girls. "You come us when we go?" The girls started looking around the island. *It is easy for them to see that it is not inhabited and has little to commend it as a place of safety and there is nothing here to eat that I can see. There is some rapid talk among them before, one after another, they slowly begin to nod.*

Christopher

*T*he others have collected any sling bullets they can, and any magic that is sensed, and have laid the bodies before me. I need to say prayers over the dead. I must do it for them, even though they were not of my faith, and their souls are certainly bound for hell. I just have to hope and pray for the eventual redemption of their souls.*

There is little chance to bury them in such a rocky place, so the bodies need to be taken down and dumped in the cove. The fishes will take care of them there, and it will not be long before there is little trace of our battle.

As long as no one sees the smoke from the dry timbers of the burning ship—and most of that is dispersing behind the height of the island in the light wind—it will soon not be easy to tell that the Brotherhood were here at all. Perhaps a fisherman will see the burnt remains of the ship and wonder. I pray not.

Thord

*T*he rest of them can take care of the bodies. It is time for a Dwarf to get *to work.* Thord produced a mallet and chisel from his saddlebags, and set to work defacing the Patterns. As the sound of his blows echoed around, he was intent on making sure that no one casually reactivated them. *I will take all day if I need to, but no one will be able to make out what was here by the time that I finish.*

Not only was he effacing some parts completely, but he even started to join up some of the incised lines to ensure that what could be seen of the Pattern now made no sense at all and could not be repaired in a workable fashion.

Hulagu

I get the first watch on the northern hump while they do all the work. I admit *to the Tenger Sünsnüüd, the Spirits of the Sky, as I fly, that I like that.* He had flown up the seaward side, staying close to the ground and landing short of the summit before moving stealthily up so that his silhouette was not seen.

Caution is never wasted, but I need not have bothered. I can see a fishing boat and two larger vessels. The fishing craft is staying close to where the village is, and the two small ships, about the size of the one now burning near-smokeless below me, are travelling, one north and the other south. Both are staying between the island and the coast, a distance of some four miles. Neither one of them is moving from its course.

Astrid

*O*nce we have completed as much as can be done, we pack what we can *take with us from the Brotherhood men:* crossbows, bolts, bows, arrows, swords, an enchanted belt pouch with more food in it than a large backpack can hold, a collection of rings and wands, and some armour.

I am trying to distribute that weight evenly among the saddles. It is not easy to balance the loads. We have three extra people to carry with us for a long distance, and two of them are not small girls. Those two will have to travel with Basil and Bianca, hanging on behind them.

After dark and the Hesperinos service they set out again. *This time we are going to go as far up the forest as we can before setting down. Despite setting out after dark, we should be able to get somewhere near Toppuddle well before it is dawn—as long as I can find the town in the dark with all of this cloud, that is.*

I am not trying anything fancy in terms of navigation. I am keeping us high and flying directly east until we reach the Oban River upstream of Ashvaria. On reaching the river, she turned left and simply followed its path in the fleeting and meagre light of the two moons, waning Terror and waxing Panic.

Chapter V

Astrid

*A*s I thought it would be, Toppuddle turns out to be easy to see, even at night. The moonlight, even decreasing, as it is this close to Midsummer Eve, reflects readily off the extensive dams and leats scattered around the town that power its mills and its industry.

It is, however, much harder to find a place to put down in the forest. There are few clearings in the wild woods that are close to the river and, keeping as low as I am, this close to the town, one that is right for us is hard to find.

It took nearly until dawn to find a spot to stop. We have ended up only a hundred or so paces from the river, and directly opposite what seems to be the most northern of the hamlets and villages around Toppuddle. From what sits around us, the clearing is probably used by a charcoal burner at least occasionally.

This settlement is a likely spot for us to start looking for a pattern. It is well away from most of their priests, but still really only a brief ride from the town itself. If it is not here, we will just move on down the river in stages, checking for a pattern each night as we go. It will be slow, but it should work.

Bianca
early in the pre-dawn of 31st Secundus

*T*he three freed slaves are looking very tender as they dismount. From what I have been able to gather from my passenger, the blonde, It Shall Come to Pass, or Pass, they have never ridden anything before excepting in a cart. That, *combined with the effects of their multiple rapes, has made them all almost collapse once we are down.*

Bianca brought her husband to them and would not, despite their protests, allow them to continue to do anything without them being healed. Father Christopher did that. *I need to get Ayesha over to examine them more closely than they will allow my husband to do. She can dress any wounds that they might have.*

Ayesha

I have dressed various abrasions, some now partly healed as a result of the Christian priest's prayers and given them some things to drink and eat. I am not going to tell anyone, but one of the drinks is a potion of False Sweetmary… an abortifacient. If their rapes have left them pregnant, they will not want a child as a memento of it. No one should have to suffer that.

It is just as well that we have plenty of healing potions. Another is of Heal-bush, and the berries are Betterberries, and between these they have left the girls feeling much improved physically. It seems that being healed by either prayer or potion is something that is new to them.

Bianca

A yesha is finished with them, why are they gathering wood? Oh my Lord, they are going to light a fire and start cooking for us. I must stop them. Bianca tried to explain about smoke and not wanting to be seen. *Just like Make, the three slave girls seem to have a very poor appreciation of the world outside the very limited areas of the kitchen and the home.*

It is strange that they are so easily shocked by things that we regard as normal. It is bad enough that none of the women among the Mice, except Ayesha, have their hair covered and that most are wearing trousers like the men, and the two who are not, Rani and Theodora, have divided skirts.

The girls rode with their dresses tucked up and it was a continual struggle to keep them from falling off as they tried to stop their legs from being seen. Wait until they get home and see bare breasts…even on the priests' wives.

Christopher
a little later

I have performed Orthos, now is the time to move closer to the river to cast *my miracle of finding. All of this hamlet will be well within range of my detection from there, and as we came in, I could see no distant outbuildings that will be outside it.*

Apart from the single example on Camel Island—and that had unique circumstances—there have been no patterns so far that have not been in a building, so I am going to assay it. If my wife and Astrid insist on coming to keep an eye on me, that is up to them, as long as they do not get in my way. It was not long before he finished. "It is in that building," he said as he pointed across the river.

Astrid

*H*e is pointing at a stable-like building that can be seen partly behind and *to the side of a substantial house on the fringe of the hamlet.* Astrid sent Christopher and Bianca back to the others and settled down for the first watch over it. *This is a job for a hunter, and one with patience.* She settled down in the leaf litter and peered through some of the shrubs across the river to their target.

We will need to know what we face when we cross tonight. Whoever owns the house is obviously wealthy and a substantial person in the community... as a matter of fact, it is soon clear that the hamlet almost revolves around the house. It is an older building, large, and with two real storeys.

It has a further storey to be seen as attic windows visible through a thick thatch, as if they are a row of half-lidded eyes. That one will be for the servants. The walls of the house are whitewashed between exposed thick, black-painted timber beams running vertically and horizontally, and also as diagonal braces. Overall it has a solid and comfortable look to it.

The stables seem to house a large number of horses, and there are a number of other buildings that are obviously there to service the needs of the house. It has a conjoined bakehouse and brewhouse. They probably serve the hamlet as well. It also has a pigeon loft, a washhouse and a domed store building.

There is a long woodpile under a timber-shingled shed, which extends sideways and has hay stacked under it in addition to a cart, and room for several more carts or carriages. There is even a large workshop, from which the sounds of a smith at work are already emerging. It even has its own well. It is a well-founded house.

The only persons who come in and out of the large house are servants, and they largely come from the rear. The only person to emerge from the front door is a servant who is repainting some of the woodwork around the door in a fresh black paint.

The building that Christopher has indicated stands isolated from the other buildings, and it looks far older than the rest, even considerably older than the house itself. Its walls are of a dark-grey stone, well-fitted but with the edges showing signs of age. Unlike most of the other buildings of the hamlet, it doesn't have a thatched roof, but one that is covered with slates. The slates, in turn, are completely covered with lichen.

Unlike the other buildings on the estate it has no windows, no shutters, and no way for light to enter it that I can see. The door is made of solid-looking timber and painted black. It opens onto a small apron of stone raised from the ground. In every regard, it very closely resembles Hildric's outbuilding at Northrode.

Astrid looked at the bustling scene in front of her for a while. *I am sure that not one of the servants goes near it, and unless I am mistaken, either consciously or unconsciously, they actually seem to avoid it and the area around it. None even walk in its shadow.*

The rest of the settlement has only one substantial house in it, one made of baked brick. It is on the road that leads to the large house and is only a short walk away. The rest of the village has typical cottars' houses, and a couple for petty trades with outbuildings. From the people to be seen, some could even be woodsmen or gamekeepers.

The houses seem to be made only of wattle and daub, even the largest, but they are well-maintained and solid looking and even have newish thatch. It is a modestly prosperous-looking settlement and completely surrounded by substantial fields. It has extensive water meadows, and its own water mill, with a huge overshot wheel drawing on a leat running down the hills behind and across to the mill on a part-stone aqueduct.

There is even a dock on the river with a large punt-ferry drawn up at it. I may not be used to horses, but I would guess that it is big and stable enough to hold several horses… I can hear someone moving behind me. She looked around to see Bianca returning.

"I will bet that this is the Count's country house," she said. "See, he can come across the river on the punt to hunt. That house," she pointed at the other larger house, "will belong to his reeve and the rest will be for his servants or peasants… Is there any sign of Count Archibald?" she asked.

Astrid looked quizzical. "How do you know whose house it is?"

"I have only been gone from Freehold for a bit over a year. Things don't always change that quickly, and unless he has died in the meantime, that is who Count Toppuddle was when I left here. I did only one trip to this town, and that was as we were on the way out on our last trip. The other girls and I were told by everyone to keep out of his sight."

"He is very wealthy, and has a reputation as a lecher who does not take 'no' as an answer from any woman. I saw him only briefly. I would say that he used to be a handsome man once, and he was renowned as a knight and is taller than you, but he is now fat and gross. I would say, from the number of horses in the stable, that he still goes hunting though."

"See that building?" she pointed. "That is a mews for his hunting birds. You can see that someone is working around that, so it is not abandoned. At any rate, it is time for you to get some sleep. I came back early. I am sick of trying to make sense of those three. If they try to do anything silly, just point at a place and make them sit. They will do that much…at least for a while."

As Astrid was going, Bianca spoke up again. *This time she is almost musing to herself.* "I wonder if Archibald found out about our books while we were here, and then arranged for us to be attacked. If that is the case, then by the oath that I swore to Saint Ursula, he needs to die and what is more, he needs to know why he is dying."

Oh dear, just what we need, a complication just like with Bryony at Rising Mud.

Astrid

I will report what Bianca and I have found out or deduced to Rani, but I will keep silent to her on Bianca's final words. However, before looking for Basil and a chance for some sleep, she did find Christopher and let him know about what had been said by his wife. He nodded and thanked Astrid.

"I had been wondering," he said. "If the planning for the attack on her caravan came directly from anywhere in Freehold, it was most likely to have come from here. We will have to see what happens now," he concluded.

Astrid
much later

When Astrid was woken up by Basil it was already dusk, and a very small fire had been lit behind a fallen tree where its light would be hidden in order to cook some food, and give them a hot drink of soup before they went to work. Around the camp was a quiet bustle of activity. "Who is on watch?"

"I have just come back, and Stefan has gone out now. The hamlet was about to go to bed when a small group arrived at the big house on horseback. Three men. From the description, one could be the Count, the others could be anyone. But I would say that one is an armsman from the way he behaved, and the other is either a mage, or a wealthy tradesman from one of the less physical trades."

"We are going to treat him as a mage," he continued. "One man who we think is the reeve has gone around the settlement and come back with three women. They didn't look very happy, but they weren't forced to go."

Rani
it is now dark

"Gather round," Rani said quietly. "We will need to see if Stefan has an up-date, but we now have two targets. The most important is the Pattern. We need to get rid of that. The second is the Count and his friends. There is one we are presuming is a mage as well as an armsman, who could be a bodyguard. He will probably be very good at that."

"It is a similar problem to what we faced at Mousehole, but on a smaller scale. There don't seem to be any guards, but with the Count about there could be servants who are awake. We will be leaving the slave girls here... Bianca, you need to somehow make them understand that they must stay right here, and that they are not to wander off no matter how long we are away or what they hear."

She paused. "If they are left behind, they will get blamed for what is about to happen. Try and make it clear to them that there shall be no fires under any circumstances." Having seen Bianca nod, Rani looked around. "Father, you need to get rid of the Pattern." Christopher nodded. "That door is probably locked. Ayesha, do you have that pick from the bandit horde?"

Ayesha felt in her pouch. *She has an annoyed look on her face.* "I'm sorry but I must have forgotten to bring it. I will never do that again."

What do we do to make up for that? "Well we do not have Lakshmi with us to try and open it stealthily. We could use a spell, but that could also trigger something. Thord...I am going to give you this ring...if there is a magical trap on the lock, it should help protect you. Use your hammer and chisel and open the door, then protect Christopher."

"Stefan, when he comes back, will be in charge of that group. Both of you obey him and do what he says...even if he says to pull out before you are finished. Hulagu, you are not even going to land. You are to stay in the sky and use your bow to prevent anyone in the hamlet helping our targets. You can also fire at anyone trying to escape the house."

"Try and only hit those who are armed or the three who just arrived." It was Hulagu's turn to nod. "Ayesha...you get to find your way inside. I think that you should try to target the mage. Remember that he has a good chance of seeing you through your glamour, but he represents the most potential to harm us."

"I will take Astrid, and Theodora will take Basil and Bianca with her. Between us we should be able to take the Count and his henchman if we move quickly. We will all land behind the large shed with the timber and carts in it. We will not move on the house until we see Ayesha wave to us out of a window or we hear a commotion." She looked around. "Does everyone understand? Are there any questions?"

"When do we move?" asked Astrid.

"We will move once the house goes quiet. I think that will be after midnight, so we will get some more rest now. We will carry out our attack, come back here for the Brotherhood girls and then move on to Oldike straight away."

Thord
31st Secundus, just

I am the one with the lucky last watch. That is the last of the three girls leaving the Count's lodge now. They will all be back in their homes very shortly. Having none stay the night makes things a little easier. Now I get to break into that building. I wonder what will happen when I break the lock. I hope that ring works. He came back to report and they all made ready.

Bianca

*S*aint Ursula, I pray for your aid that I have made the instructions to the three slave girls clear enough, and that they will not panic when they are left alone in the forest and do something silly like try and light a fire. Any fire will most likely show a glow, which will in turn, most likely alert someone on the other side of the river.

The Mice took off and circled around in a long flight to avoid being seen from the houses of the settlement as they came up to the house behind the cart shed. They hopped off their saddles and Ayesha disappeared.

Astrid has done the same. She is going with Ayesha to the house to stand ready beside a door. Silence has settled over the whole hamlet like a blanket. No lights are visible in any of the houses and, this far inside Freehold, there is no watch being kept. Now, we all get to just wait and I will silently tell my rosary.

Chapter VI

Ayesha
31st Secundus, just after midnight

*O*nce again, I take Astrid's hand and we set out. They walked towards the lodge house. *Passing clouds are reducing the light from the stars, Terror is in its last quarter, and although Panic is getting near full, at its best it only sheds a fifth of the light of the larger moon.*

I can see no obvious means to get inside the house quietly. All of the windows are closed. It will even be hard to see through them. The lower ones have shutters firm closed on them, as do some of the upper ones. During the day we saw that those that are visible are not single sheets but are made up of diamonds of stained glass in various hues.

She looked at the rear door. *That seems to be the best chance of entry. It stands in shade inside a small porch with a seat to sit on and remove muddy boots and with a place to put them.* She looked out. *It is so shaded, the rest of the Mice probably could not see inside even if the door were open. There is a simple lift latch.*

She cautiously used it. *There is no lock there and no bar in place behind it. Inside is dark, although I can see some shapes. It looks like one of the servants, at least, sleeps on the floor where they will be ready to come if they are called.* She tugged Astrid's hand and brought her close so that she could, hopefully, see what she saw and then let go.

It is time to seek out the mage...no...wait. She took off her ring and leant to where Astrid should be and whispered. "We are going to wake the servant and take him captive. I am sure that he can tell us where people are in the house."

Astrid removed her ring and carefully leant her spear against the wall. *She has the strength and speed, particularly with wearing her bracers and torque, for this work without killing him.* Astrid carefully sat down on the floor beside the sleeping form and quickly grabbed it into her lap, putting one hand over the mouth and facing the servant towards Ayesha, who squatted with a dagger in one hand and with the other helping pinion his legs.

We have a futilely struggling young lad held pinioned by Astrid in an iron grip with both his arms enclosed by one of hers. His eyes look like they will pop out of his head. My Latin is heavily accented, but that is a minor problem.

"We want to know which room the Count is in and which rooms his friends are in. If you tell us that and behave then we will not harm you. If you misbehave, we will kill you. The choice is yours." *The eyes are growing even wider, but of course he cannot answer.*

"Blink both eyes if you are going to be a good boy." *He is blinking both eyes.* Ayesha nodded at Astrid, who started to move her hand from his mouth. "Whisper only." Ayesha moved her dagger up towards his eyes.

The lad swallowed. "He…he…the Count, that is…he is in the end room upstairs. Eustace, he is the guard, is in the room next to him and his friend… Master Antonio…the mage, that is…he is at the other end of the corridor. Please don't kill me. I only took this job because I was keeping an eye on my sister. Please…"

"Which end is the Count?"

"Oh…the Count is to the north."

"Wait." She moved up the corridor and had a look at the stairs, cautiously feeling to see if the stairs were solid. *They seem to be.* She returned. "Put your ring back on and take him out to the others. Get Basil to tie him up and then bring everyone to their places. Don't come up the stairs yet, but I will wait until you are in place before I move." Astrid nodded, and keeping the lad circled with one arm, used her other hand to slip the ring back on. *To my eyes they both disappear.*

Rani

*B*attles and raids are so much easier once the fighting starts. I hate just *sitting and waiting and hoping that I have made no mistakes.* Astrid suddenly appeared. *She has a young lad literally under one arm and must have left her spear behind as her other hand is over his mouth.* "Basil dear… bind and gag him, please." She turned to Rani.

"Ayesha wants us to move to our places. It is all quiet, and the three are asleep upstairs. Our main target is at the upstream end of the house. The Count is at the north end of the hall and the guard one is in the room beside him.

Ayesha is waiting for us to get there before she goes after her mage at the other end of the house."

As she is speaking Basil has already gagged the servant who, although wide-eyed and staring around at us, is putting up no resistance. He finished that and pulled the boy's arms behind him and trussed them with some leather cord before getting him to lie down and tying his ankles together and then fastening them at the rear to his wrists. Basil stood up. *The lad has stayed still and quiet, his eyes wide with fear.*

"Let us move then," Rani ordered quietly. *Stefan leads Christopher and Thord towards their target and Hulagu gets back on his saddle and takes off, staying low, towards the tree line, his bow is in his hand with an arrow knocked.*

Astrid

*W*e head to the house with them all following me. She looked behind her. *As usual, Rani is making far too much noise.* Astrid raised a finger to her mouth before turning back and leading them to the wall and then along it to the door.

I am glad to be back to my spear without anything seeing us. Ayesha is still waiting patiently in place. Astrid grasped her spear and Ayesha nodded at her and put her foot on the stairs as she faded from view.

Astrid moved those with her around the lower hall. *These are clearly the servant's stairs and so the hall is not very big. Basil and Bianca can stand beside the two doors that enter it, and cover both them and the two ends.* She placed Rani and Theodora facing each way, so that they could fire a spell or a wand either down the hall or out into the yard while Astrid placed herself at the foot of the stairs.

We settle down to wait again. Theodora went to say something, but Astrid hushed her, holding a finger up to her lips. *Will she never learn? She may be a very good mage, but she is too much of a Princess to be a real raider.*

Ayesha

*T*hey are moving into the hallway. The other three move quietly enough, but I really need to find the time to work on our Princesses' skills. Despite their natural agility, they really have no experience in this sort of work. At least they *now know this and do what they are told.* Nodding to Astrid she started to move up the stairs and put her ring back on. *The game is on. It is time to see if they could māta, kill, the Count in his own base…Inshallah.*

She reached the head of the stairs and turned right towards the village side of the house. *It is unlikely that there are any traps, or anything that might give an indication that people are moving about when the house has so many servants in it, but you do not stay alive by neglecting precautions. The floors seem solid, and I have had felt no boards giving under me as I move, so far.*

What is worrying me more is the possibility of a locked door. She tried to keep in the shadows. *That is not too hard here, there is only one shrouded candle in a sconce at the head of the stairs and it is getting low. It is probable that part of the job of the lad we have captive is to replace it soon. I am surprised that the Count has no magical light set in place, but there could be reasons. It is only his hunting lodge after all, or he could just be tight with his money.*

Ayesha reached the door and examined it. *There is no sign of an outside lock and no turning handle. It looks like an old-fashioned door catch that merely needs to be lifted, just like the back door.* Getting down on the floor she could easily see under the door, even in the dark. *A light is burning dimly in the room, possibly in a shaded lantern, as it does not waver or flicker.*

She could see a scatter of clothes on the floor, a chair and the feet of a large covered bed with drapes all around. *They seem to be drawn back at present. With gaps like this under the door the house must be draughty in winter. It would need that sort of bed. There is nothing tilted against the back of the door.* She listened.

I can hear nothing, except someone downstairs made a quiet noise…it is hushed…and some rhythmic sounds of a sleeping man coming from inside the room. That is what I want to hear.

Standing again she drew a throwing knife with her left hand, and then cautiously and slowly tried to push down on the lever coming out of the door, to raise the latch with her right. It moved under her thumb. Slowly she depressed it fully and eventually it would press no further. She pushed quietly and slowly against the door. It opened slowly and she could see into the room.

This time the light is actually a magical lantern hanging on the wall, its light made dim by a pierced removable cover, and suited to lighting a chamber at night.

Despite the clouds outside in the sky, the summer night is quite warm, and I can see that the figure on the bed sleeps with few, if any, clothes on. All I can see on him is a large signet ring on one finger, but a sheet lies partly across his body. He seems to be an older man, and thus is probably a powerful mage.

She could see the opulent velvet of his clothes mostly on the floor. *His belt is close to his hand on a small bedside table. One pouch is open and shows several wands in it where they can be quickly grasped if needed. He might have other magic on his person, but it seems that most of what he has ready lies there.*

Despite her glamour of non-detection, Ayesha still kept her breathing quiet and made her motions smooth and stealthy as she moved to beside the man.

He stirred uneasily. *The proximity of all of my unfamiliar magic has some effect on him even while he is asleep.* Cautiously, she put out her hand and took the belt and pouch and laid them out of reach behind the table before putting away her throwing dagger and drawing the pesh-kabz for her left hand and her kukri in her right hand.

Allah, the Merciful, I pray for his soul. I have no proof that he is evil…that any of the men here are, really. It just seems likely. If he is indeed innocent, I ask that You be kind to his spirit and, in turn, forgive me for what I must do.

With that, she brought her two hands down suddenly…the kukri for the throat and the narrow blade of the pesh-kabz aimed through the ribs at the man's heart. He must have sensed something because, just before she struck, his eyes came open and his mouth opened a trifle. *His neck is that of an old man, thin and stringy and my blow is well aimed.*

Her blade went most of the way through his neck as blood sprayed out of the severed artery on the side away from her. She kept the other blade in his chest and kept a firm grip on it. *His eyes look straight at me and he shudders as he regains his vitality before teleporting to the other side of the room.* There was a faint "pop" sound as he shifted.

His hands are already holding his head in place as his body heals it back. He had two powerful contingency spells operating. The reason for her keeping her other blade in his heart now became apparent. *The cure has worked, and he is nearly whole, but as he teleports away, the pesh-kabz, which he had scarce noticed before, has left the wound it made. It leaves a narrow hole that leads straight into his heart.*

An evil look has appeared on his face and he starts to cast a spell. Suddenly, he stopped and clutched at his chest as blood began to gout out of his collapsing heart. *A look of pain and surprise now appears as his hands go to cover his chest.* He gave a short cry before desperately starting a new chant in High Speech. *It is time to stop that.*

Ayesha quickly moved to where he was on the other side of the bed. He tried to move away as he attempted to cure himself. She used the kukri and swung again at his neck as one hand came up too late to intervene. *This time there is no doubt on his death.* She struck again and again.

The mage crumpled to the floor with blood flowing from his chest and neck and his eyes glazing over in a now fixed stare of hate and pain. Ayesha stood

over him as he bled out. She was now listening to some noise coming from
behind her and outside the room.

Astrid

*T*here is a noise from above us. There is the unmistakeable sound of a
blade striking flesh and bone followed by the soft popping sound of
a teleport. "Let's go." She ran quickly up the stairs, two at a time, without
waiting to see if she was being followed. As she ran, she cursed to herself. *Oh
shit. I make more noise inside on a solid timber floor than I do in a forest with
dry leaves underfoot.*

At the head of the stairs, she turned left and went down the corridor. *At least
there is no reaction I can hear from around me.* She passed several closed doors.
Hopefully, the boy spoke true. Reaching the end door, she put subtlety aside and
just kicked at the latch with a booted foot and then followed with her shoulder. *It
is a solid door, but it cannot stand the two blows.* It swung open. *From the ruin
I have left, it may have been locked.*

*Rising from a large bed is a big man in small clothes. He already has his
hand on a sword that hangs on the bedpost from a baldric.* Before she could
reach him, he was armed. Desperately he tried to free a dagger as she came at
him. She feinted towards the blade that he held out in front him. He waved it
back and forth as she batted at his blade before thrusting.

*He is strong, but he is distracted by his split attention, and with my
enhanced strength and speed I am able to slide past his blade and take him
with half the length of my blade in the stomach before having to pull back as
his sword comes back around at my head.* With a roar, he followed up.

*He now has his dagger out as well, and although blood and worse flows
from the gash in his stomach, it is not an immediately mortal wound.* He
pressed towards Astrid as she moved to his side parrying his swing. A splinter
came off her spear shaft as she blocked. *I can sense, from the corner of my eye,
Rani at the doorway levelling a wand.*

She took a half-step to the right, and felt the heat as a fireball hit the Count
in the side. He roared and turned towards Rani taking a step as he did so. *You
fool...that was a bad mistake.* She put her blade right through his thigh, and
turned it in place, cutting tendons and muscle as she did so, and then withdrew
it. He stepped forward onto that leg and collapsed. "Do we question him or
just kill him?"

Rani looked down at the man flailing around on the floor, struggling to rise
and attack them. *He has lost his sword at least.* "Wait until Bianca comes...

and then despatch him," said Rani. "We already know that he is a servant of the Masters, and we don't have time to question him without taking him with us."

Theodora

I was going to run up, but Basil and Bianca just pushed past me. They are *running close on my husband's heels. I have to follow them. Astrid is attacking* *the end door, and Basil looks at ours and tries to open it. The latch obviously* *lifts, but something holds the door closed.* Basil backed to the other side of the corridor and, nodding to Bianca, hit it with his shoulder. The door moved, but did not fully open. Again, Basil struck the door as Bianca moved into position to throw past him. *This time the door flies open and Basil tumbles into the room,* *landing in the ruins of a chair at the feet of a large man in a nightshirt.*

The man is drawing a rapier and dagger from where they hang and looking *down at Basil.* Bianca threw her blades. Both hit their target—one in the left arm, and the other into his lower torso. *Both are good hits, but neither is more* *than an inconvenience to him. Bianca is already drawing and throwing her* *next blades.*

Theodora stepped into the room and to the side. *The blades hit him again...* *both of them in the torso near the first... She draws again. She has his attention* *all right. At least he is no longer looking in Basil's direction.* He dropped his parrying dagger, and started to pull the daggers out with his left hand as he took a step and thrust towards her, yelling as he did so.

Bianca parried the thrust with the throwing knife in her left hand. *She is* *too far away from him to use her other blade as a knife. As he recovers from* *the thrust, she throws again. What do I do? Basil is thrusting up from where* *he has rolled on the floor. Bianca has missed. My wand... I have hit.* The man was knocked off his feet.

As the man flew back and to the side he screamed. *In addition to my blast,* *Basil has struck home with a shortsword into the man's groin. Due to being* *thrown away, it does not look to be a deep cut, but it is in the groin. I think it* *has taken his artery. He is lying where he was thrown in a crumpled heap as* *his nightshirt turns red around Bianca's knives and Basil's thrust.*

Basil stood. *The man is ignoring him. He is obviously bleeding out his life* *from the groin thrust although he vainly tries to clutch at his wound to staunch* *it.* His screams continued until Basil stepped up and quickly thrust down and into his heart. *The screams end in a gurgle.*

Stefan

*T**here is noise from the house.* Stefan nodded to Thord as he pushed Father Christopher behind him. Thord quickly tried the door. *As we thought, it is locked.* Thord took the hammer and cold chisel and got to work. On the third blow, the door sagged open. A blast erupted from the lock.

'sblood... I am a hand of paces away, and it near knocked me off my feet. Again, we are right. There was a trap embedded in it, and the enchantment on the new amulet has stopped the spell. Thord stands beaming like a fool, untouched. "Father, you be stayin' back. I be needin' to a-check it out." He stepped into the room.

It is lit from a magic lantern on the wall. A pattern is drawn on the floor and there is an altar, similar to that we saw in Haven, to one side. In the clear light it is easy to see that the pattern is not fresh. I wonder if the men were coming here to renew it. There is a mirror on the wall, but that is all. He waved to those behind him.

Standing aside he allowed the priest into the room to begin work. "Thord, it now be our job to be a-stoppin' any move from rude people interruptin' t'ings." They took up a stance on each side of the door inside the room where they could see the house, with one looking past it to the front and the other to the back. *Our Father Christopher has already started drawing on the floor.*

Astrid

*H**e has his sword back and is still trying to hit me from the floor, as damaged as he is.* Astrid used her spear to knock the sword away from the Count, cutting his hand as she did so. *His eyes are darting around looking for a way out, as his hands hold his wounds closed. That is a big ugly ring that he has on him.*

"Remember Dharmal?" *His eyes swing towards me. Through his pain I can see surprise on his face.* "You do, don't you?" *I may sound smug at thinking of that.* "We took his village and asked him questions which he didn't want to answer at first. Then we killed him slowly. Now, it is your turn to die and then your Pattern will be the next to go. Eventually we will eliminate all of your Masters and all of their works and their people."

"You will never do that. They will save me. They saw my future, and they promised me. I am to be the new King soon, when we get rid of that chit of a girl on the throne. It is mine."

"Strangely, Dharmal said much the same until just before we cut his balls off. After that he was screaming too much to make out whether he had changed his mind. They didn't come to save him. We then had to go to Dwarvenholme and kill them instead. However, you just told me what I wanted to know... Meet Bianca." The Presbytera had come into their room.

"Did you hear what he just said?" Bianca nodded. "He is one of them." Her blade had always been pointing at the Count, now her gaze focussed back onto him. "You wouldn't know Bianca. She was from Freehold, an orphan who had been taken on as an animal handler and apprentice trader on a caravan, the last one you sent to its doom with Dharmal."

Astrid continued. "She escaped its rape and destruction and killed some of the people who did it. She also broke Dharmal and found out all his secrets. She wants to get to know you a lot better before she fulfils her oath to Saint Ursula and kills you."

Fear is appearing on the face of the Count. Bianca has a handful of blades and is wiping blood off them on cloth she has probably quick cut from the sheets in the next room and is putting them away as she does so. Astrid looked at the sweet smile on Bianca's face. *It is almost enough to scare me, let alone the Count.*

She mentally shook herself. "Luckily for you we are a long way from home and have to get out before you are reinforced by people who do not know about your perversions and evil nature. So, I am just going to have to kill you."

The Count's eyes are fixed on Bianca as she plays with a blade that she has just taken from its sheath and my words do not sink in straight away. Come on...listen to me. Astrid waited until he turned towards her to say something. *His hands are coming up.* Her spear thrust into his open mouth and the point came out of the back of his head.

The Count shuddered and died, and she twisted the blade around before withdrawing it. She turned to Bianca. "You did not need to do that. I have less of a conscience to be worried." She smiled at the other girl. More loudly she continued, "Time to get the saddles and rejoin the others." After a quick grab of a small box—*money or jewels?*—she began to gather the others, now crowded into the room.

They all spilled downstairs, brushing aside emerging servants. There were some screams as maids appeared from upstairs in the loft and saw them all in battle array and with bloody weapons. Astrid chased them back upstairs, beating at their backsides with the flat of her blade, leaving bloodstains on cloth as she did so. "Stay upstairs until we have left, and you will not be hurt. Quickly, now. Off you go."

65

The mages gathered a few things that seemed magical and then went outside. Basil collected some pouches of money and a small box of jewellery. Astrid turned and stood in the doorway. "Shuttle the saddles to the building with the Pattern in it. Bianca...let the young lad free after you tell him what we know about his late master."

"Make sure you tell him about the Count's treachery in trying to become King. That should cause some excitement. Let him also know about Camelback. We hold here until the Father is finished with what he is doing." She turned back to her task.

Hulugu

It is nearly done. We are getting good at raids. It only took a few minutes for Christopher to finish with the pattern, with those outside the building making their responses, and then a few minutes more for Thord to erase the names on the pattern.

Astrid has had to dissuade a few people from coming out of the door. I have only had to put a couple of shafts into the ground at their feet to stop others from coming out of the front. The hamlet itself seems not to have noticed the commotion.

At least no one has emerged from a door to come to the aid of their Count. Although a few people seemed to be peering out of shutters or doors, none have lifted a finger to help him. It is very sensible of them.

Rani

Well, that went well. We are now all mounted and headed back across the river to pick up the slave girls before flying off to the dwarves.

The girls were nearly in a panic, and they had to be gathered up as they had started to move away towards the river on hearing the noise stop. They had feared that they had been left behind. *It seems that the return home on the saddles will be an anticlimax. No one is contesting our passage as we fly away.* In the same three stages, they started to return home to their mountain valley.

As we fly, I have time to think about what has happened and what is yet to happen. If we are right in our assumptions, now we only have the Brotherhood to worry about in The Land before we can turn our attention to the last

Masters, if they were not there, and finish it all. However, while up until now we have been able to strike from hiding and so take our opponents by surprise.

That is about to change. We have actually used surprise more than capably, and although it seemed very dangerous at the time, we have minimised our risks very well. This may be our last raid. Now we have to move on to fight against a whole people, and that calls for a new way of acting. It is my time to take command in battle.

Astrid

*I*t is odd, but seeing the two together in that room, even though they are so *different in size, Bianca and the Count almost looked like they are cousins. How is that?*

Chapter VII

If it is deemed to be important enough, word can be spread among the Clans very quickly. It does not matter how far apart in the swaying grass of the Plains they are. In the Real World, after all, they are only a thought away.

Once a senior shaman or shamanka decides that it is worthwhile, they will enter the real world of dreams, call for a jirgah, a meeting, and wait for the others to become aware of their call and join. Together they will sit and talk and discuss what they need to, calling others to join them in the dream, until all those who are needed are present.

If a matter is really serious, and only then, they would call on the guiding spirits of the Umard Sünsnüüd, the totem spirits of the clans, and seek their opinions as well, not something that they ever did lightly. Those present would reach their decisions sobre, and they would reach them drunk, in a special wine that only exists in the spirit world.

They may be away from the shadow world that their bodies inhabit for days at a time if it is a matter that requires a lot of discussion. Once they emerge with a consensus it will be a foolhardy khan, of any level, who goes against their collective advice…particularly if the Umard Sünsnüüd had been consulted.

Qorhi Nokaj Jirgin (or Nokaj)
30th Secundus

I am senior shaman of my clan and respected even by the enemies of my clan. It is my luck that I happen to be closer to Glengate, or at least easier to find by those who are riding, than the senior shaman of the Pack Hunters. I have received the news even before he has.

He heard the new parts of the story of the Masters and of their activities, as well as their spread and their possible intentions, impassively, and then sat back in thought. *This Narjee is a good messenger and she has memorised the tale, as befits a bard and a böö. I see no choice for us. It falls to me to call a jirgah.*

The situation Narjee describes is so serious that I think I need to urge the tribes to unite and go to war for the first time in a very long number of cycles. Firstly, we will attack the Üzen yaddag düürsen, the Brotherhood, in the north, as they advance, and then, if it is needed, we will continue on and attack the Örnödiin.

Of course, if what my grandson and granddaughter and their friends are doing is successful then we will not need to do the latter, but they may still fail in their task. On the other hand, these Mice cannot attack the Üzen yaddag düürsen on their own. So far, they have only eliminated Patterns of the Masters which are hidden and concealed from the society that surrounds them.

If the people who are controlled by the hidden patterns have an influence in their society, it has also been hidden from plain view. Starting with where they are now among the Örnödiin, they will be attacking Patterns that are protected by the highest levels of the society where they were located.

With the Üzen yaddag düürsen they will be openly protected by fanatic sentinels as it seems, from the note I have received, the messages received through the Patterns are responsible for forming that entire diseased society, and the religion of predestination and total control of the spirit that it is based on.

Nokaj
an hour later

I expected to get support from the Bagts Anchin, the Pack Hunters. They helped in eliminating the original band of brigands and know much of the story as well as I do. Unexpectedly, he also received ready support from shamen of the Arslan, Ünee Gürvel, and the Amitan: the Lion, the Cow-lizard and the Bison totems.

These are the totems that most border the Üzen yaddag düürsen, after all. They have been observing the activities of their neighbours and are already concerned by them. The combatant parts of these tribes will soon be moving to the north.

The Ünee Gürvel had been slow to act the last time that the Üzen yaddag düürsen marched on the Baga Khana, the independent villages in the north, and Aberbaldie had been swallowed up. *Now the people of Bulga have already sent presents to them and reminded them of the relations they enjoy.*

Their little village is seeing more of the war chariots of the Brothers moving along the coast road, and watching them, and they are worried. Although they have stone walls to their settlement, they are only meant to protect them from casual raids and from beasts. One small village on its own cannot hold for long against a mighty army.

The northern clans prefer their neighbours to be Orthodox, people who did not try and enslave them, who greet them, even if it is cautiously, and who are happy to trade. We böö do not like the priests of the Üzen yaddag düürsen, those that we meet. They are not right in many ways and many stink as if their souls are long dead and rotten inside them.

It is harder to convince the other böö who have no direct experience with either the Üzen yaddag düürsen, or the work of the other servants of the Masters. Nokaj pointed out how the people that lived around them were blaming the tribes for many things that they had not done. He tried to convince them that this was the work of these shadowy Masters. *Without any direct proof to offer, it is harder for the others to accept my words.*

This left the matter to be divided: five for war, and five either neutral or against in attitude...and the Ayanga Gürvel, the clan of the Thunder-lizard, which was against war, had far more sway than its size would indicate. However, they argued, and it stayed that way until the Umard Sünsnüüd began to arrive.

They have not been summoned by the jirgah, but the Umard Sünsnüüd are here anyway. This has not happened in living memory or even within a time since the start of The Burning and perhaps not for a long time before that.

The shamen and shamanka were, at least as they perceived it, seated in a circle. Their positions in this circle were not fixed. They began a jirgah sitting next to ones they knew, grouped by traditional friendship and rivalry, but their images moved around by themselves as alliances were formed. One minute Khünd Chono, a Dire Wolf, would be seated beside Zaan, an Elephant, and the next, as the argument proceeded, could find himself beside Amitan.

Gradually, the totems arrived to stand behind their humans. Each had in some way the shape of the animal that represented them in the world, but they were not the animal, nor did they really look like the animal...they were more the essence of the animal.

None of the Umard Sünsnüüd are saying anything, although they rarely do. Usually, we of the jirgah gain a sense of what our guardians and mentors desire more than anything else. This time there is nothing exchanged except a sense of waiting. We all sit silent as a feeling of imminence grows.

Slowly the circle reformed again. Between the Dire Wolves and the Pack Hunters a space opened up, as if there were another clan there where no-one else sat. All of the totems seemed to give a small bow as, to the shock of all of the humans present, another totem guide coalesced vaguely into it.

To the watchers it was shadowy and not fully there. It was an inchoate essence of the notion of the guide. *It is obvious that it needs its people to exist to become more than potentially here.* To the surprise of all present, the new guide bore in its essence, the shadowy shape of a Mori, a horse.

Revealed in my heart is the knowledge that the Mori disappeared as a clan, along with another clan whose name I do not have uncovered for me, at the end of the last Age. It was lost because the jirgah failed to heed the signs that were seen by some of its members. The Umard Sünsnüüd had not been consulted, and they had not offered their own opinion.

The böö who were in the jirgah then acted from their own prejudice and for their own reasons. They chose isolation and non-interference over commitment and honour. The decisions that were made at that jirgah had not ended well for the tents. The Horse had gone against the wishes of the jirgah and had gone down with the other into extinction.

Their people, the Tangarag Khaalgach, the Oath Keepers, fought as they did on their own, but they had not been enough to turn aside the unfolding events. Now the Umard Sünsnüüd have chosen to act so as to ensure that this fate does not happen again to another clan, or perhaps even to all of them. They act on behalf of the Tenger Sünsnüüd. We will act as one.

Two days after being called, the jirgah had resolved three issues, when it had been called to deal with only one. Firstly, two girls, one of the Arslan and the other of the Bürged, the Eagle, would be sent to marry the young man of the Khünd Chono who was in the hidden valley in the mountains. Together with his sister by adoption they would all become the start of the rebirth of the Mori in a land far from the plains. The man would become the Tar-Khan.

Secondly, and indeed most importantly, a senior apprentice shaman of the Ayanga Gürvel Thunder Lizards would be leaving behind his totem, with the blessing of his spirit guide, and would also be journeying to the mountains. There he would marry the women of the Bagts Anchin and the Jijig Khushuu, the Axe-beaks who wait in Mousehole. He would be the first shaman of the reborn Mori…back after a whole full Cycle of time.

Thirdly, and far behind the other two in real importance, the clans were to be set in motion. That the Clans would go to war was decided almost as an aside…an afterthought. At the direction of the Umard Sünsnüüd, the whole of the Kara-Khitan were going to war against the Üzen yaddag düürsen and, if need be, against Örnödiin as well. The hammer of fate was about to provide the distraction that Theodora and Rani had hoped for.

After the shamen and the one shamanka returned to their tribes from the jirgah, three individuals were asked if they would accept the fate that had been decided for them. That night there would be feasts, and three people would think about the direction of their life while they were drunk.

Other people, the Kha-Khan, and the Tar-Khans of each Clan, would have a larger question to keep in mind, one with an answer that was urged on them most strenuously by their advisors. Would they commit their people to a brutal war to exterminate an entire nation, and perhaps take orders from people who were not of the tents when they did so?

Next morning, three people headed out of their camps with new clan signs hastily painted on their shields, and a gifting of horses from their families for their herds. They headed for the south and the east…to seek out and join together with those they were destined for.

As they left, fast riders went to the outlying tuman and households, and a drifting began in the camps as people said goodbye to those who would not be going and began to move slowly together for the northern or western edges of the camps. There they began to ride slowly in two and threes, which gradually clumped together and began to move with purpose.

From the clans in the north to those camped on the edge of the Southern Ocean, this movement went on. Between them, and sometimes being ridden, were the üstei akh düü, the totem beasts. For the first time in this entire cycle of time, the Clans, united, were on the way to war.

Some would head towards the Brotherhood, and others would hold themselves ready to strike at Freehold if it were needed. Messengers began to seek those who were not with the tribes…those who were acting as guards…those who were hunting…the whole People needed to know what was about to happen that they might take part.

Chapter VIII

A cross the plains caravans began to see war bands, which ignored them as they passed by, unless they had Khitan guards...in which case a messenger would come and talk with the guards, some of whom had been with the merchants for many years. That night, and without saying why, the guards would get drunk.

The next morning, some would apologise for what they were doing, pack up and leave, and join the passing group, regardless of which Clan they belonged to. Very few, across all of The Land, did this, and stayed with the caravans.

Some of these passing bands came close enough to the towns and villages of Freehold to cause them to bring their people inside their fortifications and to tremble in fear. None of the bands turned aside to them, but they kept on coming and passing. It seemed like the plains themselves were on the move.

Messengers arrived and gradually the towns emptied of any of the Khitan who would normally be expected to be passing through and acting as guards. As they left, many after long years of service, none would say why. Those of Freehold who consulted fortune-tellers had the image of The Chariot brought before them, time after time, along with Chance, which implies the intervention of luck and a resulting inevitability. Other cards of conflict and change were also seen.

Eventually, some of the people who were in power wondered how this fitted in with the news from Toppuddle. A young houseboy found himself brought before the Queen and her advisors. He related his story over and over again as they tried to make sense of what he had seen, what had been said, what had been done, and what had been found after he had been set free. He was even enchanted and questioned more deeply. The Dominicans began to look for answers among the people of the area.

Chapter VIII

Chapter IX

In the north, the Khitan discovered that they would actually have allies riding beside them to war. The Ariun Süm Morin Tsereg, the newly expanded Basilica Anthropoi, were about to go on campaign with their seven files that were now in the North learning how to act together as they moved. Some were still learning to talk to each other and not all were fully Human, but were Insakharl.

There were still not all that many men, only twice a hand of hands, as well as some scouts, but the bulk of them rode fully armoured horses. They could charge knee-to-knee, firing bows and casting darts as they went as a solid wall of lethal metal. They could even ride in a wedge-shaped formation designed to cut right through a line.

Due to their armour, not even a wall of spears would lightly stop them when they came on. As they passed through the villages of the north, they left messages from the Metropolitan to the villagers. These messages would cause the villages to look to gather in their own forces and begin to get ready to move off to the West.

Basil Tornikes

I was about to send the Basilica Anthropoi towards Bulga when the new men arrived from the east. I did not like the words that I was receiving from the people there. My files also record the earlier fate of Aberbaldie, when not enough had been done for that village.

Under the Exarkhos ton Basilikon, Athanasios Nichomachi and their chief priest, the Consiliarius Basil Phocas, the larger lead file was about to take the three normal files to a war that they would not have survived, when the

Darkreach men arrived, and after some time for sleep and prayer, they have all set out together.

Even with twice the numbers, they are not enough to stem the tide that threatens to overwhelm the North, but the extra men are enough to give us some hope. I do not think that the attack will be too soon, so I will allow troops to gather and follow more slowly with a vanguard of volunteers in the hope that my presence and the Icons that I bear may make a difference.

Others will follow behind when they can, or when the Mice come for them. It will take a while for everyone to be readied and to practice oft-neglected skills. It remains to be seen if we are all going to be on time. The signs say so, and we think that the full Army of the Brothers has yet to take the field, but we cannot be sure of that.

Chapter X

Theodora
1st Tertius, Midsummer Day

Carausius made his second appearance of the year at midsummer. *He has brought iron and other metals that are, so I am told, badly needed for our village to prepare us for the winter to come. He even brought barrels of nails in the cart. That has made Norbert extremely pleased; apparently he does not like making as many as we need.*

I had to laugh when he jokingly offered to kiss the trader in gratitude. It was an offer that was hastily declined. Apparently, making the number of nails needed for repairs in our village is keeping him away from far more interesting work with hinges and decorative ironwork. He hates doing them and they use up our iron.

In addition to trade items, Carausius has brought letters from the Empress to us Princesses and to Astrid, as well as a new man to join us. Tãriq ibn Kasīla is a quarryman from Silentochre with a familiar tale of personal loss that we are growing accustomed to hearing from the people who arrive here looking for a new start in life. Our Mousehole is truly becoming a refuge for the damaged and those who seek, or who are fleeing from, something else.

Both Goditha and Harald are glad to see Tãriq. Not only do they need stone for the basilica and the school, but he can also help Goditha in her work when he is not busy with his own. He had to recover from the idea that his first major task in his new home will be helping to build a Christian temple, and that he will often be working under the direction of a bare-breasted woman as he does it.

Goditha showed him what lies ahead. Of course, I have to be there to show that we are serious. I had not really looked, but even though the basic floorplan of the basilica has been laid out now, the walls are mostly the marking out of where the foundations will eventually be. Even the highest section, just a few hands of paces long, is only a pace high.

The floors, where they are done at all—and that is only in one very small patch near the short wall section—are more a sign of intent than anything else. There is just a tiny patch of still raw stone that has been put in place and smoothed out. She wants to put tiles on it eventually, but as yet lacks both the tiles and the skill to do the work.

I know that Goditha has already talked with Father Christopher, and she got me to write a very formal letter to the Metropolitan asking for someone to come and work on the mosaics and the painted icons on the walls. They will not be needed yet for over a year, but when they come, I think that they will be living in the valley for a very long time.

Ayesha bint Haritha

I saw how excited Goditha and Harald were at seeing the new man, but it is nothing compared to the reaction of the Muslim women of our village. I thought that they were being quiet on the subject, but they have been prompted into action by his arrival.

It seems that, with the help of Allah, the Patient, Umm and Hagar have decided on their marriage arrangements, but have delayed doing anything about them until a possible partner for Bilqīs arrives. It seems that our Christian priest will soon be doing some more Islamic ceremonies.

They bypassed my input, and although they have me with them for support, the three more established women are here as almost a delegation to him. It is all arranged already between them. It also seems that Astrid had far more of a hand in it than I did. She is happily becoming quite the sanie eidan al-thaqab, the matchmaker.

A little way behind the four of us are the three new women, Zafirah, Yumn and Rabi'ah standing in a nervous cluster. Asad and Atā stand even further behind the women acting still more nervously. Astrid is standing beside the men. Astrid is clearly here in her role as the sanie eidan al-thaqab and possibly even to make sure that the men do not bolt.

The two men are obviously not accustomed to the way of doing things among the Mice and being almost told that they will be married, and indeed twice so, in fairly quick succession is something beyond their experience. What is more, it is the will of Allah, the Unknowable, that there is no Imam. Even though the Imam at Ardlark has approved a Christian, albeit obviously one who is a shayk, a wise man, performing a ceremony for them, it is not something that they are used to.

The first marriages will take place soon and the second set before the assault on the Brotherhood. It seems that Tāriq has been left out of this meeting at present. Bilqīs has apparently told Astrid that she wishes to know more about the new man before she takes him, but he seems satisfactory so far.

Our tiny, and very ticklish, mage has a steely determination at odd with her outward self when she wants to display it. What kept her alive under the bandits is now turned firmly towards her finding a possible husband. It seems that she is firmly keeping Yumn aside as her second wife. Apparently, she approves of her. What Yumn thinks seems to be unimportant.

Christopher called up Zafirah, Yumn and Rabi'ah and asked if this was their wish. *Each looks at their senior wife-to-be before they answer. They have received a very direct look back from them. It seems that the three surviving former slaves have made their arrangements and will brook no dissent. It is not hard to see who will run each of these marriages. Despite being nervous all three of the new arrivals have told the priest that this was what they want.*

Next, he talked to the men. *All of the women, except Astrid and myself, have to leave when the men come forward. The priest seems to realise that they may answer differently without the women present. However, with only quick glances at Astrid, it seems that the arrangements were agreeable to the men. None look to me at all.*

They have not been looking to have their fate so quickly tied up, and expected to have more choice in the matter than they have been given, but inshallah is such a useful concept in accepting what is to be.

I have to admit that, having the woman who tied it all together for them also being the one who put together the Imperial marriage was probably also very persuasive. Even if they never even visit Darkreach again, their families will forever gain greatly in status by association. I can see letters going back into Darkreach soon.

Astrid just nodded when I brought that up. It is obvious that if she is going to have this role thrust upon her by fate, she is going to play it up. Soon, she will only have an unmarried Lādi to worry about among the Muslim women. It seems that I need no longer concern myself on such matters.

Christopher
later that evening

*I*t happens every time we are quiet. Marriages come in batches. At the Midsummer Feast, two other couples have come forward. My first are Elizabeth *and Thomas. They expressed their desire to be married now as well.*

Elizabeth said that she lacked many of the skills that a farmer might expect in a wife, but that she was keen to make amends. Looking at the beautiful woman beside him, the much more homely Thomas seems very happy to ignore any deficiency that she seemed to think she might have. He wears a very silly smile on his face.

I thank the Lord that Astrid and Verily were able to bring the next couple to me. It was Make and Arthur. In a quiet and timid voice, Make announced that she had finally decided that perhaps she was wrong after all in what she had been taught as she grew up. It took a long time and much prompting from the two guardians, but it came out in discussion that she actually decided that she "quite liked" Arthur who, in turn it seemed, "quite liked" her. I quite like their turn of phrase.

She could not think of having sex without marriage and that meant she had to find a priest. She knew that she would not find one of her own, and that even if she could, he would not be acceptable to Arthur.

At least her faith has been sufficiently shaken by what has transpired so far that she admitted that she desired instruction from the priests to help her make up her mind. From my point of view, at least her marriage will not be an instant one. It will be the only marriage to happen in my village so far that will take what any other settlement would regard as a decent time to occur.

Basil

*C*andidas *has the usual set of dispatches for me to read. I see that the Master's groups in Antdrudge and Nameless Keep are to be closed down soon and all of their contacts arrested. I will have copies of the interrogations of those who are captured sent to me… Good. There could be some clues in there as to where else we need to look.*

I must write back that we will be heading north before winter falls, and that the despatches or at least copies of them might, unless there is to be another trip, be more quickly given to me by sending them on the River Dragon *as she moves around the shore of Darkreach… and I need to mention keeping an eye out for her as well.*

Whichever way I get them, I hope that I can read them before we actually launch an attack. Every little bit of information might be needed before we go on to free Skrice. I also need to include the copy I made of what transpired in Wolfneck. It could help in the interrogations. There were several indications of contacts.

On a personal note, Candidas has delivered a written invitation. It seems that Astrid and I are invited to a wedding. She will be pleased. My wife seems to enjoy them a lot. Candidas has been accepted as a son-in-law by Carausius, and as a husband by Theodora Lígo. If we don't mind travelling in the winter, we can come to Ardlark and bring anyone we want. Candidas added that it was rumoured that the Empress is expecting as well.

This was confirmed when Basil saw his wife. She had been told by the Empress-Ambassador herself in her own Imperial note. *Fātima has obviously been taking instruction as the note is written in Darkspeech...so Astrid had to get me to read it to her. Fātima has either forgotten, or not known that Astrid cannot read Darkspeech in the newer script that is now in use in the Empire.*

Rani

I am glad of the diversion of Father Simeon's wedding, and all of the others that are going on. We even have Danelis, having decided on what she wanted, moving very quickly lest anyone try and head her off from her purpose. It seems that she has come to realise that she rather likes the idea of being a Presbytera.

My wife says that she fully intends one day to go back to her home village and flaunt herself as a returning ghost from the past and she wants to do so in style. Besides, as Danelis told Astrid, and she in turn told my Princess, Father Simeon is by far the most handsome man that we have in the village; even I have to admit that, and she would be silly to pass him up. Apparently, vowing to have no silver in her house beyond her hair is surely a minor sacrifice to make.

I am sure that we married samalaiṅgika are more sensible than the men. Like many of the men in the village, in the matter of their nuptials Father Simeon simply has looked stunned most of the time. He fled his home, and we need to think about what we will do for them, for the church. He was forced to leave his church and homeland, never expecting to even survive for long.

Now, he is not only still a priest, but he is in a different land far from home and is to marry. The men of the village gave him the fast-growing traditional sendoff from single life, and he has entered the married state happily, even if still slightly dazed. One day I will get used to sitting up the front in state for a marriage.

Parminder
2nd Tertius, very late on the night of Midsummer Day

It seems that the Masters are getting desperate for information about us. Stefan and Parminder, who were on watch that night, were disturbed by a shape appearing outside the village, possibly coming down from the falls, and moving quickly. *A Bird Demon, if I am right in remembering what Rani told us. The type Hulagu and Bianca faced.* Just as quickly, the gargoyle Azrael screamed and took off from her perch like an arrow and headed out of the village.

Later, she recounted it to her husband, one of the few to sleep though it all. "I was able to get in one blast from a wand before the two flying creatures met just outside the village gate, and there was a tumultuous noise as they joined combat. Stefan hardly needed to sound the gong. Most of the village except you, sleepyhead, woke up to the noise."

Parminder kept excitedly telling her husband what she had seen. "The demon succeeded in gating in a second of its kind before it was killed, but with a couple more blasts from me, Azrael succeeded in killing both of them almost on her own, although she did not look to be in good shape by the time she finished.

"This did not stop her from starting to eat as soon as she dispatched them, although she seemed to be having some difficulty. One of her wings was hanging limp, and she was having trouble chewing."

"Father Christopher then decided to adapt one of his cures for her, and the results were immediate as the growing gargoyle did the seemingly impossible and ate both of her kills, and each of them was far larger than she was." Her still-sleepy husband was listening intently.

"By the time she had finished, most of the village were gathered around, including all of the children. Most of them had never seen her off her normal perch. Now, she sits there almost visibly growing around her hugely distended stomach, and she waddles rather than walks. I have to admit to thinking that she would be better rolling."

"When she did eventually return back to her normal spot on top of the Hall of Mice, it was with more than a little difficulty, and slowly. It was only after a couple of tries that she was able to get aloft. When she did, she was only just able to fly up to it in stages. She landed both heavily and noisily at each stop along the way."

"I also have to admit to nearly laughing. When she resumed her perch she was as round as a ball would be if it had limbs, wings and a tiny head added to it. She is usually just ugly. Now she is comically so."

Christopher
later in the day

*W*ith *all of the weddings, or rather all of the celebrations before them, I was a little worried that the Christmas message was being lost within a few weeks.* He eventually concluded that they were celebrating birth and conception after all, and as long as that message was delivered as well as the festivities, no harm would come.

I suppose that point was driven home for me when the quartet of Robin and Eleanor, Goditha and Parminder appeared before me. Goditha and Parminder have decided to have another child, and want me to ensure conception. This time Robin didn't even try and raise an objection. It is good practice for me with a new prayer. Theodule can perform that blessing as I just don't have the chance to fit it in with my other duties.

Once we consulted on the subject, Theodule, Simeon, and I have realised that we needed to sit down and write out our standard miracles. Although new prayers come up sometimes, it is usually rare that they are needed. Every priest leaves the seminary with a small breviary containing the details of services, the canonical hours, lists of the patron saints, and a selection of generally useful and efficacious prayers. Often this is all they will ever need.

However, the situation here in Mousehole is a little different than most villages. For instance, Simeon has come straight from a monastery, and he lacks the knowledge that we have and are developing. He has even less than a normal priest in The Land has. We need more miracles to be used in the aftermath of battle than is normal for a village priest to do, and the prayers in regard to the Masters are unique to us.

Luckily for us, Carausius, realising that mages need spell books, has brought a large number of blank volumes of differing sizes on the last trip. In fact, he had an entire horse-load of them. The missionary priests up in Dhargev might also benefit from what we have. I hope that I am not trespassing on the prerogatives of the Metropolitans by organising this, but someone in this area has to take on the role of teaching and sharing.

Verily

I *am disappointed with Make. Having three more girls from the Brotherhood join them, and to the disappointment of Arthur, Make is going back to the way she acted many months ago. At least, although they had been firm believers until they left home, Lemons, actually Lamentations, Vanity and Pass now have no illusions of their role in the Brotherhood's plan.*

That disillusion, combined with their multiple rapes and other violence that had happened on the way to their planned executions, had made them eager to discard the way that they had been brought up. At least they reject, out of hand, Make's attempt to hold them to the way they had been raised, and for some reason, eagerly look to me, and my life, as a model.

Despite still blushing almost every time they see a man, and particularly a priest, they are making a determined point of working in the fields, and anywhere else if they can, wearing just a kilt. They even appear at meals in one, and with the addition of a cloak to keep them warm if it is needed. It is discarded once they are inside.

Make is left floundering, but finds no sympathy from her betrothed. "You ha' been told lies all of your life, m' dear'm," he said in my hearing. "It be plain. You only be lookin' at t' experiences of all t' other girls from your land. Verily here spent years sufferin', t'ose t'ree new girls had only week of sudden torment, but t'ey were under no illusions t'at t'ey were going to be killed out of hand."

He is a patient man with her. "You've heard how Fear was brought here, 'n' what happened to her. You heard t'at Vengeance man speak an' before him t' two brothers who be a bringin' you. Everythin' that you've seen points to t'em bein' evil. I'm sorry to be a-sayin' it, but you be raised with a 'big lie."

"It be to your credit t'at you want to believe t' best of t'em, but it be time t'at you at last give way to t' truth. You be needin' to listen to t' holy Fathers an' what t'ey say. Even t' heathen women be doin' t'at much." *My opinion of him has gone up. He is not just a dumb farmer.*

There is at least one solid advantage to be gained from having the three extra women in the valley. I am getting them to give much more up-to-date information on what was happening in the Brotherhood than Make and even Vengeance have provided to us. As far as the three are concerned, war is about to happen in the north. Rani was very pleased with what I passed to her.

They say it was once thought that they were going south, but now, according to all that they have heard, and what everyone was saying and planning, there will be a sweep along the coast. It is probably due to us stopping the Masters at Wolfneck, but the plans have now changed.

It will not be Freehold, as Svein had told us, but Bulga, Outville and

Bidvictor which will be swallowed up before the chariots turn south and sweep up the rest of the north…or 'the Lost' as they have been told to call them…and put the whole area firmly under the control of the Brotherhood.

Apparently, this is due to happen soon, no one knows when, but it is going to happen. Everything has changed and Freehold will now wait, perhaps until next summer. By then, the north will have been swallowed, and the evildoers living there will have made their choices, and repented and joined the Faith, or will have been killed, or made slaves.

According to Pass, the family that owned her had been told that their senior son is going to be moving to one of the newly conquered villages and he is already preparing for this, saying his goodbyes around their community and packing what he will take with him, and giving away the rest, and being given things in return.

He is to take his family and leave soon. He is taking no slaves. He will find new ones where he is headed. The settlers will follow straight behind the spreading out of the army in a wagon. Anyone who is free and can fight is training; either to defend their homes, or to go forth on the expansion in the army, or among the settlers.

Everyone free, male or female, is under arms. The army is being deployed with small units and new settlers leaving the village all of the time when they are deemed to be ready to take their place in the attack.

It is getting to where the village is being defended by ill-trained women, the young and the very old only…but then, in Owendale they were far from the new battle and not going to be attacked in their homes. They believe that they are the ones doing the Lord's Work, and they only need to keep up a show to keep the simple barbarians of the plains at bay. All of the priests say that to their people, even as they prepare to leave.

The armsmen who had taken them to Camelback to be sacrificed had freely talked among themselves. They were supposed to go to the gathering of the army as soon as they returned. The priests and the mage were going to stay behind and would serve as the guard to the sacred place. They will need someone else for that now.

It seems that prayers for what is called the Great Expansion are said at every service and guarantees of divine favour are made. Verses are read from their Holy Book that show such a move to be inevitable and pre-ordained. According to the broadsheets, manifestations of Divine Favour had been seen, not just by Elders and Pastors, but also by many of the common people.

Greatkin received a mention by name. Even in Owendale, Vanity and Lamentations themselves had seen a giant shape in the sky pointing east. It was not a human shape, but more like a spirit. I wonder how the Masters did that.

"I will bet that we will find that this apparition is a projection of a Master," commented Theodora when she was asked. "You will notice that these so-called *Signs* only appeared where the Patterns are. They may emerge from the Pattern or from someone being used by it." She thought for a moment before continuing.

"Granther used a similar illusion magic once to talk to all the people of Ardlark at once, but all who saw it knew it to be magic and illusion…but then some think that him using magic is the act of a god anyway and after all, it was an impressive spell to make everyone see and hear him at once." Verily shrugged at that. *I now have to explain to the girls what they saw and how it was done.*

Chapter XI

Olympias
3rd Tertius, the Feast Day of Saint Nicholas

The next day, the new crew, as well as Danelis and Simeon, some stores, and cash for more supplies began to move down to the River Dragon. *Now, at last, we can transfer to my ship and be off. Rani has kept me here answering questions for too long and I miss Denizkartal.*

For my newly arrived sailors, the trip down out of the mountains on the carpet is a novel experience. Few people even get a chance to fly at all, particularly on more than a short circuit around a town as a reward or a prize. Luckily, being sailors, they have only a small bag each to take with them and these can go down slung under saddles.

Other saddles carried the extra stores. *It is good to have some experienced crew to go with me. I am glad that the Metropolitan thought of us.* "We have been preparing and training enough," she said to her existing crew. "The new people are all experienced at sea and can learn to handle this ship on the way across the lake."

Everyone and everything is on board and stowed. It is time to leave. Hugging her brother and sister-in-law, she went on board and gave the command to cast off. The current quickly caught their bow, and, with just a jib sail set, she turned the nose of the River Dragon downstream as she gathered speed.

Astrid

*M*urmurs from the spectators here on the walls of Evilhalt show that the locals are impressed by the smartness of her manoeuvring...or at least by the improvement that has happened in our handling since our first efforts.

As they head further out, the other sails are unfurled one by one: the mainsails, all three of the sails on the spanker, and even gradually the staysails, the topgallant and finally the studding sails as they flew south across the lake in a cloud of white canvas. The locals are now even more impressed, even I am.

Usually Olympias does her practice with her crews far out on the lake where none can see what happens if a mistake is made. Having an entirely experienced crew on board, she is less worried about that, and few among the locals have seen the River Dragon under full sail before. It is easy to see that the speed this rigging gives her, still odd even to me, impresses them.

It impresses them more as the word spreads from the experienced sailors that her sails do not follow the wind that everyone else out on the lake is getting. They have finally realised that we have our own wind.

As she receded, it is obvious that my sister is again in her element and is intent on making the best time she can. She told me that she intends to be in Wolfneck well before she is expected if she can possibly do it.

Chapter XII

Rani

*A*nd now we have our own, non-Khitan, cavalry. If my wife and Bianca are to ride to the battle with the kataphractoi, then we will have two spare saddles. I can take Goditha and her wife Parminder along on the expedition.

Although both are weak in combat, they can (sort of) use a horse bow. More importantly, they are both apprentice mages and can act to reinforce a spell, or even cast one or two of their own. Parminder's ability to speak in her mind with horses and eagles could well be useful, even her talking to cats could give us information if we are in a village.

We need to take Ariadne along as an engineer. Aberbaldie and Baloo have strong wooden palisades and Peace Tower has its stone walls. If she is needed—and it seems almost certain that she will be—then we will have Goditha along. She can help the Insakharl woman with her skills and strength when it is needed, and translate for her to other workers.

For this war, I am draining the village of people, and making those that will be left behind work hard to care for all the children who will still be here, most without parents. At the same time, we need to keep the crops and animals prospering, but I don't see any choice in the matter. We need many more people in our village. At least we have plenty of spare houses.

As they flew, she realised that they would have to start transferring people north in only a few days. *With all that we are taking with us, we will need to make several trips with the carpet, perhaps double up with saddles on the way out, and we will also need to buy horses and saddles once we arrive. It will all take time.*

On the other hand, my wife is again being secretive and excited over a new project, closeting herself with Eleanor. The more time that they have in Mousehole before leaving, then the more enhanced arrows, ballista stones and wands we will have, so I suppose that I should wait and see how long Theo-dear's new project will take and see if I can let her complete it. I can, at least, start to move our force north.

Theodora
4th Tertius

*T*he *first is complete. Now I get to show off.* The newly invented spell involved an amulet in the shape of a small shield. "See," she said. "Eleanor has engraved it with the image of a mouse rampant, and it has a strap on its back so that it looks like something a person would slip onto their baldric above the buckle to show that they belong to a unit. That way no one will know its real purpose."

"I will be making one every two days, or until I have to stop. I was able to make it stronger than I thought, so anyone of ours within, say, three hands of paces of the person who wears it will probably not be able to be hit at long or even middle range with any missile, unless it is a very lucky shot or enhanced."

She looked around at the listening people. "At shorter ranges I think about one shot in ten will hit instead of nearly half. I have also given it a fair amount of protection against magic, more than most casters in battle will be able to add to their spells, so that a spell will have less than half a chance of working against you."

"It is not perfect, but it should cut our casualties a lot and I don't want any of us to get hurt if we can. This one goes with the kataphractoi and the rest will go, most likely with the kynigoi, but it could be with those riding the saddles...or anyone...as we need."

"Eventually, when this is over, I will make enough so that everyone who goes outside the valley has one...but that is some time away...like making more saddles that everyone can ride or more of the amulets that are really strong against magic." She sighed. *When will I ever have the time for all of those projects?*

Rani

*I*t *is obvious that Theo-dear will not be going anywhere until she has this project completed, but that leaves me free to gather a few people and start* *the move to the north. Getting Hulagu to where he can buy horses will be a start...and that effectively means either Glengate or Greensin where the three kataphractoi are headed.*

If I send him to Glengate to buy, then we will still need to move the horses further north, so the other option of Greensin is far better. I need to go there anyway to talk to the Metropolitan and to try and get him to gather forces for the fight.

Ayesha, Hulagu, Anahita, and Kāhina can come with me. I may as well take the whole family...if that is what they are. I am still not sure. Hulagu seems to treat his two slaves little differently to the way that he used to treat them...and they treat him no differently in public, but it is obvious that he is not sleeping with them now, and the way he treats Ayesha is different to the way he treats the other two in terms of casual affection.

We should not be flying into combat, so the children can come as well. Ayesha has now been added to the roster of those caring for them. It looks like it is something that the other three just assumed would happen, but also something that seems to leave her a little bewildered. An assassin as an aunt; I will bet that they did not train her for that.

Father Christopher and Bianca can come as well. If I am going to be anywhere near a prelate, I want to have my own village priest close, particularly since I am a pagan. I am very sure of that.

She decided that she should send someone to Glengate. *If we are going to try and rouse the north, we may as well try there as well. Even if we only get a few people to move, it may be important.* She decided on Stefan and his wives on two saddles. *He is sort of from nearby and knows some people there at least.* They were given both money and letters. *I am not sure which of those might be more effective in Glengate.*

At the same time Aziz and Verily should go to see the Cenubarkincilari and let them know what is happening, and Thord can do the same with the Dwarves. We should make sure that all of our neighbours and friends know what we are doing now. We have a few weeks and it will not take that long if everyone hurries.

Rani
5th Tertius

It is nice to arrive in Greensin to find out that our mission is not as essential as it had seemed when we were at home. Metropolitan Basil has been talking to the Khitan himself and has reached his own conclusions about what is going to happen. *The Basilica Anthropoi have already left many days before, to ride along the coast, to help prepare to defend Bulga.*

They are being followed by a slowly assembling mounted militia drawn from the area around Greensin. They have letters to the leaders of the villages that they will pass through and hope to rouse more troops from these other villages as they go. Although mostly destined to fight as infantry, many of those going now will be those who are at least mounted for movement, as Stefan used to be.

Some of the rest have practice at holding on to the saddle of a horseman as they run alongside to increase their speed. Light wagons have already left with supplies and more of these are to follow. There will be no attack until we all assemble at Bulga, only a defence that will increase in strength as time goes by and more and more troops arrive at the village.

The levy, most of the village forces, will come along behind. Stripping the villages of all defence will be left to the last moment possible. I have proposed that they come along when we move through the villages.

I hope that the new Mousehole kataphractoi were able to pick up extra mounts in Evilhalt. There are none to be found here. Even though they have most of the Mousehole horse herd with them, it will not be sufficient for everyone I want on horseback…allowing for the three spare mounts that Hulagu deems to be the minimum for each rider to keep up a running battle on the plains.

I am also glad that I have Robin hard at work fletching for us. While the local fletcher here has sheaves of arrows lying around, they are all spoken for. There are no spare arrows to be found in Greensin and we will have to provide all of our own.

This was not helped by us moving towards the enemy using the four-fletched shafts of the plains instead of the more usual three feathers of the settled areas. Stefan has been working on saddles and tack as well as training people. He will have to keep up with that when he returns from Glengate. He was even getting his wives to help, the last I saw.

While the Khitan were on their quest to try and buy horses, Rani took Father Christopher and Bianca and went to see the Metropolitan. *He is glad to see us, and even more pleased that we will be sending forces as well. He knows he is no general, so he is very happy to defer to me on that score. He is, however, alarmed to hear what I have to tell him about weapons from the Masters being given to the Brotherhood.*

"I am not sure that they are honest magic, but they cannot be like a ballista or a fire-weapon either," Rani told him. "We were not in the best position to find out as the person we were questioning had not actually seen them in use. He just had written instructions on how to use them to pass on to the Brothers from the last Masters."

"There are three of them, and they are all made of metal. They cast a beam of light that kills. We think they are designed to be used against masses of people or against fortifications. How accurate they are against individuals we are unsure, and we have no idea of their range. What I have said is all that we know." *He looks nervous about these machines. I admit to myself that I feel the same.*

"If I am there, I have prepared some spells that may help against them. They are my own beams of fire, if you will…and I do know that they will hit a single person or two at quite some range." She paused: "We don't even know enough about them to protect against these things, but knowing that they exist will keep us on guard against them, and we are less likely to be surprised once they are used.

"In return," the Metropolitan replied, "I have news for you. Firstly, I shall be leaving tomorrow and taking more forces as I go. They are the first few of the foot, but not many. Most people need to gather in their harvests, or they may win this war and then starve over winter. I will leave word that, as others gather, they are to wait for you to arrive." *Good, we agree on that without me having to persuade him.*

"Secondly, I have consulted with my brothers in Ardlark and in Erave Town and we are agreed that we need a suffragan Bishop to cover Mousehole and the Hobgoblins and any new congregations that may occur there in your area." He paused and looked at the expectant faces in front of him and paused dramatically.

We are looking at each other. I am not even sure what he means. It is Father Christopher who eventually breaks the silence. "Who are you sending?" he asked in innocent curiosity.

"No one," was the reply. "Once this is over you are going to be installed as the first Bishop of the Mountains…at least you will be the first that we know of. I hope that church you are building is large enough to be a proper basilica."

He is smiling at the stunned face in front of him. Bianca has given a small excited squeak, like a proper Mouse, and hugged her husband. "It means," the Metropolitan continued, "that you will have to take responsibility for training your own priests and eventually setting up a monastery, but I am sure that is a long way in the future."

The Metropolitan waved a hand to dismiss that time to be beyond their current concerns. "None of our long-established and declared areas covers the mountains. Thus, we are unsure as to which of us will be your guide, so we may share that responsibility. However, that is still to be worked out and can wait until this is all over with."

Basil Tornikes

I am not pointing out that we Metropolitans have decided that our first Ecumenical Council will be taking place at Mousehole during the installation, once this is all over. It is the closest that we have to neutral ground...and even I admit to being curious enough to want to see the place. We can leave all of that until later, when we see if we have won.

Rani

L ife seems to be a series of surprises. We get back and find out that the Cenubarkincilari are sending two warriors on foot down to aid us. They insist that they have to take a part in the battle to come. They cannot ride, and realise that space will be limited on the carpet, so will not send more, but they insist that they have to be represented.

It would have been good if we could have had all of their warriors, but they are right on the matter of transport. It seems that their warriors are competing now to see who will come down to stand for them.

"We refuse their help at our peril," said Aziz. "It would be a grave insult to the whole clan, and it could undo everything."

"Be assured that I won't refuse them," Rani reassured him. "I will welcome them more than gladly. I already have jobs in mind for them, and I was already wondering who to get to do this work. They can provide the guards that Ariadne needs, and she will have them to help her and Goditha in their tasks."

"If they are good and strong, they can even help carry the ballista and its stones around for her. It will make her task far easier to have help, and it will be far easier for her to work with them than with some Humans who may be scared off by her appearance. They are also going to be strong enough to do the work that few Humans would be suited for."

Hulagu
8th Tertius, the Feast Day of Saint Hippolytus

*W*e *are often at his services, he speaks wisely, but why is Father Christopher announcing that there is a special feast day for the Khitan of the valley, and for once actually insists that we have to attend his service? Annoyingly, my sister refuses to tell me anything. She just smiles as if it is all a joke and that the joke is on me.*

They sat in curiosity as the feast day of Saint Hippolytus was announced and explained. *I am impressed. We must have missed this one before, but it seems that our Khristed itgegchid even have a patron saint for the Mori. It augurs well for us here. We must make more of a proper feast of it next year; if we are all here, that is.*

Chapter XIII

Rani
18th Tertius

*N*ow we begin the move of the Mice to Greensin. Ariadne has finished her ballista, far bigger than the ones on the River Dragon. It and the ammunition made both by hand and by clerical miracles, are going up to Greensin slung under saddles. We forgot that we need to move it all, and there are no carts available in Greensin. We need to bring our own.

This means adding yet another person to the group. I have decided on Tāriq, who can not only use a cart but, being a miner, can add his own skills to the fall of Peace Tower if needed.

The ballista needs two saddles to move it north, but the cart has to travel slung under four saddles, each of which can have only light riders. It is a delicate operation and requires all of the co-ordination and discipline that Astrid has taken so long to instil in the Mice.

Rakhi, Zeenat and Bilqīs are coming as well. All are apprentice mages and even if their spells are small—for the first two they are even smaller than those who have been working on them since Mousehole was freed—they can at least use the carpet and wands as well as being able to pick up any among the Mice that fall. If it is really needed, they can also add their small stores of mana together for one good spell between them.

Once the Mice started arriving in Greensin, they were installed in the Metropolitan's guesthouse, even though he had already left the town himself. *The early arrivals have settled down to make more ammunition as they wait for the rest to be flown up. Now we hope that the horses will arrive in time.*

Although the flying saddles cannot afford to digress from the direct path to check on their progress, Astrid did eventually report seeing in a clearing in the forest a small herd of horses. She didn't fly down to check, but I hope it will be our people arriving, as time is running short for us to get to where we should be needed.

The Metropolitan is gambling that the Khitan are true to their word by leaving the place so deserted. There are far less people of fighting age left in Greensin than usual, and those that are here will eventually be coming along with us when we leave. Some are looking nervously at Ariadne and her Hob guards. Somehow, during the transfers, Aziz has added himself to the group in Greensin as well and there is now no way to send him back.

Finally, Astrid arrived with the last run on a saddle from Mousehole bearing the most recent well-wishes and a supply of medicines and arrows. *We will have to start leaving tomorrow with the cart. Hulagu found a horse for that at least. I will not ask how much he had to pay. Luckily, that is not an issue for us.*

"Our horses should be here tonight," Astrid reported "but I would say there is some form of surprise in store. Not only are there our kataphractoi and a lot more horses than I expected, but there also look to be three Khitan. There is one man and two women. I would say that some of the herd would have to be theirs, there are so many. Are we expecting Khitan? Why would they ride with our people and not with the tribes? Anyway, haven't they all left for the north by now?"

Hulagu

When the horse herd arrived, they were all out to greet their new people, and to be frank, to satisfy the curiosity of everyone.

Although all of the tribes were supposed to be on their way to the gathering, I suppose that some could have been working elsewhere and are still trying to catch up, but why would they not only travel with khanatai gazar khümüüs, town-dwellers, but also mix their horses? They drew near enough to make out details. "They bear…"

"Their clan…" began Bianca. *She has stopped and is looking at me, and I am looking at her, and then she nods.* Hulagu turned to the rest of the Mice. *I can see looks of curiosity on their faces. I need to make what explanation I can at this stage.*

"On their shield, for any who can read them, a Khitan bears the marks of their Clan," he said. "Mine still bears a Wolf." He pointed at it and then continued pointing at different shields as he spoke. "Anahita has an Axe-beak, and Kāhina shows a Pack Hunter. We refer to Bianca as being of the Horse clan, and have painted her shield with the way we think that it should be for that clan. We had thought, from signs, that it was possible that all of us in the valley would end up being of that Clan."

Astrid looked from Bianca to the approaching riders and interrupted: "Those Khitan have roughly the same picture as Bianca has... Does that mean they are of the Horse Clan as well? I thought that there weren't any others of that Clan now. Have you been hiding people from us?"

"We haven't been hiding anyone and there aren't any more people," said Bianca. "Hulagu started telling me I was from that Clan because he thought that I was Khitan, and yet I didn't belong to any of the Clans he knew of and... well...this should be very interesting."

Somewhere along their route the three khuyagt morin have found some paint from somewhere as well. Their shields, in the shape of an inverted drop of water, and which were blank when they left Mousehole, now bear stylised pictures of the rampant mouse on them. Good...they fight under their new Clan sign as well. That is proper.

Theodora looked sourly at them. "I guess this means that I need to have a mouse on my shield if I am to ride with them. Can anyone paint?"

The arrivals drew up before the Mice, with the kataphractoi giving a salute to the Princesses that showed they were from Darkreach. After this salute in the Darkreach style, Menas spoke up: "Greetings, my Princesses. We have arrived and brought more horses from Evilhalt. We have also brought others to join us."

He is waving in the direction of these Khitan that I do not know and yet who claim my sister's Clan. "With your permission, if someone can show us where to go, we will see to the horses and clean up and leave them to tell their story. They saw our shields and insisted that they had to come with us. We have some difficulty speaking, but I have explained to them as well as I can that they must get used to dealing with all of you, not just the Khitan."

Rani got Eleanor to show them where to go. *She is reluctant to leave. Along with everyone else she wants to find out what is about to happen. This is not going to be just a matter among the tribes then.* As they left all eyes gradually turned onto the three Khitan.

They are surprised that I have not greeted them in the manner of the plains. I want to know more before I accept them. The man spoke up. "Bi mendlekh emeel amidarch baigaa khümüüs..."[1]

"Ta yuu gej khelekh bükh sonsokh baikh yostoi. Ta bükh oilgokh bolomj baikh ni kheliig yarikh yostoi. Ta ingej khelj ta mendelsen baikh yostoi bol bid

---

1 "I greet the Khitan" (literally 'people who live in the saddle')...

kharakh bolno yuu khamaaran."[2]

He is looking around. He is unused to speaking of the business of the Clans in front of those who do not belong. After a pause, he begins again in a fair Hindi with only a slight accent; indeed, it is less than mine and I have been using it now for some time.

"I am called Tömörbaatar Dobun. I was born of the Thunder-lizards, but the great Jirgah of the Böö, the shamen of the Clans, have decided that I will be the shaman of the reborn clan of the Horse following our Tar-Khan Hulagu." *I can feel the eyes of all of the Mice now on me instead of him. That is a surprise.*

Dobun continues: "I have been told that I am, if they approve of me, to marry the women who are among you from the Pack Hunters and Axe-beaks, and to make them a part of the reborn clan." *He looks at Anahita and Kãhina and it is obvious that he likes what he sees.*

He turns to the other women who are with him, and waves first to one and then to the other. "This is Nogay Aigiarn. She was born to the Clan of the Lion. This is Boladtani Alaine and she was born an Eagle. As I was sent, so were they. The Jirgah decided that, if he will have them, they are to be the wives of Hulagu."

"His grandfather Nokaj has sent a message to them, and has told them that they may only be his junior wives to a woman born not of the tents...they are aware of this."

The two women nod, looking around at me and the women near me and settling on Bianca. I have Ayesha close beside me, but my sister is the one dressed as a Khitan. She takes their intent and blushes as she draws closer to her husband. "Is that the case?" He is also looking from my woman to my sister and back.

"The choice of marriage lies only with you and not with us, the new arrivals, but if we do not marry those whom we have been sent to, under the circumstances that we have accepted, we can never return to our old tribes." *He goes silent and waits. All around there is silence.*

It is Kãhina who, after a glance at my other köle, breaks it by speaking up first. "For my part, and I think, that of Anahita, I am willing to greet you properly, and talk more to you alone. I want to know a lot more about you and what you would bring to our marriage. You have sought us out, that is good, but we are women of many horses and with fine grazing. Are you worthy of us?"

"After we have heard Hulagu attempt to explain himself, we will go aside

---

2 "What you say must be for all present to hear. You must speak a tongue that all have a chance to understand and, depending on what you say, we will see if you must be greeted."

and talk. Bianca shall come with us to act as our only female relative, but what we are to discuss is no business of anyone else." *Kāhina goes silent and everyone's gaze is now shifted back to me. I am standing and shuffling from foot to foot. My discomfort is obvious to all.*

I must say something to Aigiarn and Alaine. "Before I greet you, I say that this is all news to me. I am not married...yet...but I have one whom I wish to marry...and whom my geas spoke of before I left the tents...but I know not if she will have me...and especially, I do not know if she will share me... We have not talked about such matters." *Where has my confidence gone to? Will the light of my life say nothing?*

"You stupid man," said Ayesha, interrupting him crossly. "You should have realised that if I would not marry you, I would not have made love to you. I have grown most impatient with you about not asking me, and was about to say something to your köle or your sister to have them nudge you in the right direction."

"It is more than about time you married me, before my parents find out about our open behaviour and send someone to kill us both to keep the family honour intact. As for you having other wives, Inshallah...I am a daughter of my father's third wife. Three wives is a good number for an important man and will keep him from straying."

Before she has finished that sentence, the other two women are already nodding to go along with that. The three are agreeing about me already. "It will be my job, as your soon-to-be first wife, to talk to these women and to see if they are suitable to be married to you, and what they will bring to it, while you arrange for us to get married...tonight."

"I have decided that we will be married by my customs, and our children will be raised in my faith. Father Christopher knows how to conduct a marriage for my faith. You may talk to him...now." *She pushes me away and moves towards the new-come women with a calculating expression on her face before turning to me.*

"Hurry and go," Ayesha said. "There is much to for you to arrange and very little time for you to do it. Bianca will be busy, so Astrid will help you. She knows the right things to have."

Astrid

*T**he main problem for the marriage...and one that Ayesha has forgotten about entirely...is finding a white dress and a canopy in time. Luckily, I remember all that is required.* She began to run around Greensin asking the women and explaining what it was needed for. An elaborate lace tablecloth was borrowed and would serve for the canopy, but the dress was harder.

She eventually found one that would probably fit, even if it bore not even the slightest resemblance to a Caliphate dress. *It is the Feast Day dress of a merchant's wife, and I have to promise that it will not be cut in any way and it will have to be returned after the ceremony…and that the owner can come along to the marriage.*

The seven white bowls are also hard to find, but are eventually located. They are all different, but that is not a problem. Apart from Bilqīs there are none of the other Islamic women present to attend her…the rest of that role will have to be taken by the Khitan women…her future sister-wives, and Rani can serve to give her away—the same role she took for the other women.

Theodora

It is late in the night before the wedding is ready, and Basil has had to take charge in the Metropolitan's kitchen for it to be done, but it has gone well with six women dancing the Khitan wedding dance. Hulagu and Ayesha are finally dispatched to their bed as everyone else has a last late night before riding out to battle. Rani looked around the hall that Andronicus, the Metropolitan's secretary, had arranged for them.

The Mice, both old and new, are getting to know each other and to relax. Our few guests, particularly Andronicus and the Abbot, may be bemused by the behaviour that they see, but that was not my problem. My beauty and I have a village of very disparate people to mould into a cohesive whole and become one people.

Teaching the new ones the customs of the old is a part of that. Thord and Astrid getting drunk, Astrid telling the story of the Imperial wedding and making them all laugh…even if the new kataphractoi are both amused and shocked at the same time…the dancing from different cultures. Not just the peasant dances of the west, and some from Darkreach, but also a fertility dance.

There may be no other Caliphate women apart from Bilqīs present who can dance that, but Lakshmi, Parminder, Zeenat, Rakhi, and I can and are able to give our Havenite version of that dance. I thought that some of the younger monks' eyes would fall out, although the Abbot looked on with amusement and calculation as he watched them and their reactions.

He looks on them as though it is all a test that he has planned for them… to select those who should consider careers as priests, in place of having one as a monk. Looking around at their faces, I think that there are more than one or two of the younger monks who will be having a long talk with him later.

I wish that the wedding were being done at home, but I promise that we will have a new celebration for them when we return...before the second set of marriages. After all, we still have to present Ayesha with her necklace. At least we have a substitute for the ceremony.

I cannot believe that Astrid has brought her necklace with her. At least she has happily loaned it for the night, but just the night. Apparently, she is to wear her marriage necklace into battle under her clothes and armour. She claims that, if she dies in a battle, it is essential that she leaves a wealthy corpse.

It confirms for me, once again, that in many respects the customs of her people run very deep from some old time that is long forgotten everywhere else. It is a past that I know nothing about. I wonder if Granther does. At least I know that her old village is a very different place from that of other people... whatever they had really been back then.

Chapter XIV

Rani
20th Tertius, the Feast Day of Saint Cuthbert

*T*hat may be our last night in a good bed for a while. At least Theo-dear and I had it to ourselves. Now we all set out. Somehow, I seem to have Andronicus and many of the monks and trainee priests already looking to me for guidance. It looks as if the ancient Abbot may be running both abbey and a near- empty town for some time.

Our pace of travel will not be fast. We are all held back by the pace of the wagons that accompany us. Even the foot can move faster than the train. I thought it would just be our own cart with its ballistae and engineering equipment, but as we leave, many supply wagons seem to have been waiting for us and they are all falling in behind and heading north and west. I suppose that they are taking advantage of the armed force to travel in a safer fashion.

It will take us a long time to shake down into a cohesive unit. Hopefully, we have that time. Although we have the saddles and the carpet, I want those on the ground to do their own scouting to give them experience in the role.

Eleanor has little experience with directing a group of scouts. Princess had to yell herself hoarse to give directions. She is already complaining to me about trying to remember things she last used ninety years ago. Sometimes, like last night, I forget how old my wife is. It is slow, but I am sure that gradually our people will get better.

The five kataphractoi, three men and two women, ride along and provide a very small but solid block in front of the carts and wagons. A screen of lighter horses spreads out in front and a few ride to the side and behind.

A couple of riders, all girls who look more like herdsmen than soldiers, take turns at staying near the wagons and managing the growing horse herd. Occasionally, scouts drop back and change mounts. I am glad Theo-dear has *actually done this before. I learnt to plan battles; others used to handle details like this in Haven.*

Word has passed around the area that we are departing today. As we go, we are gradually joined by people from Greensin, its surrounding hamlets, and from assarts. They clump together as an ill-disciplined cavalry at the rear or as a gaggle on foot.

What officers they have are already ahead of us with the first troops. These stragglers are the bulk of the troops who will be headed west, although few have much experience outside the practice field and hunting and the butts. As my wife tells me when I complain, country folk always have to do this, they need to stay working on their farms as long as they can in order to eat.

Theodora and Eleanor are starting to order them around, just to keep them from getting under foot. I notice that Stefan has settled his saddle to travel near the infantry, and has started organising them into units as they walk. He is having a hard task with many people who want to travel with friends and relations. He must work hard at chivvying them into some sort of order.

At lunch he told me that Evilhalt seems to teach its people far more about these things than most of the other villages do. The archers and slingers started out walking mingled in with the rest but are finally split out. He has put the spears in another group and those with just a hand weapon and a shield are in a fourth.

As they walk, he has them move into files that can be turned into rows for combat. Flying over them all are the other saddles and the carpet, with his wives running messages for him. I hope that his voice lasts the whole way. He is doing a lot off yelling. Slowly, as we gather ourselves together, the forces of the north are going on the march.

Rani
26th Tertius

*W*e *have pushed hard and have reached Bidvictor, near the coast on the Yagobe Rivulet. We are starting to see some shape being given to our march. Stefan has units staying together more, and after talking to my Princess about how the Tagma of Darkreach camp formed up properly at night to eat and sleep and keep watch.*

No longer do they break apart to find their friends. Instead they listen to the few village leaders that are with us that Stefan has put in charge of each unit. As we move along what passes for a road, the wagons have lines of infantry marching a bowshot away on each side of them, and they look less like a mob of cattle on the move. Between the spears and the wagons are units of slingers or archers, and around the flanks moves our light cavalry.

Ahead of the wagons, our few mounted infantries and the heavy cavalry move in a column, the Mice in the lead. Even Theo-dear must admit that we look a lot more like an army than we once had. We still have a long way to go, but we are started down that road.

It seems to be falling to Stefan to try and mould this force into something that can obey orders, take fire, and repel a charge from the disciplined Brotherhood chariots. It is a big challenge for him, but he is fully throwing himself into it. The common soldiers are going to sleep tired. As for Stefan, he is sometimes near to falling asleep in his saddle.

Bidvictor is a small village with large flocks of sheep. Our saddle-riders have warned the people there that the army is on the way. Its forces are all gathered and waiting for us when we heave into view. The church here is dedicated to Saint Cuthbert, the patron of shepherds, and his feast day is on the twentieth of Tertius.

The locals did not want to leave before then. It is their most significant day of the year. The most important additions to our forces here are the local mage and his apprentice. Apparently, Justin Speller has near as much power to use as I do, although as a water mage he is, of course, less powerful in battle.

Rani
27th Tertius, the Feast Day of Saint Zita

*I*t is morning, and we need to split up these people. Rani gave a deep sigh. *Just like the people of Greensin, the people of Bidvictor also want to travel in a mob with their friends like a flock of their own sheep on the move. Stefan and Eleanor need to take firm charge of them. It seems that the two must start out all over again.*

Although the people we have added have at least some training as armsmen, apart *from their scouts they are more used to acting defensively behind their earthen rampart and timber wall. They have little notion of forming as a unit in an open battle.*

Luckily it will be a quite a few days more before we reach our next stop. Also, luckily it is summer, and the days are long. Each night when we stop, while meals are being prepared, the troops are drilling. While the infantry march, the cavalry now divides into two groups: the kynigoi, and the heavier troops with lances.

They are being drilled around the infantry as they move. Only two of the wealthy farmers from Bidvictor have enough armour on their horses to take a place with the kataphractoi, but the rest can form a follow-up body to spread out and exploit the holes that will hopefully be formed in the enemy ranks from the charge of our kataphracts.

Theodora
28th Tertius

I am despairing, how Stefan puts up with it I do not know. I know that in Darkreach it is reckoned to take two years to produce a fully trained foot soldier, or kynigoi, and even more for the kataphractoi. We have a scarce two weeks to do it at the fast pace that we are travelling, and we must do it on the move without even the luxury of enough sleep.

Most of our forces know how to use their motley collection of weapons, to some degree or another, but getting them to act together and with the singularity of purpose that an army should have is another matter.

Even getting them to divide up so that those with long spears are together, and those with just a bow or with sword or short spear and shield stand in another place, is hard. Each wants to be with their friends and relations… rather than where they will do the most good.

It is lucky the Metropolitan has given out firm instructions, and the village priests seem to have the authority to convince the stubborn to listen to us, or at least to convince their local leaders enough to get them to do the convincing. We march as hard and fast as we can, and practice as we go. I think that Stefan really needs to conserve his voice.

Third Disciple, Elder Brother Joachim Nile
31st Tertius

I am surrounded by the chariots and the infantry of the Faithful and I am well pleased with what I see. As Third Disciple, I am responsible for the armed might of the Brotherhood of Believers and have been for some time. This is the culmination of my life's work and it is good. The assembly point in Greatkin is near to bursting with the power of the Prophets.

Each chariot now bears one of the new crossbows with their winches that, as a crank is turned, can spit out death far quicker and further than any Khitan archer. Our pack train has many cases of spare bolts carried along in *the wagons. We have enough for any conceivable campaign, even if we cannot retrieve them.*

Flags and banners blazoned with crosses, and images, and passages, from the Book of the Prophets fly proudly above the units. Nothing can stand before us. According to the Archangels, there is a small force of the Unbelievers near Bulga, but we will sweep them aside as we advance. The Archangels can tell us no more when we leave here, but that should be sufficient.

As the commander of the Forces of the Faithful of the Brotherhood of Believers, I am, of course, both a priest and a warrior. I am about to set in motion that which has been prophesied, and which the Archangels have personally told me has to take place. He looked at his wife, Sister Cast Thy Bread Upon The Waters Nile.

She stands proud and armoured in her own chariot. Around her are the best female warriors of our Faith. When I leave, she will head south to Owendale, and then around to Peace Tower running a continuous armed sweep with her own chariots along their southern flank.

She is also both a priest and a warrior, but as my wife, her role will be to lead the women of the Faithful in defence of our homes. It is her role to make everything look unchanged while she patrols the edge of the forest. She will keep at bay the wandering pagans, while I add to the Glory of God in the east.

I know that all will be well and that the Power of God is in us. The Archangels have blessed our work. Last night, ten slave girls were dispatched to add to the power of the blessing and the consecration of our task. More are in a caged wagon ready to be dispatched if they are needed. I personally hope that we will not need to sacrifice them.

In the field it will be hard to keep such an activity concealed. Some of the ordinary soldiers will not realise that these soulless ones are only there to be convenient to the faithful in any way that they can, and that convenience is often best served by their death. The common soldiers and those with less faith will perhaps feel as if we are killing people. It could impact their morale.

He looked at Brother Enoch and Sister Will-of-the-Lord-Malachi, the First Disciple and his wife, as they stood on a stand to view the forces of the Faithful. *Together with Brother Job, Enoch and I shared a special Holy Communion last night.*

The slave girls had been kept pure and virgin, and so, when we took them carnally, and showed the power and virility of the leadership of the True Believers as they were dispatched with the sacred Knife of Sacrifice, the gift of the Archangels to our original First Disciple, it had a special significance. The watching Archangels were pleased and even said so.

Enoch nods to me. *It is time.* He looked to where a small group of light chariots and horses carried some of the select of the Flails of God and their *special weapons. We are specially blessed by these. They are the Gifts of Heaven through the Archangels themselves.*

They will strike down the walls of the villages that we face, and any stubborn blocks of resistance that try to hold up the forces of the Lord. I have seen them tested and they can strike further than any bow, and indeed further than almost any mage. What is more, they can strike more often and more powerfully than anything else, mage or ballista.

He then looked back over the rest of the army. *At the edges of the clearing I can see the supply wagons, and then the armed men who will be following behind us with their wives, their children, and their wagons of farm supplies to hold the lands of the north in the name of God. It is all as it should be, Praise the Lord.*

Using a magic token that amplified his voice, Joachim pronounced a benediction over them all and then called their forces into motion to a vast cheer. *The few mounted Flails lead us out as scouts; then come the light chariots, the rest of the Flails, and the mass of heavy chariots.*

He took his place in his four-horsed chariot in the front of the others armed the same, and the bulk of the infantry and the remainder fell in behind. *My army cannot adopt its battle formation until we emerge from the forest and with a force this large, we will travel very slowly along the roads. It is fortunate that there is no urgency in our advance.*

He smiled the contented smile of a man who sees all his plans coming to fruition. *We have until it is nearly winter to reach Wolfneck, and the forces that we will be likely to encounter will scarce slow us down at all once we have reached the open plains. With God and the Archangels on our side, this Crusade is unstoppable.*

My scouts have told me that there is no sign of the Khitan along our flanks or ahead of us, and by the time they find out about my force, it will be too late for them, and my chariots will own the whole coast and be ready to sweep south. Our weapons of light will scythe them down whenever they concentrate and end their pestilential heathen annoyance.

Rani
34th Tertius

*O*utville *is a larger village than Bidvictor, and has more troops to give to the fight, although some of them have previously left. It is also was a port, and the village's boats are already shuttling food forward to Bulga and stand ready to bring back wounded and carry more food forward.*

Rani looked at the boats and thought of the *River Dragon. With her here we could have carried more goods and been far faster than all Outville's craft combined, although at least these can be run up on any beach to unload them. That would, however, have meant that she would have to have left Lake Erave earlier. No, it is best as it is.*

The village mages and two priests have joined us, and our experienced trainers have yet more soldiers to break in. After Princess, Stefan, and Eleanor consulted, the new troops were broken up into the existing units so that they will have someone "experienced" with these new ideas near them to help. I am sure that our time is running out to teach them.

I have also decided to force our march to go even harder, and yet break a little earlier, to give them some more drill time at the end of the day. At least now I have an idea of what sort of units I will have to work with.

Each day now there were some who ended up riding on a wagon as blisters and fatigue took a toll, and the priests and other healers were being kept busy even before the combat started. Some who could not keep up were even left behind in little groups to catch up when they could. *We cannot afford to have too many drop out, but we cannot risk being late, either.*

Few armies in the west pay much attention to these matters, but Christopher has consulted with Theo-dear about what is done in Darkreach and has decided that the priests should also organise themselves. I suppose that he is right...this is not just secular battle... In so many respects it is a Holy War as well, and the part that the priests play, on both sides, will be vital in establishing the result.

Astrid, commanding the saddles, can quickly scout over a week's march ahead, far ahead of even the rest of the army of the north, which waits at Bulga. She has told me that we have just enough time, and that the Brotherhood army, which is larger and even more unwieldy than ours, is only just starting to emerge from the Amity Forest and has not even reached their own last village of Aberbaldie.

By using their telescopes, the saddle riders are able to stay high and still see what is happening. Although there are scouts well out in front of the Brotherhood forces, it appears they are not thinking about looking up at what appear to be high flying birds. The saddle riders seem to remain unseen.

Hulagu is also relaying what he finds to those gathering in the south of us. South of the area where the battle will take place and between the Brotherhood forces and us, but staying out of the sight of their scouts, is a gathering horde of the Khitan. Now that he has the status of a Tar-Khan, admittedly of a very small clan, he at least finds it easier to get those to whom he speaks to listen to what he says.

Astrid
36th Tertius

It is easy to see that the Brotherhood army is well practiced, and from what I have read in our library at home in preparation for this, they hold a formation that will sweep conventional forces aside if they encounter them.

On emerging from the forest, they move into a battle formation with a screen of scouts ahead of their main force. Behind them, and in the centre, move compact blocks of several hundred infantry with long spears and sub-units of crossbows to back them up.

On each flank of the force are the four-horsed chariots, moving in disciplined ranks. Right in the centre of the infantry are a small group of light chariots. Unlike the other two-horse chariots in their force, which move around in small units behind the scouts, these stay bunched up in the middle of the infantry.

I am willing to bet that these bear the Flails and that they have the weapons that the Masters have given to the Brotherhood. I cannot be sure, and I dare not give away my scouting advantage by getting too close and being seen, but I am sure that this is the case from what little I can see.

Behind the actual army is a long tail of wagons that tie the army to following the road along the coast. The ones at the front of this procession look just like the ones that follow our own forces, but behind them are ones that, it seems, carry women and children as well as armed men. Some have cattle or goats or sheep around them.

All these wagons are what is slowing our enemy down to a slow walk. An army moves at the pace of their slowest, and our horses are being changed to keep them moving far faster. I cannot work out why they are bringing families to battle. Are they that confident? She asked Rani who, after hearing what Astrid had seen, admitted that they had cause.

Rani

"If a force is small or weak," she explained, "then they will simply be overrun by the lead chariots without even slowing the advance. The infantry force that comes against us is balanced so as to hold any strong opponent while the chariots swept forward and around them. It would work against whatever they would normally have run across."

She paused and thought before continuing. "It could even work against a smaller group of Khitan…perhaps even a full Clan or more. Unfortunately for the Brotherhood, they face a force that knows their disposition down to the last man. What is more, instead of facing a weaker, or even an equal force, we have the advantage of both numbers and terrain."

I have already flown forward of Bulga and selected a battlefield for us in consultation with the Metropolitan. He was very happy to leave the choice to me. At least he is conscious of his own lack of skills in this area and has no false notions.

Our forces in Bulga have moved up and are starting to prepare traps, stakes, and pits on both sides of the road, and forward of a long ridge that flanks a small creek running down to the sea. It looks like the sort of spot an inexperienced village elder would choose for a last defence instead of holding the high ground of the ridge.

Choosing to have our back to a creek looks like a mistake, but it is actually being used to hide much of what we have. It gives me a creek-bed to conceal our numbers in for a start, and it leaves us in a better position to follow up. Astrid calls it a maskirovka. Her Darkspeech has many words in it that my wife does not know, and that is one of them.

Now I must leave the training of the marching forces up to Eleanor and my wife. I need to move Stefan up to the battleground. He must get some discipline into the troops there as he starts to divide them up, as he has done with those marching, and to accord with my idea of the way the battle is likely to go.

I can leave the cavalry to the Basilica Anthropoi. They are best suited to prepare the mounted troops that are there, once I tell them the plan. Freed of the need to scout ahead, and secure in their knowledge of their opponent's moves, they can concentrate on training together and then getting the village cavalry to work with them.

Given that they are spread out and moving over rough terrain rather than directly along a road, the formation that they maintain, while it keeps them ready for battle at any time, slows the Brotherhood forces up.

They do not know that their formation is useless, as unbeknownst to them they are being shadowed to the south by the gathering Khitan force that, knowing how everything is arranged, will be able to sweep around through the extended tail, and hit the infantry from the side and the rear. The chariots will be caught between attacks from both ahead and behind. They will be expecting to sweep around a smaller opposition and surround them, but instead will have the same thing happen to them.

Surely the Masters can see the force being gathered against them. It must be that, once their people are away from the Patterns, the Masters lack an ability to talk directly to them.

Admittedly, the forces of the North are in the same position...except that the Khitan forces seem to all know what any one of their major formations finds out within a day, at most, and we Mice are able to send messages with a saddle rider.

The Brotherhood has set its war machine into movement and now is proceeding ponderously under its own momentum. It is not capable of reacting to what is occurring around it until we have contact, and may, in fact, be one of the last of the armies of the past as they move to meet our army of the future that is arrayed against them.

In my mind, which I have shared with the Khitan to the south and the Metropolitan ahead, the army of the North will only serve as a hopefully solid anvil to hold the chariots and to let the Khitan come in as a hammer to smash the Brotherhood against its immobility.

Although we will be drawing up along a dangerously thin line with our forces, the use of pits and stakes should allow units of spears to protect our missile troops along a very wide front. Those with a single-handed weapon and shield will have to cover the spots vulnerable to penetration and our one artillery piece.

Astrid has found a convenient hillock ahead of the ridge to put this on, and the same place can also serve to hide the Basilica Anthropoi and the Mouse cavalry behind it. If we have it right, we should be placed nearly opposite the centre of the Brotherhood forces if they continue to move along the road.

We will get to face those unknown weapons, and there I will hold the flying saddles with their archery, and with some of the last of our molotails raining down from the sky. Although a small force, as well as lending their ability to scout, they could be vital in the battle ahead, for the confusion that they will sow as much as anything else.

Chapter XV

Rani
2nd Quattro

Bulga lies on the eastern bank of an inlet of the Saltash River where it is shallow, but still tidal. There is a high hill to the east on which is a large windmill. The town itself has a stone wall and can only be accessed from the west over a stone bridge.

Although the depth of the river and its mud would stop a direct charge by chariots, the river is apparently shallow enough only half a day above the village to allow both horses and infantry to cross—if they go carefully. If the village were surprised, it would not hold against the force that is coming to it for longer than a day. Once taken, the chariots would have come across via the road and laid waste to its hinterland.

Thankfully, our opponents seem to think that, despite everything, they have kept the element of surprise on their side. They are even keeping their scouts close to their main force to avoid giving this away, for which I am grateful. I have cavalry ready to try and take any who come close to our line, but none have yet done so.

Rani
3rd Quattro

My chosen position lies a day's march west out of Bulga, beyond the last of the assarts lying along the coast on the small watercourses. By agreement with the Khitan, these are only put along the coast. None of these are located far out into the plains. Our last foot have now arrived early in the afternoon, just in time for the troops to be moved into their positions.

Stefan is giving our men and women some last drill and practice in place. He is making sure they know what to do and when to do it. The wagons are coming up and hot food being prepared. A generous serving of ale and cider will be provided before holding services and allowing the troops to have a good sleep on a balmy night.

They will be up early for another service and a warm breakfast before most of the wagons, and the men and women with them, retire out of sight behind the ridge. Our forces can then rest in their places. Unless there is delay, our enemy's advance should bring them to the line before lunch tomorrow, although I expect skirmishes before that.

It is essential that my kynigoi keep the Brotherhood scouts from discovering about the pits and spikes. This must be done carefully without revealing the ballista, the aerial forces, the heavy cavalry or the strength of the allied mages. They will know where the first assarts are and that is only just behind us over the ridge.

It must seem as if the Brotherhood are facing local forces only, taking up a desperate fight as far from their homes as possible. It is all another of Astrid's maskirovka. The enemy scouts have to be driven back from the obstacles. We need to let only a few infantry be seen by them, at least until the Brotherhood commits their chariots in a charge, and it is hopefully too late for them to salvage any of their troops.

Once this is done, then the majority of the allied infantry can rise from the creek bed and defend their obstacles and the Khitan can begin their advance. That is the plan, at any rate. Now, let us see if we can somehow get the battle to follow the script that we have written. If we can, it may be a first for any battle.

At least I do have the advantage of knowing exactly what their dispositions are, while they seem to know very little of ours. It even seems as if our saddles may still be secret from them, or at least their potential in a battle is being underestimated.

The Masters must be watching this battle from afar though, and even if they cannot say what they can see to the Brotherhood forces, they will be noting everything that happens for any future encounters. After this is over, and if we win, I will need to think about new tactics for the next time that we meet in battle.

Ariadne Nepina

*T*he hill where my ballista is concealed stands a good two hundred paces high, and has a respectable view of the entire battle field, and it is from here that flags will wave in a series of simple patterns to indicate some basic orders, and a musician from Outville proudly stands ready with a trumpet to tell people to look up.

The hill is notable for having on its crest a lone tall eucalypt tree, and already the soldiers are calling this the Battle of One Tree Hill. I have sighted my weapon with care. I have even been able to use my time to fire some exploratory shots just using some plain stone balls. We have recovered these, and I am satisfied with what we can do.

Even though I am a little down the slope, forward of the crest among some boulders, the height of the hill gives me an extra fifty paces of range in addition to the eight hundred odd that I can already count on. I have sighted in my shots. Some bushes have been very carefully planted ahead of me by Goditha, Tāriq, Aziz and the other Hobgoblins in a line that goes straight out.

Our enemy will not be able to see the bright-painted marks we have placed on my side of the bushes. From here I can see them clearly and they give me the ranges that I want. My weapon has at least twice the reach of the small throwers that I have seen on the River Dragon.

I have a weapon that is meant for battles out in the open. It will throw rocks that will take down stone walls piece by piece, safely out of the range of any archer. If the enemy are drawn well into my range before they begin firing the not-magical weapons that I have heard about, I will hold my fire. I can then sting them with the stone balls that Father Christopher has enhanced, and that he has taught others among the priests to enhance.

As we travelled, we gathered willow from nearly every creek that we crossed. We also used the time to weave these into large wicker baskets. Now that we are stationary, my assistants have made these into a rampart of gabions. Earth has been crammed into the wicker baskets, to add to the stones around them and make a wall.

It restricts my angles of fire, but it should help cover where I am from sight and also help against any directed magic. We even have one of the amulets that Princess Theodora made with us. I am dry-running my assistants in how to service the piece as they act out how they have to move. It may even prove that we will get a few shots off before we are found by these mysterious weapons. We need to be as quick and accurate as we can be in that time, lest we are killed by them.

Eleanor Fournier
5th Quattro, the Feast Day of Saint Ambrose

It may still be a while off for the others, but the time has come for my battle to start. My kynigoi are making contact with the cavalry outriders of the Brotherhood forces. I dismounted some riders and they have killed the first few of the enemy front riders from ambush. From the markings on their clothes, all seem to be what we know as Flails of God.

After that first clash, our opponents are suddenly much warier and harder to kill. We are able to press them back against their light chariots with our archery. The Flails are not great riders, and although brave, they lack confidence in the saddle. Despite this, I have lost some from my riders as the Brotherhood return fire from their chariots.

The advantage lies greatly with us here, as although only a few of my people can fire a weapon from horseback, we have the advantage of numbers and so produce a greater volume of fire. Those who can only shoot on foot pull back fast, dismount, fire a few volleys, and remount and retire further. They must think we are retreating, but I am really advancing to where my army is. She smiled.

Against the two-horsed chariots it is a very different matter. When these sweep forward, they come with a volume of fire that none can stand against from crossbows that fire impossibly fast. I have never seen their like before. They are not accurate at a long range…they prove to be even worse than horse bows, but against a cluster of troops they are deadly. Against a gathering they don't need any accuracy. They just shoot fast and cover a whole patch of ground.

It took me a little while to realise this, and I have prayers to say for the souls of some of my people. At least I now know how to counter it. I keep the Mice clustered near the amulets, while spreading the others out. This concentrates the fire of the fast crossbows on the Mice, who have complete protection at that range.

Luckily, the enemy leaders do not seem to want their light chariots to be too far out ahead of the bulk of the Brotherhood forces, so they keep stopping until they are well within the arrow range of their infantry.

The kynigoi withdrew, pretending to be driven away by the crossbows, but firing behind them as they went. *I can now see some of the allied infantry standing in small clumps in the centre of our line. The rest are still concealed as a part of our trap. I wish that more of my cavalry could use the small flight arrows that our Khitan are using.*

Although only two hands long, they can travel far back over the scouts and the light chariots to the four-horse chariots...and the infantry. Few do anything but annoy the enemy, but here and there a person falls or drops a weapon as they are pierced. If we could have put up a cloud of them, particularly if they had magical heads, it would have been more than just an irritable nuisance to our targets.

Eleanor looked up at the hill ahead of her. *There is no movement on it to show that the flags are even there. I cannot see the saddles. I cannot even see the carpet with the priests sitting on it ready behind the slope to care for the wounded. Though I know exactly where it is, even the ballista is hard to see.*

Calling her commands out loudly, Eleanor kept up the slow trot of the mounted archers back towards the lines, heading for the shrubs left standing that marked clear lines through the pits and stakes, clear lines that would soon be blocked by spears. *We are still firing behind us as we go. It must be annoying for them at the very least.*

Rani

*A*strid would be happy. I am just showing the top of my head and I am *the only one looking. I hope that the hill looks bare from below, but I feel naked.* Eleanor is doing a good job, bunching up her opponents and preventing them from discovering the pits that lie ahead of them, concealed by the long tussock grass of the plains.

There are a few empty saddles among the villagers' horses, one horse further along has two riders on it and there are several wounded riding back ahead of the others, but she has her skirmishers nearly back to the line of infantry now. Those without horse bows are already wheeling through the gaps, dismounting and becoming foot archers. They look as if they are stiffening the meagre visible resistance. She waited. *The time for my move is not yet.*

Nervously, she checked behind. *I can see Hulagu waiting in the distance. He is keeping his saddle down below the low ridge and looking in my direction. He is ready for his vital flight out to the assembled Clans. That attack must come as a surprise to the Brotherhood, or else we can still be ridden down by the enemy.*

There really are a lot of them. From what I can see as they fight back against Eleanor's skirmishers, the crossbows mounted on the chariots will outrange most of the bows and slings that we allies bear. Our weapons are largely used for hunting, after all, and are not meant for a serious battle and this is about to get very serious indeed.

Chapter XVI

Brother Joachim

*L*ooking ahead of me I can see clumps of spearmen being joined now by *some of the archers from among those annoying riders. It looks like they have spread out into small units to avoid being easily surrounded. They are showing more planning than I thought that they would. I had expected that my holding the chariots back would provoke a charge.*

I wonder if those heretic heavy cavalries are anywhere around. I cannot see them yet, but they probably will not appear until I commit my forces. I need to wrap them up quickly, but there are probably no more than twenty or thirty of them, and Brother Job has orders to hold his fire with the weapons of the Archangels and take them out of the battle first when they finally appear.

He looked around the battlefield. *It is almost time for us to attack. There is no need to try for fancy tactics here. We will just sweep this rabble aside with the chariots and then head for the village quickly. It is probably being evacuated as my army moves up, and this lot are trying to buy time for them.*

Some probably will not even stand when I charge but will ride back to their families and try and help them flee. I cannot have that as they will warn the next village, and they will warn the one after that. I will give them no mercy. The men must die, and the women and children pay for their heresy by being made slaves for seven generations.

Our traders, always with one of the Flails of God in their numbers, have told me that this creek bed dips, but that chariots can just ride through it, and then easily, but slowly ascend the other side to the top of the ridge. This is what we will do. Once we are there, we will continue straight on and encircle them.

Brother Joachim called out his orders and the chariots began to form up into their new positions as they moved. The light chariots shifted to the flanks, and the four-horse chariots moved up into an extended line that ran far to the left and right, two deep.

There are only two short paces between them. The second rank line up behind the gaps of the first. The books, written down from the words of the Archangels themselves, say that this is the way to sweep aside a rabble on foot. They halted. *We are just out of range of the missiles of the infantry who stand there ahead of us.*

He looked around and raised his hand with the loud-speaking token and pronounced a blessing on them all before calling his army to advance at a walk. He had scarce done so when he noticed that his crossbowman had fallen, and his loader was trying to untie him and take his place.

My chariot has already been hit by several of those tiny arrows that the Khitan like to use at long range as we move forward. Now, one of those arrows can be seen in the eye of the fallen man. A pity, the man has been with me for several years, and was a devout believer who even helped at the higher ceremonies when he was called to.

The Khitan arrows have been harassing my people, and my chariot in particular for some time, and my man has just been unlucky. Still, that luck is going to change. They moved closer, and using his magic, he called first for the chariots to go to a trot and then, once they were all moving at that speed, for the charge.

A roar erupts from my people as they rush forward into the ordained attack. It was a roar so loud that it prevented even his amplified voice from being heard when, looking ahead, he finally was able to see what was now unfolding ahead of their advance.

Rani

That must be the enemy general I see through my telescope. He is in one of the four-horsed chariots, and he puts something up in front of his face, and words come out that I can hear from here. I don't recognise what he is saying, even though I can tell it is Sowonja, but his troops understand him. They start to move ponderously forward in a chariot charge, just like in Haven.

He calls again, and the chariots pick up speed, and then again, and they are in a full charge. She spoke to her trumpeter who started a loud call to arms as the flag man behind her started to wave his green flag so that all could see. She looked around behind her and to the sides.

Hulagu is already speeding down to the south. The long line of troops are starting to stand up from where they had crouched or sat down the slope to fill in the gaps between the visible troops as the chariots began to fire. Archers are starting to put arrow to string, and slingers are beginning to twirl their rocks around, or use their staff slings.

Below me I can see Ariadne release her first stone ball. I hope that the woman knows what she is aiming at. She has fired early and before her targets have clearly identified themselves to me. As the crew below her leapt to reload the ballista she waved to the other Mice in their saddles and they all sprang aloft.

Ariadne

*T*hey are committed. I am supposed to wait until they fire, but there is nowhere else the devil machines can be. There are three chariots holding themselves apart and not firing, and there are supposed to be three devices.

She took aim at the centre chariot, as they moved forward in time with the walking blocks of infantry. *He is the one with the banner, and so is probably their leader. At least they are not in a full charge like the rest of the chariots. They are well into my middle range. A good shot presents. That is what I was waiting for.*

She fired. "Reload!" *Damn, that was in Darkspeech. My crew realise what I want.* Tāriq and Goditha sprang to the winder and began turning the spokes rapidly as Aziz twisted around to be handed the next ball by a Hob *Krukurb. Normally, it took two men to do that, but Aziz and the other Hob are both strong men. The other Hob, Haytor, stands ready with the next ball to pass it on.*

Below us, the first ball impacts exactly where I aimed, at the front of the chariot just above where the shaft joins the basket. There was an explosion as the enhanced rock blew up and shards flew out. *In the other two chariots there is consternation, and I can see their people looking for where I fired from, tracking with their weapons. They cannot see me, but they can now see the flag men.*

Suddenly, a silent bar of bright light sprang into being and impacted the hill above her. *The beam wobbles a bit as the chariot bounces and then it goes out.* The other device then fired and above her she could hear a crashing sound as the tree on top of the hill started falling. *I hope that the people there survive, but it is better that they die as a distraction than have the enemy attack me.*

Theodora

The trumpet is blowing, and the flag is waving. It is time for us to move. She nodded at Athanasios Nichomachi, the Exarkhos ton Basilikon, the commander of the Basilica Anthropoi. He nodded back and called the kataphractoi into motion where they waited patiently behind the hill and in the valley of the creek.

There is an explosion from ahead…it is far away from us…it must be from one of ours. Gradually, they accelerated up the low bank and sprang into the view of the assembled armies. *Behind us move the village cavalry. There are more than twice as many of them, armed with lances and a haphazard collection of armour, than there are fully armoured men and women.*

Athanasios called out an order, and the kataphractoi moved in their seven small wedges, their points towards the enemy along the lanes left clear of pits and stakes. *The village cavalry tuck in behind, using us as cover.*

Above me, I can see two beams of light lashing the hill as the saddles dart over all. One beam has switched its aim and is trying to find a saddle, but our experience with the dragon has served us Mice well. Astrid has the saddles weaving around as they fly. It would be sheer chance if one were hit. One briefly stabbed out towards where we move towards them, but their general has not thought ahead.

The chariots ahead of him block most of the fire, and although we are coming down a slight slope, there is not a flat enough angle to wipe us out in one sweep. Still, one man on the far left was carved in half, and another screamed in pain before the light blinked out. Suddenly, there was another explosion.

A chariot catapults in the air as its beam swings wildly before going out. We knew that we would be charging from too close to the enemy for us to use our bows, so we all have our martobulli in our hands ready to throw them. Our lances are held in the shield hand ready to be grabbed. The reins are looped on the pommel and our horses we steer with our knees

Bolts are spitting out of the chariots ahead of us at an amazing rate. I can feel them hitting my armour and glancing off or dangling from the padding I wear over it. Even if none came through I will be bruised and sore for some time. I hope none hit the open space over my eyes below the helmet and above the mail drape.

The entire fire of the heavy chariots seems to be concentrated on us. Good for the rest, bad for us kataphractoi. From the corners of my eyes I can see that some are going down, but most of the bolts are not penetrating the padding and the metal lames that are underneath. Luckily the heavier armour on the horses seems mostly to be holding as well, although some are going down.

They moved towards the gaps in the allied line and thundered on in a charge. *We should strike our targets just as the first chariots hit the pits. Ahead I can already see chariots without crossbowmen. There are others without drivers. I must aim us for a gap, to pass between the chariots and so not run into them and hurt our own horses and yet stay in the lane without pits.*

Rani

*T*hat *was close.* A beam silently flickered between the saddles and they dodged apart to reform a little further on. *It is not ideal for spellcasting to be flying and dodging a beam at the same time but casting in battle is what I have trained for. I have practiced parts of this spell for some time, although I have only cast it once to make sure it works.*

I will, without taking some Sleepwell potion, only have this one spell in the whole battle before closing and using wands. I am throwing everything into it. I had better get chanting without risking them getting closer. She thought for a while, concentrating the spell in her mind and then began to say the phrases as she opened her firepot to get the flame going in the wind rushing past her.

At least we are well beyond the range of the crossbows on the chariots, even if the occasional spell comes up towards us. All of the enemy spells fizzle out...I bless my wife's protection. Around me, others are firing arrows. At this height it is more out of hope than good aim if anything hits, but the enemy are packed so close that some must strike home. An arrow launched from this height is devastating, even without the enhancements that most have.

She kept the chariots in view... A second was destroyed as it somersaulted in pieces out of the action. *Ariadne has struck again with her stone-throwing ballista. She clipped its wheel with a ball. That was enough to doom them.* The other chariot fired again at the hill. *It is aiming at Ariadne. Now the spell is complete.*

She aimed her hand. This was not a soundless beam of light that erupted from her hand. It began as a tiny ball drawing from the flame in the firepot. It grew as it flew...larger and larger...and as it flew, it began to roar in its passage through the air. In the little time available to him, the charioteer who drove its target saw it coming and tried to turn his team and spring forward.

His own infantry too tightly hems him in and he has too little time. He has succeeded in moving the impact site from where I aimed it near the front of the basket to the middle of the basket, but that is all. It is a futile attempt, and in the end it doesn't matter. My explosion covers not only the whole basket, but even the horses and some of the surrounding infantry.

As I wanted, the chariot has just disappeared, becoming a part of the fireball. A moment later there was another explosion within the one that she had made as something that she had hit gave way. *A small cloud of roiling flame and smoke is seething upwards into the sky, growing into something like a small mushroom. A strong hot wind is erupting at those around the chariot, knocking them over. Some are on fire.*

Brother Joachim

*W*hat has happened? All was going well until suddenly there were explosions from behind me. Now I am struggling to drive my own chariot. My driver is down, and my next crossbowman is wounded as well, even if he is still firing. The beams from the Divine weapons are going out one by one. Satan must be driving the enemy. Surely, God is stronger than the Devil?*

It will all come down to the charge. There are a lot more of the enemy now, and they seem more formidable, but surely, they cannot stand against my chariots.

We are close to the enemy line and about to contact those damned armoured horses. A rain of small objects come flying from the cavalry and their lances shift from across their bodies to the ready and come down to point at us.

The objects are aimed not at us, but at the horses and they hit. Across my line, I see chariots going down in disarray as horses fall. Ahead I can see a small wedge where most of the riders have an image of a mouse on their shields. A mouse? What village fights under a mouse? He gathered the reins in one hand and drew his long-handled mace. *I am supposed to use a lance myself, but it has somehow gotten lost.*

Theodora

I can see a chariot with a large banner streaming from it that bears a flame and two crossed keys. It has only two men visible in it, and the crossbowman is trying to target our wedge. My amulet seems to be working well. Shot after shot hits me and fails to penetrate. Bolts are glancing off my armour or hanging from the padding.*

I am sure that it is the enemy general who is trying to drive that chariot. He has lost his helmet somehow and is getting a weapon from his belt. He has succeeded, but he cannot reach anyone and still drive.

She angled her wedge between his chariot and the next as their lances came down. *Neon's lance has taken him in the stomach and Menas has the crossbowman. I take the crossbowmen from the next chariot to the left, and one of the farmers with us has another person from the same.* A lance from that chariot shattered on her shield and she felt a pain in her arm. *I didn't even see it coming.*

Now we are through the first rank, and the second looms ahead. We are unharmed, but my kataphractoi have lost their lances. I hold a wand against the grip in my shield hand. I didn't drop it even with the pain in that arm.

She transferred it to her right and got in one blast as others were drawing other weapons. Her blast was aimed at the lancer braced on the chariot ahead and she hit him. *He has fallen over, dead or dying, I don't care. He will take no more part in the battle.* They closed, and after a pass were through the chariot line. Out of the side of her eye she noted an empty horse beside her. *Someone is down...Asticus.*

Brother Joachim

*A*s *I sit propped up in the wreckage of my chariot, I look up into the sky and then ahead at the line of my men. I feel no pain, but I know that I am dying. My hands hold onto the lance shaft that is buried in my vitals, and through them into the timber of my chariot floor. I feel my blood running out, but only a few of us are down. The rest continue. I pray that my death is not in vain.*

My Lord...my chariot line has disintegrated into pieces. There are screams from horses and men. I die now knowing that I have lost. Despite the promises, despite the omens, despite the preparation, and despite the active intercession and help of Archangels, I have somehow managed to lose the Army of the Faithful.

I can feel the darkness that is gathering in my eyes. It feels like there is something waiting for me, it is something dark that I sense and feel. It will be up to my wife to hold these demons from off our families, if she can. I pray to God that she has more luck than I have had. Where has it gone wrong? What had...?

Ariadne

*T*hat last beam was close. She looked out onto the battlefield. *At least the rock to my right has been cleared away and I can see more of the battlefield. In fact, it has a flat and smooth surface as if a jeweller has polished it.*

By Saint Barbara, that is a duel I do not want to have again. Aziz has a charred patch on his arm where the beam had, fortunately, ended just in time. It isn't bleeding, at least. To my relief all the strange devices are now out of action. Rani eliminated that last one spectacularly.

She could now choose her shots as she wished. *Nothing that the enemy has can reach me, particularly with my height. The chariots are going to be no problem. Although mages and priests cast spells from them, they are met by spells coming from our allied lines...admittedly a lot less of them come from us.*

Now, the kataphractoi have hit. They carve right through the enemy chariot lines to their rear. Behind them, the other cavalry spread out and begin to attack the rear of the enemy chariot line. The enemy chariots cannot turn and cannot hold against the heavy cavalry that attack them from behind. The first line of chariots is running into the stakes and pits. Even from my hill I can hear the screams of men and horses and see the carnage.

The people with the longest spears ran to cover the gaps once the cavalry were through, and now the swordsmen moved forward through the stakes to eliminate the wounded and those who will not surrender. The enemy spell-casters will have to move quickly to cast under those conditions. Some are, but they are also going down to the archer's concentrated fire.

She looked around. *We may have stopped the chariots, but our thin allied line cannot stand against the mass of Brotherhood infantry that are now approaching. Where may I best...wait...coming into sight, from my left, is a thick mass of Khitan. They are aimed at the rear of it all and the wagons. They can deal with most of the infantry.*

Someone among the infantry is trying to turn them around, to get them into a position to defend their supplies. It is time to stop that. She sent down her next ball. *Its explosion was unnecessary. I managed to catch the man in the chest. I need to keep an eye out for the next one to show initiative.* Her team reloaded.

Their foot are all well within my range, and I think I should run out of leaders before I run out of balls to throw at them, even if I have to just use plain ones. This is going to be a massacre. Good, I am sure that it is always better to have the other person die for their homeland than to have to die for yours.

Hulagu

*A*s I head toward the emeel amidarch baigaa khümüüs, I see that they are already moving. I am sure that they had scouts concealed on ridge tops waiting to see me fly towards them. I am no longer needed here. He wheeled and headed back to the fray. *I have a wife and the rest of the Mori there and I have to do what I can.*

Ahead I can see the day sky lighting up in white and red flashes, as enemy mages and priests fire spells and wands. Luckily, none of our opponents seem to have many really long-range spells, or at least the time and accuracy to cast them against the saddles, and most of their wands also seem to have too short a range.

This battle will change the way of warfare in the west. From what little I have seen in Darkreach, this sort of thing is what they prepare for. Now I see why. Some of the kataphractoi have gone down from the massed crossbows and mages, which seem to concentrate on them, but the disciplined units just close ranks, and keep on going.

The kataphractoi tear through the two lines of heavy chariots and the lighter one behind them, before wheeling and coming back into the disorder that results when the charging chariots meet the traps that were prepared for them.

The front of the Brotherhood forces disintegrates, as the few remaining chariots are either run down and overwhelmed, or else filled with arrows by the cavalry who are now using bows as well. The wedges merge into one large formation that is two riders wide. They ride along the front of the enemy infantry and shoot.

I hate to admit it, but the emeel amidarch baigaa khümüüs would not have the discipline to keep going through fire like that, and then reform and keep going.

He reached the fight. *Those of our kynigoi who can use horse bows have re-emerged from behind the lines to join in the destruction of the chariots that evaded the pits and the few enemy scouts that were mingled among them.*

He swooped to where the rest of the Mice flew above the infantry, keeping them disordered. *An occasional explosion marks where Ariadne is picking out banners or spell-casters among the infantry and felling them.*

Rani

*T*he infantry still keeps some semblance of order, but slowly their banners
are falling, to be snatched upright again, only to fall again later. The
arrows from us Mice in the sky are creating disorder more than doing any
great amount of damage.

Our sky-riders cluster around the person who is wearing the talisman of
protection. Each cluster concentrates their fire on just one person, an officer
or a bannerman, until they fall. As their officers fall, cohesion is lost among
the enemy.

Some units have started to move towards the rear and their supply train,
but others are still moving forward, and yet others moved to the sides. A
couple of units move towards the coast, and one, which must not have seen
the approaching Khitan, moves directly towards them.

Looking back, I can see the carpet coming out towards where the kataphractoi charged. The girls on it are hauling bodies on, before heading back
towards the priests. There must be many wounded. I hope they are safe diving
into the battle like that, as although they have an amulet, none wear any armour
beyond padded clothing and bits of light dragon leather.

Hulagu

*T*he more mobile among the Clans, the scouts and light-armoured riders,
have hit the column of wagons at the rear and begun to take them. Those
mounted on the cow-lizards are still moving ponderously to the rear. They may
not even be needed in this fight.

It is obvious that these wagons are, of all things to bring to a battle, family
groups. It must be obvious to the Clans as well. Unless there is resistance,
it seems that they are just going to capture the people and make them köle.
Occasionally, a man, or even a woman, makes some resistance, but those
that do are quickly overwhelmed. Mostly it seems that lassoes are used…they
aren't even killing their targets.

Leaving guards over the family wagons, it is then the turn of the real supply
wagons. Most of these have armed men who look ready to fight. Looking down
on one of them, Hulagu briefly asked himself why there would be a caged
wagon full of young girls roped together with two guards. Calling Ayesha to
him, he swooped down as he realised why.

Those girls need to be freed, and the Clans will not understand their plight, and will keep them as köle. They don't deserve that. The guards on that wagon have their bows out and are firing as we come spiralling down from the sky. I dare not shoot with the girls that close. Hulagu drew his lance out from where it was held and couched it.

They are Flails of God… He spat as he flew. *It is confirmed then. These girls were to be sacrifices.* He spitted one archer on his lance and his wife took the other as they soared skyward again before wheeling and coming back.

One man is pinned to the wagon through his chest, already dead, his eyes staring blankly, while the other has been caught in the stomach and now lies writhing in pain on the ground beside the wagon, wrapped around the lance buried inside him. The two Mice split up, one approaching the wagon from each side.

The driver has dropped his reins and is pulling out a sword and is struggling with the cage door. The girls huddle at the far end of their cage. The driver wants to kill the girls instead of fight.

Ayesha brought her saddle to a hover and then jumped onto him, allowing the saddle to just fall to the ground. *Hopefully, it is robust enough to not be damaged by that.* His body fell as Hulagu came to the front and grabbed the bridle of one of the lead horses, pulling it to a stop. Around him the rest of the Khitan arrived.

Ariadne

*A*lthough I still have a few enhanced balls left for my ballista, I finally have to stop firing. All the enemy mages or priests seem to be down, and the Khitan are beginning to sweep over the remaining infantry. Some throw down their weapons and surrender, some are trying to run, but most are dying where they stand.

There are quite a few Khitan losses as well. Few have much in the way of metal armour and the Brotherhood use crossbows for its infantry as well. Luckily, the crossbows are slow, the rapid fire weapons are only on the chariots, and the Khitan close to within effective range of their bows as quickly as they can, dodging back away from frantic charges from men on foot who lack missile weapons. It helps that they outnumber the infantry by far more than two to one.

Soon, none among the Brotherhood stand armed and all of the wagons are taken. The last fugitives are run down and they either die or are captured. There is a silence over the entire area broken only by the screams and groans of the wounded. Below me, I can see our carpet is busy ferrying the wounded back

*to the priests. Our allied infantry begins to move forward out of their lines on
the same task.*

*The wounded among the Brotherhood will have to fend for themselves.
Although the enemy have suffered far worse, there are few enough priests
among the allies to care for all the damage those damned fast crossbows have
done to our own people. I will have to get my hands on one of them so that I
can copy them if I need to.*

She started thinking about the potential... *One of those with enhanced
bolts...perhaps with a ballista as well...on the lifting sky-wagon for the timber...
with armour to protect them and a supply of hugron pir, the liquid fire, to rain
down from above and perhaps some heads from rockets just to be dropped
instead of fired.*

She smiled grimly at the prospect. *The Princesses think that their saddles
have changed the way that a battle is run, do they? Wait until I get to work on
my ideas.*

Chapter XVII

Hulagu

The last of the Brotherhood forces are being taken in hand. They are either slain or made captive. Some of the Khitan are starting to make their way towards One Tree Hill from different places in the horde.

He looked closely at them. *There are six groups moving, and from the emblems that are borne behind them, these must be the leaders of the clans that are present. The Tenger Sünsnüüd are about to witness a Great Jirgah... here and now.* As soon as he realised this, he sped off on his saddle to gather Rani and the allied leaders.

I talked to some of the Tar-Khans one on one in passing before the battle, but I am more than willing to bet that this will be a more formal meeting. At least our leaders seem to have realised that this meeting would take place. They have already agreed that Metropolitan Basil will speak for the north, and Rani for the Mice. Rani has already gotten the girls to bring the Metropolitan back to the hill on the carpet.

Hulagu was about to go back to where he had left Ayesha when Rani coughed. He looked back. "You are now a leader...a...whatever it is you are called, a Tar-Khan. Your Clan may be small...but the Horse fought here today, and so you need to speak for them. Besides, you may need to translate for us, and it would be polite if we used Khitan, unless the leaders of the Clans decide otherwise."

The Metropolitan nodded: "I can speak it well..." He smiled ruefully. "I need to in my role, although after today the tribes might look on my people with a little more respect...Do you know who is coming?"

Hulagu began to point out to those who were waiting who those approaching were. *It is, to a degree, obvious...at least as to which Clan they are from. They come in small clumps with their personal households.*

"Tar-Khan Jochi is closest." He pointed as he spoke. "He leads the Bürged and has an eagle sitting on a stand on his saddle." On hearing this, Rani started to send those with the carpet to fetch Parminder. *My new status...I need Clan here.* He added an instruction for them. "Find Bianca, some war horses and as many of the Clan as can be found, especially Dobun."

As they were leaving Rani thought for a moment and called out further instruction: "And get the Exarkhos...the Metropolitan needs to have his Secular here."

Hulagu then returned to naming the leaders as they made their way slowly to the hill. "The Tar-Khan, who has a male lion padding alongside his horse, is also called Hulagu. Janibeg is the Tar-Khan who sits on the huge saddle astride an armoured three-horned cow-lizard, with an archer seated at the front directing the beast on the two-man saddle. All of his attendants are mounted the same, and a banner with the head of a cow-lizard is attached to the rear of his saddle."

When his clan had finally arrived in the battle, they had not flinched from the spears of the Brotherhood infantry but had rolled straight over the standing units, leaving destruction in their wake. It is their charge that finally broke the squares of spears. They are slow, but unstoppable.

"Toluy you have heard of before. He is Tar-Khan of the Khünd Chono, the Dire Wolves, and he has a small pack winding around between him and his men." *Already the lion is looking at them and they are looking back. The two clans do not always get on well.*

"Tar-Khan Bo'orchu is the Tar-Khan of the Jijig Khushuu, the Axe-beaks." Those vicious birds, their heads near the same height as a mounted man, stalked alongside their people, their beady eyes looking at all the other beasts and any people who came near, sizing them up as to whether they were food or not.

"Lastly, Kebek leads the Bagts Anchin, the Pack Hunters." *The quick and active near-man-sized feathered lizards with the large claw on their hind legs and the almost-wings of their front legs hiss from their bright blue muzzles at the dire wolves, the lion, and axe-beaks, and seem to lick their lips as they look at the Cow-Lizards. They have crests of feathers on their heads which raise and lower as they look at potential prey.*

"Already the household warriors are subtly restraining the üstei akh düü as they advance," he added. "It would be a matter of shame to have such a meeting interrupted by violence. Luckily, no one here has a current major feud that I know of, and the Dire Wolves have been friends of the Pack Hunters for some time…even if their totem animals do not always agree with each other."

As the heads of the clans and the other Mice began to mount the hill or fly in, the Metropolitan spoke up: "If I remember your customs correctly among the clans, they will not want to speak to your Princess and myself. You should do all the talking with them, and if there is a direct question for us, they can ask you and you can ask us. Now, let us consult over what you will need to say."

With that he gathered Hulagu and Rani, and they talked about what might be asked for, and what they would want out of any negotiations.

When they had finished, Hulagu looked down the hill. *The Tar-Khans are taking their time and probably waiting until the hilltop looks ready. My duties…* "Ariadne… Can you light a fire quickly…before they arrive? We also need water…preferably jugs of it."

Rani

"**D**on't be slow." *Damn. My voice says that I am a teacher having words with a student.* "You are training as a mage, and you forgot it is far simpler than that." She looked around. *Hulagu is busy. Verily is a fire mage, but Ayesha has taken her away somewhere. Earth will do.* "Goditha, light us a fire, please."

Goditha sprang to get some wood from the fallen tree and had a blaze going very quickly. "Aziz…I am sure that there is water here somewhere…

Get it, please." Aziz went off. He returned before the first Tar-Khan arrived, as had Parminder. *She kisses her husband with evident relief. Where is my wife?*

The Exarkhos arrived looking tired and showing the effects of combat, and went to stand with the Metropolitan, his armoured horse held behind him. *The members of the Clan of the Horse, and Theo-dear, along with two of the kataphractoi, are not far behind. Thord stands prominently nearby. He is a bloody mess and the sole representative of the Dwarves. That is right, he fought on foot.*

"Father Christopher was able to save Asticus," said Theodora happily: the mail on her helm was held up by the nasal. "He is resting and will not ride for a few days, but he will live." *We are all looking blankly at her.* "Oh, you wouldn't know…he took a lance and was unhorsed during the battle. It was close work."

She is happily holding up her shield arm. It has a bloodied bandage wrapped around it. The armour of that arm has been unlaced from her torso and the padded cloth sleeve cut away. How dare she look happy? What has happened to her? Rani hurried over.

Chapter XVIII

Hulagu

Jochi is the first to arrive. He is a shortish man, like many Khitan, with slightly bowed legs, a near-shaven head and braided hair. He wears armour similar to that of the kataphractoi, with images of eagles on some of the lames. Hulagu stood between the fire and a few waterskins.

Behind me are Rani and the Metropolitan. The members of the Mori stand to the left, and except for Dobun, all are on their mounts. Behind Rani are several Mice, and the Metropolitan has the Exarchos at his shoulder, and other village leaders and priests to his right. It is all set up as well as we can on such short notice.

"I offer you the gift of hearth and water, and may your sleep be safe and restful here. I am Hulagu of the Horse—" he waved his hand towards the Khitan behind him "—and these are my Clan...so far...and we are here to wipe the Brotherhood and their Masters from the face of The Land and avenge their actions against those whom we would protect."

Of course, I do not mention the non-Khitan, even though there are many more of them present here than there are of us.

Jochi is looking at me, and after a moment at those behind me. He gives a small smile of comprehension and dismounts. "I am Jochi of the Eagles," he said. "I accept your hospitality and thank you for it. May prosperity attend upon you and yours. It seems that, because the Spirits will it, your business has become our business."

A rug and a cushion are produced by his men and he sits on these. His eagle is beside him on a stand and his people move aside to make room for the next arrival. A woman stands behind him. She has the clothes of a shamanka. Suddenly the eagle on the stand screamed, cocked its head, and looked at Parminder.

Jochi glances quickly at his eagle and then at where he is looking. Parminder and the eagle are regarding each other intently. Both have their heads cocked slightly to the side and held in the same pose. Both are ignoring everyone else.

The shamanka's eyes are wide, and she leans forward and whispers in Jochi's ear. Jochi again looks at Parminder and shakes his head. I think that surprised him more than a bit. He is now intently considering my allies as if assessing their potential. I may not have mentioned them, but they obviously cannot be ignored.

The other arrivals went by in a similar fashion. *Hulagu of the Arslan is very cordial.* "Never before, that I have been able to find out about, have we had two Tar-Khans of the same name. The others must all be very jealous."

He grins. He hasn't noticed that the huge maned lion standing beside him and the slight mage are now exchanging looks through slitted eyes, but his shaman does, as does the shamanka of the Bürged. It was a good decision to have the girl here. The leaders will view the Mice in a different light because of her.

When it was the time for Toluy of the Dire Wolves to be welcomed, Hulagu added: "And my greetings to you, grandfather" to Nokaj, the shaman who stood behind the Tar-Khan. "I thank you for your dream and prophesy, and I will later introduce you to my first wife. As you prophesised, what seems an age ago, she is not of the clans."

Last to come is Kebek of the Pack Hunters. When Hulagu had greeted him, he added to one of his retinue: "And I greet you, Malik. You can see that I have kept your cousin safe, and we wish to thank you for your help to the Mori over the last years."

Malik is visibly starting to swell with pride at this acknowledgement of a simple warrior in front of all the Tar-Khans, before blushing and retreating into anonymity behind his Tar-Khan. When he was settled, Kebek looked at Janibeg of the Cow-lizards. *It is time to start, and Janibeg seems to have been decided upon as their spokesman.*

Janibeg is a very stout man and the oldest of the Tar-Khans present. Both his beard and what is left of his hair are grey, and from his girth, he obviously prefers to ride in his oversized saddle over walking too far. He looks around at the assembled leaders of the Clans and quickly nods to those behind me before speaking.

"I greet our newest Tar-Khan. I hope that his new Clan grows and is prosperous…although no one has yet told me where their lands are supposed to be, and wherever it is has yet to be agreed upon. My Clan have none to spare." He smiled. *Any good-humoured effect of the smile was somewhat spoilt by it looking more predatory than jovial.*

"Now, we have destroyed this army of the so-called Brothers. It is something that my Clan have been thinking of rousing the rest of you to do for some time. At this time, we need to work out what is the next thing to be done. I want to hear more of why we have acted, although I was happy to have done so. In particular, I want to know why the khanatai gazar khümüüs, the walled ones, were able to call on the help that they did to set us in motion."

He held up his hand to forestall questions, as his shaman moved forward and laid a hand on his shoulder. "I know the spirits spoke clearly, but I didn't hear the spirits, and I want to hear what plain people have to say. I have heard so many rumours of one thing and another and I want the truth. We also need to work out who gets what out of what we have taken and will take from now on."

He paused and looked around at the people who were watching and listening to his words. "Alliances fall apart over such matters very quickly." *There is a lot of nodding over that.* He looked around again. "Does anyone else have other questions?" *There is a general shaking of heads around the circle. I am doing the same. He is looking at me.* "Well, now it is up to you to start this. Why were we summoned? What is behind it all?"

"With respect," said Hulagu, "I cannot tell you that properly. I am not a tale bearer, but my wife is. She is only of our Clan by marriage, so far, but I am sure that she will pass the tests. With your leave, I will summon her. She has been kept busy elsewhere with captives." Glancing around only briefly to see if there was open dissent, he turned.

Rani is already talking to Goditha, who jumps on a saddle and is off. Hulagu turned back. "She will be with us shortly." *The Tar-Khans are all looking at the speed of Goditha's transit as they realise that they have not seen the saddles at full speed earlier, due to the need to fight from them. Their thoughts are obviously on what they will do for both messages and scouting… and, I am sure, how they can get them.*

"The flying saddles are one of the protections that our clan and our people have. You have nothing to fear with us taking land from you. The Mori will not lay claim to any land out on the plains at all. We will always be a small clan, but we will be wealthy. We currently hold a secure upland mountain valley, with rich grazing." *They like the sound of that.*

"We hold it together with the village of Mousehole, and we will grow further in the mountains in other valleys that are there. The Mori will always be a Clan of the mountains and of the skies. We will not hold the land of the plains and the grass." *I can see they want to ask questions.* He held up a hand. "You will hear how when my wife gets here."

I wonder what to say next. I should not leave a silence. Perhaps a history of some of those with me will do. "She may not tell you this, but you should know that my wife is noble, the daughter of a sheik, as well as a ghazi, an assassin of the Caliphate, and a bard as well."

"Our village has two Princesses; they are both behind me. One is Rani Rai…she is the one in Havenite armour. She was a battle mage of Haven. The other, dressed in cavalry armour, and who fought with our kataphractoi is Theodora do Hrothnog, who used to be a Darkreach princess. She is also a mage…and possibly the most powerful friendly one you may meet. She made the saddles and many other strong enchantments."

"We have many mages in the valley and the village… Even I am studying how to cast spells as the dwellers under roofs do. We think this is a sign. We may be a small clan and settlement, but we are wealthy and strong in war. My wife will tell you more, and if she forgets, ask her about us killing the dragon of the mountains." *That statement had a big impact on the people gathered in front of me.*

He paused dramatically and pointed. "I see that she is on her way. I will stop talking now. In the meantime, it will be best if you make yourselves comfortable. You will be listening for some time. Our tale is a very long one and it begins with the Clans and the plains and is not yet ended for either them or for us."

The Tar-Khans are turning and starting to give quiet orders to their people. The people of the plains know exactly what hearing a long tale means. Food and drink are starting to appear, and mounts, and some of the üstei akh düü are taken some distance away to be cared for.

Ayesha

I am glad to leave the wagonload of girls, firstly to Verily, and now to Goditha. I have no idea how to handle that many Brotherhood slaves, but I wonder why I am summoned and in such a hurry. She came up to Rani wanting to know what was happening and was pushed towards Hulagu.

"My wife," he says. *He acknowledges my presence. Does this mean that I am now Khitan?* "This jirgah of the leaders of the Clans wants to know what has come to pass since we all started on our journeys. I have no skill in the telling of tales, but I have said that you can do the story proper justice. Food and drink will be brought to you." He waves. *Rani is sending Rakhi off, probably to the supply wagon to organise food for us all.*

Rani

I saw where Ayesha came from, but I still don't know what she was doing there *and what is now occupying Goditha in her place. What is so special about that wagon? All I see are a lot of people there.* She sent Stefan and his wives off to find out, and to gather the others up to the hill where the rest of the Mice now were.

Ayesha

*A*yesha looked around her and assessed the situation. *I am to address a jirgah and I am not a Clan member yet. No, I must be. I had better act as if I am.* She took a seat beside Hulagu, crossed her legs, and began. By the time she had finished it was nearly dusk and all had been fed and watered. She had taken pauses to eat and drink.

Hulagu has answered questions as I rest, including introducing Bianca as the first member of the Clan. She still wears her armour, and although the other horses have been removed, she still has hers with her, including Sluggard. The packhorse, with his packs still on his back, seems to have gone through the battle behind her. He must have missed her. Can there be a war packhorse?

Hulagu

I get to thank my wife and then must address the jirgah again. This is the *important bit as we do not yet have peace. With so many here, if we fall out there may still be terrible bloodshed. May the Tenger Sünsnüüd be with my words.*

"So, you can see that our Christian priest must yet destroy the patterns at Greatkin and Owendale, and then we must recover our energy and enchantments, and voyage over the seas. That may be the end of our quest, but we are starting to fear it may not be. I believe it will only be the beginning of another cycle of battles."

"Until we are sure," he said, "the Mori will be a restless Clan, and its people will spend as much time in the air or on a boat as on the back of our üstei akh düü. Whatever you decide for yourselves, this fate is what lies ahead of us as a

Clan." He looked around him at the faces. *Most of them are uncommitted in their expressions*.

"I can tell you as well, that the chief priest of the northern Christians, of the forests and the coast, is determined to destroy what is left of the Brotherhood. He hopes that you will join him in this, but you can see how well his horsemen and foot soldiers went today against the chariots, particularly his armoured horsemen, so he will be carrying on regardless of what you choose. It is up to you as to whether you leave all of the spoils to him and his people."

He looked around. *I am assessing the reaction of the Tar-Khans and they look back blankly still*. "As for what has happened today and will happen in the future, this is what I propose. All of the captives today, except those that my wife and I took, or that have been taken at the line below us, will belong to the Clans and will become köle of their captors." *I can see nodding. It is obvious to the men in front of me that this is to be a starting point.*

"What is more, of those taken after this time, they are to be given one, and only one chance to renounce their worship of the Masters. If this is done, they are to be let free to resume their life as free people. If they fail to do so, they may be made köle of the warriors of the Clans who are with us or slaves of those who capture them from the north."

"They may not consult with another about this choice and will not be told of the consequences of the two alternatives. This will not apply to any of their priests or mages, or anyone that wears the flail of the Inquisitors. They will all be questioned, and will probably all be killed." *That has general approval from them.*

"Unless they recant, the people and their stock, as well as any grain that is in store, or anything being carried by a captive when they are taken, will belong to the Clans, leaving only enough behind to keep those left free at any place alive until next harvest. They are to be allowed to keep enough stock that they will be able, in time, to rebuild."

"As well," he continued, "any gold or silver or magic that is readily found without severe questioning, or without destroying anything, will belong to the takers, if they wish to take it." *That is all only fair and in accord with long-held tradition.*

"However, the buildings of their villages, and anything else that is in them, are to be given to those who have recanted, and the northern Christians who wish to live in them. These buildings are not to be destroyed unless it is essential to do so during the battle."

"They will, by treaty, be as the villages of the north are now, neither going nor growing into the plains without permission of the Clans and making no attempt to interfere with the way of the plains, although they will be allowed to grow modestly along the coast." *They are thinking over the implications of this.*

"In return, the Clans will grant them the right of passage from one village to another along the routes of trade. There will be trade between the people of the settlements and the people of the plains. Until it is agreed otherwise, there shall also be friendship between the villages and the clans and the üstei akh düü of their local clan shall be safe from harm or taking by their local villages."

He paused and looked around at nodding heads. *I seem to have impressed them with my wisdom. I must thank Rani and the Metropolitan later. The Metropolitan has insisted on the next part as being even more important than what I have said before. I do not see why, but he seems to be a wise man so I will propose it.*

"There will be disputes." He shrugged wryly. "We are all people. To solve them, I propose the following. Each party to a dispute shall propose an arbitrator. Between them, the two originally proposed will agree on a third person. The three shall then hear each side and any witnesses and shall read anything placed before them and shall decide, by majority, who has the right. Their decision shall be binding on all parties."

He looked around the circle. *It seems that the priest was indeed right. They all seem to like that idea.* "Do any want to speak to what I have said, or do any have other proposals, or shall we get drunk now, for tomorrow at least some of us will ride out to fight again."

Although there was some discussion, the jirgah ended up drunk that evening and agreed with the proposals that Hulagu had put forward. They briefly met again in the morning and agreed again. *They all say that I made great sense, much more than they are accustomed to hearing when dealing, even indirectly, with the khanatai gazar khümüüs. I think that they realise where my words came from.*

As they were dispersing to ride on the village of Aberbaldie, Nokaj came up to Hulagu and Ayesha. After having been introduced to his new granddaughter, he went on: "I am proud of you, grandson. With what you have proposed here you have added lustre to the family honour, and I am sure that you will continue to do so. I will tell your parents of all that has been said, and I am sure that in time they will wish to see this new land of yours in the sky."

Chapter XIX

Rani
5th Quattro

I find myself in charge of the Army of the North, setting out against the Brotherhood with the Khitan as an eager part of the whole thing. Luckily, I can just plan our move and it seems that I can leave the direction to Stefan and Eleanor, and the Exarkhos ton Basilikon. My wife is even having too much fun playing with our small group of kataphractoi.

At least my plan here is simple. There is a fan of the Khitan riding far to the front and scouts riding hard to encircle the village of Aberbaldie to ensure no word gets out. It will be a couple of days before they get there. This village will be taken before those who will destroy the Patterns have to leave the others.

We will go on with our task while the main army moves on from Aberbaldie, and from there split up to go to Baloo and Peace Tower in the south and Abbey Green in the north.

The Mice that flew soon brought back descriptions of the village from above to the leaders of the allied forces. *It seems that it all still accords with much of Simon of Richfield's description, written many centuries ago and with a copy carried in my saddlebag.*

Aberbaldie is located on a small rise above the flood plain of Gumin Creek. It is only a very short distance from the mouth of the shallow creek on the coast. There is no wharf and any boats that visit it must beach on the gravel of the creek mouth. The creek comes down a long flat slope from the low plateau of the plains rising behind it.

There is a long and wide wooden bridge crossing the creek east of the village. The whole village has an earthen rampart faced and topped with a strong wooden palisade behind a ditch. According to the Khitan the palisade, although only of wood, is enchanted to prevent fire catching on it, so it is near invulnerable to their attacks…or so it has proved to date. That will change.

Ariadne

*T*hey reckon it to be invulnerable, do they? On hearing this, Ariadne began rubbing her hands together and grinning. *I have recovered from the battlefield what stones I can that remain intact. Some fully exploded due to their enhancements, but I also used some balls that were just rock. A lot of them are still reusable just as they are.*

It is hard to damage a solid ball of rock, if it is a good piece to start with, when all it is hitting are people and chariots that squash and shatter before it. As well, while Tãriq drives, the three Hobgoblins, as well as Goditha and I, are sitting in the cart as we go, working on making more balls.

I am also working on Father Christopher, and some of the other priests, to enchant a few more balls for me to use on bringing down any ramparts that we are going to meet. As well as being a mason, Goditha is an Earth Mage, after all. However weak she thinks that she is, I am sure that it is time she learnt of these things.

Basil Tornikes
Metropolitan of the North, the early morning of 7th Quattro

*T*he scouts, both in the air and on the land, speak of some families with wagons still coming into the village. Others are hurrying out of the village to catch up with their army. These are captured once they are out of sight of the settlement, as they travel along in small groups.

It seems that our scouts are fanning out more and more, as they lap further around the town to prevent these stragglers from heading back into the Amity Forest, both settlers and supply wagons. Luckily, it seems the last of them have finally all caught up with the others. No more are being reported as emerging from the forest.

Basil Tornikes
a few hours later

A few light chariots have been seen roaming around near the village, but they do not go very far afield. They only go out to the first ridge lines within sight of the village itself, make one circuit, staying within sight of the walls, and then go back to the village. Effectively, this takes them around through where they can see all of the farmed area, but no further.

It seems that they have no idea what is about to fall on them from all around them. I pray to Saint Michael that this is the case. Less people will end up in graves that way. Once again, it looks as if the people who know the most about the battlefield and where the other people are placed are going to be able to dictate the way the battle goes. The Princess Rani seems excited by that.

Once the noose is laid around Aberbaldie, it begins to tighten. First, a patrolling light chariot is taken. It tried to make it back to the village and its crossbow made great damage, but it failed to escape. Its crew are both women. Then, it is the turn of tiny hamlets and isolated farms. There are few men to be found on them, mainly the very old and the young.

Few, except the occasional slave, take up the offer of amnesty. The most eager to take it up are slave women with male children approaching adulthood. These are the ones who are about to face the emasculation that all male slaves face, and which is done so cruelly and without regard for the slave that only half or less survive. There seems to be almost one of these at each farm.

It is becoming apparent that the inheritors of the Brotherhood will be single women and children. A devotion to Saint Pandonia may become popular here. Whether they can survive in the long run will become apparent after time.

I am beginning to suspect that the numerous farms we see will consolidate their people into far fewer places with more people on them so that they can work the more productive land better and ignore the poorer soils. The people here were winnowed once by The Burning and now they are being culled again.

The first allies to be noticed by the village are those coming along the road from the east. The villagers sent a light chariot west, but it ran into the Khitan. They did not allow it to go either forward or back. The Khitan then appeared over crest of the low plateau and it became apparent that Aberbaldie was surrounded by an overwhelming force.

The village bells begin to ring, and from above, these flying Mice report that the village is in turmoil as the elderly and women begin to take up positions on the ramparts. Gradually, we close in. To me, it looks like our discipline is far tighter than theirs is. The commanders from the Mice are still insisting on training our people as we move.

A few of the scouts of this Eleanor Fournier are probing how far the weapons on the walls can reach, retreating quickly when they are fired on. Even I can see that whoever oversees the defence lacks experience. They are allowing the rapid-firing crossbows to fire at their longest range. The kynigoi of the Mice, with their amulets of protection, can close in, dash back out, and taunt the defenders with impunity.

There is one rapid-firing arbalest beside each of the east and the west gates that has considerably more range than anything else, and I have already noted the mottled Insakharl girl looking at the one near the east gate with special attention.

I heard her say that she wants to take the one on the west wall intact to learn its secrets, but she will be making an access for the allies through the east gate and all the fast-firing weapons that can reach our people from there have to go. I know leaders who would just send people charging through such fire. Saint Winifred will surely note her desire to avoid harm to her people.

She has carefully placed her ballista directly opposite the gate on the other side of the creek, just outside the range of the Brotherhood weapon. She has told us all to be patient. When she has eliminated the arbalest, she will get her crew to move her further forward. Ariadne will rely on her charm to deflect the shafts from the heavier crossbows. Then she can take better shots at them and at the gate. She does not want to waste her balls, she says.

Eventually, all is ready, and although the kynigoi still dart in and taunt the walls, the rest of the army stands still. It is a looming and intimidating ring of weapons placed outside the village and facing inwards.

Rani

I have the device that the Brotherhood general used to talk to his troops, and the Metropolitan has a man use it to offer surrender to the village and to tell them the terms. It is well that he kept his range as he is answered with a hail of fire even though they must have known that none can reach him.

I am very tempted to allow them to just let the villagers exhaust their ammunition, but we need to move faster than that. I think it is likely, from what we have seen so far, that giving them time to think will result in a massacre of all the slaves inside the village.

She gave the signal to Ariadne to fire. The first shot missed the arbalest by a few hands and flew overhead into the village.

It flew straight down the main street through the village and accidentally hit the spire of the church that lay directly behind the gate. With a crash, audible all around, this comes down into the street. A groan can be heard in the village, but a cheer from without overwhelms it. It seems that all think the shot to be deliberate. It may take a lot of heart out of the village.

Her second shot is low and impacts just below the target on the wall. It damages the wall, and if she had been using explosive balls, would probably have taken the arbalest out of action then. *It is possible to see the crew struggling to dismount their weapon, perhaps to move it to another location, but Ariadne does not give them time.*

The next shot is an explosive one and it hits the arbalest mount squarely. The machine disappears into fragments, as does a small section of the wall ahead of it, and indeed, its frantically working crew of women.

Ariadne then gets her crew, one Hob at each corner and with her and Goditha struggling on the other, to move them forward while Tāriq follows close behind with the cart. They have moved into the extreme range of the heavy crossbows, which now begin firing at her. They do not seem to be discouraged by their constant misses.

They must be putting it down to bad luck as their bolts are falling all around the crew. There is the occasional strike, you can hear the swearing in Hob from here when it happens, but at that range they are only harming people if they hit where there is no armour.

Their well-padded leather seems to be stopping much harm happening to the men. At least their constant fire enables Ariadne to locate the firing points, and one by one her targets are silenced until the only weapons that the kynigoi could provoke into firing are all single shot ones, far lighter, and obviously meant more for hunting than for war.

Ariadne

*I*t is time to turn my attention to the gate. I do not need explosive balls on that. I only have a few of them left and I have a purpose in mind for them. It takes five balls, but eventually the gate sags open. It takes another six shots to reduce it to being in enough ruin that a charge is possible against it without it providing an insurmountable obstacle. I will most likely get all those back.

Beyond the fallen gate, the defenders, all of them women, boys, and old men, are massing with a wall of spears pointing out. They will cause a problem as they fill the width of the street with their hedge. As the kynigoi still feint in and out and the kataphractoi, some of the heavier armoured Khitan and the

Basilika Anthropoi begin to move forward into the creek.

Ariadne rewarded the determined defenders with one of her explosive balls and most of the spear wielders were cleared away. *Their wounded are removed to a chorus of screams and cries of pain and it is obvious that they are trying to reform. A second explosive ball will teach them the futility of that move. After that, I can only use my weapon to attack single crossbows on the wall.*

We have become well organised quickly. A wall of cavalry is approaching the breach at a slow trot. A lightly armoured unit of people with sword or axe and shields, jogging along in their wake, follows them closely.

The rest of the infantry follow behind in columns, and on the other sides of the village the Khitan light cavalry are starting to probe forward using their bows against the weapons on the walls, and hoping to use lassoes to gain a purchase on the walls and to get over. They don't often succeed at this, but their attacks pin defenders to the walls until they can be taken from behind by the assault.

Rani
later in the afternoon

The defenders were fighting hard until the person who was largely directing the defence was killed by an archer. He turns out to have been the only priest left in the village, and after he dies the defence becomes more sporadic, with only the older men showing determination. The women are more interested in just protecting their children, and when it becomes apparent that they are not being harmed, they begin to surrender.

The same pattern that was seen in the hamlets is seen again. Mainly the slave women are interested in renouncing their religion, although two older free boys and the sister of one of them did so as well. Almost all the men and the older boys have already died, and few become köle.

Although the Orthodox priests have no mana left, after doing their healing, for a proper re-dedication of the two village churches, they are able to celebrate an open-air mass using the announcing artefact. Each of the newly-declared converts among the adults is given a sponsor to have with them, one who can speak their tongue, to talk them through what is happening and why.

Rani
8th Quattro

*T*he night has passed, unquiet as it is with some of the newly-made köle lament-
ing their lot in life, and with the cries of the wounded, my allied army begins
to split up.

Some of the Khitan, singing songs of victory, begin to head back to their
tribal lands, taking with them flocks and köle for themselves and the rest of
their clan. Many of the rest of the Khitan prepare to move out towards those
who are already containing Peace Tower. If there are any large numbers of
Brotherhood forces left, Peace Tower is where they will be.

It is essential to stop them moving from there to where there are more of
their people. We also need to stop them from gaining shelter in the forest to
then come out and harass us later, to form a rump army of people who believe
in their demon gods. We do not need fanatics who will emerge only to harass
others for years to come.

I hope that some other Khitan from other clans will already be probing at
Owendale. The Mice that have saddles will be heading there to take the Pattern,
and to see if they can reach the same agreement as the jirgah at Bulga has come to.

Some of the Khitan will also be going along the coast to Abbey Green and
then Greatkin with the army of the north to act as more scouts than just the
kynigoi can provide and to take köle and stock. The last is a big incentive for
them.

The Metropolitan has brought monks with him and one of them will stay
behind, together with a detachment of some of the more badly injured of the
army who will require more time to rest before they will be fully recovered.

The monk will serve as a priest for the village and may decide to stay and
become one rather than return to the cloister, while the soldiers will serve to
keep the villagers in line and help them to remember that they have changed
sides, and are now apostates to their faith and subject to death from it.

Messengers are travelling back along the coast to let people know what
has happened, and to find younger sons and daughters who want to take up
land. The numbers will not probably be high, so the villages here will still
have a low population for many years to come, but time will eventually heal
even that.

If the alliance with the Khitan lasts, then the people here will be a buffer
against the expansion of Freehold for the North. Provided that The Burning
stays at bay, eventually the North will continue to grow, until once again the
seacoast has villages dotted all along it wherever there is a source of water
for them to use.

In due course, the people here will live only a short distance apart from each other as it used to be many years ago, and as Simon described all that time ago in his book. There will be a future where people will live hours apart instead of it being several days or even weeks of hard travel.

Chapter XX

Gamil
8th of Tastil, the Year 546,983 since the Spread

*I*can try and sit still here in my chair, but I know that the tips of my wings are *fluttering with scarce contained emotions. As project director, it falls to me to write the official protest note that will be delivered to the Tribunal and bring judgement and retribution, and I have already begun work on that happy task.*

In the decisive confrontation, just as they did in the last era, the Adversaries have broken the Rules once again, and this time they have not only done so, but they have somehow still managed to lose the encounter where the breach became blatant. They must have been truly desperate to so openly use that level of forbidden technology.

In addition, the Renegade held back and did not directly intervene against them. Perhaps they were counting on him doing as he did last time. Now, he has only acted within Rules that he may be outside of, influencing rather than acting. They will not even have that excuse as they did before. I am excited. The consequences are truly upon their heads.

For the next millennia at least the Daveen, the long-standing opponents of my people, the Shing-zu, will be able to give no support at all from off Vhast to their people who are still on the planet. This is despite their huge advantages of people and tools in that area. They will be blocked from acting by the Treaty and the other races around us and them.

The Tribunal, even in such an open case as this, can take a hundred years or more to rule as subtleties are weighed and influences calculated. Until that is done, none can enter the arena or even influence it from outside. Admittedly, I can motivate no more actors during that time, but I was not intending to do so, anyway.

More importantly, although what the Daveen have in place on the planet, the group we call the Adversaries, can still be used, but they cannot enter anyone else, and those on-planet can only stay or leave. If one of them leaves for any reason, under these circumstances, they can never return even if, as is unlikely to happen, there is a ruling in their favour.

They cannot even replace anything that they lose or that breaks until after the judgement comes down from the judges. This would not have mattered to them if they had won; the same as it hadn't mattered two thousand years before when they had also openly breached the rules and won the battle and prevented a peaceful alliance forming.

The forfeits that they had to endure lasted only a few hundred years. It was too short a time to reverse what they had achieved without my people breaking the rules themselves. This time the prime set of pawns the Daveen have chosen, the ones that looked so promising and who secretly built power up over so long, now look as if they have lost so badly that it is a huge disaster for them.

They still have other pawns, ones that I watch in Freehold, in this so-called New-Found Land, among the Chin, and in other cultures, but I think that they can do less to further their ambitions. If everything continues as I hope, it might cause them to finally lose the struggle for influence over the direction of the project.

I am so proud of the pieces that I set in motion. They have not yet succeeded fully in what I want them to do, but their chance of success, if they do work out what the game actually is, has just been increased almost immeasurably.

Of course, the question remains, as it has for millennia: What will the Renegade do now? Will he become more active? Will he act against his own people, or will he even act directly against my people? Does he still regard the Daveen as his people? What are his motives now and what does he want from all of this?

He seems to have relations with my actors that are at least cordial. I wish that I could see inside his Palace, but like a growing number of areas, we are frustratingly blocked from doing that. He does not seem to be helping the Daveen or yet directly helping my actors. I need answers and I do not have them.

I can ill-judge his actions as his lair was the first one that now can only be seen into with difficulty without being detected. Our spy machines for seeing inside buildings are both crude and mechanical and, it seems, are vulnerable to the magic that is wielded on this world.

My technical people swear that this cannot be the case. They swear that magic cannot affect their machines, that magic and superstition cannot overcome the physical laws that technology uses, but they have not been able to bring me what I want either.

A goal of this experiment was to test this hypothesis as to which is superior, and evidence is accumulating. Now only things that are said and done out in the open can, sometimes, be picked up from above. It seems now that every time there is a meeting of two or more leaders, it is shielded from my eyes somehow.

Every one of the deliberations that the Khitan are involved in, oft held out in the open as they are, is now shielded by their shamen from me. Even devices that people sometimes wear, as some of my actors do, can cut out my getting direct reportage. Waiting is, and will be, very frustrating, as is exercising patience in this closing stage after a few millennia.

Chapter XXI

Rani
8th Quattro

*W*e fly high over the plains. The Nettlego, the river that flows to the Northern Sea from its start at Peace Tower, comes into sight very quickly. It is the largest river of the northwest. Its western bank marks the start of the Amity Forest, with trees coming down to the water's edge. Its eastern bank marks the start of the plains.

The plains do not end until the Great Forest appears just before Greensin. Apparently, the Brotherhood have never allowed any assarts to become established along the edge of the Nettlego, as it is too easy for the Khitan to slip over and raid them, and it is too hard for them to protect the farmers.

From what I can see, it might be the largest river in these parts, but it is seems to be very shallow along most of its length so far. It is certainly at least as shallow as the ford at Evilhalt. What lies deeper in the forest itself, in the way of settlements, no one knows, and finding out about them will have to wait until all the known settlements are taken.

Rani
a while later

*E*ventually Peace Tower, and downstream of it, the village of Baloo, came into sight. *There are more Khitan around this area, and the palisaded walls of Baloo (a settlement with walls similar to those of Aberbaldie, even if it is a lot smaller in area) seem to be filled with the refugees from farms that have not been surprised.*

The small settlement that stands attached to the keep of Peace Tower itself looks to be completely abandoned. All of its buildings are now derelict and mostly torn down. I suppose that people from it are inside the great fortress and its stock are there as well, or else they have already been taken by the Khitan.

Astrid is leading us towards what appears to be a group of leaders. At least there is a mixture of clan banners there and the others are giving them a lot of space.

Of course, that may have been because there are three of the great Thunder Lizards present. Around each is a large space as they tower over mere horses. Each, when upright, stands even higher than the herd of elephants, and the howdahs on them, that are in another part of the horde. I think they are larger beasts than even those back in Haven.

"The Kha-khan is here," said Hulagu as they conferred in the air before coming down to land. "I hope we get agreement on what was said earlier. Even though the first jirgah agreed, and that binds six of the clans, he could still overturn it for the rest if he wished."

"It binds seven of the clans. You keep forgetting your own status. Now is the time to take your wife and to play upon what you have done so far. He may be your…king," *Hulagu looks disdainful.* "Your superior…" *His expression gets no better.* "What is he then?"

Hulagu

"**F**ather Christopher tells me he is 'primus inter pares', the first among equals. We usually defer to his judgement, but we are not bound and can go against it. By we I mean me, as someone they are calling a Tar-Khan. My clan can do the same to me, but not to him… I will go and see him. The rest of you should wait here."

He began to descend to almost the level of the rider of a horse before coming in to the centre, staying only high enough to be able to make his way through the warriors. Ayesha followed behind on her saddle.

Looking around, I can see that there are three Clans here: Ayanga Gürvel, Mogoi and Zaan. By the look of the beasts and banners ahead, it is not just the Clans, but also their Tar-Khans who are present. The only Clan I have not met so far in this campaign are the Amitan. Their lands lay along the west coast of The Land, and if they have answered the call, they will be clustered around Owendale. I am not looking forward to having to deal with them.

There do not seem to be many Snakes present, but then their ground lies along the south coast towards Haven and they have the furthest to travel. I did not expect for them to have many warriors here at all... Just their fastest riders will have been able to make it all that way. Most of their people will be waiting around the edges of Freehold, hopefully staying clear of their scouts, maybe even concealed by the shamen from their mages, to see what develops there.

Hulagu looked ahead. *The Kha-khan and the two Tar-Khans seem to be waiting on us and it seems that a fire has just been lit. At least they think that we are important enough for that. At this distance it will not be obvious who we are, although...* As he turned to see his wife, he finally noted that she had managed to paint what they had agreed was to be their totem symbol on her shield between yesterday and today.

Dobun must have done it...the same as he has added marks to his own shield and mine to indicate our status. It is no use waiting longer. He made himself adopt a casual position with one foot in a stirrup, the belt that fastened him to the saddle undone, and the other leg crossed over and resting on the saddle in front of him. He brought his saddle to a halt in front of the waiting leaders, waiting for the ritual to start.

It is the Kha-khan himself who speaks. "I offer you the gift of hearth and water, and may your sleep be safe and restful here. I am the Chinggiz Arghun and I am here at the behest of the spirits, attacking the üzen yaddag düürsen, the so-called Brothers."

"I am Hulagu, Tar-Khan of the Mori, and this is my wife Ayesha. I accept your hospitality and thank you for it. May prosperity attend upon you and yours. We are likewise engaged in seeking the destruction of the so-called Brothers and their Masters and have been on that quest for over a year."

"We travel," he continued, "from the destruction of their army in the lands of the Ünee Gürvel at the hands of the Clans and of the army of the north. The rest of the Mori remain there. We travel towards the land of the Amitan to destroy there something that must be destroyed for both the plains and the rest of The Land to be safe. We will then return here to join again with our allies to look at pulling down this last intrusion onto the plains."

There is an exchange of looks between the three. The Kha-khan is an older man with a beard and hair more than half grey. He is armoured in lamellar made of lizard hide. It looks like mine. He indicates that we should sit.

"Unlike all others who may want to hear your story, I need to hear it. You may now begin." What followed was almost a replay of the jirgah in the north. *This time, with less leaders present it is obvious that the Clan bards are pressing forward to hear the tale. There is more active probing with questions from the Kha-khan, and even more surprise over the death of the dragon. To the Emeel amidarch baigaa khümüüs, with our age-old friendship with the*

Dragon at Dagh Ordu, this is near inconceivable as a concept.

Rani

*A*ll this time, we sit in the sky totally ignored by those below. I was expect-ing this. During the entire jirgah in the north, not one actual remark had been directed at us. Now and then, she would send someone off to scout around. *There may be a lot here already, but there are still more Khitan headed towards this area.*

We may as well amuse ourselves by flying around Peace Tower, keeping out of range of their artillery. A few spells were sent at them, but their enchanted amulets helped them deal with those. The Mice replied, almost casually, with some arrows to kill exposed crossbowmen and a few spell-casters. *They were either mages or priests.*

They have some people of power but aiming at me was an error. Between the amulet and my natural resistance, I did not even have to counter any of their magic. After that failed, there are no more attempts to attack us. If we had brought enough molotails with us, we could have incinerated most of what is below us from here. I think that there are still some with Ariadne, but I am not sure.

Hulagu

I have waited for my wife to finish the tale, and now I present what is agreed to by the jirgah in the north. I need to be careful to point out that I already have that agreement as I make the proposal, and the Kha-khan and Yegu of the Snake and Siramon of the Elephant at least do not reject it out of hand, but agree to consider it tonight. I can expect no more.

In the meantime, they will contain Baloo and Peace Tower until the rest of the Brotherhood is taken and the Mice gather to help with the siege. Although they feign reluctance to wait, we all realise that, while they have enough troops to take Baloo, Peace Tower has broken our armies several times before.

If it has even a fraction of its normal complement of mages and priests present it can do so again. It cannot be left as it is. If it remains standing, then the Brotherhood are sure to somehow rebuild everything from here, even if the rest of their land is laid waste. Though it may not be acknowledged, the tribes will need assistance to destroy it.

"We will leave you to consider what I have said, and we will fly on now to Owendale. Hopefully, the Bison have not yet taken it and we get the chance to put the same proposal to them before they move ahead of the rest of the clans. Either way, we must destroy the Pattern there. Hopefully, there are none there that know how to use it fully, or we may see more resistance there than we would expect."

"Unless they have grown impatient, they will be waiting," said the Chinggiz Arghun. *He is grudging in admitting that.* "Our messages from the spirits called for us to hold them close and keep them occupied, until more became apparent. Unless the Brothers there have been stupid, they should be encircled, but alive."

"They probably lack the strength to do much," he said. "Soon after we started to arrive a few weeks ago, a wheel of their chariots were seen coming from there and we hid and ambushed them. They were all women, and one of the survivors told us that they were the mobile force of the Brotherhood's woman general."

"She was the wife of the one you slew in the north. She had been arrogantly left to keep us at bay with just one wheel of their heavy chariots. She was to act as if all their main force was still in place and we were supposed to stay ignorant." *He chuckles and the two Tar-Khans who are with him join in.*

Hulagu joined in briefly before replying. "In that case, I will leave you until we return." *We take off and go to where the others are waiting. I am glad that Rani has been patient about this.*

"About time," said Astrid impatiently. "Don't your people have any sense of time at all?"

"It is essential that things are done correctly."

Rani interjected. "All cultures have their own patterns. It is wise to follow them when dealing with them. That way you will gain more cooperation. Didn't we let you make the decisions and lead the way in Wolfneck? Now let us go west."

"We will have to camp along the way. I don't want to arrive among the tribes after dark. It may not be safe if they are inclined to be difficult." *Seeing that we will be landing among the Amitan, a Clan the Khünd Chono have long had feud with and that the Mori may inherit, I must agree about the wisdom of that.*

They soon flew over the remains of a group of chariots. *It seems that the woman general was ambushed almost within sight of Peace Tower as her force emerged from between two low hills.*

They spent the night on the forest side of Üzen yadalt ursgai, Sundercud Creek, which runs from the forest down along its southern flank to the sea in the west. *It is only a large watercourse if it is in flood, otherwise, like The*

Nettlego, a person can easily wade across almost anywhere on its length and a horse will most likely not let the feet of its rider grow wet.

They camped on the junction of the Creek and another watercourse that fed out of the forest. *Astrid calls it Monteagle Creek. I do not know the name the Amitan give it. She has seen its name on a Dwarven map… At least she thinks that this should be it. It is the only tributary on the map that is large enough to have a name and what flows out of the forest is nearly as large as what it joins.*

The night was quiet and uneventful for the Mice, although they kept careful watch.

Basil

*B*oth Ayesha and I are here. That means that, for the first time since we *started out from Evilhalt, we have both left Theodora unattended, and without someone else tasked for the job of making sure that she is safe…and she has already managed to get herself wounded in the battle that has just finished. What is worse, she seems proud of that wound. Will she seek more danger now?*

Hulagu
9th Quattro

*H*eading west after the Christian Orthos service in the morning and it *does not take us long to find Owendale. The Amitan could have overrun it easily and they have it fully surrounded. I can see ergüül patrols along the north road to Narwood and along the south to Warkworth. Some can even be seen picking their way among the trees.*

It looks like the outlying hamlets may already have been taken and there are patches of smoke visible, probably from burning buildings. I would say that, despite their instructions, we may be just in time to stop a sacking of the village.

Despite being the largest Brotherhood village that we have seen so far, Owendale lacks walls and is spread out as the girls indicated on our map back in Mousehole. It relies for its protection on being the home of strong army units and their support priests and mages. If you take them away, as has been done, it is wide open.

None of the mages or priests and especially little of the army are there now, and after we have made a circle of the village, all that I can see are women and children, one or two possible priests, and some old men and boys playing at being soldiers behind some barricades.

I can see the banners that indicate where the Tar-Khan of the Amitan is. That is where we need to go, and then I get to meet the last of my new peers and the one I have looked forward the least to seeing. Hulagu again took the lead and brought them down to a low level as they approached.

Rani

*T**his time, Hulagu wants the rest of the Mice to stay with him, although we must remain in the background, unacknowledged, as the greetings are exchanged. There is a space made for us and everyone walks around us, almost as if we are a hole in the ground that must be avoided. No one addresses us and they all pretend that we are not there.*

It may seem very rude, and I hate to admit it, but almost the same thing could occur in Haven if I brought my people before a group of upper Brahmins and Kshatya. I would be the only one to be acknowledged. Even our other Havenites would be expected to stay away unless they were bringing food and drink to us.

We get to make ourselves comfortable and, as the familiar story is played out, I see the occasional glance directed at us as if searching out the actors in the tale. I suppose they are wondering how the small group that they can see in front of them can have done the things that are being described. Sometimes, I wonder about that myself.

While they were sitting, Rani had Parminder explore the minds of the horses around them...*to the wonder of the horses perhaps, but most horses are simple beasts and it seems that there is little to find out from them. She is just reporting thoughts of gathering and running, of smelling new smells and eating new grass.*

Hulagu

*T**ar-Khan Mongka is a man near as large as Janibeg of the Ünee Gürvel, but without his overtly jovial nature. He has a sour expression on his face the whole time we speak. It grows less and less pleased as time goes by, and his eyes seem to shrink into his face like little raisins in one of the boiled doughy puddings that Lādi makes for us.*

When I made the proposal, I was hoping for a warmer reception than I am getting. It seems to matter little to him when I emphasise that seven Clans have already agreed to it and that the Kha-khan and the other two Clans considered it last night.

I suppose that it should have been obvious before I started that the Amitan, being on their own, were expecting to take everything and everyone, and to raze the village and treat it as they seem to have done to the hamlets around it.

Mongka does not like the idea of giving anyone a chance to escape being made köle. He is very reluctant to leave a single person free to take the village and allow it to stay and perhaps to regain its size. He is known far and wide as Shunakhai Mongka, Mongka the Greedy, for a very good reason, but not to his face. Even people of his own Clan call him that.

Behind me, I can hear Goditha translating everything to Rani. I hope they realise at least one of those we face will be doing the same back when we are finished. No, I am wrong. From the glances going in her direction anything important is being quietly relayed as we continue to talk.

"I will bet," said Rani, "that after taking Owendale he is planning on using the confusion to head south and do the same to Warkworth. That way he would have no villages on his flank at all and only Freehold to the south." *She is speaking loudly. I guess that she wants to be overheard in what she is saying.*

"I am also willing to venture," she continued, "that any villages from Freehold that were on this side of the No-iu Flow will be his next target. He does not want restrictions placed on him by anyone. He wants to be the sole judge of what is right in this area."

Now I am sure that she says this deliberately and is looking for reactions, and she is getting them. He looks sourer the more he hears from the person who whispers in his ear. I need to get his attention again and emphasise the agreement of seven and the warm reception by the other three. Hulagu sighed, although he tried to not let it show.

I need to at least try and be diplomatic, to point out that although the choice lies with the Amitan and no one can force them to do otherwise, if they do not agree, they will likely be the only ones who do not. This will inevitably place them on a collision course with the other clans. I need to sound sorrowful as I say this.

If all the leaders of their Clan have been like this, I see now how the Khünd Chono have somehow managed to maintain minor feud with the Amitan for many generations despite the övs, the territory of the two Clans being so far apart. This feud may not apply to the Mori, but it is very hard for me to sound convincingly sad as I express my regret about what may happen if it comes to conflict among the clans.

"And why should we not just kill you now…and remove one of the obstacles and one of the clans?" asked Mongka. He asks as if this were the most reasonable request in the world. *The böö shaman who stands beside him looks shocked. I can hear Goditha speak behind me and a quick preparation of weapons and wands. I think that I need to not react, to treat it almost as a joke.*

"Because, not only would it anger the Tenger Sünsnüüd and the Umard Sünsnüüd..." *His shaman is nodding,* "...but moments after you gave the order you would be dead, and most likely so would any who tried to carry it out."

"Even if you succeeded in killing all of us here," Hulagu says, trying to sound casual, "which is very unlikely, you would even only kill two of the Mori. The rest, particularly my sister, would want vengeance. Remember that we have already slain a dragon. We two might die, but your Clan will be so devastated that it would be easy meat for even the lowly Örnödiin."

"Your bison herds will be left untended." Hulagu waved his hand dismissively. "You do not even know what weapons we have with us and what magics we have poised at this moment. For a start, I will tell you now that four of those who face you are mages." *They are looking from face to face. I suppose that they can see that several have hands out of sight. They could hold wands.*

"Do you really want this fate for your Clan?" *Do I sound concerned? I am trying to.* "Is it not both easier and more honourable to follow the path that the Umard Sünsnüüd counsel and the rest of the People are following?" *I am sure that I sound reasonable in my summation. At least his shaman is nodding vigorously.*

Mongka grunted as the shaman beside him leant forward and began talking urgently in his ear. *His eyes are narrowed and playing over the Mice.* He gave an empty laugh as if it were all a joke. "But that would be against all of the laws and customs...would it not? We will consider what you have to say tonight and then have an answer for you in the morning."

"We await your decision with interest," Hulagu nodded as he replied. "In order to not disturb you, I will remove the khün khanatai, the town dwellers, from your midst. We will camp a little way away so that their presence does not disturb you and we will return after dawn."

"In the meantime, we will look around the area. I believe that we might even see what the people of Warkworth have to say about all of this." *I hope that is an innocent enough smile on my face. The look I got from Mongka is poisonous and he looks even sourer, if that is possible. I am sure that he wants the people of Warkworth to know as little of this as is possible.*

Rani

*H*ulagu may be beaming, but I am not sure that I should. That might be taken as an insult. I am sure all realise that if Warkworth sends people north, they can take possession of this village and any people that change their belief. We can also warn them of Mongka's feelings and they can put their stone-walled village into a state of defence against him.

From what Danelis has told me, he is not likely to crush that little seedpod easily unless he catches the people there by surprise. Even if they did not know about it until we get there, they are already covered by the agreement of the other Clans.

If Mongka attacks them and any of the village live to tell who it was that destroyed them, then he could find his Clan set as one against ten. If we Mice go there, then they will find out about this shield that they now have in place. Hulagu has called his bluff, and now he takes his leave and we Mice get to fly off.

"What do we do now?" asked Hulagu as they climbed.

"We do what you suggested and fly south to talk to the people of Warkworth, of course. We can even spend the night there safely, with someone else cooking for us, and then we can return here tomorrow to hear his answer."

How far is it to the village? She thought a moment. "Even if we sleep in," she continued as they flew, "we will be back here well before lunch. Owendale is not going anywhere and will wait that long. Now we fly as quickly as we can." She nodded at Astrid, who led them off at top speed, moving people into a formation as they flew.

Chapter XXII

Rani

*W*arkworth is built on the top of the long cliff that is the western edge *of the plains, a cliff that is well over forty paces high for much of its length. Unlike in the north, where the land meets the sea gently in beaches, inlets and even sea-marshes, here the one ends and the other begins quite abruptly. The village sits on its cliff with its back hard to the sea.*

Around it are the village fields, centring on Pulletop Creek, as it comes off the plains. The creek ends its journey as it runs through the village walls in a stone-walled channel to form a waterfall that cascades down to the sea over a dressed stone cliff. Steep stairs go down the cliff to the beach where there are the remains of an old stone jetty which the locals are slowly restoring.

In the meantime, goods still have to be landed on the beach and winched or carried up the cliff. The houses are crowded into the compass of its walls with no room left inside to build more. They may have to extend their walls soon. Danelis described it well and it does not appear to have changed much, if at all, since she was taken.

The village wall is anchored on the clifftop at each end and encloses the whole village. They came along the coast, flying offshore and slowing as they got closer. *I can hear Ayesha and Thord talking of climbing. I would not like to do it. They think that it is possible to climb into the village up the cliff, but not if the defenders are alert.*

They flew down the coast and circled the village from the seaward side. *The villagers have even reinforced and faced much of the cliff. It may be where the cliff is weak, or it may just be to make it a harder task. Looking at the wall, the towers extend all the way down into to the sea so that they even control the beach.*

The only entrance to the village from the land is a single gate, and having circled around the village, they came down to horse height well out of bowshot among the fields and moved towards it.

We are arriving well before dusk and the gate is still open. It is obvious that there was a market going on… It is a fair of not just local farmers, but from the look of the pack animals lined up, there are even some travelling merchants. More than a couple of them are from Freehold, at least judging by their dress. More tales of us will get back there now.

"Keep listening for a Brotherhood accent," Rani said to the flyers. "This close to Owendale, we may find some of them and any we find are most likely, whatever else they do, to be spies or worse. If you find any, get Father Christopher near them as soon as you can. He can check them for their intent."

"All of the apprentices can try and check for magic, and I will as well. Lastly, if we need to do something, Basil will act. We will see their leader first to explain why we are here before it becomes general knowledge. Keep your weapons to hand. However, I want you to try to do this without seeming to threaten the village."

"Astrid, take us in," she finished. "We want to seem to be both confident and powerful, but not arrogant, please." Astrid just grinned at the last couple of words. *Why do I let her? I suppose it is because I cannot stop her.*

As we come closer, everyone at the market gradually stops what they are doing and just watches us approach. I think that others, who saw us as we circled, are coming out of the village. A group of flyers like us is obviously something that they have never seen before. Astrid leads us through the small crowd slowly.

She must not be smiling, as I can see no shocked faces, but I acknowledge with a smile anyone who looks kindly at us. I can now see that many of the people present seem to copy the Freehold clothing, to some extent or another, just as the villages near it in the south often copy Haven in the same way.

By the time we are at the gate the guards are ready and a man, dressed in a fulsome dark green velvet houpelande and an inverted hood wound around with a liripipe, stands between us and the open gates, looking a little nervous.

Wearing that garb must be hot in the warm afternoon. I am sure that someone would only wear it on a warm day if they were either very vain, or else if they are important and want to be seen as such on a Market Day. She looked more closely at the man. *He wears a wand pouch, so he may be important.*

"Greetings." *He speaks in Latin, addressing Astrid, who is still in the lead. He looks from one to another of us. Apart from Hulagu and myself, the origin of the others is not clear for how we look and dress. The skin and eyes often do not match the clothes.*

Even Parminder, with her dark skin, is dressed in a Khitan fashion in leather with a mail-draped helm, and her husband is in a set of full mail with a flat-topped great helm that encloses his face, worn over a bascinet that came originally from a Freehold bandit. She has doffed the helm, but that makes her origin no clearer. All of us make no attempt to hide our weapons.

"You come to our market this Pali," the man said, "but dressed for war, not for trade. I have to ask you what your intent is."

"Ask away," said Astrid. It is times like this that her heavy accent, rising and falling as it does, becomes most evident. "...for we would like to tell you. However, we think that it is best if you, that is if you are the leader here, and perhaps your head priest and your Captain met with our leaders in private. What we have to say is first for your ears."

She then speaks louder; she is now obviously talking to the crowd. I suppose that it is more polite than arrogant. "Later tonight our bards will be telling the whole tale to as many as can hear them. That is one of the reasons that we are here...so that all may know what is happening in the rest The Land and so find out about the war that envelops it."

Basil

*A*yesha and I conferred as we came in, and now we are watching the crowd around us. I am back to doing police work again. She looks to the left and I look to the right. I knew that my wife would stir them up when she talks of war without indicating who is doing the fighting.

We are looking for those who react...unusually. Most of the onlookers, and by now I am sure that is most of the people of the village, are just curious about us, although some appeared worried, but a couple of them have a more calculating look on their faces. I have one in mind already. We will see if Ayesha has any more.

Rani

*T*he person addressing Astrid looks concerned, he even looks out over the plains behind us. "I am Joachim Caster. I am the Mayor." Still the same man that Danelis said was the mayor when she was taken, then. "Who are you?"

"I am Astrid the Cat," replied Astrid. I may be stationed behind her, but I can tell when she deliberately smiles broadly for effect. Several of those in front of *her have noted her teeth and drawn back slightly. "…and I think that the rest of the* introductions should wait until we are in a more privy situation. It is safer," she added. *Only Astrid would think that is a confidential tone.*

With that she moves her saddle to an empty place at the side beside the wall, lands and hops off it. She has removed her nasal helm and pulled off both her mail and cloth coifs, stuffing them inside the helm under her arm, as she shakes her head to allow her long braids to fall down her chest, but she has kept her spear in hand and turned back around.

Standing, she is well taller than the man in front of her and as large as or larger than the guards beside him. She is looking down at them and, in return, they are looking up at the imposing woman in front of them. It is more intimidation than arrogance, I suppose.

"Lead on to where you wish to talk," said Astrid, "and our leaders shall follow." *I land my saddle beside Astrid's and dismount and the others follow us down, one after the other.* Rani moved quickly to stand beside Astrid. *Once landed, Christopher and Thord move to beside me. I note that Stefan, Basil and Ayesha are conferring and already heading into the crowd.*

Goditha now takes her helm and bascinet off as well and puts both helms on her saddle as she shakes out her short locks, running her finger through them to tidy them a little from the mess left by wearing a helm—curse helmet hair—before she gathers her wife by the hand and heads straight out into the market.

Hulagu makes himself comfortable on his saddle against the wall watching over the gear. Unlike our last stops, here he can afford to relax and be anonymous. He has already made it clear that this is all he is going to do here.

Basil

Stefan heads inside the walls, looking around the village to see what the village has, seeking a tavern and deliberately being the most obvious one to pump for information. Why does he have to find a leatherworker so quickly? We may take a while to move on away from the shop talk. Ayesha and I end up looking at the neighbouring establishments and trying to avoid our targets.

He is getting good at being the obvious target, a man who is both simple and approachable. Both of our men have already taken Stefan's bait and are hanging around him as if wanting to have a word with him. They stand on opposite sides and look at each other as if they are not friends… I think that they may actually hate each other.

There is not much in the village to look at. One of the nearby establishments is a gambling hall and another is a brothel. Basil thought about that. *The village must have some through traffic. If there is trade from the Brotherhood to Freehold, it will have to pass through here, but I would not have expected there to be enough trade for these two places to look as prosperous as they do.*

Our targets are staying on opposite sides of Stefan and sort of back from the centre of the street towards these establishments. I wonder if they are the proprietors of these places.

I have to move further and further away to avoid my target: I see that Ayesha is doing the same. There is a tinsmith on the cross-street where I am standing on the corner. From the sign above her, so is Ayesha. I guess that they must mine tin here. I didn't ask Danelis about things like this. I should not just assume these villagers to just be farmers.

It looks like neither of our targets has noticed either Ayesha or me. We must seem to casually move around on the street, looking at workshops and buildings, though. This is much easier in a large city. With such a small crowd I have to chat to passers-by and make myself seem to be as much a part of the scenery as I can.

Where I can, I ask innocent questions, rather than answer any. Luckily, the locals are proud of their village. It takes a lot of effort not to be dragged off to see various things. I can easily find out from the passers-by that my man owns the brothel that he is hovering near. Some caravan guards are waiting for him to open up now that the market is winding down.

Stefan has gotten tired of exchanging shop talk and the leather worker is pointing south down the cross-street and over a bridge. Stefan is heading off past me, followed by a whole train of people. It looks like the people waiting to talk to him will have to wait a little longer to do so.

Stefan is going into a tavern bearing a sign with a picture of four elephants standing on the back of a turtle. I can find out no more this way, and surely the two men will work out what is happening soon. They cannot be completely stupid. He went over to Ayesha. *We use Darkspeech, I am fairly sure it is unknown here.*

"You reward the people you have been chatting to by being taken off to see the sights. See what you can find out about these two. Mine owns the brothel back there, by the way. I will collect Stefan. The effort of acting the part of the innocent is wearing thin on him. He is too honest. I will join him in the tavern and see what we can get from them when these two decide to join us."

She nodded, and they split up. Basil entered the cool gloom of a large rural tavern. *I have seen many like it before.* He looked around the room. *The level of cleanliness is not the highest, Sajāh would not have permitted it to be this bad at home, but it is not the lowest I have seen either. The floor needs sweeping for a start.*

Inside, he grinned to himself after that thought. *It probably isn't all that bad. I must admit that I would have happily eaten and drunk here before this all started without noticing any issues, but now I am spoilt.* He grinned more broadly on the inside. *I will still check the kitchen before I eat anything much here.*

Rani

*T*his Mayor Joachim has taken us to his office. The Mayor of Warkworth has an office that any village leader would envy. I envy it. The stairs up from the beach have their own gatehouse where they come to the level of the village and the Mayor's office sits over this gate.

When the village is under attack it will be a part of the defences, but now I can see timber panels fitted into slots in the floor. They must cover murder-holes. There are wide-open shutters in the walls and a magnificent view over the Western Sea on one side, and north, south, and over the village from the other three.

It is a small but formidable keep. In the summer heat of today, a refreshing cool breeze blows softly through it, laden with cleaner salty smells than you get from the breeze when it blows in Pavitra Phāṭaka.

Father Nikolai of Saint Irene's Church and Captain Antonio Scarlatti, of their militia, are introduced to us. Then Astrid starts to introduce the Mice, proudly using Christopher's title of Suffragan Bishop of the Mountains for the first time. Christopher looks embarrassed. He hurriedly points out that he has not been installed yet. Astrid gives the three locals a quick précis of the story of Mousehole.

I started to tell it in Hindi, as I have no Latin, but Astrid interrupted. I know that I am not a storyteller, but…I am sure that I am not bad…and I am a good teacher.

"I am sorry, my Princess," said Astrid, "but you are telling it just like a teacher and sucking out all of the excitement. It is even worse in another language, and they will hear the full story tonight from Ayesha, after all. They just need the important bits now, and why we are here and how it fits together." *I suppose she is right about the last, at any rate.*

She just told what happened and then hands back to me. I will need to get Christopher or Astrid to translate my words. The priest has no Hindi.

"If you wish to send some people north," she said, "they will probably be able to take over Owendale and look after the locals there. The Khitan should give no trouble. Our Khitan leader, who waits outside with our saddles, has them tied in knots and they know that it would be cutting their own throats if they are to make the mistake of cutting yours."

"It would still be a good idea," she continued, "to keep an eye out here, but if you have people, third or fourth sons, who want land, then send them north... I will let Father Christopher explain, but any men who go to Owendale may end up with more than one wife, so make sure the priest you send is happy with that."

"I am not happy with that," said Father Nikolai bluntly. "I have only your word on the...*acceptability*...of this practice."

Soon-to-be-Bishop Christopher gets to reply to that. Rani indicated to him that he should do so. "The three Metropolitans we have consulted so far have all agreed on these arrangements for us. I can see no reason they would rule differently for any other place where there are many more women than men. At any rate, I will show you the Holy Words myself and we can discuss this later."

"If you worry about not having enough priests, I will talk to Metropolitan Basil when I see him in a few days and get you sent a replacement and another to add to Owendale as well. I have a feeling," he added in an aside, "that we will need a lot more vocations to become apparent before we are through with this.*" Father Nikolai thinks before he nods and allows me to continue.*

"We know," Rani said when she resumed talking, "that the Master's servants are spread out through the whole Land, and have found ways of hiding their evil from priests." *I can see some alarm on Father Nikolai's face at that news.* "Is there anyone in the village that you are concerned about or who may not be what they seem?"

"Jonas Smith," said the Captain immediately. *The other two are quickly nodding at his words.* "He is from the Brotherhood for a start. We see them as traders, on and off, but he is the only one of them to live here. He makes no attempt to hide this, but then you could not hide his accent. It is nearly as bad as yours."

He nods towards Astrid with a smile. She smiles back, not taking offence. I don't think that it is even possible to offend her over her deficiencies. "He supposedly uses runaway slave girls in his brothel, but they hardly ever seem to leave the building and they never have any money, except to buy necessities, when they do leave it."

"Brotherhood traders all seem to visit there, but we are really not big enough a town for more than a girl or two working on their own to ply their trade. He has six girls. Sometimes one disappears, and if that happens, another always seems to 'escape' to him soon after."

"He always seems to have plenty of money, and he is free to buy drinks for people, particularly for travellers. I don't know anything beyond that, and this is all guesswork anyway. He may be innocent, but I have been looking for a good excuse to question him for some time. Others may know more." He looks at their priest.

"He is not of the True Faith," said the priest, "so I rarely see him... Come to think of it, he does seem to avoid me a bit, but when I have been near him, he seems to me to be a good man. I suppose that is a bit surprising given his profession, but I have always thought that he was just good to his girls and that they were happy."

"He told me once, when I asked about her, that one of the girls I'd chatted to who disappeared had gotten married to a farmer who'd been a customer, and he had dowered her. He did not name the farmer and I admit that I did not think to ask. He always seemed to be genuine." *He shrugs and looks at the Mayor.*

"He carries magic...several items...but then who doesn't?" said Joachim.

"With your permission, of course, I will get my people to lay hold of him. If we are wrong, then we have more than enough money to cover over for any embarrassment that he may have if we have made a mistake in our accusation." *There is a thoughtful expression on the Captain's face.* "Are there any others you can think of?"

"I don't like Jonas, and am suspicious of him anyway, but there is another whom I have no grounds to suspect, until you think a bit about his business..." He looks at the Mayor and the priest and shrugs before continuing.

"I wouldn't have thought that we were important enough for spies to be put here, but Giuseppe is from Freehold, and our village hardly rates its own gambling hall either. If you think about it, he is like Jonas in some ways. He has no ties, no wife, and is wealthier than he has any right to be with the amount of custom that he can get from us and from travellers."

"Can we talk to him as well?" asked Rani. *The three locals look at each other for a moment before the Mayor nods.* "We shall return when we know more." Rani, Thord and Astrid wandered off to find where the rest of their people were. They needed to get together to lay their hands, for questioning, on the two dubious men.

We have their Captain with us, both to identify the two men that had been mentioned for us, and to explain what is happening to anyone who might object to their treatment. The pair of priests are off to the Church, promising to be only briefly away from the rest. I am sure that no one present, on either side, really believes those words.

Goditha

For Parminder and me, it is the first time that we have been out of Mousehole as a couple, and with a market to play in. There isn't a lot for us to buy here but it is fun just enjoying ourselves, holding hands and buying small things together.

Warkworth isn't a major town, but even such little things as ribbons and lace, that travelling traders from Freehold carry easily, are both rare in Mousehole. We have bought a quantity of them, and some braid. Goditha suddenly realised what she was seeing in great quantity.

She turned to one of the local girls...*she seems to be following us around...* and asked: "I doest not know much about thy town, but there doeth seem to be many things that art made of tin here. Why doeth that be?"

"We mine it here, said the girl, "and we have several people who work it. Would you like to meet one?" Goditha nodded. The girl looked around her...*I think that she wants to see if she can be heard by those people who are around us...*and leant closer.

"I will take you to our best if you can answer something for me." Goditha nodded agreement and the girl continued. "You have your hair cut as a man, and you act to this other girl as if you were a boy towards a girl...but you are two girls... Why is that?"

I am sure that I understand what this girl means and what is most likely behind her question. She looked around as well. *I know what it is like growing up different in a small village. I grew up in one and not everyone there was as understanding of the way I am as my brother has been. It can be hard being different to those around you.*

"It be because we doeth love each other and do be married. We even have a daughter together and doeth expect another child soon." She grinned widely at her wife. *Parminder joins me with her beautiful smile. I turned out to be lucky with my life, even if it did not seem so at the time.* "My wife and I doest need help for that part."

"No one objects... Your priest doesn't mind?" the girl asked.

"Our Bishop doth be the one to marry us...and our village hath two Princesses...and they do be married to each other as well. One of them doeth be with us here. If thou do wish to know why, then do come along tonight, and thou wilt hear our story."

She seems very excited. I am sure that she has a girlfriend...and that they keep it secret from the rest. She has taken us into the village and along the wall and left us where a man sits making a pewter plate. Then she leaves quickly.

I am willing to bet that she will be there to listen tonight...and with another girl close beside her.

Goditha discovered that this tiny village, like Mousehole, had a near monopoly on a metal. *Mousehole now produces antimony, perhaps more than The Land had seen before from one source and which Carausius is very happily shipping out, while Warkworth produces a lot of tin.*

The smith we have been introduced to, who is producing work as fine as any that I have seen, even produces thin sheets of tin that he has beaten out and put between rollers to flatten it smooth, and then bundled up into rolls for lining boxes for food to keep out the vermin.

I may have surprised him by buying his entire roll of this sheet and a pair of ingots as well, and from the way his eyes are nearly popping out, by pulling out one of the heavier purses the man has seen to pay for it with. He is not used to such extravagance from a simple passer-by, and one who seems to be a woman armsman at that.

He smiled and explained that there would be a Freehold merchant who was due in a little while who would be most disappointed. *Apparently, I need to bargain better when I buy things. I think that I paid him a lot more than the other trader does. If I want to return later, I am sure that he will be happy to see me.* She smiled back. *We can afford the coin, and I am sure that he needs a good buyer.*

My birth village of Jewvanda is used to both Freehold and Haven merchants. There they only have their carnelian, but I know that it costs more than four times as much than the miners receive when you see it anywhere else and sometimes even ten or twenty times, as I saw in a shop when we were in Ardlark.

Norbert and Eleanor will have uses for a full ingot back home. I am trying to remember my lessons on significance with all that has happened lately. I can remember that tin is an earth metal from the moon of the Spider and so it is important to me, but that is all. I think that the smiths use it to make bronze as well.

At any rate, I am sure that there will be uses for the thin hand-rolled foil. For a start, I have little in the way of lead sheet when I am working on waterproofing buildings, and this roll would serve better than that in some of the places where I need it. I just have to be careful not to tear it when I put it under other things.

Rani

Captain Antonio showed them back down to the street. *In the block towards the gate is the brothel. It seems to have people moving inside it but is closed up tight without its owner there...and with a market in town so there are trader's guards. Its owner apparently doesn't trust the girls to operate the business on their own, and that is an interesting thought in itself.*

A little further along is the gambling hall. A couple of merchant's guards are hanging around waiting for one or the other to open. Without Basil here, who do I get to find things out? It has to be Astrid herself to do it. They went near the gate as if going out and Rani had a quiet word with Astrid. *She just grins, spins around and goes over to one of the men. What have I done now?*

Astrid pointed and smirked, and with no attempt to drop her voice just asked: "Good brothel, is it?" *The man just blinks and looks at her. I admit she looks like an armsman and sounds genuine in her enquiry. I guess that he has known samalaiṅgika before, but they may not have been quite as open as Astrid is pretending to be.*

"Yes, actually...not that I want much that is special, but the girls are pretty, and they will do anything you want without charging extra...not like at home. You will find one to help you get off, if you want to...when the owner gets back. For some reason he is not here... I just wish that he would open up and let us in."

"Thanks", said Astrid, now smiling widely, "but my husband more than satisfies me." *She comes back to us. Antonio is just looking at Astrid from where he stands beside me. He looks astonished. I guess he hadn't thought about asking so blunt a question. I must admit that I wouldn't have either.*

They crossed the street to the Church to prise Christopher away from the local priest and then went in search of the others. The Captain took them to a tavern next. "This is the *Elephant and Turtle*. It is our largest tavern." He went in and stopped.

It is very dark inside here out of the afternoon sun coming bright from the west. Our eyes need to adjust to the light. He continued in a much quieter voice. "And there, talking to your people are our two friends. How do you propose that we separate them, and which of them do you think that we should talk with first?"

Basil

*W*hat is happening here? Stefan has been bought a drink and has hit on a simple solution to saying nothing. He is trying to look and sound more of a rustic than he really is. It seems that he has entirely forgotten how to speak Latin and is now working away at the other two in fluent Dwarven and very poor Hindi.

That is a nice plan. I can see the frustration growing on their faces. He is talking non-stop, saying lots, and they don't have a clue what it is all about. He is giving them the guard roster of Evilhalt by the sound of it. I am not sure what they make of that, as the names from Evilhalt are odd enough anyway.

Basil came in speaking Latin to the two. *They are quick to offer me a drink. Suddenly, I have two...Giniver from one and Rum from the other. Everything seems to be a contest between them. The two clearly do not like each other, and seem to each be striving to monopolise my attention. That is not going to happen. I want them getting in each other's way.*

One is obviously from the Brotherhood. I can recognise that accent easily now. Something about the man reminds me of Vengeance Quester. Even a casual look shows that he has the same lean and constipated look, pinched features, and an odd mixture of arrogance and humility on his face all at the same time. I suppose that is the look of hypocritical piety.

His voice has a degree of unctuousness about it, as if he is soiling himself by just talking to me. He doesn't give his name but offers to take Stefan and myself to "an establishment" he owns that has many fine and willing girls in it that will help us forget the trouble of travel. Basil smiled inside.

I wonder what Astrid's reaction would be if I decided to take him up on the offer...and I am sure that Stefan would be in even more trouble from his women. Both of us decline, and from Stefan's innocent smile he seems to have the same thought in his mind that I did.

"Don't be an idiot, Jonas," said the other man. "They are travelling with four beautiful women... What would they want your drabs for? On the other hand, I have the finest gambling in the north...cards, dice and many other games. You might wish a diversion from... What are you travelling like that for anyway, on those flying things?"

Backwards and forwards the conversation goes as the two men try to draw out what it is that we are here for. *Stefan is sticking with Dwarven and I am trying to answer their questions with questions of my own. It is a fine old time we are having; talking to each other without saying anything. Finally, we get Rani, Thord, Astrid and Christopher arriving with a man I don't recognise. Ayesha is nearly on their heels.*

"Can you come here please, darling?" *My wife talks in Darkspeech. That is even better than Dwarven. They recognise Dwarven, even if they cannot speak it. Neither has ever heard Darkspeech. I get to make my apologies and have the only Latin speaker leave. Thord has moved to take my place. I can hear his loud Dwarven as well. He and Stefan will both be useless to them.*

Ayesha was quickly filled in on one side of the situation while Basil was filled in on the other. *Thord has made sure that the two have their backs to the door where we have gone simply by taking each by the arm as he moved between them and not letting go.*

"We will take them separately," Basil said. "First we take the brothel-keeper." He looked around. "Father Christopher…I promise that we won't tell your wife, but you are about to express a desire to visit a brothel and enjoy what the girls there have to offer." He quickly sketched out a plan.

The others disappeared while Basil and Christopher went to where Thord and Stefan were. "Keep the other occupied," said Basil in Darkspeech. In Latin he said, "Christopher here does not speak Latin, but he has decided to take up your idea of a ride on a willing girl. He doesn't have a woman of his own here and none of us are willing to share. If one of your girls speaks Hindi…"

Jonas nearly falls over himself ushering Christopher away and out of the door. He is so intent on this that he doesn't realise that I am close behind as they go out of the door. Just as we are rounding the corner to the back door of the brothel, we are confronted by the man I don't know, who is with Astrid and Rani.

"Jonas," said the man, "I think that you are in our village as a spy, and this lady mage here has consented to put you to the question. What do you say to…"

The brothel-keeper is moving his hand towards a pouch and starting to mutter something as he attempts to dodge quickly sideways. Unfortunately for him, I was expecting that, and I move a lot quicker than he does. Basil hit him from behind with a sap and he fell.

"I guess he just told us that he is guilty of something," said Basil. "Now we strip him and tie him up. As soon as he looks like he is stirring again, we do what we always do to those who are about to answer questions." *This man, some sort of authority, waves his hand to a couple of other men who are waiting conveniently nearby.*

"Now let us deal with the other." Basil turned on his heel and went to get the owner of the gambling hall. He loudly entered the tavern, rubbing his hands together.

"Well, Christopher seems happy," he said. "Now let us see about your games of chance. I feel lucky today. Come on lads; let us spend some of that pay we have. Lead on." He clapped his hand to the man's shoulder and started to push Giuseppe towards the door, keeping his hand in place as he did so.

Things follow the same course with this second man, but this time there is no attempted muttering and no reaching for a pouch.

"He looked both surprised and worried," said Rani to Basil. "But he didn't try and cast anything or reach for a wand. I think that we may be safe in questioning the other first."

Once the two are stripped, it turns out that Jonas no longer feels the same to Christopher and Father Nikolai. "He now reeks of evil," said Father Nikolai in wonder. "How can that be?"

"We now know who he is working for, Father," said Christopher, rubbing his hands together. "We have sources who have told us of this magic. It hides an evil man from priests and makes him seem good. He could have hugged you every day and you would not have felt any differently about him. He just didn't trust his own magic near you."

Rani

*W*e will now do some simple experiments in magical deduction and repl-*ace items on him one by one until one ring changes the feeling about him from being evil to being good. Christopher then gets to examine that later.*

The questioning goes along the lines that we expected. With the Mayor, the priest and the Captain present, and everything that he is saying being written down, Jonas Smith rapidly turned into All These Curses Shall Come Upon You Smith, a Flail Inquisitor and priest from the Brotherhood. I was right about him.

He is quickly drained of mana and overdrawn until he is pale and shaking. He is far more dangerous than Vengeance, and unlike the man who had invaded our valley, is a truly evil man. He has simply killed some of his slaves who displeased him, or who became pregnant, and makes the others live in terror.

It seems he has them convinced that, if they run away, or give away what he is to the people here, then they will die in agony from spells that he has cast on them.

It was with some delight that Christopher tells him of the coming downfall of his religion and the defeat of its army at One Tree Hill. The man may glare and spit, but he keeps answering questions as he is compelled to.

He is still talking when Astrid comes in from what passes as the village gaol, downstairs from the Mayor's office, with six girls...all of whom are pretty, and who bear more than a passing resemblance to Make in so many ways. They clutch each other and look about them as they move. From their demeanour they are obviously very scared about what their fate will be.

For Brotherhood girls, they are wearing very little in the way of clothing. Indeed, it is not enough for decency by the standards of most villages, with skirts that scarce cover the groin, nothing at all worn under them, not even a loincloth each, bare legs and abbreviated blouses...and a head scarf... They all have their hair on their heads covered.

Some of the girls bear scars and old bruises. They all recoil back towards the door when they see the man that we are now calling 'Curses' pinioned with a rope around his wrists and hung up by his arms. They are being held over his head as he hangs from a pulley, with his feet just touching the floor. They cannot go out with Astrid behind them.

"They seem to speak only a few handfuls of words of Latin between them that are not directly useful in a bed, but they have a lot more Hindi" said Astrid. "I think that this animal forbade them to learn anything beyond what they need to get instructions from their clients and to get some information from them."

"I used his key to get in, but then I had to threaten them with a spear to get them out of where he had them locked. It reminds me of Mousehole under the bandits, only I think perhaps worse. Now, does anyone here speak Sowonja?"

"I do," said the Captain. "What do you want them to be told?"

"You will need to fill them in on their change from being slaves to being free women," said Astrid. *She does not even ask me.* "Tell them it has come a few generations early." Astrid looked at Rani. "Do we add them to our collection of freed Brotherhood slaves, or do we just set them loose? They seem to be so much like Make in some ways. They will be lost if we just cast them adrift."

Rani sighed. "I suppose that we will have to be responsible for them. We cannot take them with us now, but we can leave money to look after them and put them in the charge of Father Nikolai until we return. He and his wife can start instructing them in, well, everything I suppose." She turned to where Captain Scarlatti waited.

"Let them know that we are now responsible for them. We will be back in a few weeks with others from the Brotherhood who will explain it all much better than anyone here can, and then if you can just translate what Curses says. I don't think there is much more we can get out of him that is useful anyway."

She then turned to the Mayor. "He has confessed to murdering his slaves. Do you execute murderers here?" The Mayor nodded. "Well, it is your village, but we now know he is one of their priests and so has access to miracles. I would execute him soon, before he is able to do anything again. Then we can get on to the other one."

The Mayor thinks for a moment. There are two guards behind him. He calls them forward before deciding. "There is no time to prepare a proper public hanging, but we have written down his testimony here and that shall be available for anyone in the village who wants to read it. He had few friends anyway." He looked down at the table where a woman was writing.

"What we have here condemns him…and we have the girls as well to tell us more if we need it, so we will just hang him from the cliff pulley. Fetch Giuseppe along and we will tell him why this is happening before we talk to him." *He turns to Rani.* "You did this one. Now it will be my turn to get the next to speak."

The compulsion of obedience placed on Curses has worn off by the time we move him, and everyone else, a few doors along and into a room that is used to winch things up from the beach below, and a noose is put around his neck.

As he is being prepared, he kicks and swears, calling imprecations on all our heads, and seeking help from his God. It is just as well for us that he has been drained of his mana and it seems that his God is not listening to his entreaties either.

He is pushed over the edge of the cliff to swing in the breeze coming up the cliff face.

Without being given a good vertical drop to kill him, his neck doesn't break cleanly. Curses is taking some time to choke to death. His hands are still bound by his sides as he tries to break free of his bonds, and while he swings wildly to and fro, he is dancing a jig in the sky. I am feeling no pity for his suffering from what he has said.

The faces on his former slaves keep changing from fright, as they check around them, possibly expecting the sky to open, to joy, then to relief and then back again to fear. They cling to each other in a tight group of terror as they wait for their own end to somehow appear and doom them. One even makes a futile attempt to undo the rope, which would have doomed him anyway, but Astrid quickly puts a stop to that.

Giuseppe's story is a lot less interesting…in some ways. After seeing Curses die, he scarce needs a compulsion spell to get him to talk. He starts talking before we get back to the room. He is eager to tell as much as he can to save his life. He is a Freehold agent, but not entirely voluntarily. He was given a choice of taking the job or of being hung.

He says that he hasn't killed anyone and is just providing information. It turns out that he is a long-term thief who evaded detection in Ashvaria for many years before being finally taken in. Someone with a poor sense of humour has decided to use him for this task instead. They know that he cannot run away from it.

Going north will take him into the Brotherhood, and certain execution, and the way south is blocked by Freehold. Going east would mean risking the Khitan. He could have escaped by sea, but all boats that call at Warkworth will be going on to either Freehold or the Brotherhood anyway. He is trapped like a rat in a cage.

He lives well and has plenty of money sent to him, so he prefers his mostly comfortable, sponsored exile. His job is not just to keep an eye on Warkworth, but mainly to pass on anything that he hears from, or can find out concerning the Brothers, and he has no problems with doing that as he doesn't like what he sees of them.

All these things he freely and eagerly talked about. No one who sent him out cared about that. However, as soon as he was asked how he passes his messages to Freehold and who he reports to, he started choking, and despite the priests trying cures, and before they could assay to cast to remove any curse that has been placed on him, he is dead.

It is obvious that there has been a strong geas placed on him to prevent exactly this sort of questioning. While the obvious things, the things that anyone can guess, provoked no response, it seems that answering at least one question, the important one of who he reported to, triggered his death. Whoever did that obviously has a very cruel sense of humour and also did not place a great value on his life.

With the questioning now behind us, it is time for us to go outside to where Hulagu waits, collect the saddles and gather at the tavern. Astrid has had to go look for Goditha and Parminder. It seems that they are still wandering the streets, no doubt hand in hand, poking in shops, buying quantities of small things, and looking around.

Now they are back, they get to sit with the local priest and his wife and the former slaves as they are fed. They keep looking around them in wonder at what is going on. Goditha and Parminder spend most of the night trying to converse with them and learning as much Sowonja as they can...even a few more words could be useful...as translations of the tale go on.

Astrid

*T*he Elephant and Turtle *is not a very lavish establishment, but at least it is fairly large, and it seems to have the entire village gathered inside it, in addition to merchants and some of their guards. The story that Ayesha is telling tonight now has a new, if short, chapter about Warkworth added to the end.*

The villagers are enthralled about what is happening in the larger world outside and a few of the men, the sons of poor farmers and the younger sons—those who, like Stefan and Arthur, stood to inherit little—seem to be talking earnestly together by the end. I guess that the men here will head north instead of east to us.

It shouldn't be hard for the Mayor and Captain Antonio to find volunteers to go north to see what is going to be available after the fall of the Brothers. Good land always attracts people, particularly if it has already been cleared and is ready to be just moved on to, and this land may even have wives available, maybe even more than one each.

That is a rare thought, and I would venture that the women may not seek a high bride price, and maybe no price at all. Few younger sons have such a chance presented to them. Not as good as I can offer, but far better than most younger sons face, and it is all just a short trip from home.

Rani
10th Quattro

*I*t is very early in the morning, even before the sun is properly up, when we make our goodbyes and quickly fly north. I want to be outside Owendale to hear what Mongka has decided in regards to a covenant and to be there when he actually makes his attack. We leave behind a village that is starting to wake up to the changes in The Land just as it is preparing to wake up to a new day of work.

Already, in the pre-dawn light, there are armed people, mainly young men, starting to saddle horses and to prepare a cart. They may not have slept at all. They have some chickens in boxes and a few other young animals with them to replace what the Khitan will take and to start building up their stock.

Christopher pointed out as they left that two priests were headed north with them. *Perhaps one can be persuaded to go on to Narwood, the next village of the Brothers to the north of Owendale...and one that the Khitan might decide to go on to and sack as well.*

For those who are not going, it will be some time before Freeholders will be totally trusted again in Warkworth. The downside is that, with the market day traders in town, the tale of what is happening will now also be carried into Freehold from here as well as from Glengate. Who killed the Count will soon be well known in Freehold. I wonder what reaction that will cause.

Chapter XXIII

Hulagu

*W*e *arrive outside Owendale just as the Amitan are about to make their attack. There is a light summer mist drifting in from the sea and the village can only just be made out from where the Clan has gathered.*

Hulagu and Ayesha led the flight and took the Mice swooping down in front of the line of advancing warriors. Their move forward petered out before it could become a charge as the Mice flew across the front, spooking the horses and angling in towards where Mongka rode.

"Greetings, Mongka, Tar-Khan of the Amitan. I see that we are back here just in time. What decision did you come to last night and this morning?"

"I see you Hulagu, Tar-Khan of the Mori." *Mongka shoots a venomous glance at the shaman riding beside him and almost spits out his reply. It is as if he is already regretting what he is about to say and that he has been forced to say it. The man beside him looks grimly back in return. I am glad that Dobun and I already have a far better relationship than this will ever be.*

"We have decided that, although we do not agree with it, it was best if we fell in with the other Clans and agreed to your covenant with the baga khana." *He pauses.* "I suppose that you are going to insist on allowing the people here a chance to convert as well?"

"Yes," *I need as many to hear me as possible.* "There are priests on the way here now from Warkworth and men who will take over in the village once you have taken what you are due." He paused and looked around at the Amitan. *Most of them are trying to listen to what is being said.* "Now, it is time to go and add to your legends and tales...and to pick up some wealth besides." He grinned at the last.

As he said it, he took his saddle up into the sky and waved them forward. *I know that it looks like I am the one telling them, rather than their own Tar-*

Khan. I guess that is because I was. It isn't lost on Mongka either.

He has shot a look of hatred at me and then gone on to wave his Clan forward, although most are already moving in the direction of the village and do not notice him. I guess that the Mori have one minor feud brewing for us already. Hulagu rose higher and smiled inside... *And we are not even properly set up yet.*

Rani

I wonder if Hulagu meant to offend him like that. Such behaviour would not be acceptable in Haven. I am already regretting what I said yesterday. The Khitan really do act differently to us. Their Clan leader hates Hulagu, but he still agrees to the treaty. Did Hulagu really back him into that much of a corner that he had no other choice?

"Astrid...you know where to go, take us in fast. We want to take that building and the Pattern now, before any priests that are left get a chance to try to do anything to forestall the attack. Such an attempt will probably mean that another girl will die."

"Flat wedge in close, mage in centre, priest behind," she calls loudly. *We start to move our saddles around. Hulagu has the point out in front with his bow in hand, and next comes Astrid. Three others stream out to left and right, with me in the centre and Christopher right at the rear between the two end riders.*

"Forward, fast. Keep fifty up." *Hulagu leads us off fast, keeping only just above a church steeple. The village quickly becomes more visible, and it is obvious that the attack from the Khitan has been seen. I can see people running around already and people are calling to each other. Again, it is mainly women and old men that I see in arms.*

None of those hiding behind buildings and obstacles seem to notice us flying silently above them, although our archers are shooting as we go. They will be trying to pick out anyone who looks like they were giving orders or who are in a good position to fire as we pass by.

Astrid

We only get in two shots from the archers before Hulagu brings us down beside the building that the Pattern is probably in. and we are only just in time. Those two men in leathers are dragging a girl inside and closing the door as we descend. They didn't look back so have probably not seen us. They are going to kill her...screw them.

Astrid was off her saddle in an instant and hit the door with her shoulder. The lock shattered and the door flew partly open, colliding with something behind it. *I bounced. I will bet there was someone behind it.* The door swung slowly open all the way. With spear in hand she strode into the room that was revealed, moving to the left, clear of the door as she did so.

A man is moving quickly towards the door. He was the one behind the door trying to bolt it, and he bounced further than I did. He is now returning to try and secure the entrance. He is already closing the door as I slip past him and I hear a latch click. I can also hear an arrow thud into it as he does so.

Another man is struggling with a young girl, trying to throw her onto a table, one like the one that we saw in Pavitra Phāṭaka. She fights back and is starting to scream. The man closing the door is armed but doesn't have his sword drawn. He can pay for that. Astrid, ignoring the other man and the girl, quickly cut across his body with the point of her spear's blade.

I don't have the room for a full-strength thrust, but a short cut with the point is possible. It is nice of him to provide me the room I need by yelling and stepping back away from me as he tries to cross-draw his sword.

Astrid grinned at him and thrust under his arm into his stomach. She twisted her wide blade as his hands left his sword and tried to grasp her shaft. Astrid kicked him in the chest, and he flew off the blade, tripping over and landing on the floor screaming. *I guess he feels the pain in his gut, and his face shows that his impending death is sinking home.*

Astrid stepped forward and followed up on her first thrust with another straight to his throat. With a muttered gurgle he thrashed around briefly, pinned to the wooden floor by the blade, before quickly expiring, his neck nearly severed by the wide blade.

I can hear the door behind me re-open explosively and in almost complete ruin. That sounds like Thord is coming in. Astrid looked up from the dying man. *Yep, Thord is drawing his hammer back again after hitting the door. He runs towards the man who is still struggling with the girl and who has his back to the rest of the room.*

Thord is not giving him a chance to correct this error, and reaching high up, brings his hammer onto the man's leather cap. It is like kicking a melon. The man jerks in a spasm and falls to the ground. The hammer stays buried in his head as he topples. The girl gave a final scream and collapsed in a faint, splattered now in her attacker's blood.

I don't blame her at all. That was messy. Christopher comes in through the door and immediately gets to work. The altar is on a stone-faced central section in the middle of a timber floor. He knows what he is doing, and he has Thord anyway. There is nothing else for me to do here. It is time to get my bow out and help where I can outside.

She left the building. "Goditha...Parminder... There is a girl in there... She has fainted. Go look after her. You can now say some words of their cursed language at least. What is happening here?"

The two that I name look at Rani. She nods. They run inside. The Mice are kneeling behind their saddles or pressed against the building. Women and children are running around in every direction. There is total confusion. There is the sound of screams, the pounding of hooves, and the clash of combat coming from the edge of the village.

Rani has us ignoring anyone who is unarmed and shooting only at those who look ready to fight, regardless of age. With the Mouse girls inside and caring for the slave girl, now Thord joins us and takes a place with his bow. Behind us, in the building, Christopher can be heard loudly praying preparatory to his actual casting of the dispel enchantment.

The first Khitan are in sight as one of the women notices that we are not shooting people. She has run behind Rani. She has realised that we are a safe place and is calling others to her: boy and girl children and some older girls heed her call and soon we have a largish group of scared villagers huddled in our midst clutching each other. The Khitan ignore them and ride on past. The village is still being plundered, but Rani keeps us here in our places.

It is easy to know when Christopher completes his casting. The now soundless scream in our heads is familiar to us, but it terrifies almost everyone else. Around us, combat and flight both stop completely as people, both Khitan and villagers, pause to watch as...something...a misty red parody of a human face, perhaps—something that shines red and wet in the morning light— ascends high into the sky with a look of pain and surprise on it.

Saint Anne, I pray you, protect us. Everyone is shaking their heads at the sound that echoes in them. Some hold hands to ears, others raise them in prayer. A couple of women scream. Some of the amateur defenders throw down their weapons, and yet more run towards us as a safe place that is just holding still.

This Pattern makes a sound when it dissolves that is louder than any that we have previously experienced. The mana that has been freed here must have been larger than any we have encountered before. Perhaps the Pattern here has been fed with more sacrifices than the others, to bolster its power. Astrid shuddered.

Once the noise and image had left them, the Mice proceeded to ransack the shrine, finding soft velvet robes and objects of precious metals and gems. *There is another of those knives that we found in Haven and Rising Mud, among other things. Like the others, this will be disenchanted when we can get home and do so safely.*

Rani

*T*hey found a variety of treasure in the form of plates and golden goblets. *I don't really want to know for sure what the goblets are for, but they suggest to me a form of communion that was not of the symbolic form that Christopher has his followers practice. He said they, simple golden goblets with no magic that I can sense on them, feel evil to him.*

The Pattern is disenchanted, and the resistance seems to be over. Now we can talk to the captives. It is a slow process...At last we find a woman who can speak Hindi fluently. Once we have her, it becomes a similar scene to that in Aberbaldie. It takes a while but, once again, most of the ones who are willing to change their religion were slaves before.

Most do as they are supposed to, but some of the Bison warriors seem to be reluctant to bring forward all the captives to be asked the question. It looks like, whatever Mongka's opinion of their actions, the shamen and shamanka of the clan are co-operating fully with the agreement as they push forward with their captives.

Eventually the survivors are sorted into two groups, and the larger group are being moved away. It is only then that they realise their fate and try to break free, but it is too late. They had their chance and, as agreed, it was only the one chance to keep themselves free.

The thin sea mist of the early morning had burned off by then and wailing captives and protesting animals could be seen being herded out to the plains. *Those who are left behind have their fate explained to them and expressions of relief appear on their faces even as some reach out towards some of those who are leaving.*

Hulagu

*H*e was not here while we sorted the captives, so it remains to be seen *what Mongka will do next, and I need to find out. I think that I need to gather my wife. Together, we need to go and find him and watch what he does.*

He is already preparing to return to the plains with what he has gathered. When they came up to him, he was directing the loading of a heavy box and several small sacks onto some packhorses.

It is very obvious that they contain coin. Mongka looks at me as if he is expecting me to make an objection to this. One has been dropped near a building as they were brought out of it and is on the ground. I carefully point it out. You would think that it is a trap I prepared. Mongka gives me a wary sidewise glance before returning to his task.

It seems that the sack is over, and he begins to gather his people. The whole time he keeps looking up at the sky where the face had been apparent. Perhaps he expects it to return. As least he may better believe our tale now. The bloody apparition above us seems to have shaken him more than a bit. Perhaps he will better abide to the Treaty if it has shaken him enough.

It is only two hours before lunch and almost all of the Amitan have left the village and can be seen heading south-east. They are travelling slowly as they have over three hundred people on foot with them as well as a lot of stock. The entire attack and sack was over in almost no time at all. Less than three hours have passed and most of that time was taken with sorting the captives.

Rani

W*e still have over a hundred people with us, most of whom are weeping or otherwise grieving as they have lost friends and relations, either dead or taken away, and all of them are in shock. Their whole world has just come apart around them and with no warning.*

At least they will take orders and obey them. When I start giving them, getting them to find what is left and to get food together, its snaps some of them back to a more normal mien. They are eager to obey. It seems that most of them are used to being given orders and it has a comforting familiarity for them.

It is not just food we need to arrange. I also need to have them gather all the bodies outside the village near where the creek meets the sea. They can be burned later using stored wood and the remains swept into the creek.

Although there are only a few dead, less than you expect in a battle, for the Bison preferred to capture rather than to kill, there are still too many who resisted for us to bury easily. The villagers weep and mourn as they pick up the bodies and our priest is busy consoling and praying over the remains. Some are so young.

Christopher and the others that can heal are also busy with the many minor wounds that these people have taken. Just like the previous slaves we have freed from the Brotherhood, most are not used to having people pay attention to their wounds.

Christopher called me over at one stage and got me to order the girl he is treating to lower her top. She meekly stripped once I made myself understood. She has been badly whipped. It was probably just last night, and the wounds are still oozing blood. He'd seen the blood staining her dress. I hate these people we fight.

That night, after Hesperinos and then Apodeipnon, which progressed slowly as most of those listening had to have it translated for them, the survivors were given a compressed version of what was happening, which again had to be translated.

When it is revealed that they will be left in a couple of days there is panic. It is only partly allayed when we tell them of the men from Warkworth coming in a week. It takes most of the night for the survivors to be calmed down. They insist on sleeping together and have taken over the soldier's barracks so that this can be so. It required a fair amount of cleaning up as the most resistance to the Khitan was around it.

I realise now that we cannot leave this village untended. We must wait until the men from Warkworth arrive. With the Khitan not having moved on to take Narwood, it would be simple for an armed group from the Brotherhood to come down the coast and quickly recapture all of these people and to take them back north.

We could even see some of the Bison, for some are still waiting around the village, to gather them all up and disappear back into the plains. It may even be that the waiting tribesmen are hoping to do exactly that. I intend to disappoint them if I can.

Rani
11th Quattro

*O*ur healers are still hard at work. If we are to stay a while, we now have more time to recover, and Christopher is being more lavish with using mana to heal. I need to send scouts to keep an eye on the Bison heading further back into the plains and to check on the progress of the men moving north, as well as to see if anyone is coming south. We need more people and that means more saddles.*

Perhaps realising that we will be staying for a while, most of the Bison still lingering in the area are now dispersing. The men from Warkworth are coming towards us as fast as they can, and no one seems to be within a day's hard ride of the village from the north.

We have been to the outlying hamlets and assarts, and some stock have been brought in from them that were missed, although we find no more people. The village is gradually coming to order and more stray animals are found. Goditha and Parminder sit in the middle of the village with a woman who speaks Hindi. Goditha is intent on learning some more of this tongue.

Christopher
15th Quattro, the celebration of Pancake Pali

*T*he men from Warkworth have arrived. They have moved quickly. It is of great relief that no one has appeared from the north in that time. At least I have no difficulty explaining Lent to the villagers. Their religion practices it as well.

However, I do have difficulty explaining what Pancake Pali is. The idea of a festival that is just for fun is alien to them. I do not think that fun is allowed in the Brotherhood, at least for slaves. Astrid has a more practical approach. She has the women organise a festival, even if they do not fully understand what it is all about.

They are too few for a parade or anything like that, but particularly with the men now in town, and obviously ready to defend them, it is hard not to get into the spirit of things. They all seem to like pancakes and there are lemons, sugar, and cream to go with them. It is the first time since we freed them that the children have actually sounded like children.

For their part, the men are looking around keenly at what they see. They can see that they have a largely intact village in front of them. Some of the women have claimed buildings or farms already, mainly those women who are older and have several children, but most of the other places are unclaimed.

There are many women…far too many for that few men, but some are older and show no signs of interest in any man. Several are younger and interested in the men from the south. All of the local men who are left are former slaves, and so all of the adult men are eunuchs.

Despite this, with those newly arriving, Christopher smiled. *I suspect that the priests from Warkworth, both of whom speak a little Sowonja, will be very busy in the months ahead. I know how they feel.* He made sure they knew what he had been through, as he pointed out the challenges that lay ahead of them.

Chapter XXIV

Rani
16th Quattro, the Day of Ash Tetarti, the start of Lent

*W*e *are leaving, and it will now be up to the young men that came from the south to keep watch on the north on their own. The priests have taken charge of everything in the village for the moment, but I am sure that will change from some of the questions starting to come from the women.*

For the moment though, it makes it far easier that at least the women in Owendale react well to being given instructions both by priests and by the wife of the one, slightly older, priest who is already married. It seemed that the priests of the Brotherhood expect to be obeyed instantly...and their wives seem to be even more used to being obeyed.

We will now have to hurry to accomplish what we want. The northern forces will have taken Abbey Green long before now and be almost at Greatkin themselves. The extra time we spent at Owendale means that we only have a couple of days to locate and destroy what we seek. As well, autumn is pressing closer and that brings us to our other deadline.

Luckily, the woman who speaks some Hindi was the slave of a trader and has been to Greatkin several times looking after horses for him. She has at least given us an idea of where what we seek is in the town. She saw a building, similar to the one in Owendale, but larger, that is treated the same as the building there. It is rarely entered, except by the senior pastors.

It seems that it was more ornate than the one at Owendale, and it has guards, and as she describes it, should be easily findable from the air. I hope so, as after we make a brief reconnaissance from the air when we first approach, we will be flying in at night to destroy the Pattern with very little other preparation. We will have very little chance to correct any mistakes that we make.

They flew along the coast west of the Amity Forest and went high over Narwood, so high that they could not make out people on the ground. *In our formation of a wedge, if we were seen with a telescope, it would have been, as usual, as if we are a very fast-moving flock of geese headed in the wrong direction.*

The land bulges out into the sea after Narwood. We fly over forest before seeing Fenwick, the next village north and half the size. We keep well clear of that as well. It is well before lunch that we come in sight of the cleared area around Greatkin. Staying high we can barely make out the smaller buildings and cannot tell a person from a sheep.

This is likely to be our most dangerous attack yet. I need to make a plan that will make it safer. I will send Hulagu and Ayesha east towards the approaching army, the others back to the edge of the forest, and Astrid and I can slowly circle lower, hopefully looking like a pair of raptors to anyone who might look up casually.

The pair circled slowly lower. *Eventually, we can easily see the building that was described to us. I cannot make them out, but Astrid says that it still has guards. Even with most of their army away, it is given the status of two armed people to walk around it. She says that no other building in the town seems to even have one guard.*

"I will bet that they are Flails of God," Astrid called out loudly. *At this chill height, and with the wind whipping about our ears, it does not matter how much noise she makes. Anything she calls out will not even be heard as a whisper on the ground, even if she uses the Brotherhood General's calling-out device.*

I can see that Greatkin lies on both sides of the lower reaches of Cangi Creek, a few hundred metres from where it enters the sea in a small bay. The creek straggles out of the forest to end in a natural harbour, only a small one, but well shaped according to Astrid. From what we have seen, it is the only place capable of providing shelter on the entire northwest tip of The Land.

It seems that the Brothers so ignore the sea that there is not even a wharf there, even if the caravel that we destroyed at Camel Island must have called here often. I guess that everything is loaded and moved by small boats. Possibly their lack of other natural harbours keeps them away from the sea, but for whatever reason they pay it little attention.

There do not even seem to be all that many fishing vessels for the number of people that must be in those houses. Perhaps their leaders see the sea as a way of people escaping their control. I don't know, but at least that is one thing less for us to have to worry about.

One very wide street leads east and west, crossing the creek on two separate bridges. They also seem very wide. Perhaps they want room for their chariots to travel in columns. At the creek there is a short street that runs along each side. It all leads to the town having just two shorter streets that are north and south of the main one.

Although there are many farms packed all around it, all of this leads to the main part of the town having just four large blocks, incomplete on their outward ends and four separate short lines of buildings in an almost symmetrical arrangement. It must be that very few people live in the town. They must all be in the farms around.

Our target lies in an eight-sided building in the middle of the southwest block and behind what is clearly the largest building in the town. From the look of it, that has to be the main church of the Brothers. It does not look like a temple that I am used to and not even like the Orthodox ones. It is just a big box sat down in the middle of everything.

There is clear space without even a tree all around our target, and no one approaches it while we circle except for the guards, who pay more attention to one side than to the others. That is probably where the door is. Even running, it would be impossible to get close to it without being seen by the guards as they move around.

Unlike everywhere else, where we checked for a Pattern before attacking, here we just have to hope that we have the right place. We will not have time available to us to do anything else. At any rate, it looks like it should be the right place. Having seen all they could see from up in the sky, Rani and Astrid spiralled back up, as if in an air current, and then went in search of the others.

Thord was drifting around in the sky, and came up to meet them and bring them down to where the others waited. *They are at a small clearing with a farm that seems to have been recently abandoned.*

I am not used to judging the worth of a farm, but from what has been left behind, broken and discarded, it does not seem to have ever been a very prosperous place, and its owners may have been among those who went east with the invasion. Hoping for a better life, they just left their crops behind them. It is all abandoned and untended.

Apart from some kitchen vegetables, the crops seem to consist only of small fields of lavender as well as other herbs in some quantity. They must have once been expecting to sell these herbs and the oils that they produce to buy grain or potatoes, as I am told that there is little to be seen in that line, and not much provision for livestock beyond a small chicken coop, and a barn that looks like it once held a donkey, from the small size of it.

There does not even seem to be provision for a cow, which all these northern farms seem to have, and the storage for fodder is almost completely empty. If they went east, they took everything they had with them. At least there is a well and a roof for us to shelter under. Thord went back up into the sky to keep an eye out for anyone approaching through the forest and for the other two riders.

Eventually, he brought Hulagu and Ayesha down, while Parminder took a turn on watch in the sky. "The first of the army was about two days away when we left them," said Hulagu, when they had come down to the others. He went on to give a report of all that had occurred.

"They took Abbey Green yesterday, and they think they are still moving faster than any news of them is. At least they don't think that anyone has gotten away from them to the west. They are using the carpet to ferry people forward to hold the road and to prevent anyone from escaping. They have taken several couriers that way and unless the Brothers are using birds to carry messages—and they have seen no sign of that—nothing has gotten past them."

"We told them what has happened in the south, and the Metropolitan said that they will swing south to Owendale before sweeping back round to Peace Tower and home. They have already sent some people along the road from Abbey Green to Fenwick and we must have just missed seeing them due to the thickness of the forest."

"Your chief priest says that he thinks some people may have escaped into the forest, and that will keep the Basilica Anthropoi busy for some time trying to find them all, once this is all over. He said that he fears that there will be some forest bandits around for some time to come."

"There are still more than a few Khitan, from almost all of the clans, with the army. They are taking advantage of the covenant to gather a good bounty in captives and stock, but it means that the Brothers are well outnumbered and casualties on our side are very low, even if the priests and the böö have been kept busy."

"Our own horses and the carpet are working with the army in the north, but your wife decided to send Ariadne and her people down to the south with the ballista and the cart. We didn't go back to Peace Tower, but they will most likely be there by now, or at least soon. She said that they would be needed there." *She is very likely right about that.*

Rani thanked them and sat everyone down and outlined what she wanted to do tonight before they settled into a routine of quiet watch and sleep for the day and the early evening. *Christopher conducts services as usual. Even I am used to that. It has a comforting familiarity to it. I miss my wife and our bed.*

Astrid
18th Quattro, very early and just after the Midnight service

*T*he army should be within a day of us and we have had a day to rest. No *one has come near us in that time, there has been no change that we can see in the town, and now we attack.* Those that had slept woke and ate. *Basil has a hot meal ready and mugs of kaf. It is good to have this kaf. How did I live so long without it?*

Around us is the brightening night that occurs just before mid-month with the full moon of Terror. It is very late summer. There is little cloud overhead and the moons and stars shine down on us clearly. We will have no cover for our attack from clouds, but on the other hand we will see everything better and we are expecting trouble anyway.

They took off and were almost instantly out of the woods and out over the cleared fields. *This time I am keeping us a few hundred paces up. At this time of night there should be few casual walkers around to see us. Greatkin is clearly ahead of us. A few buildings still show lights, but most lie dark in the night.*

There are a few patches of brilliance in the night. They mark where there are outdoor lights. They are so bright that they must be magical in nature. Astrid steered them slightly west before angling back. *I want to come up to it from behind the building, from the other side to where I think the door is.* They came closer.

"Damn it," she said, "Almost all of those bright lights are clustered around our target like squid lights. The slave woman would not have been out at night, so she wouldn't have known. We will have to get down quickly."

Because we are in the centre of a hostile town, and not just in an isolated village, we need to have the saddles with us to get out quickly once we are done if we need to. This means that Ayesha and I cannot just sneak in on foot and remain invisible from some distance away.

At least I can clearly see that there is, indeed, no door on this side of the building. There is not even an opening of any sort anywhere low on the wall. There are some windows very high up near the roof that would let in light but could not be seen through. They are coloured glass anyway. It is hard to see thought that.

Astrid brought them down quietly against the wall. *We must come down out in the open and will be very exposed in the light being cast from the buildings around us. What is more it is hard, with the light shining as it is, to make out any targets that might be in those buildings…and we are in the darkest spot that I can find.*

Getting off their saddles, Astrid and Ayesha clasped hands and put their rings on, fading out of sight of the others as they did so. The rest of the Mice were prepared—when they heard anything—to move from the small area of comparative dark where they landed. They sat on their saddles with arrows nocked in their bows, and wands or weapons in hand, and waited for the two to prepare to move around the building.

Ayesha

*W*ith the aid of Allah the Victorious, here we go again. My teachers were *right. It does make you lazy in your approach if you are invisible.* She looked around. *However, there are no shadows to hide in. If we didn't have the rings, the lights near the front are so bright we would be casting at least three shadows all the time.* She looked down out of reflex at the thought.

I am now casting three shadows. She looked at Astrid, clearly visible beside her. *I can see her plainly.* She looked back at the rest of the Mice. *There is an expression of dismay on Rani's face as she looks straight at where I stand. I had better not point it out to Astrid. She might laugh at our Princess, and that would not do.*

The rings stopped working as soon as we left the tiny area that is more shaded at the rear of the building. Whoever set up the lights has done so deliberately to make sure this building cannot be easily attacked. Not only do the lights eliminate shadows to hide in, but they also include a cantrip to allow the invisible to be seen.

It is a very smart ploy. It is much smarter than I expected from the Brothers or their Masters, and far better even than what they did in Pavitra Phāṭaka. She pulled on Astrid's hand. *She realises it as well and has stopped and is looking at me.*

"We are just going to have to be fast and silent," said Ayesha. She put her ring in her pouch and leaning close to whisper. "Instead of doing what we were going to, we will split up. I will go this way," she pointed, "and you will go around the other way.

"Once you are past the others you will start to run. You will make more noise than me in that mail shirt that you have come to like so much, so I will travel slower. As we go around this building, they should be looking for the source of the noise…*you.* You take the first with your spear. I will take the other from behind."

"And if there are more than two for some reason?" Astrid asked back in a whisper.

"Since when have odds worried you?" *She grins.*

Astrid

A strid grunted, smiled and nodded before heading back towards the others. "Change of plan," she said nonchalantly as she walked past the others, moving anti-clockwise around the building, its stone wall on her left and blowing a quick peck of a kiss with her hand in the direction of Basil as she passed him. She looked back. *Ayesha is looking at me and pointing my way. I know what to do, girl.*

She started to run, her spear held in both of her hands. *As soon as I leave a careful glide, the mail starts to make the unmistakeable noise that it always makes if a person moves at any speed.*

This building is much larger than most houses, except those of nobles, and whoever is on guard will, if they are awake at all, have some time to prepare for my arrival. I expected them to be taking advantage of a corner of the building to shelter behind if they are a right-hander and...I am right. She had swung a bit wide as she approached the last corner before the front.

There waiting for me is one man, equipped with sword and shield, looking cautiously towards my arrival as he uses the building as cover for one side. There is a door behind him in the building and another man armed the same stands on the other side of that. He is also looking at me. She ignored the second man.

I hope Ayesha is quick. I have come around the corner far enough away from it that my man has to step forward from his cover to meet me, and that gives me the advantage of reach. My opponent seems hesitant...perhaps he lacks the experience of being in an actual real fight. She feinted with her spear at the man's face...*he reacts and raises his shield quickly...so.*

Astrid changed the direction of the feint into a thrust down for a quick stab at the man's leg. He soon realised that the first blow was a ploy and brought his shield quickly down to try and cover his lower half.

He is fast, but not fast enough. He hit Astrid's spear shaft hard just as the tip of the blade pierced his right thigh. *This converts my straight and otherwise light thrust into a long gash down the length of his leg.*

A scream of pain came from his throat as he brought his blade around towards Astrid. His attack was affected by having to cope with pain in his right leg. He was pivoting on it for the blow and Astrid was able to get her spear shaft up to block most of his attack. The rest fell harmlessly on her mail. *The first flurry goes to me.*

With that cry, the game is up as far as secrecy is concerned. Our attack will be soon known, if anyone is awake. She moved back and freed her blade. He came forward and, as she had hoped, nearly fell. *I must have severed something.* She thrust forward. *He is only dressed in armour of padding and light leather. It only helps him a little.*

His near fall coincided with her thrust so that her blade went into the base of his throat above the join of the collarbones and sank deep into his chest from above. His sword hand flailed forward, more out of inertia than anything else, and the blade again slid off the mail of her shoulder onto that on her arm as he gave a final gurgling scream that rang out around the lit area.

Ayesha

If I can hear that noise clearly, the guards must be able to hear it even better. It doesn't matter how quietly she runs, that "shing-shing" noise of soft sliding rings is unmistakeable. She came up to the corner and quickly peered around. *Yes. Both guards are looking at where Astrid has just appeared.* She quickly, and quietly, stepped behind her man.

I was expecting the guards to be wearing mail themselves. I have my pesh-kabz ready in my left hand. As the man moved forward to try and help his friend, Ayesha was able to quickly and silently move up to shadow him. She took position behind the man and was about to stab when he must have sensed something and started to turn.

It meant that she could not get her hand over his mouth as she had intended, and she changed her point of aim so that her blade struck home, slipping between his ribs into his chest.

Inshallah. I was taught that this is one of the deadlier blows, and so it has proved since I started using it, and it slips nicely between his ribs. I scarce feel it going in and his turn towards me pulls my blade out of him all by itself. As he brings his shield and sword into play that look of astonishment, one that I am getting used to, appears on his face as his heart collapses.

The man dropped his sword and almost his shield as well as he clutched at his chest with both of his hands. *His mouth opens either to cry out for help, in pain, or to make a prayer. He is steeped in an evil belief, but may Allah still have mercy on his soul.*

She stepped in and carefully placed the needle-sharp point of the blade into his wide-open mouth and up into his brain before rotating the point. He fell...*almost instantly dead*. Looking up she saw that Astrid had dispatched her man just as quickly, although he was still thrashing on the ground. As Ayesha watched, the larger woman put her foot on her man's shoulder as he lay in front of her and pulled her spear from his body. *Around me the others are arriving on saddles.*

"That was quiet then, dear," said Basil as he hopped off his saddle and ran to look at the door. "It's locked." He proclaimed.

Rani

"Go get your saddles," Rani said to Ayesha and Astrid before turning to the others. "Basil, check the guards for a key... Otherwise... Thord, no time to be subtle, take this amulet and use your hammer again. The rest of you take shelter. It will almost certainly be trapped. It all depends on how strongly they have made the trap."

While Ayesha and Astrid were running around to get their saddles, Basil ran his hands over the bodies, "Nothing," he proclaimed.

"There be heads that be looking out of windows across the way at us," said Goditha. "Doeth we shoot?"

"Thord, get the door. Everyone else, don't shoot at anyone before we are shot at. Until we shoot at them, we are not necessarily going to be their enemy. The longer we keep them confused as to who we are, the better it is for us."

Thord

Thord looked at the door and grinned. *Ayesha gave me her magic lockpick before we started out tonight. This time she remembered to bring it. It is time to see if it works. There are, in fact, two large brass-bound doors that open in the centre. Once they are unlocked, they will swing wide enough that we will be able to fly a saddle inside easily.*

He looked at the bronze-alloyed lock and went to work. *I can feel the lock sliding... It is almost instantaneous, even with my lack of skill in picking locks. The lock yields in a series of soft, but audible, clicks. Now the doors are coming loose, and I can push at them to start them opening. This is easier than breaking them apart.*

The door was opening, but something was triggered. It was a trap that the picks had not neutralised. As the doors began to swing open, there was loud explosion of wind, almost a thunderclap, and Thord flew away from the door to land in a heap near Basil.

Basil

T *hat was quite a blast. It near knocked me over as well.* Basil leapt onto Thord as behind them the doors gaped open a little. "He is alive... Unconscious, but alive," Basil cried out. He began ministering to the Dwarf, taking a potion bottle from its pouch on its belt and beginning to dribble some of it down Thord's throat.

"T'at must ha' been one powerful spell," the Dwarf said as he shook his head and weakly grabbed for the bottle for another swig.

Astrid

I *have returned to the front of the building just in time. There still could be guards or other traps inside.* She sprung up the steps and hit the doors with her shoulder before Rani could say anything else. *At least Thord has succeeded at his task and they swing open smoothly.* She peered suspiciously around the room that was revealed.

A point source of light hangs from the ceiling. It isn't as bright as that outside. The hanging charm is giving about the same amount of light that a large candelabrum would give. Most of the building seems to be taken up by a single, nearly round room, although there is a balcony around the building three paces up and the area under that has rooms built into it.

On the floor are mosaics making up the Pattern, with shallow glazed tile troughs rather than painting to mark the lines. They are not clean. Between the lines are the names of the so-called Elder Gods laid out, painted on large glazed tiles and a table altar stands to one side for sacrifices. Troughs run from the table to the pattern.

"Come in. This will take a lot of work." People began to fly their saddles inside the room. *Christopher has taken out a chalk and has already begun praying as he moves in.* Astrid went out to help Basil with bringing a still-shaken Thord inside. *Last in is Goditha. She has flown in with my saddle and she is here just in time.*

A bolt lodged itself deep in her shoulder as several others stuck into the saddle or failed to pierce her armour. *She moves the saddle over to one side before landing it. Luckily it is not an explosive shaft, but it is in deep.*

Goditha

"**S**hit." Goditha grimaced and reached for her belt. *Lakshmi made sure that everyone had at least one flask of Healbush potion on them, and it is just as well.* "My love, canst thou be pullin' this out please." Parminder ran over with a look of concern. "Don't thou be worryin', my dear. I don't think it hath hit anythin' important. It just hurts a bit."

It hurts more than a bit, but I am not telling her that. As Goditha sat on the floor, her face pale, Parminder put her knee on her husband's back, took the bolt in both hands and pulled. Parminder was not very strong and she had to put all her strength into what she did. The bolt eventually came out with a wet sound and Parminder nearly fell over as it did.

Ayesha has already loosened my belt and is trying to get my mail over my head. "Come on, Parminder," the Ghazi said… "Help me get this off her. We want to make sure that the bleeding has stopped, and that the wound is clean and has nothing in it."

"I don't need help" *Why are they both ignoring me?* The mail came off and Ayesha got a good look at the wound. *That is why. I can feel her pulling at threads from my gambeson that the bolt carried into the wound. I am glad to not see that. It feels bad enough. Now, I can take a sip of Healbush. I can feel the bleeding stopping already.* "Thee canst now stop fussin' my dear."

Astrid

That was a quick response from the people outside. Already more bolts are coming through the open doors, hitting the woodwork opposite or skidding across the floor. Astrid pushed the left door almost closed as Hulagu pushed on the other.

"Now we get our bows," Astrid said to Hulagu, "and then we try and keep them away from us for a bit." She peered out of the crack between the two. "It won't take them long to rush us if we don't fire back, and Christopher needs a lot more time to do his work."

Stefan

*T*here is a set of stairs leading up to the balcony on each side of the room. He took them in his stride. *The balcony has a walkway around it at the top four rows of seats and, wonder of wonders, a narrow window every few paces that is covered in stained glass. Saint Sebastian is with us. They have given us arrow slits.* He smiled.

He moved to the window above the door and kicked the glass out. *There are some people coming down a paved path from the big square temple that is in front of us. Both men and women and all seem armed.* He had his bow in hand and it only took a moment to put an arrow into one of them. *The others dive for cover but there isn't any to be found in the well-lit area.*

"See if'n you can bar t' door. We be havin' good firing points up here 'n' it be safer." *There is noise below me and soon the sound of several sets of feet on the stairs. It looks like, before enough of the Brothers can get in place to rush us successfully the door will be barred, and we will have several archers in place.*

All this time I can hear Christopher at work on his disenchantment down below. His voice is rising and falling as he prays while he draws his own pattern to counter the unholy one that the place is built around. I know that he learnt from Gil-Gand-Rask and has flasks of sanctified water standing ready for afterwards to help complete what he is doing.

Rani

*E*ventually Parminder, Goditha, Ayesha, and then finally Thord join those on the balcony. I can hear the constant sound of bows being fired. I am near the doors with wands ready in case something happens and they are forced open. Before she went, Astrid found a pair of iron, floor-mounted candlesticks, obviously ceremonial, given the light coming from above, and has jammed them through the handles. They should hold a while.*

Basil, who has no distance weapons that can reach beyond throwing range, is noisily investigating the small rooms. He is breaking things open and dragging some items out onto the floor if they looked interesting. I hear splintering timber. Rani looked around. *I can see a blade, another like those found in Haven and Owendale, more of the golden goblets, and elaborately covered books, undoubtedly sacred texts of some sort. Basil is calling me…*

Several of the rooms, taking up almost the rear half of the building, are cells with beds, comfortable looking, but with no handles on the inside of the doors and sliding panels on the doors to see in. I wonder how many young girls have spent a last terrified and pain-wracked night in them. Far too many, I warrant.

Each of the beds has padded shackles for hands and feet attached to them and other equipment as well. All to better help these loathsome men rape their victims before they kill them. It is so nice to be killing these people and destroying their twisted beliefs. Anyone who would use rape as a weapon is not human.

She looked around. I am no priest, but even to me this place reeks of despair and pain. Looking at Christopher, he seems to be a little haggard as the miasma of wretchedness has some effect on him. Outside I can hear yells and the occasional scream and sometimes an explosion as one of my Mice thinks that a target deserves it... They all do.

There is a slow, rhythmic thumping from the barred doors. Astrid calls from above: "Sorry, too many of them came on at the same time. They have a ram at the door, and I cannot get the angle to fire at them now." Rani looked. There is already a small gap there and through it, I can vaguely see people rushing towards the door.

The ram hit the door again and the gap widened. Rani stuck a wand into the crack and fired it without being able to see exactly what was there. At least I am rewarded with screams. I can be sure that I hit someone. She fired again and again, now checking through the gap each time as she did so, until there were no more sounds of movement at the door. The timber that they were using as a ram is lying on the ground and it is surrounded by bodies.

"That should slow them down. It was nice of them to make such a defensible location for us. Slow down your fire if you can. I suspect that we will be here until the attack goes in. All of their people must be outside this building now, and if we try and fly out we will become pincushions, even with our protections."

This was confirmed soon after. Astrid, who is above the door, is cursing and, at the same time, calling on Saint Michael. "They have one of those repeating crossbows set up opposite me. One got in and I have a bolt caught in my mail...I don't think that it broke the skin, but it is going to be harder to keep them at bay if they use that to cover any rush at the door."

She is right. It is impossible to safely fire out with one of those playing on your window and bolt after bolt coming through. Whoever is using it knows exactly what they are doing and soon an almost constant stream of the bolts is coming through the gap above me.

They stop an archer using the slot to fire out, but that is all. It is lucky that they cannot depress their fire down to floor level, and they are flying well over *where Christopher works. They are hitting the opposite wall, sinking deep into the wooden panelling there. The timber there is starting to look like a pincushion.*

Another attack on the door came soon after, and Rani again fired her wand. *One wand is used. Time for me to pull out the next.* This time many of the screams were female. *Their women are as fanatic as their men.* The attack stopped. *The doors are a little wider apart now, half a hand at least and they refuse to close any more.*

The wooden pole that they are using as a ram is jammed into the opening and the iron stands holding the doors closed are starting to bend. This is not good. They are not broken, so at least the doors serve as a barrier.

Eventually Christopher completed his ritual and, with the now familiar scream, a tortured face erupted from the pattern through the roof and presumably into the sky. *It was even worse in appearance than the one at Owendale. At least the destruction of the Pattern seems to cause a pause in the attack from outside for some time.* It eventually resumed. *I think that it seems less intense.*

The night proceeded with sporadic attacks being repulsed and the Mice receiving the occasional bolt in return. *None hit anything vital on anyone, but we are halfway through our potions, many are wearing a bandage of two, and I can see Christopher is muttering to himself. I am sure that he is debating taking some sleepwell potion to regain his mana.*

Astrid

*T*hrough my window I can see the sky is fast getting lighter all around us. *Dawn is here.* With the dawn came a series of loud noises and shouts from the outside. *That is a welcome sound. I think that we have held out long enough and the attack has started. We have probably kept them busy and so it is coming as a real surprise to them.*

"I think that the armies of the north are attacking," said Rani from below. "They must have moved quicker than we thought they would. Can anyone see anything?"

"We are being ignored." *Finally…he got careless.* She put a last explosive shaft into someone she had been trying to get at for some time. He was an older man who had been directing the attacks all night from near the temple, and she thought that he was a senior priest. *He looked like one of their priests. He is thin, balding, sanctimonious, and mean-looking. Well, he is about to be a former priest.*

He lay there shrieking as he tried to hold his stomach together where the arrow had exploded. *I will give him that he is determined. He is trying to get something from his belt. That will be a cure then, one I don't want him to have.* She followed up with more normal arrows until he lay still and ceased reaching for his potions.

A woman, wearing a female version of what the priest was wearing, boldly ran towards him with a flask in one hand and a shield in the other covering most of her body. *No, you don't, you harridan. You can go to hell with him.* Astrid aimed at her legs until she was brought down to the ground and then made sure she was dead in turn. *No more come out.*

Soon cavalry, some Khitan, some Basilica Anthropoi and some from the north, are riding through the town and becoming visible to the defenders. *That is a welcome sight. Oh look, those are our kynigoi even. There is Eleanor giving directions.* Astrid called and waved out of her window at them. *They see us.*

We have succeeded, I hope, in eliminating all the Patterns in The Land, and it is not yet the start of autumn. We still have to clear up the rest of the Brothers and organise ourselves to reach Wolfneck in time to board the River Dragon, *and whatever presents itself after that, but it seems that the most important part of our work is finally done for The Land itself.*

Chapter XXV

Bianca
18th Quattro, just after dawn

I am finding out that there is a quiet after a battle, quiet that is, except for the wailing of captives and the cries of the wounded. It is when the survivors among the victors catch up with each other and make sure that the ones they care about are still alive and well. People mourn those who are lost or wait in pain hoping for relief.

It is when those whose job it is to care for the wounded are at their busiest as they frantically try to save lives and repair the damage done by blades and missiles and magic. It is when stories are told between friends as to what they did and what they saw, both teller and listener happy to be alive. In themselves, the stories that they tell each other are unimportant. They are more an affirmation of success and of their personal survival than anything else. So it is with we Mice.

I am more than pleased to see my husband again, and he is happy to see me, but once he has confirmed that I am well, he bustles off to look after those who are not. I must be resigned to that. Trying to change Christopher's nature is near impossible and I would not want to anyway. It leaves me free to look around.

Theodora and Rani are useless for some time, as they just hold each other and murmur things to each other between kisses, each happy that the other is fine. Astrid sighs, muttering something about the Princesses havering, whatever that is, and chases everyone around as she organises a place for us all to sleep and eat.

Stefan has his Bryony and Adara to worry over him, and for him to worry over them. Hulagu has Aigiarn and Alaine concerned over him, and over their elder sister-to-be, and the wounds that they bear from our attack.

The others will have to either wait until they are home, or at least until they join Ariadne and the cart. This night that we will have together is only a temporary break. The next morning, we will all be busy once more. We will all be riding or flying off in different directions, once again. At least we will have tonight.

Theodora

*O*ne thing that we are able to do today is to ransack the library of the Elders for anything that looks like it might be interesting. I am not the only one to find almost all the books interesting, for one reason or another. It seems that it is not only the former owners of Mousehole and Dwarvenholme who were interested in collecting volumes.

The Elders of the Brotherhood have been doing it assiduously and for a long time. Furthermore, they have been looking after what they have gathered far better than the Masters have. The most interesting-looking books are in a locked cupboard where a casual reader could not see them, but there are a goodly number of others as well.

Theodora looked at what they had gathered and wondered if their Masters knew about this collection. *Of course, once we have gathered the books of interest, we are left with a little problem of transporting them home.*

We already had collected some beasts to carry what we have been able to salvage of the weapons of light, not that there is anything much useable left of them. The loads on those beasts are getting bigger and the horses that are supposed to be remounts are now starting to become pack animals as well. I am not sure if Hulagu approves.

Thord

*O*thers can look at the library. I will see what they find later. I am sure that there is more that lies buried under their Temples than there is visible above ground. It is where I would keep things secure against being found by magic. I am taking the lockpick and then going looking through armouries and secure storage chambers.

Thord
several hours later

I may now be a little singed in patches from some places that were trapped, despite my caution, but I have come up with some interesting finds and now have a lot of packages hanging from my saddle. These are packages I need to be very careful with. I need to talk with Astrid and Basil. I think that they will help me carry home some of the finds.

Basil's saddle will have something of great interest on it. It is hard to disguise a very large two-handed sword wrapped up in cloth and strapped securely lengthwise under the saddle. At least no one will see the details of it, and that is the important thing. I suspect very, very important from what I can read of its inscriptions and what was on its case.

Rani

*W*e *have destroyed their army. We have taken Greatkin, and we have destroyed both of the Patterns of the Brothers, and it may mark the end of that problem for us Mice, but from the point of view of the allied forces it certainly does not bring the campaign to a complete finish. Indeed, I think that we are quite a long way from reaching that point.*

For a start, the villages of Fenwick and Narwood have yet to be taken. Indeed, such has been the pace of the attack that those villages may even still be unaware of what is happening, but it will not take long for them to find out and try to do something about it.

More importantly, Peace Tower has yet to fall. Until that fortification is gone the Brotherhood can still return to haunt us all. What the Brotherhood have left in the way of an organised army will still be inside its walls. In addition, there will be individuals, as well as perhaps families or even small groups of soldiers, still in the Amity Forest.

If they become brigands it could take years to eliminate them, even with magical assistance through the liberal use of location spells. The Amity Forest is just a little too big to be quickly searched. Besides, too little is known about it by anyone except those who live there. From what we have seen there are little clearings with farms in them sprinkled all through it.

If Peace Tower remains untaken, then the people inside its walls could unite these scattered people into a force that will be able to come out and threaten the newly freed villages. Apart from Peace Tower, that is a problem for the North. However, we need to deal with the fortification before we can completely leave this area.

Theodora

*F*or most of the Mice, the fall of Greatkin marks the time when we should start heading back to our home. I made this clear to the Metropolitan on our advance to the west. There is much that we still have to do, even if all of the known Patterns are eliminated. Now it is a case of getting rid of the last of the so-called Masters before other matters concern us.* Unconsciously, Theodora rubbed her stomach.

If even one of the Masters is left alive, they will set up more puppets and perhaps even create more beings like themselves. Additionally, it seems that we still must use the carpet to pick up more girls from Warkworth and get them, and the other freed sacrificial slaves from the caged wagon that had been outside Bulga, back to Mousehole.

These last girls are supposedly currently under the protection of the ballista crew and so should be at Peace Tower. Rakhi, Zeenat and Bilqīs will be running a constant shuttle with the carpet all around the northwest of The Land over the next few weeks. Goditha, Parminder and Ayesha have already taken the three girls down to Warkworth on saddles, with the carpet rolled up as luggage.

Goditha and Parminder are there to translate, and once it is clear to the freed girls from the brothel what is happening, the girls on the carpet will start with transferring them from there back to the valley and Goditha can join us at Peace Tower. We may still need her there. The journey from Warkworth will be the longest trip and the one that is best gotten out of the way soonest.

Christopher, with Astrid back to looking after him, will be consulting with the Metropolitan before going on and Hulagu will be talking with Clan chiefs. The rest can go straight on to the siege, leaving the last two villages to the forces of the north. It is time for me to stop just having fun being a simple kataphractoi and go back to being a Princess.

Chapter XXVI

Basil
19th Quattro, the of cial start of autumn

*W*hen we have done what we all need to, all the Mice on the flying saddles will meet at Peace Tower, but this time I will be letting Theodora take my saddle, and I will ride with the horses with that sword. I do not want it out of my sight. My skills are less likely to be needed in a castle assault than Theodora's are.

I will have a word with Ayesha before I ride off about keeping an eye on our charge and not letting her get too close to any artillery that might be in a fortification. We have already allowed her to be wounded in the battle at One Tree Hill and that was too close. She has even fought several more times since then, but she seems to have not come close to harm.

The library and some of the other items were loaded onto packhorses. *My wife, with her new-found interest in learning, has made me promise to look after them well. It takes most of those packhorses that we can find, mostly former chariot horses or animals that have been freed from carrying the food supplies that have been eaten so far.*

To carry everything we want taken needs ten horses in total, and more would have been needed if one of them had not been Juggernaut, who carries more than two of the normal beasts. Can we perhaps borrow a Cow-lizard or two from the Khitan? That would make it all easier.

Basil
26th Quattro

I must admit to being amused with the dynamics among the riders as we set out. For a start, Hulagu should be pleased that his clan is being shaped without him having to do much of the internal work, although he has laid the foundations with the other Tar-Khans. Bianca has assumed control of the Khitan who are riding, even Anahita and Kāhina are now deferring to her.

Even if they want to, none of Dobun, Aigiarn and Alaine have a chance of usurping Hulagu's authority. Moreover, Bianca does it as matter of "Hulagu would like it done this way" or "the Tar-Khan wouldn't like that".

The authority is always laid off to Hulagu and Bianca, as his sister, is always deferential to what she thinks he will prefer. What is more, Dobun doesn't seem to have much of a chance of taking a stand against his wives-to-be. It is immediately obvious that the two girls like what they see in him and they flirt outrageously and publicly.

A certain amount of joy and abandon is to be expected from them. After all, with their background, they had once been looking at a bleak future of certain death. They now have a future husband who is, in all likelihood, going to be an influential shaman and seems to be a promising young man.

They have a goodly amount of wealth as well, and have collected far more in the north as they went. They have decided that they have the same right of pillage of any of the other Khitan and they are concentrating on taking horses, with any treasure collected being only incidental.

It is just as well that they are doing that. We are using many of their horses to carry the books in improvised packs and other arrangements. Although their marriages to him will be waiting until they return home, it seems that they are not holding back in finding out if they enjoy each other in bed.

Next, there are the Darkreach kataphractoi: Neon, Menas and Asticus, and their relations with the single girls. It seems that they have been sent west knowing all about the conditions that apply in Mousehole, and they have set about trying to seem a good match as well as they can.

The only girls from the valley who are with us, who were not yet committed to another person, are Maria, and the new girls Zoë and Loukia. The men are not unhappy to have women from their own culture to pay court to, but this is outweighed a little by the fact that Maria, although small, is just so stunningly beautiful, with a heart-shaped face and honey-blonde hair and blue eyes.

I am amused to see all three men so unsure as to which of the women to court and why. Anywhere else in The Land but Mousehole, the two former Darkreach women would have been counted as more than attractive and both are accomplished in their trades. Indeed, they are both good catches in their own right.

My wife has talked to all three of them and I know that all the girls are well aware of the indecision of the men, and are content to just flirt with them until the men are willing to make a commitment. I am willing to bet that nothing will happen between any of them until we all return home and there is more time.

They are all young and seem content, now that we are more secure in our future, to sit back and wait and see what happens next. Until the Masters are defeated, none of us can be sure that we will still be alive. Darkreach culture lacks the same traditions that Astrid's has in such situations. The girls can see no reason to hurry into a relationship, let alone commit to a marriage.

I am, at least, now more certain what the relationship between Stefan and his wives is. Although when Stefan is around, they are both as attentive to him as any wife should be, it is obvious in his absence that they also follow the path of the Princesses.

Thinking back, that should have been obvious even when Stefan is present. They are not acting behind his back in any way. Oh well, they all seem to be happy. That is the most important thing. At least I don't have to worry about that. What happens between the people of Mousehole, in private and in public, is often more than enough to make anyone's head spin.

Chapter XXVII

Ariadne
22nd Quattro

*T*he walls of Peace Tower look to be quite strong, but they are meant to
keep out the Khitan rather than someone who knows how to deal with
them. The Khitan seem to know little of such things as sieges and, if what I
have been told is correct, even with the backing of their shamen, they will get
bored and move on rather than sit down to wait out a long investment.

*This is already evident as we arrive with our cart, and with a full company
of the infantry of the Northern Army around me for protection. Some of
the Khitan have already started to leave the area around the Tower. Long
experience has told them that they will not take the citadel on their own and
that they are wasting their time.*

*As soon as I start unpacking, they begin to drift back. They can perhaps
see that the rules have changed, or at least they are curious about what I am
doing. Unfortunately for me, this time the advantage of height lies with the
defenders, and but for the fact that it seems that the devices mounted on the
walls are smaller than mine, the defenders of the Tower would have held a
distinct advantage.*

*I am slowly pushing my ballista forward, and it seems that those on the
walls have only one-cubit devices, sufficient—indeed ideal—for keeping
Khitan at bay, but not with a long enough range to break a serious siege. They
trade their range for a much faster rate of fire. It is a pity that I do not have the
makings of a serious siege, just one engine and some men and women.*

Ariadne remembered what she had been told in her lessons before she had
begun concentrating on how to make bricks. *A defender should always have
the longest-range artillery possible. Rockets are best for this, and are ideal
against cavalry, but they are not known west of the mountains and you work*

with what you have.

Even with the height advantage that the defenders have, I am able to creep forward until I am well within my mid-range while they are just unable to reach me with a normal shot. Some shots that bounce off the ground gain some extra range but, as their devices use bolts, rather than balls, most of them stick into the ground rather than ricochet.

Once I have my wicker gambons, packed again with earth, in place at the front, the chance of being hit by such a shot is very low. Still, we can expect a collection of bolts to begin to appear in the gambons soon.

Bolts are far better than balls against their normal opponents, but things are not normal now. It is made worse for them by the amulet that we Mice have, but the defenders do not know that. None of this stops them from trying to hit my ballista and my people.

They must realise that it represents the worst threat to them in their stone walls that they have ever seen, so they keep firing at it. They must have huge reserves of bolts. They have probably been adding to their stores for generations and it may well be that it is almost impossible to run them out of ammunition.

Now that I am set up, it is time for me to open the gate. The advantage of my low and flat trajectory ballista is that misses are usually either high or low, and very rarely stray far to one side or the other. In this case, I am not firing at a point target, such as a single person. A gate that leads into a keep is a very large target indeed.

At the range I am firing at (now that I am properly in place), a miss to the left or right is only going to be a couple of paces anyway, as the rounds of a ballista follow a long, narrow path when they land. A gate that is made for large chariots to have access through it is far wider than a couple of paces in width.

As well, seeing that I am aiming for near the top of the gate, what would be long or short in a field battle just translates into hitting near the base of the gate, or else attacking the wall of the castle that is in place above it, to break through into where the murder holes are. I am just as happy to hit either one of those targets as well.

She started with a few unenhanced shot to get the range, and to gauge the strength of the defence before moving on to explosive balls. The gate began to disappear into splinters and rubble in front of her. *It is not as thick as I thought it would be. It is probably enhanced against fire but is not as strongly protected from what I am throwing at it.*

The Khitan around me are vocal with their approval. Peace Tower, being deliberately placed far out in the plains on one of the few real hills here, has been a thorn in their side for years. It will take some time, and I will have to make more shot as I keep firing, but eventually I will open a path into the keep. It depends on how many gates and other impediments there are for me to remove, but it will be done in time.

I am sure that I have the first piece of artillery ever with a seated audience watching from behind us, drinking from bottles and leather bags, making bet, on where the next shot will go, and cheering each shot and calling out comments to the defenders.

Soon the rest of the Mice began to arrive. The ballista crew quickly got to work. So were those making more shot for it and there were many volunteers for that task, even from among the Khitan. Some Khitan were left on their horses to guard against a sortie by the garrison, but the rest of the allied army sat down to rest and repair for a while.

Rani
23rd Quattro, the Feast Day of Saint George

Theodora and Rani flew overhead and considered the options. *Ariadne will clear a way into Peace Tower. That much is inevitable, but it will still be hard to force the breach, and many of those first through the gap will die. Even my wife remembers that from her training, and she admits to not paying a lot of attention to many of those classes.*

Although the words I was given by my teachers are slightly different, we were both told that, if you are looking to have victory, never leave your opponent with no choices but to fight. If that is an opponent's only choice, then they will have to fight. You need to allow them to choose to not fight you and perhaps to keep living.

If we are to smash a hole in at the front of the castle and then and go in through that hole, then it will be as if we are trying to force the cork into a strong bottle instead of taking it out. The further it goes into the bottle, the harder and harder the job is. We do not have the people to be able to do that when we only have a single company on foot.

Thord and Astrid had some things to say and what they said opens up a lot more options. We have time to consider them. We still cannot do anything until Hulagu rejoins us to talk to the Khitan who, apart from their interest in Ariadne and what she and her crew are up to, are still happily ignoring the rest of our Mice when they can.

Hulagu

*T*his army has a steadily reducing number of people in it. Casualties, troops used to hold areas from anyone who might be lurking in the woods, and unasanid, riders returning home to the open plains from the close horizon of the enclosing woods, steadily deplete the numbers.

However, it is still a quite formidable force and the number of warriors left behind by the Brothers in Fenwick and Narwood, most of them women, is not sufficient to really slow them down. Well before we are needed at Peace Tower, all organised resistance has been crushed and the Army has ended up at Owendale.

With its arrival, the last few of the Amitan left and those emeel amidarch baigaa khümüüs who had been with the Army of the North ever since the battle before Bulga, now that they were finally out of the woods, began to stream back to their övs, taking with them their new riches in köle and herds. It is time for us to join the others at Peace Tower.

Basil Tornikes

*F*or the first time in a very long time, my Communion, indeed perhaps even my own area of the North on its own, now holds more land than the church in Freehold…except of course for this other land to the west of The Land that they hold that I have been told about, and that my new priest, the wolf, seems to come from. If you add in Darkreach, we will perhaps have more than that as well.

However, if we leave aside those in Darkreach, we still have far fewer people than Freehold does, and those people that we have are very spread out and share most of their area with the Khitan. We have not a single real city and most of our towns are really just villages, but our situation is now much better than it has been at any time since the Schism.

Although I have been acting as if I am the leader of the north during this campaign, I know better than to expect that to continue. The heads of the old villages are far too accustomed to their independence, and although I am sure that whoever ends up heading some of the new villages will defer to me for some time, that situation will not continue forever.

I cannot even rely on the Basilica Anthropoi to back me up and to enforce *my will. They are sworn to defend the faith, not any one leader of it. Most of the time I can rely on them to do as I ask them to, but their obedience is not, and never will be, guaranteed.*

Trying to use them to enforce my dictates on others of the Faith would be something that definitely will not have their support. I am always going to be best off acting by persuasion and moral force rather than attempting to impose anything on the people. It is how I have acted my whole time as their Metropolitan and it has worked most of the time.

One thing is certain and that is, with the power of the Brotherhood broken, Freehold will want to be paying a lot more attention to whatever manages to succeed it. They may even think about extending their influence north and rebuilding their Northern Reaches.

He sat in quiet contemplation for a while. *I think that I can see a way out of this situation. I can call a conclave for everyone to express an opinion on how we should organise ourselves. I can let everyone know that there will be one voice for each village, and one for each spiritual leader. That means the Abbot and myself, and perhaps Christopher…and one for the Exarkhos ton Basilikon of the Basilica Anthropoi. That should be acceptable to everyone.*

I will invite the Princesses, and the Dwarves of the Northwest, to send someone along…and perhaps the Khitan can come along as well. That way they will know we are not forming an alliance against them. Janibeg of the Cow-lizards has the most contact with my people and he seems to have the respect of the other Tar-Khans, and perhaps the leader of the Pack Hunters as well. They will be good ones to send an invitation to. They may not come, but this way they will not feel slighted.

If it is all done after winter then these other matters the Mice talk of should be concluded, and it can be wrapped up before the meeting of the whole Ecumen in Mousehole, and before the Mice go off on their next summer campaign…wherever in the world that might be taking them…They are close about that…even to me.

With that decided, and then placed into the hands of his secretary Andronicus to organise, he turned back to the immediate problems at hand, smugly satisfied with his idea.

Rani
late in the afternoon

*D**ealing with the Khitan is frustrating. If you are not one of them you can sometimes talk with one ruler, but when there are several together, they* *prefer not to acknowledge the presence of anyone else, anyone who is non-Khitan. Sometimes they speak as if they speak to the air. Sometimes they listen as if the air replies.*

It is as if, when several are present, they all compete to be the most Khitan of them all. Dealing with one Tar-Khan is sometimes easy, but not always so. It depends on many things. It is easier to get the Clan of the Horse to relay messages. Of course, this makes it hard to discuss tactics for the battle to come but I may eventually have a solution.

She had Hulagu call a meeting of the Clans present at Peace Tower, and made sure that the Mice were established in place and seated before the others arrived to the places left for them alongside Hulagu and Ayesha. Cushions had been laid out for the others in a circle.

Now that Hulagu has greeted the Clan leaders, I can speak only to him while he can speak to both the Clan leaders and to me. The Clan leaders speak only to Hulagu, although they sometimes do continue to pluck words from the air around them. She sighed. *This seems to work and gradually we can put a plan together.*

Ariadne

*I*t has been a day since I blasted apart the last attempt to rebuild a barricade across the gate. All I can do now is to wait for the next part of the attack. We wait and fill in the time with making more ammunition with the help of any priest or earth mage I can convince to help me. At least Goditha is getting better at it, but it is slow with only one person doing the spell.*

Now, however, it is time for the saddles to fly over the fortress, staying out at long range for any missile weapons. This is fully sufficient for the talismans they bear to do their job and, while some of the better crossbow users sometimes hit one of the Mice, they fail to penetrate their armour. Besides, firing a weapon into the air above your own people like that sometimes has consequences.

When we started doing this, the occasional spell had come up at us, but Rani has been cruising the sky doing this every day, and each time a blast of magic comes at her, she replies with the fireball spell that she used against the Brotherhood chariot at One Tree Hill.

Each time she does that she kills anyone near where she aims. After losing several mages or priests, as well as anyone that is around them, it seems that all that the Brotherhood has left are a few casters without the power to do much to harm anyone. She can only kill one group of them each day, but that is proving to be enough.

Goditha
24th Quattro

*N**ow, instead of just shaping balls, I get to actually do something. I knew that I was learning to speak this tongue for a reason. There are others who can speak it better, but they cannot fly a saddle. I have my speech written out and have practiced it. I hope that I do not make too many mistakes—even if I do speak with a very heavy accent. I even get to use their own General's speaking device.*

"I send greeting to the people inside Peace Tower," she said, trying to speak slowly so as to not blur her words. "If you keep watchin' what we do using a telescope, you will look that today your village of Baloo will fall down to us. Once it has gone, the fortification you are in will be the last place left standing of all of your people's place."

"All of the rest have fallen down," she continued, "and all of your holy places have been destroyed, and you have been abandoned by the demon that have seduced your leader. The same fate awaits you soon. That we sail over you and have opened your gate to the world, despite what you have tried to do to stop us, show that what I say is truth."

"Your devil god have abandoned you with the failure of your army, and the rest of the north is arrayed against you out of disgust with what your priest and the Flail have done. Anyone who leaves your keep, by any means, before the attack comes in two days will have their life spared. Bring no weapon with you. Anyone who leave with weapon will die."

"When you leave you will be asked to abandon your false god. You will not be forced to, but you will be given that choice. If you chose to surrender when we make our attack, then this will be accepted as well, but I warn you that you are likely to die before then. The choice of which way your destiny flow now lies with each and every one of you."

A few more shafts came up at her while she spoke. *It is apparent that at least one more priest or mage has lain low, or has been healed, because a ball of fire is coming up. I was told to expect this, and I bear several of the devices for protecting me against magic, even priestly magic. I am nervous and hope they work. I must hold still.*

The explosion rocked around her but caused no harm. *I had charms on me to cure me if the protections didn't work, but I am pleased that they succeeded.*

Rani had been expecting something like this and had stayed well away from Goditha and carefully timed her casting. *She can cast almost straight away and the area where the spell had been launched from, on a roof inside a diagram, is soon bathed in a huge explosion. There were three women standing there, possibly female priests combining their powers.*

Theodora is following this up, in case a contingency cure is in effect for them, with an air bolt, which is using stored mana. Oh my God! It is so powerful that the roof there is cracked open and falls in on itself over most of its area. Below me, I can hear wailing from somewhere in the keep, but the charred remains of the three women, what I can see of them, remain still and unrecovered.

Everything is according to plan and now I need to make the rest of the speech. "I hopes that you all saw that. I let the so-called miracle of your fire-priest wash over me, and we then replied with impunity and have crushed them flat. So it will be for all of you…unless you surrender." *With that I fly off to reassure my wife that I am fine.*

Ariadne
a little later

Goditha is finished, now it is my turn in this show we are putting on. The ballista is packed and ready to go on the bed of a dray that has been reduced to being just a small and precarious platform. My assistants are on the platform with me. I hope that they hang on tight. It is not as good as the idea that I thought of earlier, but this is what I have now.

Eight saddles are, hopefully, lifting us the short distance to Baloo where I will help everyone to repeat what happened at Aberbaldie. The saddles will then lift me back to the keep itself. We will need to make more trips for the ammunition. Baloo is a very small settlement, with not a lot more people left in it than Mousehole now has attached to it, but it still must fall.

The ballista arrived there on its platform and started the attack by firing at the crossbow mounted on one of the gates. From what happened next, it seemed likely that whoever was in charge of the defence had placed themselves at the gate directing things. *Of course, from here they would not have seen what I did to the Tower.*

The weapon that had been placed above the gate was quickly knocked out by Ariadne using an enhanced ball, and the crew, and several others standing there, disappeared. The gate was next opened with solid shot and anyone on the wall facing her with a missile weapon was killed. *That is done, now*

Goditha makes the village a short offer of surrender.

Most of the Khitan in the area have ridden over and are now sitting around just out of crossbow range waiting to see the result. I think that they like this game. They certainly cheer enough each time that I fire. Someone inside the little village is obviously more sensible than any we have encountered so far.

A woman was trying to gather what is left in the village into a defence, but another woman came up behind her and hit her over the head with an iron frying pan held in both hands. She has fallen and soon there is a stream of unarmed women and children coming out of gate, bringing the felled woman with them. Soon there is no one left in the village.

Unlike other settlements, they had a mix of free women and slaves to contend with here, and almost all were willing to forsake their birth faith. *The Khitan gain few köle from Baloo. According to the gossip running around, last night they witnessed their first execution of a girl-slave by the priest who was at the gate as he tried to contact the so-called Archangels.*

It seems that this shook many of them. We were all speculating on this one night around the fire, but it appears that their priests keep what happens well behind the scenes from most of their people. The folk of the Brotherhood are, as most people are if they have the chance, essentially goodly at heart and human sacrifice does not sit well with them.

It was his wife and fellow-priest who'd been felled by the frying pan, and although wounded and with a bloodied head she is, unfortunately for her, still alive to be questioned after the village is taken. It seems that she was not popular with the villagers in the first place, and many blame her for reporting friends and relatives to the Flails of God.

The next day she was questioned in front of her old parishioners by Rani, and the village found out what had happened to cause many of the pretty girls (both slave and free) from the area to disappear, and she revealed how pressure had been applied on fathers and slave owners. The village had previously been encouraged by tales and had been led to blame the Khitan for these losses.

The Khitan present are very interested in hearing that. She is almost the only priest from the whole Brotherhood to be captured, and while the others died of wounds, she is the only one to be executed in the whole campaign, and she is executed by her own people. The villagers asked the Mice for that right and, when it was granted, they stoned her.

She died unrepentant and trying to call on her Archangels for help. When the Khitan finally left Baloo with their few köle, they also left more of its flocks and grain than had been left behind at any other settlement. *It seems they approve of the way the women of that village handled themselves. The woman with the frying pan is already getting the others organised as we go back to Peace Tower.*

Rani
that night

It seems that word of the fall of Baloo has an effect on them. Several people are fleeing Peace Tower. There are not many of them, but they reveal that some within the Tower are trying to stop others from leaving. I wish that there was more we could do to help them flee, but I am not sending my people in there to what could easily be a trap.

Some of those fleeing are escaping down walls on ropes and a number of these are killed by defenders with crossbows when they are seen. Only one has made it out of the front gate alive, and that is a young slave boy. A larger group escaped from a sally port at the rear, leaving it open behind them. A few more came out of there later before it was slammed shut.

Maybe we should move Ariadne and her machine around there and open it permanently? No, she needs time to make more balls for when we make the final assault.

Goditha
25th Quattro

Morning comes, and I now fly above them and read out my next set of lines. This time it is short, and I tell them they have one more night before they will be taken. I make sure that, if they missed it, they know of the fall of Baloo, and the stoning of the woman priest, and exactly why she was stoned. No more spells come up at me. They have learnt that much.

Rani
26th Quattro, morning

Last night we have had another fifty people escape...or try to. It looks like that door is now permanently open. Someone set it on fire, and it looks like they used oil to make sure it burnt. Some of those escaping revealed that there are still around two hundred people left inside. Some of these would like to surrender but cannot. There are Flails of God still inside and they have taken control.

One group of slaves has killed one of the last priests, a very junior trainee, and they have brought his wife with them as a captive during their escape as an offering of sorts to us. I wish they hadn't. She is very young, just turned fifteen, and has only been married for two weeks. She is not yet ordained as a priestess even.

She is very scared. She is crying and making no effort to resist when she is handed over, and it is obvious that she has been beaten by her captors. I am reluctant to just execute someone who seems too young to be guilty of very much at all. She fainted from the terror of what may happen to her as soon as she saw me. I had best just put her aside under guard until later when we have some time to properly question her.

The escapees revealed that the Flails had taken control of the gatehouse and the area around the postern gate and that they were rigging traps there. *We will deal with that.* Early in the morning, the Mice took their saddles up to see what could be done about those areas.

Peace Tower is a large rectangular fortification with square masonry towers. It has a larger outer area and a smaller inner keep with a separate internal gatehouse leading to the outer keep. It is that second gatehouse that has had its roof stove in by my wife's air blast.

The larger gatehouse at the main gate has lost some of its stones to Ariadne's ballista, but it is still largely intact. According to the last escapees the few dubious elements of the population left, the slaves and others who most likely want to escape, are locked up in a storehouse inside the inner keep. That should, at least, keep them safe from the combat, but the two gatehouses still dominate the castle.

Although there may only be, at most, two hands of Flails inside, it will not take many to hold the wall, and those two strong places and that inner gate cannot be forced by Ariadne's shot.

"We need to open the main gatehouse. My dear, can you repeat that blast and knock the roof in for us?"

"It is lucky then that I recharged my storage device yesterday," was the reply. "I have one such spell for a day. Are you sure that is what you want it for?" Rani told her what she planned before getting Hulagu to go and make "suggestions" to the Khitan.

While they are essential in keeping the garrison contained, their horses and other mounts will be nearly useless in the assault. They still have a part to play in engaging the wall defences and perhaps climbing the walls using their lassoes if they have the chance, but the actual attack will belong to the few northern infantry.

I only have a company of them, all armed with a sword, mace, or an axe, and a shield. They came this way with Ariadne instead of going west. With so few of them, possibly only a few more than there are defenders—possibly even less—it is essential not to lose any, and the advantage in such an attack always lies with the defenders.

Stefan may be on his saddle, but he will be with them as their officer with his armour on. By now, even the only village leader who was present at the siege, Laurence Woolmonger from Bidvictor, is used to Stefan giving them all orders and is quite content acting as his lieutenant and passing on what is given to him.

When the Khitan had started their harassment of the few people who were on the walls, and all else was ready and in place, Rani nodded to her wife. Theodora flew over the gatehouse.

Theodora

A few bolts from their crossbows are coming from the keep towards me as I approach. I am flying relatively low. Ariadne has discouraged that with an explosive ball into one of the embrasures that the fire is coming from. I guess that they are out of wands, or at least don't have any close by. Theodora gained her position above the gate and began chanting.

As she was finishing, she could see a trapdoor below her starting to open. *The defenders are starting to emerge onto the roof to try and stop me doing what I am doing. They are too late. I used the shortened range to boost the power of my spell and the whole roof is collapsing around the emerging defenders.*

There is still some movement there, but they are not going to be doing much more than trying to get free at present. Bolts are starting to come at me from the second gatehouse by this stage and several have come close to hitting me, but I have my husband's helmet. They either go past me or else fall out of the sky. Theodora started to return to the where the rest of the Mice were.

Rani

N ow the next blow falls and it will fall hard. Rani waved Astrid and Thord off on their mission. They approached from higher up. *It is obvious that they are not seen, as no bolts come in their direction. Thord goes for the internal gatehouse and Astrid for the main one. Flying saddles are ideal for dropping things, and Thord found a supply of molotails in Greatkin.*

The two begin carefully dropping these into the caved-in roofs of the two gates. They spread them out, and looking from outside the main gatehouse it is soon evident that the entire main upper area is full of fire. Not only can flames be seen licking out of the embrasures, but burning chemical is dripping down through the murder holes.

The Flails must have had combustibles stored there as well, to use against the assault, possibly even more molotails. There is a series of other explosions and new fires burst into existence inside the clouds of smoke that are boiling up into the sky. The screaming that started does not take very long to stop.

In its place, the smell of burnt flesh begins to lay heavy in the air as the oily blackness of roiling smoke ascends. The flames still drip down, and the remains of the outer gate and the inner gate begin to burn. The latter was open; now it will never have a chance to close.

The iron-bound wooden portcullis on the inner gate comes crashing down in flames, as its machinery begins to melt from the conflagration. Soon it too will be gone. Stones above and around both entrances begin to crack with loud explosions from the heat.

Once he has dropped his burden, Thord starts to fire at some of the wall defenders from inside, where they have no protection from his shafts. Ayesha, Hulagu, Parminder and Goditha join him. There are few embrasures facing inside, and to fire at the attackers the defenders have to come out into the open. Some did and paid for it. They cannot dodge as well as a saddle can.

Parminder took a crossbow bolt in the leg, and retired to the concern of her husband, but she was the only casualty. The Mice then took turns to contain the defence, not allowing any to come from the inner keep to the outside, until the inferno had died down.

That takes over an hour, and the fires are still burning, although much reduced, when the first infantry, holding their shields over their heads, run through the gatehouse. By then Khitan are starting to appear on top of the walls and none come to oppose them although there is still some attempt to keep them out of the corner towers.

In close combat, the defenders are not lasting long. Few of the Flails seem to wear more than light leather armour and they are not used to serious combat, only intimidation.

The northern infantry started to search the outer bailey, but the resistance must have been centred on the towers and the gate. They encountered no opposition. *Except for the gatehouse, it seems that the whole outer keep has been abandoned.* When they were able to make into the inner bailey, fighting alongside dismounted Khitan, their enemy crumbled before them.

They discovered that some of the surviving Flails had, instead of manning the walls, tried to get into the storehouse to massacre those they had locked within there. *Why do they always want to kill their slaves rather than let them go free?*

One of the eunuch men inside had realised this and had organised a barricade, and when that was being forced, fought desperately against them with a flour-bin lid as a shield and a large kitchen knife while others used other improvised weapons, even bread ladles, to aid him. He fought hard and had held the gap in the doorway for just long enough. He had died almost as the first of the allies found and killed the last of the Flails.

Most of those inside the storehouse are slaves and they are all glad to renounce their faith. They have seen several of their number sacrificed over the last few days as the last senior priest tried desperately to contact his Masters for aid. It must be that the destruction of the Patterns cut them off from their chance to communicate or gain help.

Rani
later that afternoon

*W*ith the fall of Peace Tower, the Khitan soon begin to disperse after sacking what they can and taking some of their new köle with them, along with everything that can be taken. I am glad for us to join in the sack. They can have the coin and magic. We are mainly looking for any books that we can see, but we also find another of the obsidian blades.*

While most of the Khitan left, some of the Elephant clan stayed behind with the strongest of the few köle that they had taken and with some of their great totem beasts. *They are all already hard at work, and they have a lot to do.*

To add to the insult of their defeat, the newly-made köle are now going to be used to dismantle Peace Tower piece by piece so that it will no longer exist as a threat to the plains. It will take a long time, but the Elephant clan has endured the insult of this building and its sheltered warriors for many generations. They seem prepared to take that time to be rid of it.

It is time for us to move on. I can hand over the village of Baloo to the priest who has been delegated by the Metropolitan to take charge of the area, and we can begin the long task of getting everyone home and ready for the next part that we must play. The time that we have available to us is running out faster and faster as each day passes.

Chapter XXVIII

Olympias
3rd Tertius, the Feast Day of Saint Nicholas

I *have only fourteen people to crew for a full-sized ocean-going vessel. I will be working very short-handed and it is no use complaining about it. I must work with what I have, and what is more, I now have more than I expected. What is it that the Ayesha woman keeps saying with a shrug in such circumstances…? "Inshallah" …That is it. I have heard the same from Muslim crew before.*

On the positive side, I have a good ship with a solid hull and good sails. It has two different forces of magical wind. I can even calm the sea for a while, if need be. I also have artillery and magical weapons on board.

My crew are almost all (except for two girls and a boy) experienced sailors, and none of them are complete novices by now. It is more than many captains start out with. I have a large supply of money—an amazingly large supply of money—to help me act the part of a merchant, and I have a deadline of winter.

It is a little over eight weeks until the start of autumn and I want to be in place in the north at around that time. The Land may be girt by sea, but we will still have to sail near halfway around it in that time. My crew will not get a lot of sleep, but I think that we can do it.

Even though my coxswain—I refuse to call him my mate (although my sister uses the term to the exclusion of others, all of the time, and with a smirk)—shares a cabin with me, the captain and the bosun and one of the leading hands sharing the other, it will be irrelevant. Unless we are resting in a port, none of us will have the time or energy to get up to much except sleep.

Olympias

By now she had a fairly good idea of what the bottom of Lake Erave might look like along her path and was starting to build a real chart of it. Although she kept the soundings going, she could make good time once the sails were all set.

The question is what do I do once we reach the other side. As a matter of courtesy, there will be a brief visit paid to Erave Town—the Princess Theodora has made that clear and has given me a letter that I need to deliver—but should we stay the night there or just keep on going?

Eventually, she decided not to waste any light. *It has not been very long since my last transit of the river. I will hope and rely on the soundings that we made during that trip and just keep sailing, and trust that we will find out about any new problems before it is too late to do anything about them. Whoever has the wheel will also have to take notes of any new soundings as we go.*

At least this time we will not need to take as many bearings and the river is unlikely to have changed its speed. However, until the others join us in the north, I only have seven people on each watch. One will have the wheel, one will be doing soundings, and one will be on lookout for shallows… That only gives me four for the sweeps.

That is not enough to be safe on a river transit, even with a jib up and with our own wind available for us if we need it. She thought on the problem and eventually made up her mind. *Until the crew are too tired, I will travel both day and night with near as full a crew available to me. I may not have saddles, but I can at least rely on the light at the masthead.*

That will mean that one can read the records and do the writing. Shilpa is supposed to be the supercargo—that would normally be her job anyway—and I will then have enough people for the sweeps.

One can be kept off watch so that they can sleep and feed the others as we go. When the others stand down, that one will have to keep the boat secure until the rest wake up again. That should work. The silver-haired new Presbytera, Danelis, can take that job.

She can even keep us awake by playing music; she has already shown that she can play well. She can help us sing work songs. Denizkartal or I will need to teach her the songs as we go, but that will help and we both have good voices. Come to think of it, the Hindi woman plays a drum a little as well. Better and better.

Olympias
4th Tertius

The stop at Erave Town was very brief, with no trade goods to declare, and nothing being taken on board; there was just a letter to deliver.

We do, in fact, have goods, but they are hidden well away in the secret hold along with most of our money. There really is not much in the way of trade items anyway, only some spices, antimony and rubies, but I have decided that it will take too long to work out what is owed on them, and we will not be trading here on this trip. At least most of the crew got a chance to stretch and rest...but not for very long.

Olympias had only a bow rope, loosely held in place on a bollard, for the few minutes that the letter took to deliver as Shilpa found the Mayor at his work and then, with a flick of a rope by Denizkartal, they were on their way again, twirling the ship around using the flow of the river and headed downstream with dispatch.

Night fell, and they kept going. *Father Simeon has to step away from being a leading hand to perform his Offices as we go, walking around the ship to administer sacraments as he does.* They were well past all the little settlements now, and the masthead light and the deck light were uncovered.

To add to that, the moons are both waxing and that gives us about half of their light when they are both full... That light will get better as we go further down the Rhastaputra. "Danelis," Olympias ordered, "head below and try and get some sleep. I will need you awake in a few hours as those on duty need to be fed."

As they sailed south, Olympias realised that there was one major problem with the masthead lights. *While they are useful, in terms of travelling, they shine brighter than the moons do themselves, and so every insect on the river seems to think of them as home. Clouds of them are hovering permanently over the ship. We must be careful what we breathe in when we go aloft.*

Several of the crew already have tied cotton clothes around their faces to help them. It is just as well that we have Dadanth unguent to keep the biting ones at bay. Shilpa needs to buy more of that in Sacred Gate when we get there. We need as much as she can find. It seems that we need to buy it by the firkin along with wine. It is just as well we have plenty of money.

She kept a close watch on her sailing notes from last time as she steered her way through them. *It seems that there is very little difference between the readings that we are getting this trip and the last time we went up and down.*

Admittedly it is only eight weeks ago that we came up, but I have seen the Butsin, on the mainland nearly opposite the island town of Antdrudge, change its course enough to make my normal craft have difficulties there, and it drew far less than the River Dragon *does, in far less time than that.*

The Mulwherry, the river that comes out of the mountains at Pain, is even worse. It changes its rocky course every few weeks, as the smooth pebbles of its banks shift around each time there is a storm. Still, none of the Darkreach rivers have as large and as constant a flow as the Rhastaputra. In the whole Land probably only the Methul carries anywhere near as much water.

The two rivers, between them, drain almost the whole western side of the Great Range and this is the side of the mountains that most of the rain comes from. Still, I am not going to trust that all will be well until I have made a lot more transits than this.

Olympias
5th Tertius, late at night

I think that it is finally time for me to call a halt. We have done remarkably well with the distance that we have managed to cover, but now we need to rest. My crew are tiring and they are starting to make mistakes. I cannot afford for that to happen on a river.

With two anchors set on the bow holding the *River Dragon*'s nose into the current, the crew were fed and then they all collapsed exhausted into their hammocks.

Danelis
6th Tertius

The front light is left lit to shine back up the river to watch if anything comes down in the current, and the deck light stays uncovered. I can see that all is well, even though it does make me a better target for a good archer, anchored as we are in midstream. With weapons in hand I must keep turning the sandglass and noting times and make watch notes in the logbook.

I get to leave everyone to sleep until dawn unless something happens. I have a whistle to blow if I need to, and hopefully that will stir the rest from their slumber. As it turned out the silver-haired priest's wife had a quiet night on her own, watching the banks and listening to the noise of the forest and of the river as she swatted away insects.

I get to wake the crew with jugs of kaf and tea, and the smell of bacon, eggs and porridge. Once they had eaten, it was then the turn of their priest, her husband, to hold a service while the rest of the crew drew in the anchors and started down the river again. *I had work to do before last night, so after a full night awake, I will not have any trouble getting to sleep today.*

Shilpa Sodaagar
8th Tertius, the Feast Day of Saint Hippolytus

*W*e have reached Garthang Keep. *Once again, we are met by a proa of the river patrol. The officer on it, the same one that we saw on our last trip, has come aboard the* River Dragon *and started looking about without asking.*

I think that her name is Apinaya Sarin. It is important that I remember things like that. As the supernumerary of the ship, and indeed only one of the two awake who speak fluent Hindi, I must take the lead now for the ship, and not the Captain, when we are dealing with the local authorities. It is a while since I have taken that sort of role, many years.

"No need to look too hard, Subadar Sarin…" *I must be right about her name. She need not know my caste, and I have deliberately worn no marks of it, although as a trader I am not too far beneath her anyway.* "The Princess is not with us on this trip. You will no doubt hear the result, but she is campaigning in the north for the foreseeable future."

The subadar looks a little suspicious. She looks hard at Anastasia, who took the rope from her boat. Of course, she is new crew and an obvious Insakharl. "Remember," said Shilpa, "that we did say that this ship was meant to be mostly a trader when we were here last."

We didn't, but confidence often works in such matters. She saw me then. She can easily see Denizkartal as well. He was one of the more prominent paradēśī *from the last trip and is now very visibly holding the rope to the proa.*

"We are not needed in the north at present, and we come to continue some of the trade we made last trip and we hope to extend it. We only have money with us now, but we intend to spend a fair amount of that, and to buy goods in Pavitra Phāṭaka, and then take them on to the south and further around to Darkreach. We may be gone for quite some time on this trip."

I saw her look at our freeboard as she came aboard. She waves, in a desultory way, at one of her crew and he begins to have a nominal look around the ship while the subadar charges us a small transit fee for the trouble of her and her crew.

She chats while he works, and she is using the time to let her eyes roam all over as she does so. Our ship is rare in Pavitra Phāṭaka itself, let alone here on the river and she is still curious about it. I am being very polite but at the same time I am making every effort to answer her questions only with vague generalities.

Olympias

*S*hilpa seems to have the officer well in hand. I am not going to slow down *unless I have to. Her craft can trail along beside us as we continue on the way. We are not even stopping at Garthang Keep unless we must.*

The *River Dragon* made it to the south of Peelfall before they stopped to have their next sleep. Olympias kept the sails up, and even used their own wind to fly down the stream, as the lookouts peered ahead and kept close watch on the notes that had been made on the chart.

The shoals and narrow stretches seem not to have changed here either. We are lucky not to have encountered problems or met any craft coming slowly the other way up the river. Our speed both worries and excites me. It is an exhausting way to travel, given the level of alert that we must maintain, but it should be saving me several days over a more leisurely and safe run.

With any luck at all we will make it all the way to Sacred Gate on the next leg. Hopefully, the crew can catch up on all the sleep that they are losing once we hit the open sea. At present we are all drinking an awful lot of kaf.

After we pass the town of Shelike, both Shilpa and Danelis can go to sleep, along with Father Simeon and Vishal. It will be up to them to do the purchases in Sacred Gate while most of the rest sleep. Despite having allowed time for this stop in my plan for the voyage, I want to be out of the city as quickly as I can.

It seems it is safe enough to go fully with the flow of the river from here on in. I will switch from using our lesser wind to the stronger and give us even more speed. Although I have another of my new crew, Habib, taking soundings, we have found no bottom anywhere along this stretch since last we were going down and up. The surface of the river is thick with traffic, none of it following anything in the way of channels.

Eventually, she stood more of the crew down to rest, so that they could stand guard over the ship while they were docked.

Shilpa
10th Tertius, the Feast Day of Saint Kessog

It would have been nice to have the reassuring presence of the group of Mice that were around me the last time I was making my way from Ante to Vyāpārī.

My new lover is armed, it is true, and he certainly looks the part of a well-armed and prosperous guard, and both the priest and his wife are in heavy mail and have hammers and shields, but the obvious menacing bulk of Aziz and Astrid has a more direct affect upon bystanders.

Still, this time all I really have to do is let the word get around that I am looking for more goods, and with the amount that we spent on our last trip, merchants will soon be calling on our ship with their wares. That will account for the bulk goods and the herbs and spices. They were told to be there soon after lunch or they would miss out.

This time, knowing that we are headed to Ardlark, I need to try and look more at the luxury trade. I want silk, and lots of it, but I will still not despise one hold full of quality rice as well. I have the space after all.

On Olympias' advice she bought everything that the instrument maker they had been to last trip had in stock. *I do not have much of an idea what most of it is, but Olympias has assured me that the quality is good. Good quality precision work will always turn a profit in a major city a long way from where it is made.*

She came back with six wooden boxes with odd-looking brass objects in them nestled in their packing. *It is a very hard job bargaining for something when you are only pretending to know what you are buying, and that applies to a few of the things I bought. However, Olympias seems more than happy with the purchases and that will have to do.*

The time pressure of getting out fast is playing on me. I am glad that I made an early call at the providore I used last time and made sure that supplies are brought to the ship. I emphasised to him that we will be passing through the city regularly and want to have a reliable fixed supplier of good quality goods.

It is no guarantee, but it should help stop poor supplies from being foisted on us. He seems to be very keen to have my trade, but then we pay well and want good quality, so he will make money from us. If I had not done that first, I would not have been ready in time to cast off.

It is coming on to dusk and we are already headed out to sea. By Varuna, we have only been in port for a few hours and the ship now rides much lower. I am still making sure that it is all stowed away properly as we sail out. The holds are more than half full, mainly with sacks of rice, and we have a call to make at Southpoint next. I will find what they sell there when we arrive.

She went over her bills of lading thoroughly before she went back to sleep, totalling up what she had spent and where it was all stowed. She smiled. *Life is so much easier when you are a rich merchant. Karma favours you so much more than when you are poor and trying to scrimp and save on the last Anna.*

I have the capital available now to make some real money. Even if it is only a cover for what else the ship is up to, I am going to try to be diligent in what I do, and besides, it is much more fun that way.

Compared to those who fight the battles going on around me, I might only have the role of a part-player in some great tale-teller's story, but there is nothing that says I cannot enjoy myself while I am playing that supporting part.

I have decided that, after what came before in my life, it is time for karma to come onto my side for a change. She smiled a satisfied smile at her lover. *He is much younger than me, very fit, and quite willing to be taught. He smiles back innocently, not knowing the thoughts that are going through my mind. Later, I will show him a couple of things I bought.*

Olympias

With the wind coming steady and strong from the southwest, Olympias let the *River Dragon* make one long reach out past the end of the delta. *Birds are already following behind us. I will rotate the watch through wheel duty, to give them all a feel of it. They all need to learn how to follow a constant bearing for the whole night.*

Only the lookout in the main top could see any land at all as they went the whole way out heeled over under the last constant wind of summer, and that sighting was only visible as a dark line on the moon-lit horizon in the night.

There is little for those on watch to do except sit around and talk and actually get to know each other. It is a pleasant break after the run down the river, and we can afford to run short-handed shifts to allow everyone to get back in time with the others of their watch.

Apart from the curling of the water under the bow and the soft thrumming sound made by the wind in taut cables, the only real noise was the call of whoever had the duty of turning the glass, striking the bell and then casting the log. *More useless soundings of "no bottom" are written in the ship's log along with an unchanged course.*

There is little enough trade that would be going in this direction and at this bearing that, although there were several ships in sight when we left Sacred Gate, we now have the ocean entirely to ourselves. One other vessel had also headed east, but it was definitely hugging the coast as it left and it kept doing that.

From the masthead it can be seen that two larger craft are heading west, but the rest are just small local boats. Now, apart from the sea birds and a few feathered lizards that soar along in our wake hoping for scraps, the ocean itself is empty.

Once they were surrounded by a large school of fish, which broke surface trying to escape a pod of large fish-lizards. *It is hard to tell them from dolphins when it comes on to night...until you see their tails or their huge eyes.*

Olympias
11th Tertius

*A*part from the schools of fish and fish-lizards, the day breaks with news *from the masthead that the line of land to our port is now disappearing completely, and that he has no sight of the sail of the eastward-bound ship, or any others, against the coast. It was only a single-mast ketch and carried far less sail and was far slower than us anyway.*

Olympias made a note of the time and called for a new bearing. *If the chart I found in the Mousehole library is correct, that bearing should put me nicely between Zim Island and the land south of Southpoint; hopefully closer to the latter than the former. The wind is now coming fine off the rear starboard quarter. The square sails are up, and the spanker stands out taut to the port.*

With the ship heeling less now, their speed soon picked up with the extra wind that they were catching, and they began another long reach across a nearly flat ocean. *The swell beneath us is long and very low. It has little effect on our speed. The water itself is clean and flat and so unaffected by wind that you can clearly see the fish below.*

In the middle of the first watch of the day, Thomaïs, one of the new crew who had the watch aloft, called out to Olympias and pointed down to the port into the ocean. "We are sailing over a city," she called. "You can see it through the water. We are well above it...but look." Those who were awake rushed over to look.

Where there is shadow, and the light is not reflecting off the sea and dazzling the eye, there can be seen the outlines of buildings and streets. Below us a huge city is clearly to be seen. It is laid out under us as if we are flying low above it. It would not be hard to imagine that perhaps there are still people in its streets.

Oh damn. Now we are well rested, I get to remember the injunction that I was given by the woman who is now doubly my Princess. With reluctance, those who were not doing anything useful were gathered together where Olympias had a small pile of slates out. "Wherever we have come from, we now all belong to Mousehole.

"I have been told by our Princesses that there is a cardinal rule for our village: "Everyone works, everyone fights, and everyone learns". I am sorry to say that the Princesses want me to make sure this continues during our trip as well. We were too tired to do this as we came down the river, but now we have lots of spare time. They think that language is the most important, and easiest, thing for us to learn as we travel, and I am afraid that I agree with them.

"Those of you who cannot speak Latin will be learning it from Father Simeon," Olympias said. "Those who cannot speak Hindi will have Shilpa. Those are the lucky ones. I am told that both of those two can actually teach."

"Unless someone has a better idea, I am the one who gets to teach Darkspeech to those who don't have it. There is a reason that I left for the sea as a child instead of going to a real school." She smiled ruefully. "You are about to find out what it is."

From then on during the trip, when it was quiet, one group or another could be found sitting around having lessons. They concentrated on learning words that applied to the sea but tried not to totally neglect the rest of the languages.

Harnermêŝ has the hardest lot of everyone on board. He needs to work on all three languages and often, when on watch, sits high up in the masts keeping lookout while, at the same time, talking to himself in one tongue or another.

They went swooping across Iba Bay in one day and in a single reach. *It is so much better as a trip than the last time we crossed. Then, when we were headed towards Haven, it took us near ten days of hard beating into the wind.*

As the sun was setting, the lookout could see the very top of Gil-Gand-Rask, Zim Island, the peak listed on the map as Giant's Drop and the smaller volcano next to it. *I wish I could make out its name on our old map.*

We are nearly even with the southern end of the Great Range and all of its peaks are clearly visible running up in a long row into the distance towards where Mousehole lies. There are three peaks at the very end of the range that are supposed to be very important for our navigation. Olympias was checking her distance from them by measuring angles and comparing what she had there to what was on the map. *If the map is accurate, and there is no way for me to be sure of that, and if the wind keeps up, and that is even more uncertain, then we should be in Southpoint in the morning.*

Olympias looked up and ahead. *The volcano will be visible to us all through the night. In the growing dusk its top shows a reddish glow that is coming from within the mountain. A column of billowing smoke rises high into the sky from it, shot through with a baleful red glow.*

From time to time there was a bright flicker as lightning coursed down and through the column of smoke, and some time later, a distant muted grumble sounded. *Some trails of fire mark molten rock being flung into the air. Down one flank of the mountain a long tongue of red glows in the dark. Luckily, with the way the wind is blowing, the ash is being borne away from us.*

The course we are following needs very little correction. The current under us seems to be travelling within a few points of the same direction that we are headed and keeping clear of Zim Island should hopefully be easy, even at night. When she had finished her work, she looked up at the mountains, their peaks catching the last of the afternoon sun.

Somewhere, just behind there, lies the town of Dimashq and the Caliphate. With the way the wind is blowing the ash, it might be unpleasant living in the far south of that land at the moment. I wonder how it will affect the crops there, although there is at least not so much as to block out the sun as I have heard can happen.

The night itself was uneventful. The only thing, apart from the readings, that was noted in the log was the occasional pulse of light from the direction of the volcano and the reflected glow of the cloud near it. Several times lighting struck through the clouds, making them pale and lighting up the scene briefly.

We must ask the women from the Caliphate what the name of the volcano is when we next return to Mousehole. If it has a name, we should know what it is. When it is like it is tonight, they should be able to see its glow over the range from Dimashq itself, and even feel the pulses of its explosions through their feet.

Olympias
12th Tertius

As the first lightening of the skyline was becoming a reality, Olympias began to take readings again. The wind was unchanged, and they had passed Zim Island many miles to the starboard. The Land was only a mile to the port, and they had lost sight of the volcano behind the low range that lay along the tip, although its smoke could still be seen towering skyward and as a high cloud far to the north.

The map that I have available seems to be fairly well drawn, and when I compare it to what lies before me, the four peaks are lining up as they are supposed to. Once the three on the west line up directly behind each other I must make my next turn. Quickly, the bay that Demaresque Creek emptied into became visible off their bow.

The push of the ocean current can now be felt on the port side. I must allow for that as we sail. It is not a wide entrance that we are headed towards, but it is deep enough and not as rapid as some I know of. It might be tricky with a southeast gale blowing or if you are beating your way into it, but it will be easy under most other conditions.

The angle I am approaching the town from this time is the same one that I left on last time, but then I lacked this map. However, what is on the map accords with my log and observations from the last trip and so I am well pleased.

Chapter XXIX

Olympias
12th Tertius

*I*n *the few weeks since I was last here, it is already apparent that there are changes afoot in the small, and usually much ignored, town of Southpoint.* In the small and sheltered bay that the creek emptied into, a pier was being constructed, so that ships need not do what they had been in edging their way up the stream.

At least six hands of Army engineers; Humans, Alat-kharl, Insakharl, and even two Insak-div for the heavy lifting, are all hard at work under a couple of their officers, and from the look of her, an engineer mage, probably an earth mage, the normal sign of such specialists. She stands there looking at a scroll, probably a plan of the work to come.

As they work down the side of the creek, they haven't reached the shoreline yet, but it is plain that when it is finished, the pier is going to come right down one side of the creek. It will use the water that is coming down the creek to keep itself dredged deep along that side, before it ends in the bay. I suppose that enough comes down the creek to make it work.

The engineers pause in their work to watch us pass upstream. They are probably wondering whose ship this is. Most of the crew might look like they come from Darkreach, as they do, but the vessel is of a very unfamiliar type here, and what is more, it shows no banner.

This time it was harder work for them getting up the creek using the sweeps. Olympias looked down at the speed of the stream as it curled past the ship. *There must have been rain upstream recently.* She decided to unfurl her front jib and use her lowest magical wind to slowly nose her way up the waterway.

She kept the sweeps deployed, just for better steering and balance, as they came further up the narrow channel of the creek. Denizkartal stood ready in the bow with a painter to tie them up and Cyrus and Sabas, two of the new crewmen, had the wool filled bags at the side. Irene, Sabas' wife, was calling the depth. *The custom's official, my mother, is waiting and cheerily called her greetings to her son-in-law as he slid past.*

Olympias

"Greetings, daughter," her mother said as she came aboard. "You have no Princesses on board your ship this trip, then?"

"No, she is campaigning against the Brotherhood, as are most of our people." Olympias concentrated on watching her crew get the ship square.

"And you are not?" asked her mother. "Is your brother there with his wife?" *I can hear in her voice the question of why her daughter is as far away from battle as she can possibly be.*

"We are and we are not…and yes, Basil and Astrid are with her. I have to get the *River Dragon* to the north before we can take the next step with her. Along the way, we trade, and get our crew more used to the ship before we brave the ice seas. Astrid is the only one who knows those waters and we could be going anywhere there."

Somewhat mollified by the answer her mother nodded. "I did notice that you are much deeper in the water this time. Do you have anything to sell to us from out among the várvaros, or are you still just looking for cargo to take on to Ardlark?"

"Probably the latter, mother, but let us put that aside. Shilpa will look after that. It is her job and you need to talk to her. Once that is all done, we are laying up here for the day. I want you to show me your town. At least without a Princess on board for your Governor to worry over, it should be a less stressful visit for us all this time."

Having arrived in Mousehole with very little baggage, my new crew (and that means most of those on board including me) will be glad of a chance to buy some more clothes that are in a style we are accustomed to. I need to hand out money to everyone. At least Shilpa knows how much and can keep count of it all in case an accounting is needed. The shopkeepers will soon be very glad of the custom that they are about to be given.

Over a lunch of crabs, the renowned local delicacy, Olympias had a chance to relax with her parents for the first time in many years…*if it can be called relaxing when your mother is giving such broad hints on the subject of grandchildren. I had not thought that my mother was like that, and she possibly wasn't when the only grandchildren she had were those she could not see in Ardlark, but seeing my brother's children must have set her off somehow.*

Not content with having sent young Menas to the school, her father was interested in whether there were enough crew on the ship for what was needed, and he was giving broad hints to see if he could find any of the local people some work on board.

I am in a bind over how to answer that. Particularly when negotiating the river, having more crew would have made the task easier. The problem is that I am not sure how much authority I have to make promises to anyone signing on with her. What can I offer? Will it be a full share of Mousehole's riches or just wages? I don't know.

In fact, when you think of it, I am not even sure how I stand on the matter. No one has actually said anything about pay to me. I have just, somehow, been tricked by the Emperor and my sister into being the Captain of a foreign ship. Despite my ship, I could still be on the Imperial payroll for all that I know.

I am reluctant to ask the Princesses, but suppose that, when we get back together, a subtle question from me to my sister might get an answer. Not that my sister will be subtle about the matter from then on, but she will know how to find out an answer, and I will not have to approach the delicate subject for myself.

Eventually she compromised. She would have liked another ten people to train but she decided to let her father find three people for her. *There are at least two crew members that I urgently need to help work the ship and I will add them to our complement. I am sure we can work out pay details later. I also need a person to be my cabin boy and apprentice.*

I have Danelis doing some of that work, and Shilpa more of it, but they are supposed to be sailors, not running around doing errands. They don't know any better, but that does not matter.

Once her father had her agreement on getting more crew, he left the table and quickly walked off into the town, calling out names and giving instructions. She sighed. *For a little while it had been so nice just sitting here. Now I will have to spend the afternoon interviewing people.*

It was with some degree of humour that she applied to her own father for entry papers for the *River Dragon* into Darkreach. *I am glad that it is my parents that I must apply to. They will at least understand the circumstances. Due to how Denizkartal and I arrived in Mousehole, I do not have any of the usual exit paperwork and that could have been interesting…particularly if someone decided that they had to check with the person who my brother is sure performed the spell that sent us out.*

Olympias
13th Tertius

*W*e leave with the Kichic-kharl sailor, Gundardasc Narches, and his Insa-kharl wife Galla, on board and I have another distant cousin, Adrian Climacus, with us as my apprentice. He is two years older than his brother, who was sent to the school in the mountains, a bit old for the job in my opinion, but he seems to have a lot of the right skills.

Gundardasc's name made her smile…*It is just that he has another of those kharl names just like my brother's that are given out, or are taken on, as much in jest as they are in seriousness. This one means "Mighty Cook" and, if he has another name, he refuses to use it. I hope that he can live up to his name as that skill is one thing that I forgot to check for before we left Evilhalt, and although everyone is trying their best…well "trying" is such a good and descriptive word.*

His wife has experience both with sewing sails and in working with wood… another two skills that the permanent crew lacks. We have not needed them up to now—but if we are sailing into combat and heavy seas, then it is inevitable that we will at some time need someone who knows what they are doing with a needle and with a mallet. Hopefully we don't need both at once. Most warships have at least one person in each role. Some have several.

Olympias
13th Tertius

They left before the sun set to be clear and sailing smoothly towards Ardlark while there was still enough light to clearly see the coast to their port side. *I notice that the* River Dragon *is nearly down to her full drawn depth when I boarded. Only now, when we have sailed, and the ship is settling into its routine, do I get a chance to ask Shilpa what she has added so much of to the cargo.*

The answer was even more rice, of a different sort this time, as well as the sugar and hemp paper and cloth. *I expected those. I saw the fields of both crops outside of the town. The rum is a small surprise and the firkin that is put aside for ship's use shows that it is a very pleasant surprise, particularly since we just seem to have a supply of limes on board as well… What a coincidence.*

What I really hadn't known about Southpoint is that it has perhaps the finest maker of spilk in The Land. At least that is what Shilpa says the maker claims of himself. Once she saw what was there, she was inclined to agree, not that she had much experience in the area. *Normally it is well outside my price range.*

On board we have several small bolts of different colours. Spilk only comes in small bolts and each is worth a fortune. Apparently, what we have is worth far more than twice as much as the very best silk. Some of the normal traders that come down here to the isolated town will apparently be very upset when they eventually make it back down to the far south.

Not many traders sail this far down the coast, across so much open water, and those that do usually only make a few visits a year for the luxury goods, such as the spilk and the rum. *They leave the gaps between each visit to the town for as long as possible to try and drive the price down. A visit from a trader is long overdue and it seems that the producers in the town were very happy to find another buyer for some of their produce.*

She grinned. *It means at least one very upset trader when he gets into port. Perhaps I won't let Shilpa sell that spilk. The Princesses may want it for the people of the valley. It may be worth waiting to find out.* Taking another sip of the limed rum, she debated keeping all of that as well.

As they settled down after eating, they discovered that there was another advantage to having Gundardasc on board. Not only had they just had the best meal that they had eaten so far on board, using some of the delicious crabs from Southpoint, but he also played a fiddle, and his wife could dance a sprightly jig. Jennifer was already trying to teach Harnermeess how to do that as well. *The islander may be a good runner and competent sailor, but he has a lot to learn about dancing.*

It seemed that Gundardasc's fiddle had also been locally made. *Apparently Southpoint is where some of the best of those are made in Darkreach as well.* Shilpa had not found this out before now and promised faithfully to pay attention to that on the way back. By the time she had finished apologising for missing a trade opportunity, Danelis had her instrument case out and was starting to join in and Thomaïs had emerged with a selection of small drums.

We head north along a straight course, with the steady wind coming from off our port quarter in the warm night. For those not on watch, with a drink of rum and lime in hand, and both music and dancing, it makes it hard to believe that we are sailing off towards a battle.

Olympias
14th Tertius

O nce they lost sight of the Great Range in the growing dark, it was as if they had the world to themselves. The sea kept calm and the swell was almost imperceptible as they rode up and down its low rises. They kept up a steady course to the northeast all during the night, but the wind began to slowly fail as they moved further and further away from its usual path.

By morning, with the grazing lands of the Beneen Plain only just visible in the distance from the lookout, their sail was sometimes just flapping emptily. Olympias ordered their stronger wind to be activated, and the *River Dragon* immediately picked up speed again and the water began to once more cream away from under her forefoot, the only white to be seen below and around them.

Some time after the wind was set free, Harnermeess, in the maintop with the telescope, reported in a puzzled voice that he thought he could see a town. It was the first sign of any settlement in the flatness to their port. *That would be Brinkhold then.* She then climbed up to check her bearings and down again to make some notes on their progress.

It was only an hour after the sighting of the town that he next reported that the land was disappearing from view. *Good, we are coming to the Reach.* Olympias nodded in satisfaction, and made more notes in her log and on her chart, as she paced their way across it with a pair of dividers and made some notes and calculations on a slate. *We must have picked up the following current. We are making good time, better than I thought we would.*

I have not sailed this way before with a ship boasting its own wind, but we are already crossing the Oirmt Reach, the great shallow gulf of the sea that leads deep into Darkreach with the town of Silentochre at its head. The Oirmt Reach is the feature that makes much of Darkreach almost an island, as it cuts off much of it from the rest of The Land with its watery expanse.

This damn gulf combined with the lack of winds around most of this coast explains why traders are often reluctant to sail too far to the south. It is far too easy to be trapped against the shore here, and if you have to run into the Reach for any reason, and the winds are wrong, you might be stuck there for quite some time and the many reefs and the shallow water inside make it hard to tack out.

Olympias
14th Tertius

They flew north over a sea as smooth as a pond. *We have all of our sails set and yet it is still so quiet for us all that, except for the lookout and the helm, we may as well start doing lessons as we go. Even the crew who are on duty can do their language lessons instead of just sitting around chatting on the deck and along the yards.*

The quiet continued until later that afternoon when (as if providentially arranged to provide them with a little excitement) a sail was sighted in the distance far ahead of them. Olympias took herself aloft. "We are meeting a fleet vessel."

It looks like a large naval dromond with those two huge lateen sails. It is on a slightly different course and our two craft will not meet unless one of us changes direction. Like us, it is sailing with no oars out, and without regard to the current calm around us. Having now had experience with a vessel with a magically supplied wind, I don't know why more ships don't do the same.

Admittedly, such a set of spells could perhaps cost as much to install on a vessel as the whole rest of the ship took to build, but surely it is worthwhile in the long run. It is very rare with merchants, and surprisingly, very few of the naval ships have the ability to do what the River Dragon *and the vessel ahead of us are doing.*

They kept on their path and it soon was evident that Harnermeess was a better lookout than his naval equivalent. It was quite some time before the dromond ahead altered course to intercept them. *I now have a decision to make. Basil told me about the stolen ship in the north. Have the Masters taken another ship? Is this a friendly intercept for us, or should we run?*

She finally made up her mind. *Surely the navy will not have allowed a second ship to go missing, and besides, the navy often sends ships down this way, and depending on the captain they will either hug the coast, or else do what I am doing, make a long straight run along a compass bearing to save time.*

Seeing an unfamiliar-looking civilian ship this far out at sea will come as a shock to the person coming towards us and they will be curious. If I try and avoid them and move away it will look suspicious, and they will probably follow us anyway.

She looked around. *Better get ready and look presentable.* She sent her cabin boy to get her commission, and she brushed down her clothes and ordered some ropes tidied, the deck swept, and a few other minor pieces of housekeeping done.

I only just climbed out of a uniform once I was able to buy more clothes at Southpoint. I rather like the white lace ruffled blouse and scarlet silk waistcoat that I bought, and the white stockings and contrasting green breeches suit me well. I am not going to change them for a passing vessel, whoever is on board. I suppose that I will put my green coat on. It has a naval cut to it, at least.

The River Dragon *is presentable, and although I am on board, she is not strictly speaking a naval vessel, at least not a Darkreach one. Being presentable is all that really matters.* When Adrian came back, he also handed her best hat to her, a bicorn with a large red feather held on with a broach that was providentially a silver mouse.

At last the two ships dropped their winds and hove to alongside each other, gliding to a stop under sweeps. As the other vessel prepared to launch a boat, Olympias manoeuvred closer, and when they were a vessel's width apart, with her crew keeping the ship steady with the sweeps, and watching the other vessel preparing to launch a boat, she ran the carpet from the valley across to the other vessel.

I hadn't believed such an extravagant item had even been made when I was told about it, but I am glad now of having a chance to show it off on the flat sea. It has not been used much until now and this is an ideal chance. Nothing speaks of power quite like having a piece of rare and frivolous magic available to you. As long as the crews keep their ships still relative to each other we don't have to worry about bosun's chairs or jolly boats.

We are set to impress. She lined up those of her crew who were not keeping the *River Dragon* steady, and prepared to see who would come aboard, as the people on the other craft gingerly tested the carpet with their feet.

"Kapetános Várka Akritina," said a familiar voice. Being out of uniform, it was all Olympias could do to not salute. "What are you up to now?"

"Drungarius Styliane," *I am surprised... My old squadron commander. What is she doing here on her own?* She recovered quickly, however, and continued in an almost modest tone. "It is, however Epilarch Akritina." She held her hand out beside her. Adrian realised what she wanted and put the leather wallet in her hand with her commission.

"I am on detached duty, however, and until I am able to get around to where I am needed and am able to find some other ships, this is my sole command... Perhaps you would like to come with me..." She handed over her papers and watched her old commander's eyebrows rise as she read the unusual commission.

"I suppose this is in connection with the Empress' friends..." Olympias nodded, scarce keeping a smile off her face... "and you cannot tell me anything about it."

"Almost right, ma'am," *Did she notice the staged sorrow?* "It concerns the Princess and my brother, the Tribune, and the missing dromond. More than that I think I can say…" *Damn her, I don't like her. It is time to annoy her a bit.* "But I am sure that you can ask my brother's Strategos when you return to Ardlark, and it may be that he might be able to tell you more." *That perky answer and smile is rewarded with a glare. It was well worth it.*

"That would be Strategos Panterius, then? I don't think so," was the terse reply. The Drungarius looked around her. "This is a Freehold ship, I am sure, and my mage says the magic that is on board makes him almost itch…" She looked down. "This carpet came from the Caliphate." She looked at Olympias' crew, lingering on Harnermeess "…and at least some of these people are from well outside Darkreach…" and then Gundardasc "…and others are not" … then at Denizkartal "…and at least one of your old crew" and then up to the masthead.

Danelis has put one of those silly Mouse banners at the masthead, hasn't she? "…and that is the emblem of a mountain valley." She shook her head. "I hope that one day I will find out what this is all about. We hear so much about the Empress, but there is so much left out… I suppose that is secret as well." She looked at Olympias.

If I keep looking at our flag, I can pretend that I didn't hear. "I hope that you enjoy your cruise…and my congratulation on what I am sure is a deserved promotion…Epilarch Akritina." She nodded and headed back to her ship, nervously looking down at the water as she trod a path that seemed as firm as solid ground. Once the other woman was across, and with a smile on her face, Olympias had the carpet called back in and they parted and resumed their previous routes.

As they sailed north, Olympias made no attempt to hide the continued grin on her face. *I really did not get on well with my former commander, and the issue of Denizkartal is only a part of it. Nonetheless, I suppose that we should take the banner down.* "I think that we are supposed to be a little more inconspicuous as we travel this way. I am not ashamed of our banner, but it is possible that for the present we need to be a little…*careful* about who can see us for what we are."

Father Simeon Alvarez
20th Tertius, the Feast Day of Saint Cuthbert

The feast of St Cuthbert has come and almost gone unnoticed. I am afraid that the patron of shepherds has little to say to sailors. I just need to remind the crew about what will be happening some time soon along the north of this Land. Most of them know little about the valley whose ship this is and some know nothing at all.

From now on, with every service I perform, I will have prayers said for the Mice campaigning in the north…and possibly about to go into battle. I have no idea when they, and the people that fight alongside them, will need those prayers, but it is sure that they will at some stage. Indeed, we could need them soon as well.

Olympias
23rd Tertius

*W*e make landfall again near Seardip, the most easterly settlement in Darkreach, as we are supposed to. I am pleased with my navigation with effectively new and unused instruments.*

I have been here before, and anyone looking to the settlement that we have found, if truth be told, will see that it is only a large village, and really all that can be clearly seen from out here is the amphitheatre, and a tower. I can see the banner that flies on it that at night will change to a light. Even the port itself is hard to make out from here.

However, even from where we are, well out at sea, it is possible to feel the summer heat that is blowing off the Great Plain, and we can all taste the acrid dust that is borne out to sea in the wind. Mind you, they say that there is a benefit to be had from that dust. The water is littered with craft taking advantage of the rich fishing here.

Olympias
23rd Tertius

The course was changed by several points to the port and they continued on, sailing around the coast until the village of Grono on its cliff in a bay came into view. Once that was in sight, Olympias brought the ship's course around even further.

When you look towards the shore, there is a tinge of green starting to appear along the coast rather than the endless dry grasses and browned shrubs of the land that lies further south. There is even the occasional small clump of trees to be seen.

"It is like my home village of Warkworth," said Danelis to her husband upon seeing Grono, "built on a cliff and with a waterfall…but it is so spread out… and…where are its walls?"

Olympias heard what she said. "Unless you are on the frontier, or in Ardlark, there are hardly any walls on the villages and towns of Darkreach. We are a land at peace, so what would we need them for? Instead of walls we build amphitheatres and schools."

Olympias went back to considering her options on what to do next. *I have been slowing our passage as we go. With the ship's wind blowing I must do it by reducing sail until we are travelling with just the mainsail up, and that is heavily reefed. I have decided that I want us to arrive in Ardlark in the early morning light, and it is not yet dark.*

So far, we have made very good time, far faster than anyone will expect, and we still have five weeks to go before the start of autumn. That we travelled down the river as fast as we could has certainly paid off for us. By shaving perhaps a week off what I would expect to be our normal transit time, we have missed the uncertain weather that often occurs in the south at this time of year.

Having managed to miss the poor seas and contrary winds, we have covered over half of our journey in just twenty days since setting out, and a week of that was spent crawling at a relatively slow speed down the river.

Now, I have questions for myself. If I avoid Ardlark, then we can probably be in Wolfneck in two weeks. However, do I really want to do that? What if there are messages waiting for me in Ardlark? Will it even be an advantage to be that early, or will it draw unwanted attention to what is planned next?

From what my sister has said about the Emperor, after I was sent to Mousehole, I might be being watched even now by him, and perhaps even by others. Without thinking she looked up in the sky and then all around her before grinning to herself. *Not that I would know if I was. I can see what looks like a bird high up, but that is all.*

Chapter XXX

Olympias
24th Tertius

In the end, I sail into Ardlark with the sun rising from the east behind me and lighting up the sail on my craft. We pass fishing vessels heading out as we go in through the entrance to the harbours. I hold a commission from the Emperor, but the River Dragon *is not an Imperial vessel.*

It even belongs to a foreign village as its "navy". That village has a Treaty of Mutual Aid with the Empire and so I could probably claim a place in the naval harbour if I wished. On the other hand, my craft is also the village of Mousehole's sole merchant vessel, and we will definitely be wanting to trade while we are in port, so we will be best to dock in the civilian, rather than the military port.

With a sigh Olympias, for the first time in her life, sailed past the familiar entrance that led to the naval port and the arsenal and went on to the much smaller, but very crowded, merchant port. *I am not as familiar with the arrangements here, but it is likely to be different each time we arrive.* She moved forward and surveyed the craft docked about.

Around me I can see some of the trading boats of Darkreach. Some of the fishing craft are still tied up to the docks as well. Unlike the military port, where the River Dragon *would have been only a mid-sized vessel, it seems that here she will be one of the larger craft.*

Coming closer, she revised that in her mind. *Today we are going to be the largest ship in the port. None of the areas of The Land are great users of the sea for trade or even just for travel. I was taught that Darkreach, with its long coastline, is one of the larger users of the water, but most of its goods still travel by land and the vessels that do the coastal runs usually have but a single mast.*

They are also usually built with just a fore-and-aft sail, often with a gaff, and jibs, but sometimes they have a square-rigged sail on them as well. I have the only craft in port with more than one mast. I am sure that this, at least, will attract merchants who will be eager to buy what I have to offer.

Only just in time she remembered the protocol for coming in and cut the wind to allow a long boat to come out from the entry fort and lighthouse with the harbour pilot on board. *Darkreach may not have a huge marine trade, but it is crowded enough here in the port that, long ago, it became policy to have someone come on board to direct incoming ships to a berth.*

She called out for the port rail to be pulled open just in time for a part-Kharl to clamber aboard. *Oh no. The woman is looking around as if she owns my craft. This is one of the ones who are full of their own importance. She is just like that one my sister likes to talk about in control of the Gap, who I managed to avoid.*

As she moved towards the woman, she beckoned to Adrian. "The warrant and other papers… Get them fast." *He must be learning quickly.* He just handed the wallet to her with a grin.

"Ploi_gós, navigator, welcome aboard my ship. We need a berth where we may conduct some trade and buy supplies before sailing on. We will need to pay some duty of course, but this is my first time into this port in Ardlark." *I did stress the word "this", but the woman seems not to get the hint.* "Where would you have us go?"

"Your ship is not from Darkreach, is it?" replied the ploi_gós, without even acknowledging what Olympias had said.

"No, but most of my crew have come from here, and we have our entry papers all correct, so…"—she pulled them out of the wallet and held them out—"…where would you have us go?"

The woman does not take the papers, and she is looking around again instead of getting on with doing her job. "Some of you," she looked at Harnermeess standing with Jennifer, "are from among the várvaros, the barbarians. How do I know that you are not spies or pirates?"

"I do beg your pardon. You have not even given us your name. You have come from the pilot station, but are you the ploi_gós, or have you suddenly become Antikataskopeía, one of Strategos Panterius' secret people?" She continued tactfully: "If you are that, perhaps it would be best to let us know."

"No, I am not one of those." *It is hard to miss the emphasis on that last word.* "I am simply doing my job."

"That you are not." *I am losing patience with this woman.* "You ask questions that you are not entitled to ask, and you put yourself in our way. Just direct us to a berth, and then get off my ship. I have the right papers, now get on with it. Get us docked." She went back towards the wheel and stood with her hands on her hips.

The woman looks like she is about to explode at my impertinence. She is obviously not used to having her authority questioned by a mere jumped-up trader like me.

"I can order you out of this port and refuse to let you land," the ploi_gós finally said.

"You are right," Olympias replied. *I am sure my sister is having a bad effect on me.* "That is something that you can do. Why don't you? You have not even looked at our papers, even though that is not your job either. I look forward to sailing out of here into the next harbour and docking there." *I wonder…Perhaps it is time to change to Latin.*

"Father Simeon, do you feel anything from that woman?" Olympias smiled at the pilot as the priest moved closer to the woman. *The woman has her faced wrinkled in curiosity as she looks the priest up and down.*

"Do not speak várvaros. I want to know what you just said," the woman said. *Father Simeon is shaking his head, but reluctantly.*

"Why?" *I am sure that my sister would be proud of the innocent smile on my face and the way I asked that.* The woman's jaw dropped. *She is obviously not used to such treatment from someone with no authority.*

Father Simeon took advantage of the silence to speak in Latin: "She feels as if she has a good soul…one that is much better than the way she is acting. It is…puzzling."

While she speaks, the woman is looking at our priest, who looks like just a sailor. She seems almost openly hostile to us. "I want to know what you are talking about. Who is this várvaros? Who are you? What are you doing here?"

I have had enough. I have very little experience in dealing with a merchant pilot, but I do know that these are questions that I do not need to answer to one. That this woman persists is…curious at least. In her mind she tossed a coin and looked around the port.

I can see a vacant berth of just the right size ahead of us. In fact, from the look of it the telóni_s, the customs officer, is already standing there waiting for us with some other people who could be anything and, I am sure, include both curious idlers and some of the Antikataskopeía.

Let us keep her guessing. It will all be in Latin from here on in. She obviously does not understand it. "We are going to dock." She went to the rear and took hold of the wheel. "Don't let her leave the ship. Set the forward jib." *Denizkartal's eyes have opened wide and the woman, perhaps realising what is happening, has started to splutter.*

Denizkartal moved to stand beside her, and once the sail had been set to give them headway with the restarted wind, he gestured to others to take the bow and stern painters. *Sabas and Gundarasc already have the wool-filled fenders ready.*

"You will stop this ship now. I will have you all arrested," said the ploi_gós. Seeing her words have no effect she tried again "It is only I who can tell you where to go in this harbour, and I will not do it until I am satisfied that you are safe to allow in."

Olympias ignored her, and still using Latin, started directing the *River Dragon* in towards the wharf where they were expected. *The ploi_gós has moved back to the rail, but her boat has been left far behind. She turned and Denizkartal just grinned at her. I saw him wave them away when I took the wheel from him.*

The ploi_gós' crew must have assumed that the boat is now moving under her direction, and with oars rising and falling, and making no attempt to look back at her, they are already intent on returning to their station.

The *ploi_gós* continued in her attempts to direct things all the way to the dock. Olympias ignored them. "Denizkartal, come back and take the wheel now, but get ready to restrain her when I say." She moved to the still open port rail as they moved towards the wharf. *There are several people standing there, not just the telóni_s.*

As they were drawing near the dock, Olympias decided to keep casting the dice and called out to the dock: "If there is one of the Antikataskopeía present, I would like to speak to you. If there is not, could someone fetch one quickly, please?" *The ploi_gós woman is looking more nervous on hearing that. She is licking her lips out of reflex.*

One of the women to the rear of the group standing on the dock has opened her eyes a little wider and moved away as the others waiting there look at each other. Someone calling for the attention of the Antikataskopeía is not something that you hear every day. Doing so from an unknown ship coming into port has to be even more unusual.

Olympias slowed their approach slightly. *The ploi_gós looks like she might try and jump across the gap and try and escape. A woman on the dock, the one who left, was quick at returning to where we will tie up. She has a uniformed man trailing behind her. It is now time to bring my craft in.* Olympias then brought the *River Dragon* into the wharf, dropping the wind as she did so.

"Welcome to Ardlark," said the *telóni_s,* as the sails rattled down around them, and ropes began to be made fast or coiled up. "Can I see your papers please, and what do you want one of the Antikataskopeía for?" he asked, looking curiously at the ploi_gós who was now being held fast by Harnermeess and Habib.

Olympias handed the entry papers over to the *telóni_s,* the customs official, with a smile. "I am not sure that I can answer that for you, because I might be wrong. In the meantime, we do have goods to declare." She waved towards

Shilpa, who had her manifest already in hand. "My supercargo will take care of that matter with you."

She then turned and looked at the insignia on the uniform of the newly arrived man and nodded. *He is a junior man in the uniformed branch of the Antikataskopeía.* "Greetings Primus, I might be wrong, but if you would humour me a little, please come this way."

Everyone was now ignoring the ploi_gós, who was more seriously trying to get away from the two crewmen holding her and failing, while she objected strenuously to her offhand treatment. The two kept her still where they were.

Olympias moved to the other side of the ship. *The woman from the dockside is following as well, but she seems to want to be ignored, so I will do that.* She handed over her warrant, addressed only the uniformed officer. "As you can see, my papers are somewhat unusual. I cannot be sure why, but this woman was behaving…strangely when we arrived."

The Primus only glanced at it before handing the warrant to the woman behind him. "I am…on an important mission and curiosity like hers is unwelcome to us. Can I ask you to have her held, please, while we contact your Strategos? I am known to him…as is my mission." *Both sets of eyebrows ahead of me rise at that.*

The woman from the dockside now spoke up. "Epilarch Akritina…you are not related to Sergeant Akritas, are you?"

"My brother has not been a sergeant for over a year now. He is now Tribune Akritas, and I suppose that both he and I now have the same subject." *I hope that I am correctly using the words that my brother uses to refer to Theodora.*

"I am Praetor Ampelina," said the dockside woman, revealing that she was also Antikataskopeía, even if she was not wearing a uniform. "I used to be your brother's superior. I have heard of you from him but did not know that you were detached in the same way."

In reply, Olympias jerked her head in the direction of the palace looming above them as she answered. "I have him to…ahh…thank for that. He likes my sister-in-law and he met me at the wedding." Out of the corner of her eye she saw the Primus' eyes widen rapidly at that. *I suppose that being at the Imperial wedding is not something most people casually drop into a conversation.*

"When he wanted a simple sailor, I think that I was the only one that he knew. My sister-in-law says that he likes to keep things in the family." She looked across at the ploi_gós woman being held fast by her crew. *She is now very definitely trying to escape and getting more desperate in her struggles. Even Denizkartal must help restrain her.*

"My supercargo is busy doing her real job, and she is the only one of us with experience in dealing with reluctant prisoners"—she held up her hand—

"Don't ask… This woman makes me more and more suspicious. I suggest you strip her of anything that could hold a charm, and get a priest to see if she suddenly feels evil."

The Praetor nodded, and the Primus quickly ran off. "I see that a talent for this work runs in the family. If I may, I will find out more from you later." She smiled.

Olympias smiled back pleasantly, "If I may, I might even tell you."

It wasn't long before the ploi_gós had been taken away. *As this is done, I am seeing some interesting, and very pleased, looks on faces in the neighbouring ships and boats. The ploi_gós woman is obviously not well-liked among those who have regular dealings with her.* Olympias then turned to the more normal activities of a docking captain.

We are nicely docked, and Shilpa is still busy in a hold with the telóni_s, and I can hear an active discussion going on over the amount owed in customs fees. It is the same discussion with the same raised voices that everyone always hears in every port when the subject comes up, so I am not concerned in the slightest.

While there was no one else on board or in earshot, she gathered her crew together. "That ploi_gós woman was too curious… I may be wrong but then I might not… I thought that we would be safe here, but I could be wrong on that, as well. Be careful what you say. If any ask it of you, the ship is from Haven and belongs to Shilpa. That is what the papers we have shown here say."

"If you are from here originally," she continued, "then you ended up in Haven after travelling as a guard, and were glad to get paid for a trip back home on the water. I am sure that most of you can talk convincingly about what a long walk it was." She smiled and then looked around.

"Make a careful note of anyone who is too curious and let Shilpa or me… or that woman who was just on board, her name is Praetor Ampelina and she is of the Antikataskopeía…if she is around…know about it as soon as you can. I want you to stay in couples the whole time, and do not go far from the ship unless I know about it. Stay armed."

I can see looks of concern on several faces. "You have all… Well, most of you have heard what Ayesha said back in the valley. They are not just stories. You may have just hopped on board or walked the long way, but Denizkartal and I were sent directly to the valley by the Emperor himself in a major incantation."

"I am not a storyteller to tell you all the whole story, but I assure you that this is all very, very serious and there may be people here who would be very happy to kill you for just a few words of what little you might know." With that she laid out the details of the shore watch and let them go about their business.

Shilpa

I cannot believe how much they charge. "Captain," Shilpa shook her head ruefully, "that was eighteen of your gold Imperials that lot cost to bring in. I have had to promise not to sell the spilk or the rum...and it is marked that way on our manifest and will be checked before we leave...or it would have been another two Imperials on top of that."

She shook her head in disbelief at what she had handed over. "I had better make a good profit from selling this lot or I will never trade through here again. Are you sure you want trade here? I am not sure if even Haven would charge that much... Well, they wouldn't for a Haven merchant."

"We don't have to make a profit, you know," replied Olympias. *I hope that my horror at that idea shows on my face. It seems to from her reaction.* "Never mind." Olympias continued, "I am sure that you will do your best."

"Now, while you are trading," *Olympias is changing the subject,* "see what you can find out about that woman. When she was taken away, the neighbours looked very pleased. I want to know why. My brother usually has himself and you and Ayesha and Lakshmi. I only have you. I may have to keep you very busy, but you need to do for me what all of you would do for him as well as your own job."

Shilpa smiled happily and unconsciously rubbed her hands together: "And here was I thinking that this would be a boring trip until we got to the north." She shook her head and turned to warmly greet the first of the arriving merchants who had come to express interest in what she might have on board as cargo.

Looking at him, and the man behind him, it is just as well I have worked hard on both my Greek and Arabic, as well as my Darkspeech. It is always better to use a man's own tribal tongue to bargain him up or down to the price that you want. Using a third tongue does not make him feel as comfortable.

Shilpa

Shilpa had only just sold her bulk goods and was about to head off with the brass navigation items from Haven, and had gone to fetch them, when a plain sedan chair arrived on the dock. A pregnant woman dressed in Arabic garb with a veil as well as a headscarf got out and moved towards the ship.

Vishal, who had been given the gangplank duty, moved to intercept her.

She looked him up and down and then spoke past him in a clear voice: "I was looking for a ship full of Mice and yet I cannot see any at all. I must ask, where are they hidden? Do you have them in the hold with the cargo?"

She spoke in Khitan. Danelis' and Shilpa's heads both jerked up and looked around at the woman immediately. "Fātima?" they asked at the same time. They moved quickly and soon the three women were embracing each other tearfully.

Olympias

F̄ātima? Olympias whipped around and looked at the dockside. *There are a suspicious number of large Insakharl and Kharl of various tribes around at present just innocently taking the air along the dockside and gazing at the assembled craft. Several are looking at my crew and others are just looking around like my brother does. Latin will do…*

"Everyone," she spoke quietly and clearly in Latin. "Do not change the way you are acting. Act normally. It is just an old friend coming to visit a couple of sailors." *I hope that they all have enough Latin to get the gist of what I said.* She looked around for who might not.

Cyrus is being pulled up from going into a deep bow by his partner Anastasia. Olympias surreptitiously kicked Adrian. *He is just standing there staring ahead at the visitor.*

"But that is…" he started to say in Darkspeech

"…an old friend of Shilpa and Danelis who wants to catch up with them. Pardon him, Fātima, he is the second cousin of my brother Basil and myself, and he is a little slow and we are looking after him as a favour for his parents." She pushed him ahead of her, covering his protests before whispering to him why he had to behave as if nothing was happening.

Shilpa

F̄ātima nodded and looked around the ship before again talking in Khitan. "Are you two the only real Mice on board? Where is everyone else? My husband told me that you had a ship, but why is it here?"

Shilpa and Danelis took her aside and sat her down on one of the hatches and told her what was happening and what had happened in the village with babies and relationships, how it had grown and what changes were there.

Before long an embarrassed-looking Adrian appeared with a tray of kaf and some biscuits.

"Gundardasc says that this is all he has ready…ah, miss. He is making something else though and says he will be as quick as he can." *He is rewarded with thanks and a smile. He retreats but he has a look of awe on his face. I don't think that the boy has any idea of dissembling. At least we can call Simeon and Vishal over and introduced our partners so that Fātima can inspect them.*

It did not take very long at all for Galla to appear carrying two trays of finger food. "The first has cheese, dragon salami and koupepia on it, and the second has some warm food: keftethakia, tiropitakia, some small hot balls of meat and gasparin, and some tiny and delicate pastries stuffed with some of the crab from Southpoint." *Adrian is trailing her with more kaf. The smell of it and the food is almost the smell of our home.*

"If you please, ma'am, the cheese is from the valley itself. I was told to tell you that Giles made it, and the salami is from our own dragon, and there is some for you to take home if you want and the gasparin and the kaf are from the valley as well." *She cannot help starting a bob but manages to stop herself in time.*

Gundarasc Narches

I cannot help congratulating myself on having brought some live Southpoint crabs with us in a cage over the stern of the ship. It has been a nuisance making sure that they are safe from larger fish that may try to eat them and their cage, but I am sure that I am serving the Empress herself, even if I have never seen her before and cannot officially acknowledge it.

There are not all that many cooks who get to make something for the Imperial family, and I am very, very pleased that I have the right things to do it with. I knew that I was doing the right thing starting to get ready for visitors as we came into port…not that I expected this particular visitor, but it is best to be prepared.

Olympias

Fātima is still here talking and Praetor Ampelina is already back to us. I noticed that she has shown something to one of those on the dockside and climbed back on to the River Dragon *through the open rail. She nodded at Vishal and he had the sense to let her pass. She is looking around and then taking my elbow and not very subtly moving me to the rear of the ship away from others.*

"This is a curious ship…and it has interesting friends…and enemies. My superior sends his greetings and says that you were right. She is one that we missed, and we are going to be spending a long time discussing how much information she has passed to her friends. He also sends his apologies and says that we have a lot of people to check."

"While you are in port, I am to be your liaison, and I can see now why you might need one. My name is Procopia, and either I or one of my people will be on ship while you are here. Now, if I remember your papers, you entered the Empire through Southpoint. Is that some of their crabs that I can smell, and who do I have to kill to get some?"

Shilpa

*N*ow that the Empress has left, it is time to sell my more specialised wares. It feels strange to even think of her like that. She, a girl I have seen raped in front of my eyes, is now the Empress of a third of The Land. She shook her head. I have to get used to the strangeness of my life. I will take Vishal to carry them for me. He is a strangeness I am quickly getting used to.*

Look, we have an escort. Most would not have noticed the men and women just drifting along near us looking at shops and behaving in an innocent manner, but it is the sort of thing that Basil is getting me used to doing myself, so I can see that Vishal and I have several shadows. It may embarrass them somewhat, but if I am in doubt as to where to go, I am not wasting time guessing. They are welcome to shadow us, but they can make themselves useful and also give me my directions.

She and her younger partner were excited by everything that they saw around them. *Ardlark is several times the size even of Pavitra Phāṭaka and it is so much cleaner. There are no beggars or starving people sitting around. The smells are very different, the people around us are very different, and I admit surprise at this, but there are very few armed civilians around apart from us.*

What is more, and it is certainly something that I am not used to in a city, no one seems to be looking at sizing us up to steal from us. Mind you, I think there are many curious about our appearance. You would think that they have never seen a sari before, and Vishal is nearly the only one to be seen without a shirt on.

Danelis

*O*ur *Empress friend has left and now my fun is over. I think that it is time* *for my husband to have his. He has put on his best clothes and has* *waited patiently for me to finish. Now that I am free, it seems that we are off to* *see a Metropolitan. I have already seen one, and I am sure that they are much* *the same anywhere, but Simeon has a letter to deliver.*

As they went, they gazed around them in awe. *Simeon has been to New* *Ashvaria in the Newfoundland before coming here, and it is a very large town,* *and he came into The Land through Sacred Gate and it is larger…but Ardlark* *is a real city and it is huge. It seems to be far bigger than the Havenite city,* *from what I can see.*

I have much less experience in a city than he does, and we were both born *in small villages. I think that we both feel lost. It is very lucky there always* *seems to be someone around who can speak one of our languages and can* *point us in the right direction when we need it, and now that the dome of Saint* *Thomaïs is in sight, it is very hard to get lost.*

Once they were nearly run over by a huge humanoid with dark-green skin trundling an equally huge wheelbarrow along the street, and had to dive aside. It had a tinkling bell on its front to warn people of its approach. Apart from that, they enjoyed their walk. "The streets are much cleaner here than in New Ashvaria," said Simeon.

Danelis agreed with her husband. *Speaking of things being cleaner, I need* *to relieve myself and there are no handy bushes that I can see. With so many* *people around, they may even disapprove of that. I should ask someone.*

It is lucky that there are so many helpful passers-by here. I have been *pointed towards a building with an odd sign on it. I think that I have seen* *several of those along the way. Inside it has toilets that are just like the ones* *at home in Mousehole. There is an old Insakharl woman here. She obviously* *looks after the facilities and produces towels and hot water and other things.*

But why does she just stand there with her hand out when I want to leave? *She is keeping herself between me and the exit. Why?* The two moved one direction and the other for a few moments. "Why do you not let me leave? What do you want?"

"Oh, you are foreigner?" The older woman asked. "You do not have like me at home? I look after here, and you pay me for how nice I keep it, and how well I look after you."

"How much?" Danelis asked.

"That is up to you. Do not worry. You are foreigner. You will learn. I am privileged to serve you. I have never had a foreigner here before. I will tell all of my friends tonight. They will be very jealous of me that you did not choose their places."

Embarrassed, Danelis dug in her purse. *We were all given money before leaving the ship and I must have just given far too much. The woman is now very co-operative and friendly. She is bowing and asking me to visit her again. Her face is all smiles. I think that I have now given her far more to talk about than me just being a foreigner. Still, her toilets were very clean and smelt nice.*

Danelis
a little later

My husband has said where we are from, and we were very quickly being ushered before the Metropolitan. Now I discover why Bianca warned me about such meetings. She excused herself from the pair of men. *I will swear that neither of them has noticed me leaving. Simeon can find me when he is ready to leave. I will look around the Basilica, I think.*

It is vast. I am sure that all of the buildings of our whole village could fit together under the dome and yet still leave space to move about. She gazed up into it and its mosaics and icons in awe. *People around me are talking, but their conversations were swallowed in its immensity.* Her ears began to fill with a rich sound of music. *I have never heard anything like that before. It is the sound of heaven brought to earth.*

When Simeon eventually came looking for her, she had several of the basilica's musicians monopolised and had promises that books of liturgical music would be sent to them with Carausius.

"I also have the promise of plans for a smaller version of this marvellous machine," she said. "It is called an organ. Hopefully they will be done before we leave. I hope that our artisans can make one for our own basilica. Mind you, it will be useless if I cannot remember what they have told me about how to read what the music says."

The idea of writing music down is strange to me as well. You learn music and you play it. That is all that I have ever heard of people doing. I have promised that I will be back here every day until we leave Ardlark. I will work hard on that skill and try and learn how to play…at least to start to play and how to read these sheets. She looked at the one in her hand that she had been given.

Olympias
before midday

*P*raetor Ampelina says that she has a surprise for me. I am not sure I like being surprised by the Antikataskopeía. She has asked to show me something and *I am being taken into the Palace and through a maze of corridors.* Olympias was just about to ask where they were off to when her guide knocked on a door.

By the time she had left that room she had her own small talisman to show to people in Darkreach to gain their co-operation and instructions from her brother's Strategos to keep her eyes out and report any more people that she found equally as suspicious as the ploi_gós had been. *Well, it seems that I am now in the Antikataskopeía myself. Is that how it is done all the time?*

Olympias
a little later

*I*am going to take advantage of my connections. What is the use of having them if you don't use them? She found her way to the office of the Magister Ploi_gós, the keeper of all the charts and navigation aids for Darkreach.

I may have had to introduce my shadow, the Praetor, to his assistants to get my way and see him, but I am starting to appreciate how my new sister goes about doing such things and I am not reluctant to follow her example. It seems to work for her. After all, it is not as if I have to worry about getting my Drungarius upset any more.

When she left the Magister, it was with a promise for a speedy delivery of the most current set of charts ringing in her ears as people were already starting to scurry around in her wake.

Olympias

*I*still don't know whether my crew and I are full citizens of Mousehole with access to their almost unlimited wealth or whether we are just paid servants, but I have decided on a compromise and there is none here to gainsay me. She gave everyone a purse of money. *It is a lot more than several months' normal* *wages...more like a year in a bag.*

Shilpa may have complained about handing over all that money for the port charges, but when I asked her for the equivalent of sixteen Imperials and two denarii for each of the crew, except Adrian, her eyes nearly popped out. It is lucky that there is a moneylender near the wharf to let us change some of our coin over to more convenient amounts.

Adrian still got ten and three, but he is not getting it himself. His purse is going to be given to whichever adult he is with when he goes out. I am sure that he will still manage to come back with a lot of sweet food and other such joys of the young. I suppose that it will not hurt. It will really only happen here.

Olympias
28th Tertius

Shilpa and Danelis were whisked away from the ship to visit their Ambassador. *They have returned to say excitedly that the battle has not yet started in the north for the rest of the Mice, but they won't say how they know that much, and I do not suppose that it is a really good idea for me to press too much for an answer.*

Everyone has enjoyed themselves while we are here. We have stayed longer than I meant to. Father Simeon wanted to see how a Saint's day was celebrated in a basilica and Saint Zita, the patron saint of servants and housewives, was conveniently close.

I admit that I did not protest too much. The delay has let the music and organ plans, that Danelis wants, be copied out. I suspect that many back in Mousehole will feel the same. Far more importantly, a newly updated set of charts has been delivered to me now, so I am not unhappy to wait just that little bit longer. Good charts are important.

We are sailing out in the early morning directly into the sunrise. This time, as we leave, the River Dragon *is sailing out of the harbour at the same time as the fishing boats leave. We are heading straight out to sea with the smaller craft trailing behind us like little ducklings wallowing along after their mother.*

Olympias checked behind her. *There are two huge flags clearly visible on the shore near Ardlark...one to the north and the other to the south of the city. At night, or in poor light, they are replaced by lights, one green and one red. There is one...and there the other.*

Olympias pulled out a small wooden device with three arms that she had obtained in the city and began looking over it back towards these marks, correcting their course as she went. She showed the others what she was doing, and when the angles between them and the flag on top of the Palace were right, she ordered the *River Dragon*'s wheel put over hard to port and they settled into a new course that should, with a long ocean transit, take them straight to Antdrudge.

Although the sailing is easy on a smooth sea, I need to be continually mindful that it was while sailing on the reverse of this course that the fire dromond disappeared, and with the end of the month coming, and the gradual disappearance of the moons, the night sky is getting darker and darker. We cannot relax our vigilance. In fact, we need to increase it.

Chapter XXXI

Olympias
31st Tertius

*A*t least we are having delightful weather all the way north. Our sailing work is minimal, and my crew get to spend their time continuing to learn their new languages, or rather struggling with them. Most of us put such schooling behind us when we went to sea. In many ways this is harder work that handling a ship.

As a reward for all their work, Olympias allowed some dancing and music each night so as to also have some fun to mix with their work. On one of the nights, Adrian was trying to tell tales and Olympias, who had the wheel, nearly missed what he was talking about.

I have been ignoring him, as although he may be keen to entertain, he is not very good at it at all. He muddles his stories up and must go back several times when he realises that he has forgotten pieces, usually important pieces. I just caught the tail of this one. She waited until after he had finished and then called him over. "You were talking about Zim Island just then, weren't you?"

Adrian nodded "Our fishermen have to avoid it all of the time. The fish are bad around the place where the gods fought ages ago."

"What do you mean when you say that 'the gods fought'?"

Adrian shrugged. "That is what our bards say in Southpoint. There was once a fair city there where the old Gods lived. It had another name then, but that is forgotten, and it was from there that the Gods rode into the sky in their chariots. An age or more ago, the Gods argued and fought about what would happen to the people."

He looked at Olympias to see if she was really interested, and seeing that she was, continued: "We know that it is just a story, and they could not really have been Gods, but it is said that they fought so hard that the city was destroyed, and those who lived there died, and the people in The Land were abandoned and left on their own for many years."

"The bards say," he continued, "that before that time, the Gods were all the same and they were kind and looked after the people, but since that time they are mainly either good or they are evil. However, some also say that several Gods, most of the forgotten ones, hold apart from the others and weep at what they see."

He stopped and looked at her. "Is that important? I thought everyone knew those stories. I mean they are just stories, after all. The priests say that other Gods are not real, and that there is just the one God, and Jesus is his Son."

Olympias wondered what to say first. "I guess they are not real Gods," she said, "but they may be powerful mages for all we know, and other people don't tell those stories. I grew up in Ardlark and I have never heard it before at all. The stories, they talk about 'old Gods'... You are sure about that?" Adrian nodded.

"When we get to the north and the Princesses join us, I want you to tell them that story, as much as you can remember of it. While we are travelling, try and remember as much as you can and, when you tell it, try and get it all in order as well. Even if I forget, you have to remember to remind me. Somehow I think that it may be important."

Adrian looks puzzled. He is wondering how an old story that is told to children can be important for anything. I am not going to tell him. The less he knows about what I think, the better. At least he is nodding to his Captain.

Olympias
36th Tertius, just after midnight

*T**he presence of Antdrudge is visible and written in the dark night sky well before the town itself comes into view from the sea. Its beacon light is a great pillar of flame permanently erupting high into the heavens from the centre of the great six-sided citadel on top of its mountain in the sea, and it is visible from many, many, miles away as if it were a small volcano.*

On the River Dragon *we see it clearly. I have seen it many times before, but it is always a surprise to the first timers. Firstly, from afar, they see the glow that the town makes on the underside of the clouds. It is like the glow of a massive forest fire. Next, a full glass later, the light of the flame itself becomes visible.*

However, even with our own wind behind us it is not until morning dawn that we came level with it and can hear the roar of its flame. Those who are not on watch are eagerly looking at the sight. It is one you can see nowhere else but here. How the people who live nearby can tolerate that constant sound, I never can understand.

Antdrudge, with its permanently burning flame and its massive architectural feats, is generally acknowledged as one of the wonders of the world, except, of course, by the lands that lie west of the mountains. Even in my crew there are people who have never even heard its name, even though they have heard of its products.

Olympias

They had to sail past the town and around the island. *The only entrance to the harbour, that is the only one that is suitable for a large vessel to use, is an approach from the north. The southern approach to the port was blocked centuries ago for such ships as mine by the huge stone bridge that links the islands of the town to the mainland.*

The crossing starts on the coast with a small fortification and then jumps via a series of long stone arches, first to a small island in the channel, one with its own substantial keep, and then on to the main island on a series of piers that are sunk deep into the sea bed or that land on small islands. There are two piles in the first leap from the shore from a tall cliff.

The cliff, which runs for some distance to the north and the south, is the reason that the town, while there are some small hamlets and assarts built near rivers and streams further inland, really exists only on the island itself. The land near the bridge is arid and waterless and there is little access to the sea from the plateau running along the coast.

Fishing boats and the smaller coastal vessels, my old boat for example, can sail straight under the centre span of this first bridge, but I prefer to take the safer option now. The passage is deep enough for a great galley to show no bottom, but they mount lower masts than the River Dragon *does, and they are ones that can be lowered if needed.*

The second, and far longer, part of the bridge has five piers in it. That section of the bridge slopes down markedly to land on the island of the actual town at a second keep and each of those spans has far shallower water running under them. Only the very small fishing craft would venture to go under them.

They came around the island. Those who had not been here before were staring at the features of the town. *There is the amphitheatre on the southern end. Beside it is the only real open space on the entire island, a space which is used for markets and festivals and games of ball. I cannot chide them for looking. I forget how strange this place looks; I have been here so many times.*

It is not just one thing even. Next there are the houses, all made of brick and stone, tile and slate, and all leading up cobblestoned streets from the encircling bottom street to the top one that runs most of the way around the keep at a level that is over three cables above the high-water mark. There is not a single timber or straw or mud construction to be seen.

On the ocean side of the island can be seen the Megas Fabrika, the great works, where the thick black liquid which comes from under the ground is made into the hugron pir, the liquid fire for the molotails and flame throwers of the army and the fuel for countless lamps. It runs in a huge dark wedge from the keep down to the sea wall.

It is also the place where the war rockets are made, with all the greatest dangers kept together in one place. Despite the spells of the mages, accidents are common, and all the works have a sort of charred-around-the-edges appearance. Its buildings do not so much look like other normal buildings as like Dwarven mounds and tunnels.

Occasionally a chimney or a pipe exuded a flame with a roar that punctuated the constant noise of the flame that erupted from the huge metal chimney pointing skyward from the top of the keep. These small explosions of sound and light never seem to be accidents, but just normal events that the local ignore.

It is an odd sight, and the smell that blows off the land to where we are sailing is pungent. It makes several wrinkle their noses in reaction to it. It is no wonder that Ariadne wanted to leave this place and take another profession. To most people, working in the Megas Fabrika would be more like working in hell than a normal job.

The Megas Fabrika faced the sea and was connected to the keep above it by walls, and the keep itself crowned the hill. It dominated both the works and the town itself. Once the works were passed by, the buildings of the town resumed and kept going around until they joined with those that they had first seen.

In the mix of buildings could be seen a cathedral and a church as well, a mosque and a Temple of the Living God. They, and several other buildings as well, are all large and, given the likely uncertainty of life there, the temples were all probably very well attended.

Gradually, the two great stone breakwaters that made up the harbour came into view. The southern one—the one that attached to the island itself—was half a mile in length. Both walls were tall and solid enough to be capable of sheltering a fleet from the great storms of the north, if they swept down this far.

The two magical lights, the red on the island side of the opening, and the green on the land side, were clearly visible on top of their own small fortifications. Olympias pointed the way between the lights and Simeon spun the wheel around and, heeling her over, headed the *River Dragon* into the port as Olympias began ordering the sails to be brought in.

At least, after talking to the people whom I saw in Ardlark, I now know that all of the officials here have been cleared by Strategos Panterius' staff. This means that I am able to keep up my own wind rather than rely on the sweeps. It makes the task so much easier than relying on the fickle breeze that is all that is usually here once you pass the great walls of the breakwater.

Hopefully there are no other spies that have appeared here. From what I was told, it is unlikely. It seems that more of the Masters' servants were scooped up here than anywhere else in Darkreach, even Ardlark. I was told that it is believed that our foe will have very few secrets left hidden behind in Antdrudge.

The long wharves were nearly empty, although she nearly headed to the military end, with its huge slipway for the fire ships to be hauled out of the water to be checked and refitted—*one of them is there now*—instead of the civilian end. She brought her ship into a berth at the far end of the harbour near the great bridge, its stone arches around the same height as her masts.

As they moved closer, they could see a set of wooden rails coming down the hill and along the docks. *These were the magical rails that let them safely move the inflammable and explosive things that were made here from the stores of the Fabrika down to the wharf where the ships that are going to carry them wait.*

The teló_nis are here waiting, but unfortunately for them there is nothing that we want to sell here and Shilpa is happy to have all the goods left in a single hold under bond. Even though the telóni_s were curious about the *River Dragon*, they seemed to expect that ships calling in just to buy and not to sell was the normal thing for vessels visiting this port.

After all, I am only landing here to purchase things, and one thing in particular, and purchasing as much as I want would not normally be possible without the authority that I now have.

One hold of the *River Dragon*, the one closest to the centre of the ship, had been completely cleared of everything else and Galla stood ready now with lengths of timber, nails, wedges and a hammer to make sure that what was soon to be put into it would not shift around, no matter what sort of sea they encountered.

Shilpa

*N*ow *it is my turn to negotiate. Denizkartal can have the crew make the River Dragon ready as Olympias and I head off. I have a rather large value of coin in a remarkably small purse and we are going to see the person that they call the Curator Pyrkagió_n, the keeper of the fires. Even I had heard of this place. To actually be here is exciting.*

They looked around as they walked up the steps of the main street. *Here the prosperity of the town can be easily seen in its taverns and its kaf shops. There are many shops selling meals in different styles. There are pastry shops and even a confectioner's. From the people going in and out they all seem to be well patronised.*

I can sadly contrast the happy bustle around us with what is seen in Pavitra Phāṭaka. We have picked up a follower, probably an official one, but there is no one looking at our purses, or even at us, to see if we can be taken. She sighed. *Anyone who looks at us is obviously more curious about the way I am dressed than anything else. Even more than Ardlark, they probably have never seen a sari and choli before.*

What is even more unusual is that the streets are so clean. There is even a small Kharl, one who looks like Gundardasc, who has a little trolley with brooms and bins and other things on it. He is occupied with sweeping the other side of the street from us. People greet him as they go by and he returns their greetings. Everyone seems to know him.

I can see many Kharl, who are a bit like Ariadne, but even uglier. I suppose that these must be full-bred Alat-kharl. They have real tusks like a boar, and these seem to often be inlaid in a way to proclaim their wealth.

Suddenly there was a loud hooting noise like a surprised cow audible through the low roar that came from the top of the hill, and everyone drew away from the centre of the street and the wooden rails that were there. A cart came rapidly down the hill with a person who looked like a mage sitting at the front in a little seat.

It must be moved by an artifice or conjuring of some sort. The little cart had boxes tied onto it and it moved smoothly and quietly down its tracks. *Once it has passed towards the harbour, still making its hooting noise, the normal bustle of the street returns as if it had not stopped. No one has remarked upon the sight. It seems that this hooting cart must be a very regular occurrence.*

Eventually they reached the top of the hill and came to the wall of the castle that surmounted it. The gate stood open, but there was a guard mounted there. Olympias walked across the small open space to the entrance and spoke to an armed kharl who stood there.

I guess that they are the guard. I wish she would not speak Darkspeech so quickly and softly. I cannot follow her at all. Now she is showing something to one of the guards. He pointed to a building. "Come on," Olympias said. "Let's see what we can get using the influence of our friends."

She grinned and showed Shilpa what she had showed the guard. *She has a small green cylinder in her hand. Where have I seen something like that before? That is right, Olympias' brother has one that is just the same.* "It seems that I now have some of my brother's friends as my friends now," explained Olympias.

Olympias turned around and looked at the people near them as if she had just thought of something. "Is anyone following us?" she asked suddenly. Shilpa tried, without being obvious, to indicate who the person was.

Once she knew who he was, Olympias went straight over to the man and showed him her sigil. *I obviously needn't have bothered with any subtlety.* The man saluted the Captain and turned away. *One look at that and he is just leaving us alone. We are no longer of interest to him.* "It works," Olympias said when she returned.

Shilpa
an hour later

*H*ere was I thinking that I had made some large deals in Ardlark. Here I am returning to the *River Dragon and I am leaving behind two old mithril coins, each about the size of one of our Havenite hundred Mohur pieces and several platinum ones, all the size of a ten-Mohur. All of them have markings from long ago on them.*

It seems that I have bought for us a large supply of hugron pir in molotails in their special boxes...a very large supply. I have only ever seen deals involving, at most, a box or two of the substance before now. From what I saw, it went down as we came up; I think that it will take several loads of the hooting cart to deliver them to the docks for us.

Olympias

I hope that none of these boxes break loose in the northern seas. I am giving *them their own hold and Gallas will be fastening them into place with timber as almost a second floor to the hold, but I am still very nervous about this cargo.*

I always hope never to have an accident, but seeing that the boxes will be secured below the waterline of the River Dragon, *this time I really do hope that we run into nothing that will fracture the keel of my ship or even pierce the hull. I need to keep a good watch for the floating ice that my sister tells me about.*

I am going to take advantage of my new status. I am taking my crew to look at the dromond on the slip. I want my people to know what they could face, and this one will be similar to the one that was stolen. The ship is over three times as long as the River Dragon, *and its entire hull is covered in bronze and copper right up to the rails.*

Olympias pointed this out to her crew. "That is something I want us to have," she said, "when we get the chance to do it. Not only does it help against fire, but it also stops her fouling as much and means you do not need to careen her as often. You can keep a higher speed with your vessel without seaweed growing on your hull."

The ballistae that it mounted on each corner, and that hung out over the platforms they were on, were much larger than those that the *River Dragon* carried, or could carry, and it had an onager on the stern as well. It was not fixed but mounted on a turntable that would let it fire in any direction if the mast was down.

It is made to throw special bombs of the hugron pir. Unless you are stationary, or in a restricted place, you can sometimes evade that one if you are quick, but it can throw a long way. What makes the ship most dangerous are the two tubes mounted at the front. They can poke out through hatches that lift to reveal them.

"Those throw the fire out in front," she explained. "If a vessel is within sixty paces, and sometimes even more, it will just catch fire and burn. Sometimes, instead of a thrower like this one has, or in addition to it, they carry rockets at the front. These fire one after the other and cover a huge area with fire or explosions. Basil told me that the missing one has rockets."

"They reach out far further than anything we can throw, and indeed, far further than most mages can cast. All we can do if we see it is to run and hope that we are faster on the water than they are. So, we need to keep someone aloft and watching the whole time. When the Princesses join us, they may be able to help us, but I am not sure how. Astrid may know. She led the Mice to kill the dragon and this craft we will face is truly a dragon of the sea."

Simeon

I *have another letter to deliver here. This time it is from one Darkreach Metropolitan, Tarasios, to another, Petros Lydas. He is the second of the four Metropolitans of Darkreach.* With his wife in hand, he excitedly made his way around the hill and then up the hill in search of the Basilica. *Surely the basilica must be close to the bottom of the hill where it is easier to level the space required.* He didn't have far to go.

He eagerly ended up, once more, in a deep conversation and series of explanations as his wife slipped away. *It seems that the idea of an Ecumenical Council is getting all the ecclesiastics excited. It has been so long since one has been called, and I am hoping that the one whom I will now have to learn to call Bishop will be as pleased as I am that we are going to be hosting it in Mousehole.*

That night the crew got to enjoy the food and the entertainment of a town that, if it was not making things that either exploded or burnt, was making its money from the people who made them.

Chapter XXXII

Olympias
1st Quattro

*A*gain, we are leaving port in the first rays of the morning light. I want to time my run past Neron Island so that it is full daylight all of the time. I have no protection from being seen, so it seems likely that a mage will be able to find out about my ship if they want to. I want a chance of being able to see what is coming at me.

It seems quite likely that somewhere in the waters that we now must sail in order to reach Wolfneck, there is a possibility of finding the stolen fire dromond. The last I heard...from my sister...is that it was at the Shunned Isle...but that was months ago. It could be anywhere now, and without a flying saddle on board, I want to have as much warning as I can if it is here.

Olympias
much later in the day

*T*hey moved smartly to the northwest along the coast with the peak of Tor Glannen, the last mountain of the Great Range and one of its greatest peaks, quickly becoming clearly visible. *It is a while since I have seen it. Perhaps I should tell Vishal what else to keep a watch for. He has the watch at present. My sister doesn't seem to have mentioned its inhabitants to anyone, although she must know of them.*

She looked up at the masthead. *Vishal's gaze is fixed only on the sea ahead and to the starboard, but there could be other dangers as well. It is very* unlikely that they will be around. They are rarely seen, and it is the wrong time of year, but it is best to be sure, particularly with the cargo we have on board.

"Ahoy, the watch…" Vishal looked down from the watch platform high up at the mast head. "That mountain," she called out and pointed at the one she meant, "make sure you look at it and around it as much as you look at the sea; there are three dragons that live near its peak in a cave." *He nearly fell from his perch in surprise.*

"Three?" he called down uncertainly.

"Yes…but they are rarely seen. I have only ever heard of them coming out in the spring when the great whales come past and through this channel. That is what the dragons prey on. Apparently, they are not quite as big as the Mousehole one. They are smaller green ones, but there are three of them and they almost always come out together."

She grinned. "Why eat skinny sailors when whales are so much bigger? I mention it just in case these Masters can rouse them."

After he heard this, Vishal keeps casting nervous looks up at the mountain, not just during his watch, but even afterwards. *He is not the only one.*

Olympias
an hour later

*T**he weak breeze, which has been drifting all around the compass for some time, has begun to pick up. The waves, which now are coming from the north, have also started to rise.* By the time they had Tor Glannen directly to the south and East Zarah, the main mountain on Neron Island, on their forward starboard quarter, the waves were high, one third as high as the masts and perhaps even more.

Harnermeess, who next had the watch aloft, had tied himself onto his platform and Olympias had ordered the *River Dragon* to be turned more towards the island lest it be swamped.

Olympias
a little later

I do not like this sea. Even with our magic to calm the sea and wind in place, people are still being thrown around on the ship. Outside our little circle of relative calm, dense streaks of foam are being blown off the tops of the waves and their crests are toppling over, tumbling and rolling. The wind is becoming a storm.

From the deck I can see very little due to the spray and the height of the waves, and to make it worse, what I can see is a solid wall of rain that is sweeping down on us from the north. Olympias soon had everyone scurrying to take in sail and make sure that everything was battened down and made safe for the coming gale.

Great, this is just what we need. We are coming into an early northern storm and I have a hold that is full of explosives. She took herself below to check on them again. *At least they are well and firmly fastened in. There has been no shifting.*

Soon East Zarah was lost to sight, but, as vision of it was going Harnermeess called out. *His voice can hardly be heard…* "Sail ho"…*He is pointing straight ahead.* He had to repeat the rest several times to be understood. "It is a single sail…as small as ours or smaller…and it is coming this way before the wind…a low boat…with a row of oars…from the west of the island".

Olympias acknowledged him from the raised stern. *It sounds as if it is one of these northern boats that my sister has talked about sailing. With a row of oars, it would be a…drakkar. It is just possible that it is an innocent vessel, but I don't think so. From what she has said, a drakkar is not meant to be a cargo ship.*

Anything that is coming out of port in this brewing storm (and they would have known of the wind before they left Skrice on the west of the island) must really have to be out at sea, and that can only mean they are a problem for the River Dragon. *At least in this weather the dromond should be kept safe in a harbour, unless they had a very, very, good weather mage on board.*

She tried to remember what she had been told about the magic of the Masters. *I must start paying attention to more things than ships if I am going to be caught up in these affairs. I am sure that I was told that they are air mages. They can control weather, then. Damn. Still, this weather might be beyond their ability to calm. This sea is possibly even more than the Princess' magic can cope with.*

The ship lurched heavily over a wave. *Possibly a lot more than it can cope with.* Below on the deck she could see Danelis, *her priest-husband's arm is tight around her and a rope is around her waist and she is already leaning wretchedly over the rail. She has fallen prey to a sea-sickness that she had not shown so far on this trip with lighter seas.*

Olympias looked up. *The rain has arrived, and I can now scarce make out my own lookout.* She looked beside her at Denizkartal on the wheel. *His eyes are fixed on the compass ahead of him rather than trying to see ahead.* Again, she weighed her options. *We are making way against the wind, but only just.*

Our own magical wind is just a trifle stronger than that which is coming from ahead of us, so the River Dragon *is heading into the wind, but across the sea as it drives in from our starboard quarter. If I turn to port I can make it to Cold Keep, the most northerly part of Darkreach, but if I miss it, and that is easy to do in a storm, we will be caught by a strong wind that can easily get stronger against a lee shore with an enemy vessel coming from our windward.*

No, I think that our only hope is to hold our present course, perhaps even turn a little more to the north and head more directly into the waves and then, when in the lee of the island...which hopefully we will see, we will swing around and run for Wolfneck. Hopefully we will miss the other vessel in this gale and, if we do not... She felt in her pouch.

Rani gave me three wands and the Princess gave me yet another. She sighed. *They will do no good sitting here in my pouch, and from the deck I can see nothing anyway unless we are on the crest of a wave.* She looked up.

Harnermeess is the one who needs them. "Shilpa," she beckoned the woman over. *She has discarded her dress and is just in her trousers and top. She is already drenched, her clothes cling to her and you can see the wind buffeting her slight form.* "Can you make it up the mast with these?" Shilpa looked around and nodded. Olympias gave her three of the wands and instructions on what to do with them.

Olympias had lines rigged along the deck and now called for sail to come in even further. *Most of them are down. The* River Dragon *sails on with just a tight-reefed mainsail slewed around. Having your own wind is good but, when it is opposed by the natural wind, it is still hard to handle. Under these conditions it is best to calm the gale and sea as much as I can and only use the natural wind for the moment.*

When all was ready, she sent those who were not needed below. *There is no use them getting battered by the wind and spray and possibly going overboard if they don't need to be here. After all, they are only one hatch away if they are needed.*

Again, she looked up, trying to keep her own feet. *Harnermeess has tied himself to his post and has his legs around the mast and is looking ahead.* To the side... *Denizkartal has lashed himself in place and seems comfortable at the wheel. I have Habib, Cyrus and Irene ready behind me to do anything that I need, all with ropes holding them to the ship. The rest are just below.* She looked further around to make sure all was ready. *All of the stone balls are secured in their lockers now. That is one risk less.*

She looked again at the glass that was covering her compass on its post. *It is swinging wildly in this sea as the ship responds to wind and wave. I must judge when to turn and I have little information to go on.*

The deck rose beneath them suddenly, then... *At our most exposed...*

Olympias was lashed by stinging spray and rain. *There is a brief glance of the waves with spray flying... I can make an attempt to see what else is out there. Is that the top of a mast or is it just a glimpse of a lost bird tossed about by the wind?*

With a lurch, the *River Dragon* slumped forward and over to the starboard and slid down the face of the wave. Ahead there was only the trough of the wave and then the bow was driving into that water with a shudder that ran through the ship and crew. Then again there was the sudden climb up the next wave. *Over and over comes the rise...the fall...the shuddering halt.*

Suddenly, there is a cry and a flicker in the dark of the storm...two flickers... Lightning or...? One was from us, I think. She looked up. *Harnermeess is standing now. He is clutching the mast...his gaze is on the port quarter. The lightning came from somewhere over there. I felt it strike the ship; I can feel the tingle.*

Harnermeess is still there, but now he is struggling in the wreckage of the topmast. It is his turn to fire. Lightning is striking out from the River Dragon, *and again from where the other ship must be, but that passes harmless to the side.*

Damn, I don't have a wand out. She struggled with her pouch on the tossing vessel. Her feet slipped on the deck and she risked losing both the last wand and her footing. *Now we are on top of the wave and I can see what is happening. There is another craft on the next crest only a few cables away.*

She used the wand in her hand to cast a blast of fire as Harnermeess and someone on the other craft did the same with lightning. The *River Dragon* lurched down from the crest. *We are struggling in wreckage. Now the top of our spanker mast is down and my three on deck are trying to get Denizkartal free from under it so that he can keep steering. Blood is running from his head. If he loses control, then we will broach and we won't need the other boat to sink us with their magic, the sea will do it for them.*

We are rising, and again Harnermeess and the other craft exchange bolts... this time the River Dragon *escapes damage...again the crest...* Olympias looked abeam to the port. *There it lies...its mast is down, and I can see its crew struggling with wreckage...* She cast fire again. *The air is full of the feel of lightning from the other two wands, and even in the rain, the sharp smell of its passage stings my nose.*

They all reeled as the sky itself now crashed and paled with lightning from the storm itself. *My God, we were lucky to not be hit by that. If we manage to live, I owe candles to Saint Christopher... We all owe many candles.*

Another blast comes from Harnermeess overhead and nothing comes back from the other... Another blast, and another comes from Harnermeess without a reply. We are back on a crest. What I can see is no longer a boat over there.

It is a mass of wreckage with people struggling to survive in it. Another blast came from it, and Olympias and Harnermeess both replied.

Harnermeess is calling something, but I cannot hear what it is. They rode up the next wave. *Somehow, despite the driving rain, my fire bolts have set something on fire. The wreckage is all that is there, along with some struggling figures.* She fired again and saw a person outlined by flame as they were directly hit. *I can see them fall into the water with a faintly heard scream.*

Suddenly it is over. The River Dragon *is back to battling just a storm and clearing wreckage from the deck. We have survived one battle. Now we have to survive our next one. We have defeated the first enemy, now we must fight with the storm itself, and survive the rocky shores that are somewhere ahead of us.*

Night is already falling on a very long day, and although we should have been nearing our destination, we are still at sea fighting the elements. Up…lurch and down…shudder…the pattern that continues. Is it lessening? Harnermeess called something and pointed direct ahead before waving frantically. *That must be the shore… It must be time to come about.*

Olympias ordered the wheel put over, and the pattern of the waves and the lurching changed as the mainsail swung around as well. *Now we are running before the sea with the gale coming off our starboard stern quarter. Is it time to bring our own wind into play, or do we just run before the gale?* The climbs, the lurches and the falls were now all further apart and gradually they fell into a new rhythm as Olympias adjusted the sails.

Olympias had memorised the bearings that she wanted to hold. *If I am right, and if we have turned at the right spot, if I have allowed enough for drift and reefed enough then, sometime just before dawn Harnermeess should see the Wolfneck light not too far off to the port. There are far too many times that I just used the word "if" when thinking about our situation, and that is a hard lee-shore that is somewhere south of us.*

Still, I am glad to be in this ship and not on a galleass or a dromond. They would have been lost some time ago. It is remarkable that the drakkar made it out to the battle. Maybe there is something to what my sister says about their seaworthiness.

I suppose that we were lucky to have spotted it before the storm. If we had been taken by surprise by it, we would have lost that battle before we even knew that it was happening. The drakkar would then have sailed back to safety, leaving us behind in the water to drown instead of it being the other way around.

Before dawn, the gale suddenly died away to become just another strong wind. *If it had not been brought on by magic, then what we have just faced is not a full winter storm that lasts for weeks: it was just a first loving blow from the ice-lands to the north to tell us what lies ahead if we dare to test the sea.*

Harnermeess cried out, and now they could hear him. *He is still tied on at the masthead and he stands draped in the wreckage of the topmast. He is pointing portside.* "A light." With relief, Olympias ordered the helm put over following the direction of his arm and sent a relief up to him. *Damn, he is coming down using only one hand. His left arm is completely broken and hangs useless.*

"Father!" Simeon was quickly hard at work. He had already dressed Denizkartal's gash, now the more serious wound needed attention. *It looks like we have made it to Wolfneck in time. Now we must repair the ship and stock her so that we are ready to sail when my brother and sister and the Princesses bring the other Mice to us.*

Will we face the dromond while we are docked here or will the loss of the drakkar give them some pause? They have lost one vessel and possibly lost a mage as well. I suppose that whether or not they are on the defensive depends on what is happening elsewhere and that we have no way of knowing. I wonder how the rest of our people are faring in their battle.

Chapter XXXIII

Olympias
2nd Quattro

Olympias brought the rest of her crew out on deck into the new day. *The lowering clouds in the sky and the gale have swept past us. They now batter the northern slopes of the mountains that lie to our east, leaving behind just tattered remnants in the sky. But the seas are still running very high in their wake.*

Luckily, it is largely a following sea. By keeping our own wind up and adding that to the wind that comes from nature, the River Dragon *is almost travelling with the waves like a dolphin, occasionally catching the crest of one so that it drives us on before we slowly slip off the rear of the wave—until we are caught by the next. If the main and spanker topmasts were still in place, we might have been able to balance the winds with careful sail setting and hold the crest of a wave.*

Once the storm had cleared enough that it would not be too dangerous to work aloft, they recovered what they could of the damaged cord and masts. Olympias went quickly aloft with Galla as the damaged sections were cut loose from the whole.

We were lucky in several ways. Both hits from the magical strikes were above the join between the topmasts and the lower masts, and we will be able to recover almost all the topsail rigging. We lack being able to set topsails or the spanker gaff, but we can go without those sails. The main worry for us is the stability of the masts from the lack of stays, but we are carrying very little sail at present, and so the lack of fore and aft stays should not place too much stress on the masts...I hope.

From above, Olympias could see how their opponent would not have been able to get a good hull shot from their low craft in the high seas.

It is just as well, given our cargo. She looked down. My crew are winding up what cable is let down to them, stacking the timber and making the ship as presentable as they can in this sea. Denizkartal is already moving both ballistae to the starboard side mounts to cover where we will be docking.

Wolfneck is supposed to have been freed of the influence of the Masters, but it has been nine weeks since any of the Mice have been here to check on them, and a full month since the River Dragon *left its home port. Anything at all can have happened in the village during all that time. The Mice oft move quickly from one target to another and there is nothing to say that our opponents cannot do the same in turn.*

Olympias
later in the day

Having tended to her lover and made sure that he was comfortable with his broken arm, Jennifer had now taken over the lookout role in the main mast, and using the glass, she reported that there was some movement at the dock, but that it did not seem to be any sort of preparation for war. "It is just people milling around," she said. "I can even see children."

Mind you, that is just what I would want to be seen myself if I were preparing for a sudden attack. Once the ship was set up as she wanted it, she had the crew arm themselves and stand to. Even those on watch had their weapons about them.

Let us see what happens if we hoist that silly banner. She ordered the Mouse flag raised. She looked at Shilpa, working a sail in the rigging, and down at Danelis in the waist.

They both look at it as it goes up and both have an odd expression on their faces. I suppose that we are now all Mice. Maybe we should fly it all the time to make us all feel more of a part of this absurd village, instead of thinking of ourselves as still having our home in Darkreach. I will have to consider this.

We have made excellent time on our voyage. Despite the time that we spent in Ardlark, we will still make port well before anyone who watched us leave Evilhalt will have expected us to. This could give us an advantage of surprise. For all I know, the ship that we defeated last night was a desperate gamble by our enemy to delay us.

According to what my sister has told me, the Methul has no bar at its mouth, but I am not taking any chances. Astrid admits that the deepest of the boats that call in here draws far less than a fathom, and so the lead is being cast all the way in and the depth is being called constantly. It is better to be safe than sorry, and even running onto soft mud could be a problem with our masts.

Around me, the water changes colour abruptly as we encounter the outflow. Suddenly it goes from the deep green open northern sea to a near black colour of the river water as it pours out, laden as it is with tannins from the northern swamps and marshes. There are many rivers like this in the north of Darkreach, not as big, but with the same water.

The *River Dragon* rode a full fathom deeper in the water than any of the northern boats. My *sister was almost correct. The shallowest that we can find is near a full four fathoms and we found that only briefly. She is a deep river.* Olympias looked at the flow past them. *And fast.*

They passed the spits of land on each side that made up the mouth, and while the surf, the remnant of the storm that had battered them, still could be seen and heard pounding the beaches on either side of the mouth, for them the waves quickly disappeared and the *River Dragon* began to glide smoothly up the watercourse, slowing quickly as the flow of the river pushed hard at them.

The strength of that flow would make it hard work to pull against if you were rowing any craft up the stream. You would hope to have the wind behind you as well.

They passed the harbour light. *It is mounted on a tall and strong-looking timber pole. It looks like the whole trunk of a large tree, which is, in turn, on top of a small hill. It is strongly braced with other huge timber beams against the storms of the north.*

A narrow wooden set of stairs winds around the pole and there is a watch platform near its top and someone is standing in it exposed to the wind and rain. It looks like they have a short pole sticking out above them to hoist banners or lanterns from. Above that is the globe that lights up at night or when it goes dark.

The person on the watch platform seemed unconcerned at their passing and waved down. Several of the crew waved back. Olympias looked around her as they went.

This river is not as wide as the main channel of the Rhastaputra at the island where we dock, but still it is ten or more cables wide and generally seems to be far deeper. Astrid has told me to come up the river and dock with the prow facing upstream. It will be easier to turn as we undock than it will be to turn in an unfamiliar river and then dock as we move downstream with the strong current pressing on our stern. As far as Astrid knows, the dockside has at least a full two fathoms of water beside it anywhere, even at low tide.

Olympias then looked ahead. *The village is entirely built of timber, or of what looks like piles of earth with houses under them. I can see grass growing on several roofs, which often reach down to the ground, and more than a few* have odd-looking sheep grazing on top of them. Some are grazing from right beside where smoke drifts up from a chimney.

Despite that, the real houses are solid, often being built out of untrimmed whole logs with, presumably, clay in the gaps. Many of the houses even have two storeys. Several great jawbones, presumably of whales, stand on their ends, framing each street as it leads off the dock.

There is a welcoming group assembled on the dockside. I can see several obvious priests and other people there, none of them in armour, although most are armed. The number of children running around put paid to any idea of being ambushed and she ordered her people to stand down.

She could see several large dogs tied up in a row near a house, barking with excitement and being answered from elsewhere in the village by at least three other packs. *I wonder if Simeon will be able find to find anything out from them. Do werewolves speak the same tongue as dogs? I have never asked him. Will it be insulting to do that?*

Several of the people in the village, even at this distance, show that they are indeed Insakharl. From what I see, I doubt that any of the girls here are anywhere near as pretty as my sister. She looked out at the buildings and the chaos ahead of her.

Children and chickens are running everywhere through the village. Despite some of the faces that look back at me, it is a madcap village scene totally unlike anything I have ever sailed into in Darkreach.

Siglunda the Wise

The Captain of Wolfneck looked at the banner flying off a yardarm as the strange craft came slowly upriver. *This must be the ship that these Mice talked about, the one that will take us to Skrice.* Siglunda chased the villagers around to get them ready for the visit. *It has either been in a battle, or else it has suffered badly from that little blow.*

Looking closer, she could see that only the tops of the masts looked shattered. *They look like the top of a tree that has been hit by lightning, not one that has been broken by wind. Those are not just simple breaks. I think that they had to fight hard to come here to us and they must have won. They look happy, despite their damage. I can see one bandage on the head of a kharl and another on that black man's arm.*

At least the side that I am forced to be on seems to be winning. By going along, not entirely voluntarily, with everything that Astrid and her mage Princesses have done in my village, I have now tied myself, for better or worse, to the venture that they are on. I suppose that my continued hold on the office I have held for fifteen years depends on what comes next.

It is a tenuous hold. So many families have been affected by death and exile that the bitterness lies deep over them. She looked around her. *If it were not for the playing children, oblivious as they are to the unfolding events, I would have retired and given someone else the mess to handle.*

Mind you, I am not sure that there is anyone who can do better than I have or even anyone that wants the job. Old Magnus still has everyone's respect, but I have cautiously sounded him out on the subject, and he has made it very clear that I have set my sails and now must see the course. He will support me, but he wants no part in plotting the route.

Father Simon, his priests and their families are the only ones who are truly happy. Despite having sent Astrid's brother, Father Thorstein, south to this village in the mountains, it appears that several others among the young men are possibly interested in vocations.

Moreover, there is now attendance at church such as they had not seen for many years. Even I have decided that I need to go every day and be seen there. It seems that my village's brush with evil might have started some of the residents thinking more about their futures.

Now, as they had not done for many years, the bells proudly ring out before each service, even that at midnight, and no one objects. I would love to say no. My bed is far too close to them. The testimony of those who were questioned publicly had shocked the whole village. It seems that a brief chilling touch from what may have been their old religion, or more likely may not have been, was enough to provide a lot of support for the Church, even among those who don't like me.

Father Simon and the Church have been strong in their support of me, so as far as my public words are concerned, they can do no wrong and I have to be seen to support them in anything. She turned and prepared to open her village to this strange ship…and to take her people to the battles that its arrival presaged.

Chapter XXXIV

Rani
27th Quattro

*W*here is Sajāh when I need her? Organising a battle of thousands is far easier than getting my people to where they need to be, and shifting them around like pieces on a chessboard. Someone like Sajāh makes it look so easy. At least Eleanor should have the cavalry back to Bulga by now. I don't have to worry about that.

It will not be until some time in Quinque that those on horseback will return to Greensin. I have until then to work out whether to send them home directly or to Wolfneck, although I am sure that I can keep track of them. I can let Astrid do that. She will be missing Basil anyway and will want to see him as often as she can.

I am glad that I gave them instructions to ride fast. They will not be riding as hard as the Khitan clans, but then they still have fewer horses each. I now appreciate what Hulagu has told me on that point. Lack of remounts is one of the deficiencies of the Haven cavalry, and perhaps either one of the reasons why they don't venture far from home, or else one of the excuses for that.

I must admit that now I am not sure which one it is. I have not specifically asked for help from Haven, but I did let them know everything that is happening in that letter. Since I have come north there has been not a single sign of any of Haven's troops coming outside their land at all. Even a few Battle Mages at our side would be useful.

Are they going to be content to just sit there and allow others to fight the battles that need to be fought rather than to risk contamination? It is beginning to look like that will be the case. Having sent me out, almost as a sacrifice, perhaps they feel that they have done enough.

To be fair, I may have felt somewhat the same before I was thrust outside and had my life changed, but what is happening (and I know that both my Princess and I have stressed this fact) is not just some small-time bandit raiders attacking trade caravans to try and make money. I am starting to seriously wonder if Haven has gained its reputation as a refuge just by isolating itself, and then being lucky that conflict has somehow managed to wash around it and leave it alone.

Already Ariadne and her artillery people are headed back home. With Tāriq driving the cart it will take a long time before they get back. They should be fine. I have had to promise to try and get Aziz back to Verily quicker if I can, and I want him on the River Dragon when we go to Skrice anyway. If we could be facing Insak-div, we want as many strong ones along as we can have.

I wonder if we can get the other Hobs…what is their name? I must admit to myself that I think of them as the ugly one and the even uglier one. Their names even make fun of their looks. That is right. One is Krukurb, or "strong frog" and the other is Haytor,"pretty bull". He might be pretty to a cow, I suppose. I had better not say that to my wife.

At any rate, they will be safe from the Khitan wherever they travel. They are flying a Mouse banner on a spear shaft attached to the cart, so even with the wagonload of former slave girls behind them, they will not be touched. The Khitan seem to have decided that they like the ones who bring down the walls that fence in the plains.

According to Ayesha, Ariadne and her crew of Humans and Hobgoblins even have their own name among the Khitan now. They are now being called, or more likely given the language, have called themselves, the "Devartetilcu Yamyam" or "wall-striking monsters". To be a Yamyam is now apparently a good thing on the plains. It turns out the Khitan give them an honour they extend to no other outsider. They will freely talk with them as if they are Khitan themselves.

The first three girls from Warkworth are already on their way back to Mouse-hole with a note to Sajāh and Father Theodule about what is happening. Bilqīs, Rakhi and Zeenat are flying them on the carpet with Goditha, Parminder and Ayesha on saddles to bring the three flying the carpet back to make for a quicker return.

Each trip will take them several days before they return to us. They are long trips and having three who can control the carpet makes them less likely to become exhausted. They are going direct to Mousehole, sleeping and then heading back here to pick up more people.

I hope that having this many Brotherhood girls arriving will not raise more problems with Make, but there is no other choice for us. With three Mice on the carpet to reassure the girls and to allow changes in who controls the carpet on such a long trip, there is only going to be room for three more people, so *five more trips are needed to get all of them back, and now we are taking this young woman priest as well.*

Rani sighed in resignation. *That will take until after the Feast of Rath Yara and nearly to my wife's feast of Easter. In the meantime, all the freed women get to stay with the wagon and follow the Devartetilcu Yamyam.*

Oh, Ganesh grant me wisdom. I have just referred to one of my religion's major festivals and then, almost in the same breath, to a Christian one. The closest that I will be to Jagganath and the chariots on Rath Yara will be to the two wagons that are being driven back east from the battle, but on the other hand, it will be certain that I will go to an Easter service.

She smiled wryly. *It seems I am already taking part in some of the Christian rituals, whether I want to or not. For some reason, my wife has given up on having sex for this Lent. I admit that, seeing that we are away from Fear and now are safe, this worried me enough to mention it to Father Christopher.*

He just smiled that quiet smile that he sometimes gets, as if there are secret amusements that he is keeping to himself, and innocently replied that people are meant to give up some of the things they most love for Lent. It is supposed to remind you about sacrifice. He then spoiled it by smiling even more broadly as he turned away, thinking himself unseen.

Rani shook herself. *My mind has strayed far from where I mean it to be.* Dismissing those feelings, she returned to her previous thoughts. *The rest of us should start off along the coast to bring news of victory, and of the opportunities to the west, and then to Greensin and finally to Wolfneck.*

We have left Wolfneck alone for too long. Who knows what has happened there in over a month? Has Siglunda, despite the way Astrid spoke to her, resiled from her promised support? Have the Masters again sent forces there? Perhaps they have sent more this time in order to overwhelm her. I want to be in place to greet the River Dragon *when it arrives in the north and to make sure that it comes in safely.*

She looked around her at the Mice. *We have finished packing up our encampment. People are just idling around as if they are waiting for me to make up my mind…and I have. Now I must get them moving.*

Chapter XXXV

Gallas
2nd Quattro

After they had been welcomed to Wolfneck, Gallas quickly took over control of the ship from Olympias and began doing what she needed done.

Captains are in charge at sea. They only think that they are in port. If the ship is damaged, it is the carpenter who must take control of her, and ensure that she is repaired quickly so as to be able to go to sea again. At least my captain seems to understand this and has put up little resistance to what I want done. I have suffered under captains who have not understood the way of things before.

That is the good news. The bad news is that I am not impressed with either of the people who have seasoned timber available. One is a little better than the other, and yet they have good timber growing here. I just don't like what they have in store. Their timber was meant as masts and spars for these excuses for ships that they use here. Overgrown whaleboats are more like it.

She had finally decided to buy some timber meant as masts. *I will trim them down for the lighter pieces that I want. That will take time, but I seem to have plenty of that and at least I will have exactly what I want. I am glad that the woman who was the carpenter on the last trip of the* River Dragon *had put her time in Haven to good use. I have a good selection of tools and equipment to use in the locker.*

She established her workshop on the dockside and set to her task. *It is a pity that I cannot just copy what has gone before. My captain has already told me that she will be taking this opportunity to increase the rake of the masts by a couple of degrees to gain a little more speed from our craft.*

The crew are already hard at work on this with the side-mounted backstays, although they cannot complete the work until all the stays are ready to be put in place. If the raking is to work and not break, I will need to use a thicker and stronger timber for the topmasts to take the extra strain of what my captain wants.

Gallas
20th Quattro

*A*ll this time and there is no sign of any other Mice arriving here. Gallas was close to despair. She had been sitting idly and happily after working for several days on the first topmast. She had it ready to hoist into place on the next day when she realised that the village lacked a shear-legs.

I have never been in a place that expected to do repairs on ships which lacks this most basic tool of a dockyard. I have well over eight paces of stout timber shaped and ready to lash in place on the spanker mast and yet there are no means to raise it into its place. Do I have to make my own shear-legs?

Galla shook her head and wondered how the locals coped and went to look at some of the craft near the *River Dragon*. She shook her head again.

They don't need to. The mast on each vessel, whether they are on the smaller whale boats and faerings, the low, narrow and speedy drakkar with their few and wide planks or even the deeper and far wider knorr with the cargo space and maneuverability of a trader, can be unshipped and laid down whenever they want. None has a tall enough mast for it to need to be permanently shipped. No wonder the local yards don't have what I want in the way of timber.

She was musing glumly on what she could do when she saw the old man who had been introduced to them all as one of the more powerful of the local mages.

When I came along, I was worried about the language problem in the barbarian west, but at least in this village we can talk to the locals, even if the people do have a thick accent that sounds very up and down and almost like the person you are speaking to is chanting or singing and, even worse, their writing is strange and unreadable.

"Sir…" She approached the man respectfully with her sea cap in her hand. *You should always be respectful before mages, particularly ones who could be powerful.* "I wonder if you can help me …" And she explained her problem.

Magnus looked at her and smiled in a fatherly fashion. "You are a very lucky young girl. I am far too old to go out and fight in this war that you are taking part in, and I am not much good at battles anyway. I was wondering what I could do to help, so I thank you for asking me. I am a mage of air, and one of my enchantments is designed for lifting heavy things. It isn't needed much, but when it is it is very useful."

He is waving vaguely in the direction of the church as if that in itself is an explanation. Looking at all the timber making up the roof and the spire, and the height of the roof, over twice as tall as a normal church, it may well be at that.

"When you want a mast set in its place, then you come to me and we will get it all arranged. If your Captain thinks that your mages will not mind, I will use their pattern and we shall get it all done very easily indeed. I do indeed have a very good casting for that sort of thing." *He is rubbing his hands together quite happily. It looks like that problem is solved.*

Chapter XXXVI

Basil
28th Quattro

I *do not think that I have ever seen as profound a shock from the behaviour of those around them as our three new Khitan are experiencing from being exposed to the rest of the Mice. Admittedly Rani still has troubles with other cultures, and perhaps I did not notice it with Hulagu when we first set out from Evilhalt, but these three are a source of perpetual humour with the way that they react.*

Looking at the Khitan and their interaction with the rest I suppose that, when we were on the way west there had been a serious concentration on the battles that lay ahead and a focus for activity as people learned to act together as units. There was a lot less time free for purely personal concerns to surface and become apparent.

Now, although another battle lies ahead of us, it is some way off, and many of these people may not be fighting in it. Most seem to realise that, for better or worse, they are thrown together and need to learn to act together as a community of a different kind, and not just an armed band. Now they must form friendships and even families.

Although, as a matter of routine, we take precautions against ambush, I know that my wife would regard them as being laughable. For a start, we are riding far too fast to show a goodly amount of caution, and I know what she thinks about that. What is more, the whole group has an almost festive air about it.

Although Bianca tries to make the Khitan feel more at home with the others, and they defer to her as the sibling of their Tar-Khan, she often must act more in lieu of her husband than her brother. I wonder if she even realises how she changes in her speech and manner as she switches from one role to the other. I do not think that she does.

Anahita and Kāhina's behaviour are obviously a shock to the three people fresh from a tribal life. The two girls have changed much in their time away from the Clans. They have lost much of the normal isolation from us walled ones. Looking at the two girls, they have irrevocably changed from being what would be regarded as normal for women of the Clans.

They spend as much time sitting, talking and drinking with Adara and Bryony as they do with their Clansmen and, what is more, they expect the other three to do the same. They have lost that separation from the rest of the world that we have seen with most of the tribes. Mind you, I have noticed that they drink only little beer.

Tömörbaatar Dobun

*F*or once in my life I do not know how to act. I did not expect this when I set out, but my whole life has been overturned. My probable future wives, and they still have not fully committed themselves to that path, expect me to spend as much time with Basil and Asad, and even with the Khuyagt Morin men from Darkreach, as I spend with them.

Also, neither of them shows the proper deference that I have been raised to expect to be given to a man of status from his wives. They expect me to listen to them as much as they listen to me. I don't mind that they are pregnant to my Tar-Khan; they already have other children to him from being köle. It is the lack of respect that matters.

He had cautiously raised the topic in a general way and been greeted by laughter and had been horrified to discover that his Tar-Khan's sister was brought in to share the joke and she found it just as funny. *If I am going to be a part of this clan, and it was seen that I would, then I am going to have to learn a new way of relating to the women around me, several of whom only act as women ought to act when they choose to.*

For instance, I really don't know what to make of the cousins that are the two hunter women from Yavakh Bolomjgüi Gazar. I know that some among the women of the Clans are of two spirits and follow the same path that they do, but while these two are loud in proclaiming that they miss their husband, they are also very open in their physical affection for each other as well, behaving more like a besotted husband and wife than as sisters, even while they are openly discussing names for their children to their husband.

Basil
that night

*T*he Princesses have made none of us oversee the rest. That is a mistake. If we had someone making us learn and study and practice, it could be better, but we have a lot of idle time on our hands when we set up camp for the night and none to direct us how to use that time.

I suppose that, to make it worse, Kāhina and I both brought drums with us, Bianca always has her flute handy and Eleanor has somehow managed to bring a lute intact through the whole campaign of skirmishes, and even a major battle, in a hard leather case tied onto one of her saddle bags. This means that at night Valeria and Maria are always intent on dancing, and in teaching the men the dances that are common in our valley.

It did not take long for me to be dispossessed of my little drum. After all, I have only been playing it since the Princess decided that I needed to learn, and Lakshmi and Aine are both better with it. It means that I am pressed into dancing. Neither Asad nor Dobun has ever danced with a woman before and neither Aigiarn nor Alaine has ever danced with a man.

It may be foreign to their cultures, but cultural reticence has never saved any man from a female Mouse who is intent on dancing, and this often means all of them that are not on watch, asleep or playing instruments. Every place has its own peculiarities and music and entertainment seem to be a characteristic of our valley.

When we were passing through the village of Bulga, Kāhina even managed to unearth, from somewhere, a mandolin. While she normally plays an oud, the two are not dissimilar in the way they are played, it seems. This means that she and Eleanor can now take it in turns to dance and to play.

If a fourth man is needed, then either Adara or Bryony will fill the gap… badly. Both keep dancing the wrong part instead of the one they are supposed to be doing, colliding with others as they go the wrong way around and loudly regretting that their husband isn't here. It has ended up with them not being allowed to dance together as a couple, as they will constantly forget whether they are a man or a woman this time, and can easily both dance the same part, causing any group that they are in to disintegrate in chaos.

Aziz

F *or Tãriq, Ariadne, Krukurb, Haytor and myself, the trip back to the mountains is a different experience in very many ways. The horses have galloped off ahead. They have left us to return along the coast alongside the foot soldiers of the Army of the North. We no longer require much in the way of supply wagons with us, only needing to carry enough food to tide us over until the next village.*

Now that we are away from battle, Ariadne has retreated into the shell of quietness that she lived in back in the village, and the other three men are near as bad. No one else wants the job, so by default it seems that I am in charge of them all, as well as the girls from the Brotherhood in their cart.

I have no experience in that sort of role, and as a younger hunter in Dhargev, and of an age with the other two, I never expected to ever take a leadership position. Although three of us speak Hob, I need to make the other two try and practice their Darkspeech and Greek, not that I am an expert in either. We need the Greek to talk to the few girls among the Brotherhood who have another language than their own. None of them has more than a few words, so they are learning as well.

Unless we are in a village, and there are not many of those, we are forced to rely on our own resources. Luckily, the rescued girls do most of the cooking although Tãriq has some experience and Ariadne and Krukurb at least have an idea how to boil water and know enough to help, but we lack supplies and equipment.

We are all glad when there are taverns to go to, despite the looks that we receive from the other customers in them. If, except for Tãriq, we had not been thorough in going to the local church at the first available service after we arrived, and being vouched for by soldiers of the Army of the North who saw us in action, I am not sure if we would be served.

When we are on the trail, I am finding that I am leading the morning prayers before we set off and the evening ones before we go to sleep. I am now used to them daily and find that I am uncomfortable when I don't have them. I must admit that I do miss having a priest say them for us. It is odd what we get used to.

Seeing that he was leading prayers, Krukurb and Haytor wanted him to confess them. *I have had to explain that, even though I know most of the prayers for the night and the morning, I am not a priest. There is still so much we Hobs do not know about our new religion. It keeps coming up, and we have the ignorance of the Brotherhood slave girls to deal with as well, as they try and join in. At least, as time goes by and girls are gradually picked up by the carpet to go back to the valley, the number of them to worry about grows fewer.*

As we travel, Tāriq and Haytor share the driving of the carts and the care of the horses, while the rest of us generally walk. The Brotherhood girls stay together, and I go ahead of the others to keep a watch out unless we happen to be walking with several other returnees ahead of us.

This means that the other two, Ariadne and Krukurb, are usually left walking along together. I have noticed that this seems to have given them time to find out that, despite the differences in their upbringing, they actually have several things in common with their skills and pastimes. As time passes, I notice that they seem to be together more and more, even when we are all in camp. When they sit, they sit closer and closer together.

Well, that may be one less husband to find, that is if either of them can overcome their shyness, something that my Yųmųkimşe and I never had a problem with. Rani said why she wanted the groups kept together like she has, but I miss my little Yųmųkimşe. I hope that she is safe without me to look after her. We have not been apart this long since we first met.

Chapter XXXVII

Rani
30th Quattro

*A*strid *is looping her saddle back towards us as we fly north along the Methul. The sea is just visible as a growing line ahead of us where the green ends and an endless grey begins. What is that girl up to now? She is laughing about something.*

"They have beaten us here. Olympias must have pushed them so very hard to do it, but the *River Dragon* is tied up beside the wharf." With that she swooped back around and ahead as she headed down towards the village of Wolfneck, for Rani just becoming visible in the distance. She could see the smoke of its fires rising, but little else.

I am sure that I will never get used to how good her sight is. At this distance I would need a telescope to see what she sees straight away with just her eyes.

Olympias

*T*he *River Dragon* was indeed in dock. It was looking as if it were new from the shipbuilders. *I have kept my crew busy with the endless round of holy-stoning, painting and mending that are the lot of a sailor in port. We are now a familiar part of the Wolfneck waterfront as the normal life of the village goes on around us.*

I have been thinking that, if the Mice are much longer about their business in the Brotherhood, I should have to start to train some of these northerners in how to sail this larger ship. Several have been restive about not being allowed to take their ships and boats to sea to fish and hunt, and others are just getting very bored with doing nothing. Now that the Mice are starting to arrive, things will hopefully change.

Rani

O lympias has a watch up the mast and it must be keeping a good eye to the south. She already has Siglunda waiting nervously for us as we land. Allowing the rest of the Mice to talk with the crew (and for Christopher to be introduced to Simon and his priests), Rani and Theodora, taking Astrid with them, went into an immediate discussion with Siglunda.

Without much in the way of preamble, Rani launched straight into their purpose here. "The Brotherhood is now completely destroyed," she said. "It may well be that the Masters on this island of Skrice are all that remains for us to complete our geas. What sort of armed force do you have ready to go with us?"

Siglunda

I have given much thought as to how to answer this question, and Father Simon has been exhorting the village at every opportunity to get them prepared. I have been around, and sounded out possible people, and the early arrival of the River Dragon *after its victory at sea has certainly helped in my asking. The story of the sea fight in a storm spreading through the village has not hurt either.*

Having taken them to a quiet spot in the tavern, the Brodir Lind, she explained this and continued: "Having said that, the only ones I can definitely commit are the Rangers…and even with Atli, one of our mages who is keen to go, that is only two hands of scouts. I think that you will get many more, but it will be best if you…or even better, if Astrid asks."

Rani

A strid is already nodding. She has already told me that, like the Hobs, the people from her village will far rather follow a leader rather than an idea or a cause. It looks like their village leader thinks just the same. "What you need," Siglunda continued, "are enough who have their own ships to commit to coming so that you can take a fleet with you."

"Perhaps," said Rani cautiously. *I would have been happy with another two hands of useful people. Indeed, in my planning I was only counting on having that many extras on board the* River Dragon *along with our people. If we take more than that, then we will need to crew extra ships and we will be slower.*

I will, however, never admit to that, so I will get Astrid to ask and we will find out how many are willing to go on the raid in their own ships. However, we will only take the fastest of them. I will then see what tactics I can come up with depending on the numbers that we have with us.

"More ships," muttered Theodora to herself. Rani turned to her. *Theo-dear's eyes are glazing over, and she is pulling a small slate out of a pouch.*

"Pardon my wife. She has obviously thought of some spell that will help us." Drinks and food began to arrive. Theodora abstractedly started nibbling on some pickled herring and onion without really looking at what it was she was eating. *Astrid has tried to get her to eat these disgusting things called rollmops before along the coast and it didn't happen. She is not noticing what she is eating, so she is deep in thought already.*

"We will just leave her sitting down here and she can get on with thinking about it," said Rani "She will tell us what it is that she has thought of in due course." *Siglunda looks sceptical.* "She is the one who made our saddles. Have you asked your mages if they could make them yet?" *I must sound cross. Siglunda now looks abashed.*

"I see you have, and they said definitely not, didn't they? She has also made something to hide what goes on in our entire valley and for a long way around it...again something your mages, and few anywhere, could do. She will have something useful in mind. Let us eat, and then we take Astrid and go out to the village, and we will see how many we can get to come with us."

They left Theodora sitting and thinking and went outside into the autumn sunlight. As they left, Siglunda beckoned over a man with a spear in his hand. Like Astrid usually did if she were moving about, he also bore a bow across his back in a woollen roll with a quiver. She got him to round up the villagers into the trader's area outside the wall.

Astrid

*T*hor Thorsteinsson is still the Sergeant. At least he was not tainted by the whole Old Gods thing. While he is going around the village calling *out to people, I will get my saddle and bring the Mice out to the caravan area while I think about what to say. If getting people to confess to their sins, even when they know that it is likely to get them killed, is all about playing on their fears to make them cowards, what do I have to say to get them to be brave?*

I thought that this moment would come along eventually. I think that I did the right thing talking to Father Christopher about it. Surely a priest learns something about talking to lots of people and I have always found that his sermons before battles make me feel eager and prepared, so I hope that what he has told me to do will help.

Deliberately she was wearing her mail and had left her helm on her head, her braids hanging loose from it.

Astrid

A s the stragglers arrived, Astrid looked around at the people of her former village that were assembling in front of her. *Unlike the last time they were all here it is now full daylight and at least there is no one tied up and accused of crimes lying on the ground, but it is easy for me to see there is still a mix of resentment and fear on many people's faces. The bodies may just as well still be in front of us.*

I can see that some people are directing looks of open hostility towards Siglunda, and indeed towards us. People stand around in groups, with one group almost ignoring the next that is right beside them. They wear arms and glare at one another if they are jostled. They do not stand as one people. As the skalds say, it is a hard crowd.

My old village is one that carries grudges and resentment for a long time, sometimes for generations, until they are resolved, usually in a fight or in getting drunk or both. On one side of the village's people, and to the rear, are my father and my brothers. Father is glaring at me. My brothers shuffle their feet and look at everyone but me.

Up in front of the gathering and facing the crowd on my right are the Mice. The ship's crew and the saddle riders are all mixed together and closest to the wall and the entrance. In the centre of those at the front are the priests and me while Siglunda and the Rangers stand to the left of us, but still seem to be separate.

Apart from Atli, who stands with the Rangers and Magnus, who is behind Siglunda, the other village mages have not committed themselves. Grim, Leif, and his apprentice Bjarni stay in one clump while Guthorm, who was Ketil's apprentice, stands on his own with a small space around him in the crowd.

He does not look happy at all. I will bet that there are rumours about him and his master.

She had arranged for a large box to be placed beside her. *I am tall anyway, but with several hundred people here, I want to see them all, and to be clearly seen by them. My voice is not as loud as I would like it to be for this, but I have decided against using the talker thing of the Brotherhood general. It is far too loud.*

She had a long look around. People have finally stopped filtering in and the children in the crowd are starting to get restless, as the rest of the village watches those in the front and wonders what is about to happen. It looks like they are ready for me to start. Without anyone introducing her she just jumped up on the box and the crowd largely fell silent.

I can feel hundreds of eyes just looking at me and the silence is impressive. I can see my father still talking (deliberately I am sure) to one of my brothers and with his back to me, but I will ignore him. It is time for me to start.

With her spear in one hand, Astrid started talking slowly in a clear and loud voice, looking around as she spoke and trying to momentarily catch the eyes of some people as she did so.

"It has been two and a half months since you last saw me here," she started. "Before that, it was nearly two years since I left here running in confusion from a beast. That beast corrupted this village and he was to blame for many of you losing some of your kin. It was the fault of no one else apart from him, and of them. No other left in the village can get the blame for their deaths or their outlawing. He has paid for that and so have they."

"Of course, they should not have listened to what he said, and maybe you could have stopped them, but all of us are sometimes weak. For myself, I should not have fled Wolfneck back then, but instead I should have stood up to my father, and to the beast, and said no to a marriage I didn't want." She paused and looked out over the crowd.

"Since I fled here, I have grown up and become wealthy beyond dreams. Not only am I married and a mother, but I have killed a large pack of black wolves. I have helped free an entire village of slaves. I led the attack that killed a dragon and then we took its gold. I have been one of those who found Dwarvenholme and its lost hoards." *All heroes are supposed to boast of their achievements.*

Astrid continued. "I have sailed to the islands of the south and killed servants of evil in the Swamp and in Haven before coming back here and helping you clean up your mess just in time. We have raided into the very heart of Freehold and killed more servants of evil there including one of its Counts. We have just come from conquering the Brotherhood and tearing down their castles and temples and bringing away even more treasure and making thralls out of most of their people."

Astrid paused and looked around her gauging how people were reacting to her words. *I have chosen to just speak, and speak slowly, rather than try and yell or scream or plead. I want them to think on my words as I say them. I can see on the faces in front of me that most are doing that.*

"I left here as a scared little nithling..." She smiled a little when she said that—*It is obviously something that now I am not*—"but I have returned to you as a figure that skalds will tell stories about. They are stories that will last for a long time. You ask Solveig and Hrolf if you want" —she named the town's two skalds as she waved in the direction where they stood near the mages. "But Astrid the Cat will figure in the legends of The Land for a very long time, and people are already singing songs about me in other towns and villages, even among the Dwarves."

I didn't ask them, but they are both nodding, and others are seeing that. I hoped that they would be getting rumours and it seems that they have. "It is not just me who has changed. One of us left a monastery as a new priest" —she pointed at Father Christopher— "and he is about to be appointed as the first Bishop of the Mountains. Another"—she pointed at Hulagu—"left his home as a young and unknown man, and he is now a Tar-Khan, that is the leader of one of the clans of the Khitan."

She kept pointing and ticking off people. "Thord the Dwarf is now the Crown-Finder, and the most famous Dwarf in The Land. Our mages both left home unknown and are now Princesses. My husband is now a senior man in the Darkreach army, and one of us has gone from being a slave to cruel men to being the Empress of that land. Stefan here went from being a homeless leatherworker to being regarded as one of the great captains of the North."

"This adventure has made us all famous...and even more than famous. We are not only rich, but we will live on in the stories and legends for all time." She paused dramatically on her pedestal and put her free hand on her hip, lifting her chin into the air and deliberately striking a pose with her spear.

That should look heroic...I hope. A pause to give all that a bit of time to sink in, before I start off again by looking around and briefly trying to catch the eyes of person after person among the listeners. I need to look at the ones that are important: the furrier Vera Frakkkvinne, the weaver Hrolf Vidarson, the notary Jaap Josefson, the weaponsmith Gerolt Mikelson and the rest of those that people look up to.

"Now, we are about to go on to the next stage of our battle. In the last stage, against the Brotherhood, the Metropolitan rode with us along with most of the forces of the North. We had with us the men and women of Greensin, of Bulga, of Outville, and of Bidvictor. Even far Warkworth had a part to play.

All of the villages and towns of the North have had a part…except one."

She paused again and kept up trying to catch people's eyes as she went on. "It is now Wolfneck's turn to join in and to become a part of the legends. In return for what they tried to do here, we are about to go on to raid Skrice, for it is on Neron Island that the last of these so-called Masters lives. I am not telling you to do anything, nor am I forcing you to do anything against your will. However, I am asking for volunteers to go with us."

"Some of you may just want the adventure, but some of you have a point to prove to yourselves." She looked directly at Guthorm, the mage, and made sure that everyone saw where she looked. "Some of you may resent what has happened in your family, and because of what they have done, have a cloud hanging over you with the neighbours whom you have known all of your life."

She looked at her old friend Gudrid's family. *That sank home with her father.* She allowed her voice to build a little. "Now is the time for you to wipe the slate clean. Now is the time, possibly in the last battle of this whole campaign, for you to take a chance to make your mark in the tales, to fight alongside a fenrir priest, a pair of mage-Princesses, and a whole slew of heroes who are walking straight out of the legends to ask you for your help with this battle."

"I cannot speak on what is right for you to do, but I am sure that any who say no to this great quest risk being labelled nithling not only by their neighbours, but even by themselves and for the rest of their lives. For your own sake, when your grandchild asks what part you had in this Great Raid, make sure that you can tell them that you were there when you were asked to come and when you were needed."

Astrid stopped and took a last look around. *I can see people talking now and some heated discussions have already started between husbands and wives, and between sons and mothers. I think that I have said enough to get people stirred up. It is time now for people to work out their own destiny and decide what they want to do.*

More conversationally she concluded: "If you want to know any more you should talk to me, or you can talk to any of our people but for those who want to come already, don't see me, see our Princesses, or else see Siglunda or Magnus. Come now, or come when you have talked to your family, but for your own sake, I urge you to come. We are not going to be leaving for a few weeks, but you will not get another chance like this in this life."

I think that I am pleased with that speech. Astrid jumped down off the box and let the crowd dissolve into chaos as people started to argue and discuss what to do. *Already I can see people heading towards those I named. I am pleased to see that my brothers are all moving towards the front as a group, despite our father trying to hold them back.*

Astrid

After everything had died down, Rani came up to Astrid. "I need to thank you. You spoke well. I could not have done that." *Rare modesty.* "It looks like, once everyone has had their arguments, that we could have a hand of hands filled coming with us. That is a goodly force. Now, I must ask you, what is a nithling? I thought that I was getting to know Darkspeech, but that is one word I have never heard before and you have used it a few times."

Astrid shook her head. "Darkspeech seems to have lost so much. First, it isn't written right now, and it is losing words as well. A nithling is a person who is less than a worm. They are a little burst of nothingness, and totally unimportant in the way that things are. It is nearly the worst insult that you can call someone. It is like calling someone a coward, nekulturny and a waste of space all at the same time. It means that they are not even worth stepping on, unless they put themselves under your foot as you walk. It is a good word."

Astrid
that evening

It took a long time for everyone to make up their minds, but eventually people had largely stopped asking questions. Ayesha was telling the tales of the fall of the Brotherhood in the Brodir Lind when Theodora started to pay attention to the world again. *She ate almost without acknowledging us, and I made sure she had plenty more rollmops and pickled octopus.*

"Tomorrow I am going back to Mousehole," she said. "It seems to me that it is easy to defend an island because even Astrid cannot easily sneak up on it. There is no place to hide. A good spell will let you know who is coming very easily. I am going to make a spell that will hide a ship from magic." She looked around at those watching her.

"If they use their eyes, they will still see us, but the Masters seem to be lazy. Magic will work well almost all of the time, and that is all they will use at night and it is what they will be using to make sure that we are still here."

She turned to her husband. "You will make a plan," she said, "so that we will move at night and then they will not see us. It will take me several days anyhow to make what I want. Now, how many do you want me to make?"

Rani

In Wolfneck, as Rani was sitting in her working space, a table in Brodir Lind, Olympias came up to her with the young cabin boy. *He is yet another cousin from Southpoint. It seems that it isn't just Hrothnog who thinks of family first, as Astrid alleges he does: his brother is already in our school. Adrian…that is his name.*

"I need to tell you a few things I found out from the Antikataskopeía… Basil's people," Olympias said. *She looks a little bashful as she says that. I wonder why.* "But firstly…on the way north Adrian told us a story," said Olympias. "I don't know if Basil knows it, but apparently it is a tale that is told to the young ones in Southpoint. I have never heard it and no one else on board has ever heard it."

Olympias then prompted Adrian to tell the tale about Zim Island. When he had finished, she looked at Rani. "So, what do you think of that?" she asked. "Do you think that this is all connected? We are fighting some ancient evil, and you will have noticed that the story is about the 'old gods' and what happened to them."

"It struck me: What if these are the same people who built the city on Gil-Gand-Rask? What if they are the names that we are not allowed to say? We need to get back to Ardlark and Mousehole and look in the records and see if there is anything for us in them."

Rani nodded. *This is all new to me. If it were a widely known tale, this is the sort of story that would have been relayed around, at least among the staff at the University, and I have never heard it before. Why have I not heard of it before?* Olympias continued.

"I told Hulagu to look, but he is not a book person, so my sister told me to give him a note to give to the schoolteacher as well, and my sister tells me that she is a book person and will look through our old books." Adrian was sent back to the ship and the two sat to discuss the implications of the story and what else Olympias had discovered about their foe.

Astrid
3lst Quattro

The next morning, leaving Stefan with Rani, Astrid decided to take Father Christopher with her before he disappeared into the church to teach the younger priests and was not seen again until the attack had to happen. "You need to send me Eleanor," said Theodora as they left. "You have to get her back to Mousehole as quickly as you can. I cannot complete anything without her." Astrid agreed to send her when she could.

They were headed west to check on the riders, and incidentally, to see how their spouses and the rest of the Mice were. *I should have guessed that we would not make it. Christopher has convinced me he needs to talk to the Abbot about his elevation and what he will need to have in place. It is hard to argue with that, and so we will stop briefly at Greensin.*

Hulagu

Theodora returned to Mousehole, taking Thord to North Hole on the way. *Astrid has made me go with them. I wanted to go west to my people with her. It seems that this will not happen.* "Do you want to explain to Ayesha," Astrid said, "that you allowed Theodora to go on her own without having protection along? What happens if she starts thinking too much and gets lost?"

"It is just the same for me," she continued. "I usually have to look after Christopher with Bianca not here, so without Basil and Ayesha being along, Theodora is your responsibility." He gave her an odd look. *I had not thought of some of the obligations my marriage would place on me, but she is right. It is now a family duty.* He just grunted in acknowledgement.

They were warmly welcomed at North Hole by Baron Cnut Stonecleaver. *Once again there is little interest expressed in much of what has just happened to the west, as it did not directly affect the Dwarves. Thord's curiosity about the world outside their villages is showing itself, more and more, to be very unusual among the Dwarves. The Baron is more interested in what is about to happen, and Thord has promised to tell him everything before we return from the south.*

Astrid
the morning of 34th Quattro

*W*e *will only stop briefly in Greensin, my arse. I suppose that I should have expected this after all this time. Despite my trying to urge hurry on him, we have not left here by the time our cavalry arrived themselves a couple of days later.*

Christopher was more than happy to have Eleanor take his saddle, and she agreed to leave in the morning. "Theodora needs me to make jewellery," she said.

Christopher thinks that this means he will have more time in Greensin. He is not so happy to discover that he will not be left behind in Greensin until he is picked up. There is no time for that, and he will now have to ride a horse along with the rest of the Mice until someone brings his flying saddle back from the valley.

Chapter XXXVIII

Theodora
32nd Quattro

*T*abitha *is on watch outside the valley and she is nearly jumping up and down with excitement as we arrive at the lookout.* "We have been expecting you for a long time. Ever since they started bringing girls back… Why do you keep sending girls?… We need men… We have been waiting on you… Where are the rest? I suppose that I will have to wait until tonight, won't I?"

Theodora was overwhelmed. *The quiet girl, who most notice only because of her odd-coloured eyes, is being taught more than how to use a spear and bow by Astrid. She seems to be picking up some of the directness of her teacher as well.* "Tonight…I will tell all tonight."

It was more of the same inside, and Hulagu was left to answer the questions as Theodora quickly went to see Fear. She then closeted herself away in her study while she prepared and wrote out the first draft of her new spell. Having finished, she sat back and looked at what she had written.

I have set out the wording as well as I can. Once again, I will be straining my resources. I will need a fully charged storage device and my charged diagram, but at least it will be an easier enchantment for me to cast than making a flying saddle, or indeed, the conjuration that hides the valley from prying eyes.

The main problem with it is that both of the aspects involved, that of creating a magical device and the form of the hiding itself, are earth-based spells…and I am an air mage. It will take me so much more power to overcome that obstacle. I will need to start charging storage now. I should have been doing it as we returned.

Theodora
34th Quattro

While Theodora was glad to be home and to see Fear, having her in the large bed was not the same as having her husband there, and she slept fitfully. *When Fear cuddles up to me in bed, she is all elbows and she still has bad dreams sometimes.*

I cannot even concentrate on just casting my spell, despite having laid out a number of suitable gems from the store. Eleanor has still not arrived in the valley yet, and there are far too many things pressing for attention and distracting me. Everyone wants a Princess to see what they have done, and we have not been back to inspect things for quite a while.

For a start, more and more of these Brotherhood girls seem to arrive. Have we really rescued so many? What will we do with them all? There seem to be as many of them as we first freed when we killed the bandits. Most are seemingly useless except as housekeepers. Robin is trying to teach them how to use a bow, but Ruth seems to have more success with the children from the school.

There is a new priest in the village, it seems. He is Astrid's brother. Did I even know about him coming here? He and Theodule are trying to teach them to speak Latin, and to read and write all at the same time, although that does not seem to be an easy task, from what I am hearing.

They are reading to them from the real Bible, not the thing that I read bits of in the villages we passed through, and using that for their language lessons, and at least that goes some way to holding their attention. Pass and Make have a little Latin, and Dulcie and Danelis have a little Sowonja, and that has to do for the moment to talk to them.

At least they seem willing to turn their hand to any work they are told to do, and the fields are getting better and better prepared for the winter. What has previously been only an outline of new fields in the grass of the lower valley is now more complete, and the path that leads firstly to the mine and then onwards, leading up to the falls, is now fully outlined with growing stone walls on the flat.

The new fields lack gates, but then the walls are not high enough yet for them to be really useful, even to hold sheep in. Some of the girls have adapted to wearing the kilts and some have not. The latter are usually given less active work with the sheep or cows or in the kitchen, and the former in building things.

In the half day dedicated to work by the students, they are more than making up for their lack of skill with their numbers and enthusiasm. Atã has even found that he has helpers to cut timber from the forest, bring it in for firewood and to season for construction. Robin goes along to chaperone, and to look for new wood for the number of bows that he will have to make over the next few years.

He even joked to me that Asad would be going away more often, if each time he leaves this much ground is cleared away for him and Arthur to farm in the next year. Although several large stumps still remain and are piled high with brush around them, waiting for winter to make it safer to burn them out, there are several virgates of nearly flat land cleared of timber down below the level of the road.

I am told that they are suitable for plantings of a rough corn such as maize, at least, as a first-year crop. It meant a lot to Arthur when he told me that. Although there are still many rocks left in the stony ground and will be for very many years as they come to the surface in the frosts, some stones have even been put aside in rows and heaps for the start of farm buildings and for walls.

Verina has also been hard at work. Apparently, she has decided that the mill will be at the very entrance to the valley, inside it, but only just so. She says that, unless she builds on the far side, there is nowhere to run a leat, so it would be an undershot wheel and have no head, but the river is a fast one anyway, so she says that she will still have plenty of power for her small stones.

She has been labouring hard and has the area that she wants to use laid out in the shape of a mill. She has Thomas helping her, as he knows something about masonry, and as Goditha flies in and goes out again to bring the girls in, she is apparently offering advice and showing them how to do better work.

Despite the difficulty and danger of working in the fast-flowing rivulet, they have the wall of the mill that is against the river sunk down under the water and firmly anchored against the solid rock, and the floor of the mill and the outline of its walls are already complete. Apparently, it should all be firm and secure before spring brings the rush of water from the snows melt down our river.

Verina may know how to use a mill, but she has never actually had any experience with making one before, so Dulcie is working on the wheel and the gears and hopes to have it ready in time. She has never made anything as complex as this before, and she has made herself a series of little models from small pieces of scrap timber.

It seems that the first several models that she made hadn't worked, or at least had shown serious problems when she tried turning them with her hand, and she was hoping that the latest one she showed me will be more successful when it is finished. It was all a process of trial and error, and a lot of it seems to be error.

Aaron has also started work on a more modest structure outside the valley for his tanning. He already has tubs knocked together, mostly made by just hollowing out felled trees and then dragging them into place. He has found out where the small drain for Mousehole's toilets leads, by looking for a small noisome swamp, and is using what came out of that small putrid stream for some of his work. I could happily have missed being shown that.

Other skins lie ready for use in the torrent that comes out of the valley, and yet more lie soaking in tubs with oak bark or leaves from some of the bushes in the upper valley and on the hillsides. Of all the things that we need, at least we should have enough leather for our purposes.

The usable space inside the valley is gradually filling up and, until we repair the long-fallen bridge over the stream in the valley, we can do nothing to utilise nearly a third of our land. It is easy to see where it once was, carrying a path over our stream. Its remains lie near to the base where the path goes up to the top meadow, but even its foundations will have to be rebuilt for it to be used again.

Unlike my husband, who gets to plan things, this may be my most important work as their Princess. They need me to inspect all this work and declare that it is good. I don't have to understand what they are telling me. I just nod and remember what they say. It is essential to let the proud workers show off what they have done and what they still plan to do.

I am truly pleased with their efforts while we were away, but I am even more pleased now that Eleanor has flown in at dinnertime. I think that Tabitha has flown straight out to replace her with the riders and to let Christopher rejoin the River Dragon, *but that is all up to Astrid to arrange. I can get on with my casting.*

Astrid
34th Quattro, in the afternoon

After spending the night with her husband, Astrid returned to Wolfneck to a scene of grim preparation. *It is rare to see so many ships being stocked and made ready for sea this late in the season. There might be one or two vessels going west to Bidvictor or even, very, very rarely, east to Cold Tower in the north of Darkreach, but they would only be doing a quick trip. They'd be ready to quickly try and beach somewhere if a severe storm came along while they were hard pressed against the lee shore.*

What is more, a large fraction of the people of Wolfneck, perhaps even a sixth in total of the number that live here, are actively practicing and drilling with their weapons. They work with throwing or thrusting spear, or bow, with a sword or axe and a shield, or even with the great bearded axe that is held in two hands. I must have spoken better than I knew.

Mind you, I don't have much of a chance to see how the preparations are going. Rani has a task for me. She seems glad that I am back so soon. As soon as Astrid had eaten and had a nap, and confirmed that she was willing to fly on, she had her ring on and was flying invisible and with her amulet against magical detection towards the northeast with her instructions.

Astrid
around dusk

With Neron Island clearly visible ahead of her, Astrid felt a familiar tingle that told her someone was looking out and trying to find something. *So, they are looking for us, are they? Were they looking for* me, *or were they just checking on where the saddles were generally, or even just looking for anything coming near them? It could make a huge difference.*

She looked at the first glimmer of stars and at the positions of Tor Glannen and East Zarah. *I hope that I can see them on the way back. If I feel something at the same place, it will be from a general field.* She looked at angles and distances and remembered what Olympias had told her and had a quick think as she flew. *If it were a general field of detection, perhaps set up to look for anything at a certain range, then maybe it would even have picked up the* River Dragon *in about the right spot to have put that drakkar in its way.*

It would have to be a powerful field, but I suppose that Theodora could do something like that, if she wanted to. If the general spell worked all the time and picked up something, it could just be a warning. Then they could use a more focussed spell to find out exactly what it is that is coming to them. That would be a good way to do it, providing always that the opponent they were looking for wasn't as sneaky as we Mice are. Astrid unconsciously smiled the focussed smile of a hunting cat as she flew along, returning to watching ahead.

Astrid
an hour later

The night is chill. Gradually, what lay ahead of her was becoming both clearer and yet more of a mystery. In the glowing gloom of the early autumn night she could see that there was something very strange ahead of her on the island.

On the very peak of the mountain of East Zarah there is a glow. It is very bright, and it covers quite a large area. I can see it clearly from here and I am nowhere near the island yet. I will eventually be checking what is up there, but first I will make landfall over Skrice and check out what is there as I was asked to do.

Coming to shore and looking down, she could see four boats and two ships drawn up on the beach in their bay, and the racks for drying fish and for seaweed for both feeding the sheep over winter and for the people to eat in their soup. *There is no sign of the great Darkreach ship that I am supposed to look out for. Does that mean that we will not face Kharl when we attack them?*

Skrice is nothing like Wolfneck, although the two villages are about the same size. More of its people stay on land and tend herds of four-horned sheep or grow hardy crops of oats. Less people go to sea, hunt or become traders. It has always been more self-sufficient or, if you want to put it that way, more isolated, and so it is forced back on to its own resources.

I can see that some of its buildings look to have been burnt down. It looks like the churches and some others, and an area north of the village has been cleared in a huge circle. I am sure there was a small forest of stunted trees there last I was here many years ago. There is what might be a stone circle there...one like the people in the Swamp or the Bear-people use.

I am not to go any closer, Rani has emphasised that, although I am sorely tempted. I will be a good girl and go along with what she said. However, I think that it is likely now that the most important part of what I am going to find out lies ahead where the bright light is, and I have not been told to stay away from that.

She flew towards the peak and, mindful at least of the general idea of Rani's instructions, drew herself up a good bowshot away from it. She stopped her saddle in the darker sky to the east, drew out a telescope and prepared to use that if she needed to see what was there in more detail. *There are four lights fixed around a large rock on the summit. Those are what I could see as I approached.* She circled around until she could see more. Using just her eyes, she could see one of the giant Insak-div and a Kharl. *He is probably an Isci-kharl, but the rest are Humans, locals by the look of them. There are four of them.*

She sat still and invisible in the night sky, watching what went on. *It is obvious that they have just fed themselves and are tidying up for the night. One is giving orders and four, the Insak-div and three of the Humans, are preparing to sleep in a tent that is pitched against a large rock near the summit. They use the rock to shelter them from the northwest wind. I don't blame them up here.*

The Kharl was standing up and looking around on top of the rock. *He seems to have the physical watch standing there beside something on legs that is a few hands across. The one who was giving the orders has climbed up there as well.*

The man pulled something from his pouch and suddenly, but casually as if he was not expecting a result, swept it around in a circle as he walked around the box. Astrid felt a tingle. *I have you. You have something there in your hand that should find me or my magic. You are a mage...I will bet on that, and you rely on the device you have been given. If you looked carefully with your eyes, you might have just seen me out here through my glamour.*

Having done that, the mage climbed clumsily down from the rock and went over to the other Human. *He has left the Kharl looking around at the sky for anyone trying to creep up on them. I don't know what the other Human is doing. He seems to be just sitting there on a stool staring into a small box that sits on a low table set up in front of him.*

The two talked for a while and then the mage took himself off to the tent to sleep. *The man who is left keeps just staring at the box.* Astrid used the telescope and even moved around to get a better view, but it was no use. *The thing on top of the rock is a sort of small flattish circular box standing on three legs and it is near to the height of a man.*

The lights make it possible to see that something is running from it down to where the man sits just staring at his box. He is not an experienced hunter, is he? Occasionally he looks up, or rubs his eyes, or yawns. It is early in his watch and he is already bored. No matter how much I look, I can see no more than that.

*What is the box on legs, however? Why peer into another box? I itch to go up and see what he is staring at, but Rani has pointed out, very strongly, that our opponents are well aware of how to stop invisible stalkers from coming too close to them and we can no longer count on that advantage. I don't want to betray my interest in them or that their magic failed to pick me up so far so...*she sighed*...it may be time I flew back to Wolfneck.*

Astrid
another hour later

As she flew, she kept checking where she was, and with the small amount of moonlight available at the end of the month, she thought that she was in about the same place as she had been on the way in when she felt a familiar tingle again.

Does the box on legs that is up on the rock look for things? How about the box he looks at? It is not magic I am used to, but it could be that way, I suppose.

I don't understand magic, but I know that it can look for things.

Astrid
very early on 35th Quattro

She arrived back in Wolfneck at around midnight. Rani was still awake, and in the tavern nursing a leather tankard of what smelt to Astrid like warm glögg as she sat staring into the distance.

"My report can wait," Astrid said. "Even with the cloak of warmth on, I feel cold. I want one of those before I will say anything and perhaps another one or two more after that. We must teach Aine how to make it." Once her first drink had arrived, she sat down and, with the aid of a wet finger on the bench top in front of her, she outlined what she had seen and deduced.

Theodora
the evening of 2nd Quinque

Eventually, Theodora and Eleanor had completed their work and they had eight small rock crystals mounted in a series of little brackets so that they could be fastened to a piece of timber, like a ship. *They are all cabochon-cut, and it is not important that they are nearly all different sizes.*

"I will need to check these tomorrow," Theodora told Eleanor. "I need to make sure that they work before we set them in place, but what we have should be sufficient to cover enough boats for what we are about to do…and with some left over to distract our enemy."

She settled down to enjoy a night with nothing set aside for her to do. *For once I can just sit in the Mouse Hall, quietly listen to music and watch the dancing with a growing Fear curled up happily in my lap. Not that there is much of my lap left over. She is getting so big.*

Theodora
early on the 3rd Quinque, the Feast Day of Saint Philip

I have people standing around in the area outside the village wall where they can be clearly seen with at least thirty paces between them. Some of them have crystals on the ground under their feet and some do not. I do not know which do and do not. This should work. She smiled.

Theodora turned her back on them as she cast a conjuration of clairvoyance. With eyes closed, she turned around to face where the spell was cast. *In my mind, I can see many people there, but there are gaps in the pattern of people.* Opening her eyes, the gaps were filled in, she closed her eyes again and they disappeared in her mind. *The crystals work.*

The question is whether to leave tomorrow or to wait for those bringing in the Brotherhood girls to finish so that we can all go at once. I am not sure when that will be, but it will have to be soon by the look of the numbers of them around. I thought that we had worked out that it would take at least thirty days to get them all here.

I am sure that it is only thirteen days since the fall of Peace Tower and— She added up the numbers in her head from what she had seen and where she had been told that they came from *—there are already twenty-four of them here. I think that there are only another six to go. How are they doing that? They must be riding double and carrying nothing they don't need to take.*

At least Ayesha and Goditha are in charge and they are both sensible girls, so it must be safe. I can always spend the time making wands. Hopefully, I only need to wait another couple of days and all of them will be back. She smiled to herself. *If I have it right, then the sermon tonight should be interesting. It should be the Feast of Saint Mary Magdalene, the patron of sinners and those hoping for redemption...particularly the redemption of fallen women. Given the history of many of the women in Mousehole, it is a sermon that has always been preached with compassion and a sense of appropriateness here.*

At least in the past those listening understood the language of the sermon and what was being said. I wonder how it will be preached in translation. I am sure the next feast after this one will have even more of a special meaning for Theodule and his helpers. It is the feast of the Saints Cyril and Methodius... the patrons not only of the defence of the faith but also (and more importantly in this case) of translators. I am sure it will be preached with feeling.

Theodora
5th Quinque, the Feast Day of Saint Thomas

Two saddles had arrived in Mousehole the night before, and now five, four of them carrying double loads, and with a carpet rolled up across the last, flew out. *No more people will be brought to the battle from the village, but as many as can be transferred north from among the riders will be. Our new Khitan and kataphractoi will be bringing all the horses back to our home.*

I am sure that we will even try and bring in most of those who are with the carts from further back. Having experienced crew to man the ballistae, without taking away from handling the River Dragon, *might be important in what is to come. Even its little stone throwers, much smaller than the one Ariadne used against the Brotherhood, and really only as strong as the dart throwers were on Peace Tower, can far outrange most wands and battle spells.*

Theodora

When they arrived in North Hole, Thord had news for them. *More than a dozen Dwarves are on the track ahead of us led by Stonecleaver himself. The Baron has considered that, seeing these might be the last of the Masters, he wants to be present when they die. Apparently, it is a matter of honour. He has even taken a druid and a mage along with him. Never get between a Dwarf and their honour.*

Rani
11th Quinque, the Feast Day of the Saints Cyril and Methodius

People are arriving in Wolfneck from all over and the taverns are filling. The village is more than full of people. They stay with locals, or in taverns, and they camp in the caravan area.

Once my wife arrived with the crystals, I had three nailed down on the edge of the docks. They will stay there, at least for now. Between them they will cover most of the berths, and the ships that are tied up alongside, with a protection from being spied on by magic from afar. From now on, unless someone physically flies overhead and actually uses their eyes (and I have saddles aloft to try and stop that) our enemies will not know how many ships are actually in the port or when we leave it.

It should give us some measure of surprise over our enemy if the rest of my plan succeeds. Surprise may not be essential, and it cannot be total, but even a little bit of surprise and uncertainty will help. If we can keep our opponents off-balance, then the people of the North are likely to be hurt less when it comes time for the battle. If we can make our enemy die and yet save our people, that is the best way to run a fight. The serious business of getting everyone familiar with the plan and their part in it now must take place.

What I learnt in Haven as a Battle Mage, and what Theo-dear learnt in her lessons (the ones she admits not paying much attention to) are skills that are rare in The Land. The idea of co-ordinating an attack from different directions, and using different troops for different roles, is alien to most people.

It seems that all over the West, people just arrive on a battlefield with their forces and only then look at what they face. If they can, each side then moves their forces around until they are happy and then, almost by mutual agreement, they attack each other. If you arrive ready to fight on that piece of ground and without having to move your forces around first, as the Brotherhood tried to do, you will usually win, even if you are outnumbered.

We will be taking the five largest ships, each with a crystal affixed to them. Besides the River Dragon, *there will be a drakkar and three knorr. It will be crowded on all the vessels, but we will all fit, if we have good weather. The men and women from Wolfneck, apart from the Rangers, will be on the other smaller craft and everyone else will, somehow, cram onto the* River Dragon.

To make the crowding worse, Ariadne has insisted on bringing the larger ballistae on board. Not only had it been slung under saddles and moved here, but somehow Astrid organised for the carts and their drugged horses to also be lifted by using most of the saddles. They were taken to outside Evilhalt for Tāriq to take on home when the Khitan bring the other horses through there.

I had to defer to Ariadne on this. She quite sensibly pointed out that although Astrid had not seen the missing dromond yet, it can arrive at any time and her weapon has double the range of the lighter ones. We could need that extra range if the other ship has war rockets as well as flame weapons.

I do notice that she neglected to say how she would use her giant rock-throwing crossbow from the crowded deck of the River Dragon, *but I am sure we will do what needs must. If we need it, we may have to aim by turning the ship around a fixed line. I can imagine Olympias' reaction to that idea in the middle of a battle.*

Rani
15th Quinque, the Feast Day of both Saint Simon and Saint Dymphna

*E*verything is ready, and no more people are arriving to be crammed on board somehow. We could have gone on any of the five days before now, but it is not until today, and the night before Easter that the seas have been deemed to be calm enough for the heavily overloaded craft to set out. At least the delay will make our enemies even more unsure as to what we are doing.

At the Hesperinos service at sundown, Father Christopher led the service for the Orthodox present, including a good strong blessing as he did so that used all the power of all the priests before we set off. They will be sleeping as we sail, and regaining their strength for the healing that they are sure to be needed for.

The crowded boats were soon underway, while overhead flew the carpet and the saddles. *Siglunda is with us and I have left Old Magnus in charge. He is the only one with the respect necessary to get obedience from those left behind. He will be trying to get those in the village to make the place look as normal as possible to anyone who watches.*

At least the people here understand about this maskirovka. People have been getting on boats and staying there for a few hours over the last few days, and so I hoped that will cover if anyone happens to be watching when people board, and a good attendance of the faithful at church has been fairly normal over the last few days as well.

Whilst the rest of the flyers kept close around the ships to stay covered by the spells in the crystals, Astrid and Ayesha, with a rope held between them to keep contact, put on their rings and flew ahead on the first stage of the attack.

Although the two women are confident in their task, I am not, and both of their husbands seem concerned as well. I think that it is a lot to ask the two of them to attack up a mountainside in the night against far greater numbers, but they are still the only ones with the magic and the experience for this necessary task.

Astrid and Ayesha just turned to each other and grinned when I explained their part to them. I suppose that it is, after all, one of the roles that Ayesha trained for, and Astrid, may the demons take her, just thinks of it all as fun, as something to keep her amused.

Chapter XXXIX

Astrid
15th Quinque, the Feast Day of both Saint Simon and Saint Dymphna

As they climbed, Astrid looked back and saw the ships settling into their formation. *The* River Dragon *is in the lead. Svein's former drakkar, still trying to dance through the waves (although it has more than twice its normal crew, and a freeboard of only a hand) is leading the other three lumbering craft with most of the people on board.*

The Wolfneck vessels are supposed to stay together, and Siglunda is in the drakkar to try and ensure this. With the wind coming nearly from the west, the northern craft are beating along a nice long starboard tack. We really did need to have fine weather for this. I just hope that it stays that way. Even losing one craft would be a big loss for Wolfneck.

Already the River Dragon *is pulling ahead of the other four as more sails are raised on her. I can see almost all our people with any experience are up in the masts. I am sure that it is far better standing on a rope and hanging onto a yard than being below in one of the holds.*

The River Dragon *is supposed to reach somewhere around where the detection barrier probably is, the place where I felt a tingle, well ahead of the others. The ships from Wolfneck are not expected to get to the same barrier until near dawn. By then the* River Dragon *should be making landfall off the east of Neron Island and we will have finished our part.*

Astrid turned away from the ships behind and went back to paying attention to how tight the rope was between the two saddles. *If it is too tight, we risk pulling it out of each other's hands and if it is too loose then we will collide.*

It is hard to fly in formation with someone that you cannot see, and when only one of you can be heard.

They flew on through the night. *The moons are well up, and although Panic is but a declining sliver, Terror is near full and provides a good supply of light when there is no cloud in the way. There is, however, a good supply of cloud and around half of the sky is covered. Hopefully that will help us when we arrive, as will the wind.*

Looking below, Astrid could see that the wind seemed moderate and the waves had many frequent white horses on them. Even though Ayesha could not reply to what she said, she kept up a stream of talk as much to keep herself awake as for any other purpose.

Astrid
much later that night

A strid felt the tingle of the field of detection around the island and called out to let Ayesha know that they had reached that point. *From now on we cannot risk taking the rings off.* They kept flying ahead through the night with the light on East Zarah now clearly visible.

While they were still far enough away, Astrid slowed them down and quietly explained what she wanted to do. She had noticed a sort of path winding up to the summit, but she wanted to avoid that.

I can see that tonight the Insak-div is the one who has the watch on top of the rock. We will circle around to where the tent is in the lee of the prevailing wind, land and move up the slope with the wind in our faces. She tested the temperature outside the cloak. *It is a cold night and the wind will make it far colder up where he is. Hopefully, that will slow him a bit.*

Given what happened to us in Greatkin, I have to assume that, once we enter the light we will become visible. We will land out of the light and then, using our normal skills, stalk our prey up the mountain. I will tackle the Insak-div and Ayesha can start on the others. She can take the box-watcher first and then try and work her way through them.

Hopefully, she will have the good luck to take the supposed mage first. Magnus has told us that, even assuming that all of the mages are still alive and no more have been brought in from somewhere, there are normally only seven mages living here on the island. I have been there many times and I did not know that.

Magnus said that, seeing that detection is usually a specialty of earth mages, it would make sense for the one on the mountain to be of that ilk. More importantly, Magnus also said that both the most powerful and the least are earth mages, and it is not likely to be the senior one who will be sitting bored on a cold mountaintop.

Ayesha has the pendant that'll protect against most magic. It hadn't helped her in Haven, but Rani said that the spell that was used there, cast as it was from the other side of The Land by compulsion, would have had far more mana in it than the crystal had been made to deal with. It should work here even if it is some of the more normally powerful magic that she faces, say something from one of the stronger local casters.

I can see a spot outside the lit zone behind a rock that will be a good place to leave the saddles. They won't be seen there from the lookout. Whispering instructions, she slowly led them down to it. She landed and looked up. *I cannot see the Insak-div from here.* "Good luck." She hopped off her saddle and soon felt the rope drop. *Ayesha is down and moving as well. Now we go to work.*

Ayesha

*T*his is frustrating. Astrid can talk to me and I can say nothing back. Yes, her ring is less powerful than mine, and she needs her cloakpin as well to stop any magical detection, but we both move silently enough that we should not need the extra misdetection. If we are to keep doing this sort of thing, it is me who needs to have a new ring made and not her.*

Allah akbar, Astrid has brought us down to a good spot, drawing in the rope as she did so. A whisper told Ayesha that Astrid was off her saddle and waiting for her to move. She used the only communication she had and dropped the rope before heading off to the right around the rock. Ayesha adjusted her headdress so that only her eyes were visible as she moved.

We are on an old mountain. It has alpine fell-field vegetation and cold-eroded, lichen-crusted rocks pushed bare of the soil by endless cycles of frost and thaw. Between them are growing hardy cushion plants and mosses. Underfoot the soil is moist and soft. I feel at home. Allah is Merciful and there is cover everywhere if a person is careful and is willing to take their time instead of rushing.

Ayesha did not even think of drawing a blade. *I assume that I became visible the instant that I rounded the boulder. I am using my hands to help me move up the steep slope almost as much as I am using my feet.* She looked up.

The watcher above can see something down on the shore of the island easier than he can see me. He stands on a huge boulder with the box-on-legs and he would have to come right to the edge and look down to see me, and he doesn't seem to be doing that as I have not seen him since we landed. As a matter of fact, as I have moved up the slope, I have heard the wind bring me the sound of him stamping his feet and loudly blowing on his hands, even though he is unseen.

The same wind I feel will be far stronger on the top, and it will be making it seem far colder there. It seems that he has not learnt to ignore the cold, and from what I saw as we came in, he does not seem to be well enough dressed to help enough overcome the chill. Suddenly there was a loud sneeze from above. *Yes, he is cold up there.*

It was not long before they were in the lit area. *Bright lights always lead to there being shadows. I can use them.* Ayesha looked around her whenever she reached a good-sized boulder and was finally rewarded by seeing a glimpse of Astrid off to the left. *We have moved well apart.* She checked around. *No, I cannot be seen from above.*

She waved broadly at Astrid and the sudden movement at the edge of the other woman's vision eventually attracted her attention. She grinned and waved back before going back into her stalk. *She does not move up the slope as I do. She moves more like a hunting cat instead of a person, even with her spear in one hand.*

At least we both now realise that we have lost our invisibility. After Greatkin we expected that, and it is now confirmed. From what I can see, I should be coming up to where the watchers are camped with the tent between me and the man with a box.

Astrid should come up near what she had said seemed to be the place where they go up and down to the top, but from what little I have seen of the Insak-div, he stands well over six hands taller than even Astrid does. He might just jump down anywhere and ignore the ledges that the others use to go up and down. They are probably too narrow for his feet to be comfortable with, anyway.

Ayesha reached the last part of the climb over a talus slope of tumbled boulders lying where once a pinnacle of stone had stood, until it had gradually crumbled away and fallen, leaving the boulder above as its last remnant.

The frost and snow are now slowly reducing the smaller boulders into becoming the dirt in the fell-field slope below us. She felt the rough dolomite under her hands. *At least the going is quiet unless I slip, and these boulders are not likely to allow a foot to slip if I am careful. Allah, the Just, has been good to me.*

Soon the tent was visible. She cautiously looked up. *The Insak-div still cannot not be seen at all…* and then, just as she guardedly looked across, *I can just see the man with the box. He seems to be sitting on a stool and facing where the path comes around the boulder. From the glimpse that I took earlier, Astrid is moving at about the same speed as me…* She briefly looked up at the stars.

We have been a long time about our task. It is a hard stalk up a hill, and what is more, we don't know when the River Dragon *will hit the detection barrier.* She decided to wait a few more minutes, to allow Astrid more time, and so settled down as she cautiously chose and drew her weapon.

Earlier I had thought of using the pesh-kabz for my left hand and the kindjal for the right. However, the stabbing dagger has served me well so far on its own, and although the target wears no armour that I can see, I will try to grab him across the mouth with my right hand, to stop him calling out, while I use the left to find his heart.

Ayesha
a few minutes later

I think that the time has come for me to start. She left her kindjal in its sheath and moved forward. Above her, she could hear the Insak-div grumbling as he stamped his feet, blew on his hands, and sneezed a massive sneeze again.

It is blowing far stronger where it is exposed up top, but even here below, the wind whispers roughly among the rocks and my movements go undetected. Even the faint crunch of gravel between the cushion plants that make up much of this platform is disappearing. She reached a position behind the man.

The box he looks into is on its own table ahead of where he sits. It doesn't make sense. There is a series of pale green circles visible on it, and a green line sweeps around in a circle. It is a ghostly green colour on black and it shows…nothing.

On the same table there is a gold and sapphire amulet, and another made of opal and what looks like iron. She thought about what Theodora and Rani had told them. *The first will be some sort of detection device and the other one is possibly a talker. I still have no idea about the box, but a rope or cable of some sort leads from it up to the boulder.* She stopped and thought again.

The way he slouches, his heart is too hard for me to reach if I hold him still. She changed her mind and crouched down. *Allah akbar.* Covering his mouth with her right hand, she plunged the pesh-kabz into his brain from under the chin through the top of his spine and stirred it around in a circle. As she did that, she moved him softly backwards.

I am lucky. His death throes are only a brief spasm, although I can smell that his bowels have let go. Moving him back has knocked over the stool that he sat on, but the mossy platform of low and soft button plants muffles any noise that it made as it fell.

She laid him aside where she would not trip over the body and put the stool beside him. *Now it is time for the tent. Someone in there snores, only softly, but they snore. Some light spills in. It is more of a lean-to than a tent and it has to be tall to let the Insak-div in.*

Wiping the blood from the pesh-kabz onto the watcher it came from, she put it back into its sheath and prepared to change blades. *From here on in I will be fighting more than just killing.*

She drew the kindjal and made sure that there was a dagger ready for her left hand when she needed it. *In the meantime, I will keep it empty. A light is blinking…* She turned back towards the box. *The sapphire is pulsing with a cold blue light and on the green circles there is now a dot at the edge. Whatever the box is, it sees through Theodora's spell.*

As she watched, the one bright dot was sometimes joined by others. *They are tiny and far harder to see, and they flicker in and out. Whatever the box is, that will be the* River Dragon *and the saddles that it is finding then. It seems that I have chosen to move in to make my attack only just in time. Allah has indeed been very merciful.*

Astrid

I am angling my way up to the left. It is hard for me to move with my spear in one hand. I didn't even think about bringing my bow as well. I really need both hands to safely move up and over the boulders. Luckily, there are some patches of this terrain within the area that Wolfneck sometimes patrols, so I am not unfamiliar with it. She looked up.

Most of the time the Insak-div cannot be seen, and when he is visible, his back is often towards me. He is mostly looking west. I am in the lit area now and must assume that I can be seen. I am above most of the boulders, and the ground is soft and damp beneath my feet. The soft squish of the damp moss will be inaudible above the sound of the wind.

The problem for me is not just the shaft, but also the blade on my spear. If the angle is wrong the bright lights will glitter off it and be seen. She tried to stay behind boulders as much as she could as she went up and around.

Something is moving. Ayesha is waving from behind a rock. Well, that is clear then. The Masters don't like us being invisible. She waved back and returned to the task. *Ayesha is at around the same level on the slope as me.*

That is good. Now, I don't like it, but there is no way forward without using the path. She looked up.

The man with the box is around the corner of the boulder and the Insak-div is looking the other way at present. He is a big boy, isn't he? She grinned. *I cannot imagine little Ayesha trying to take him on one-to-one. She would come up to his elbow and would have to tackle his groin or legs as she could not reach anything else.*

I now have no choice in how I get to move. I have to make a quick rush up the slope. She gave a soft sigh of relief even as she shifted. *Even to me the crunch of the gravel on it is soft and almost completely absorbed by the damp ground and my soft leather hunting boots.* She was soon pressed against the boulder. *My heart is pounding so loud it feels that someone must hear it.*

She inched around to where the handholds were for a person to come down off the rock. *Now to wait; until the Insak-div moves, waiting is my job. Ayesha has to take care of all of the others on her own. I have the one that, even with my size and strength enhanced by charms, still has the advantage of me in both reach and strength.*

This could be dangerous, even for me. After I flew past earlier, I knew that it would be dangerous. Even if Basil and I had not said anything about risk to each other, our lovemaking last night had a certain intensity to it.

Did I hear something around the corner, a soft clatter? She resisted the urge to peek. *Like a mountain lion poised to strike, I am one with the rock behind me. I am beneath a slight overhang, and even if he looks down, the Insak-div is unlikely to see me.*

I need to just be still and focus. I need to listen hard. Calm the breathing. Time passes. A hunter must wait for the shot, and I might only get one. It is like waiting for a bear with a spear when there will be no chance to use a bow, and I have done that.

Saint Kessog, the patron of those who fight against monsters, he will be my patron. Surely this man-shaped thing above is a monster. Bianca likes Ursula, but I fight monsters. Sometimes they are human-shaped ones, but they are still monsters, and I haven't been a virgin for a long time now.

Astrid began silently praying to her new patron Saint, asking him to forgive her late choice of him. *You should think of it, instead of being late, as being a careful selection as I have been mulling over this choice for a year, and as I am sure you realise, the choice of a patron is not a choice that a person should make lightly.*

She promised to get an icon of him as soon as she could. *Bianca bought a beautiful miniature mosaic one under a crystal cover in Ardlark that she wears at the centre of her crucifix…I promise you one of those. It cost a small fortune…* Astrid kept her senses alert even as she silently sought aid from her new patron.

There was noise. A gurgling scream like that is quite clear in the quiet night. Overhead I can hear movement. She gripped her spear and her heart again began to pound as she said a few final words. *A brief amen and then I grip my spear in both hands and get ready for action as a crunching noise made by heavy feet in nailed boots on rock comes from above.*

Ayesha

*E*nough *of the lights, they will wait. Now for the people in the tent.* Ayesha looked into it. *The bright lights outside are partly cut out by its overhang, but it is still far brighter inside than it would be on even the brightest night. Beside the entrance is a big empty spot. I guess that is for the Insak-div, and another further along is for the dead watcher.*

A tarpaulin is laid over the bumpy but soft ground to keep them dry from below. Four other bodies lie in a row with their heads under the rock and their feet sloped slightly downhill. The snorer sounds like they are the last one on the other end of the tent.

The floor of the tent is littered with clothes, armour, weapons and boxes and pouches. How they move around without falling over, I have no idea. Maybe they don't and perhaps every time they move, they wake someone else up; whichever it is, it will be hard even for me to move without something shifting underfoot. I have to try...

A glance behind showed no sign of Astrid, and the sapphire was still blinking on the table. *I hope that this location is the lookout for the entire island. If it isn't, then the Masters know about the attack well before they are supposed to...*

She felt forward with her feet, moving things aside and carefully transferring her weight forward. She came up to the first of the men and knelt down beside him. *He is a big man with a beard and braided hair...a local man who is at least as big as my husband, or Astrid, and a full three hands taller than I am.*

Shift the kindjal to an overhand grip and get my left hand ready to put over his mouth...strike into the heart with the blade...I have to try to keep him silent... It didn't work. A strangled cry erupted out of him in a muffled yell. *His lungs are already filling with blood from his lacerated heart, with a blade pinning him down so it comes out already as a despairing gurgle of doom.*

The man's body fought her even as it died. Arms and legs flailed, and he hit the man sleeping beside him. She glanced along the row. *He is stirring...as is another Human. The Kharl is still snoring, but that won't last long.* Taking the kindjal from the man's mouth, she quickly pulled her dagger out of its sheath with her left hand.

"What the fuck…?" The sound erupted from the one beside the dying man as he turned over and saw what was happening beside him. *He is trying to sit up and grope for a weapon at the same time…* "Orn… Wake up, damn you… wake the Kharl…" *He is getting louder as he goes on. The man beneath me is only moving feebly now.*

She leapt onto the one who was calling out as he clumsily drew a sword from beside him. It tangled in the blankets and his mouth opened again in another cry as he saw a dagger flashing for his face. He tried to dodge and scream but Ayesha was too quick. *While he dodged that one, he doesn't see the other larger blade, now held underhand, strike into his chest under the sternum.*

Don't wait to see the result…roll clear…the next one is getting a wand out…too late to do anything but…Allah the Merciful… Ayesha felt something wash over her as a spell of some sort hit her and recoiled back onto the caster. *The ring worked. He has fallen back screaming and grabbing for something beside him. He is hurt badly.*

She changed her focus again. *The one beside me has his sword out now, and holding his other hand flat on his stomach, he strikes at me. I collect it on my dagger…At that angle it lacks power.* She was able to return the blow with a thrust from the kindjal that took him in the throat. *His eyes go wide, and a bubbling scream erupts as he drops the sword.*

His hands hover. He doesn't know what part of his body to try and hold together. I leave him with that dilemma. She looked across. *The mage has an axe in his hand now, and he is coming for me on hands and knees, just waving it ahead of him hoping to fend me off as he moves. He is hurt badly but the Kharl…yes, an Isci-kharl as Astrid had thought…is standing up.*

He sleeps in his armour. He isn't much taller than I am, but he is wide. He is already up and advancing and inside a tent is no place to face him. I am light on my feet and need to dodge rather than trade blows while I trip over bedding. Ayesha retreated outside, slashing at a rope with the kindjal as she went. *Away with the dagger and out with the pesh-kabz. He wears mail.*

The tent began to collapse as he emerged, and she took advantage of that to dance off to the left Ayesha stood on the collapsing tent where he could not see her. She planted the pesh-kabz into a kidney with a quick twist, withdrew the blade, and ducked down as the bent Kharl slashed blindly from under the cloth to where he thought she should have been.

He missed me, and the sudden turn has twisted the tent around his head. I stand and use the pesh-kabz on the flailing elbow and block left with the kindjal towards his blade. The first struck and grated on bone to a brief, accompanying scream of pain. The second briefly held his sword as he yelled again and used his knee to hit her in the groin and knock her over onto the ground.

Pain… She managed to keep her grip on her weapons, even as she lay there turning over to rise. *One arm hangs useless on him, the sword still locked in his hand. He is trying to get the tent away from his face. The mage is crawling out of the tent. He looks better. There is a flask in one hand. Allah help me.* She went for the Kharl again. *I have no defence, just an attack as his arm pulls the tent away from his head.* His eyes registered what was ahead of him and his mouth opened wide…

Ayesha thrust firmly as the kindjal went into his mouth and the pesh-kabz prodded across Ayesha's body, seeking his heart. The sharp-pointed blade ignored the mail and probed in, and the kindjal cut off his voice into a strangled scream. She pulled back. The Kharl fell writhing and clutching his face.

He is dying in a mess of gushing blood, enough of him. Now the mage is out of the tent, and on his feet. He is unsteady and weak, but he is up. Ayesha danced back and around as he came on, and as she hoped, stumbled over his dying friend. His eyes involuntarily went down.

Ayesha leapt forward. *The pesh-kabz is too fragile to use for a parry against a determined stroke from that axe, but it can hold pressure against a haft and just keep the weapon out of play.* She closed and stood face to face with the mage. *His breath reeks.* She drove the kindjal home under his ribs, reaching up towards his heart.

She held it in place and wriggled it before stepping back and pulling it free with a faint sucking sound. *It seems that they always look surprised as the pain and the imminence of death strike them. Does he have a contingency in place? No, he is just crumpling. Perhaps he has already used it.*

She stepped forward and slashed across his throat. *He bleeds out like a butchered goat.* She turned her head. *The last one… What is he doing? He holds his guts with one hand. His throat bleeds, but it is obviously not fatal, and he is drinking from a bottle.*

"Mawmas" he said in Arabic as he groped again for his sword in the ruins of the tent.

Ayesha was surprised. "No…I am a ghazi and servant of the Allāh wadhu, the one God, bringer of justice and your nemesis…kāfirūn pig. Die and go to visit Shaitan, your lover." *I am not going to risk the footing in there. Outside I hold the advantage.* She slashed at another rope and again at the next as she moved.

I have been so absorbed in my task that this momentary inaction allows me to realise that there is a roaring from behind me and the clash of weapons, and it has been there for some time. Astrid is still fighting… I have time. She changed the blade in her left hand to a dagger and held it down against her forearm.

This one is being cautious and cutting his way free without moving forward. He is now free from the waist up. He took another swig of the bottle and shook it. *It is now empty, and he throws it away. He is intact again, but he will still be weak from the cost of healing. Cautiously, he edges forward. He is feeling his way.*

She feinted at him and he struck out with his sword. She caught it on the dagger in her left hand and trapped the blade of the sword between her smaller blade and its brass hilt as she struggled to keep pressure on it. *He pulls it back to free it as he is moving…and stumbles and falls forward. The last one on their feet wins…*

She quickly knelt onto his back as he fell and plunged the dagger towards his heart. *And again…and again…He is struggling and screaming and trying to turn.* She stayed on top and he lay flat beneath her, face down. She dropped her kindjal as she used that to hold his right arm and steady herself as he struggled.

He is starting to shake me free. I need better-enhanced blades. Another blow to his chest…He shudders. Another and he goes limp…and another, to be sure. Breathing hard, as if she had been in a long race, Ayesha rolled over in the blood and wreckage, her right hand feeling blindly for her kindjal as she noticed the struggle still going on before her.

Astrid

I *can hear footsteps above. He is going to jump.* A mass appeared in front of her from above. *I felt his landing through my feet. His hands are above his head, holding something.* Without thinking, she stepped out from the rock and thrust forward in a lunge. *We both have mail on and mine is riveted…Is his? No, it isn't.*

As he landed with his hands in reflex above his head, holding his weapon in both hands, her spear blade hit and plunged into his torso for well over a hand's depth, driving her back with the force of impact as she thrust inside him. She then pulled back and out as he spun around, roaring. Astrid nearly lost her blade as, spinning, he struck out with something in his right hand.

It was a clumsy blow. What is that weapon? It is sort of like a curved sword on a stick or a very long axe with one end held against the haft. It is held again halfway along its length at the end of the shaft and the rest projecting forward into a point like a spear. She dodged as it swung again. *If I parry that with my spear haft, I will lose my spear.*

The two feinted back and forward for a moment as each assessed the other.

Still, he is wounded. I might have cut one of the muscles of his back. I think that it only just slows him a bit. I was probably quicker to start with, but he is still far stronger.

I cannot oppose his blade directly. I have to shunt it aside with my blade held forward. My blows are restricted by my need to defend. He has his left hand covered by the curving blade and his right on the bare haft, and feints forward and back.

"You come to Murgrątt, pretty girl." *He speaks in Darkspeech.* "Murgrątt got plenty for little girl." He was swinging as he spoke, and Astrid was frantically parrying. "Give me little spear, and I give you my big one." He leered and swung, and she parried with her blade, steering his towards the ground. *'sblood he is strong.*

"I break your little spear so no use to you and then I fuck you. I can fuck you alive, or I fuck you dead, you still be warm. Which you want, little girl?" *He is quicker there...*As Astrid dodged and ducked, his blade slid off her mail and she felt a stab of pain along her back. She thrust even as she felt it, and was rewarded with a great yelp, as she slashed the tough and scaly skin of his leg with the point of the spear.

They both pulled back and settled into a series of blows, backwards and forwards on the small platform. Astrid felt the pain in her back. *The blow didn't penetrate the mail, but it feels like a rib or something is broken. It hurts, but his side is streaming blood and he seems to be slowing. Damn him; a Human would have died from that first blow.*

He has realised that he is losing. His pace picked up as he just roared in rage. *No longer can I attack. Just barely can I defend as my mail has to take several of the blows. I am hurting...a lot.* She was stepping back and back and then... *My feet are on the path down. Suddenly, he has run out of puff and I am able to resume. Now, it is his turn to be forced back and back.*

He was near to the rock and his blade, drawing back to strike, caught on the rough surface beside him. Momentarily it was held. Astrid thrust straight ahead with all her weight on the blow and watched the blade sink to its crosspiece in his chest through his mail, which now had several rents in it.

He looks down and gives the huge and windy roar, such as a wounded whale makes when it knows that it is dying in sea surrounded by bloody foam. His hands drop his strange blade and come towards my shaft to break it.

Frantically, she pulled back and twisted as he tried to stop her. Astrid's blade came free as his hands grasped at it. He now screamed a curiously high-pitched scream as he lost a finger, and his eyes started to glaze. He looked directly at her.

I swear that I can see a mix of hate and lust and pain all combined together in them. She thrust forward again, this time into the base of the throat. He died, and she had to keep her hands firm on her spear shaft to stop it being torn from her grasp as he did so. *His face is like a huge, dark green-scaled bear, with the look of a small hurt child painted on it.* Astrid looked up to see Ayesha staring at her from twenty paces away. *Thank you for your blessings, Saint Kessog.*

"Sorry I took so long. I guess you have taken yours." She stepped forward over the body of the Insak-div. *The world is swaying. Is it an earthquake? No, it must be a reaction to the excitement of the fight. I feel weak.*

Ayesha came running over. "Drink this," she said, and thrust a bottle at her. *Not sure why I should...I suppose I should be good.* Astrid complied. She went to give it back, but Ayesha made her take another draught and then another... *My head is clearing...* "Feeling better now?" Astrid nodded. *I am.* She looked down.

There are rents in my mail... Big rents. My enchanted coat that had once belonged to Thorkil, now needs a lot of work done on it. I can see rapidly healing skin clearly through the rents, and I can feel the already-drying blood coating my side. She winced at the feeling of new-healed skin and the still-broken ribs.

Ayesha

"**Y**ours was harder than mine were, I think." Impulsively, Ayesha hugged Astrid. She was rewarded with a wince of pain. "Sorry... Now look at this." She led Astrid over to the box and together they looked at its green circles with the line that swept around and around and a small bunch of dots. *The sapphire is still blinking, but nothing comes from the opal and iron object.*

"That will be a talker, and we will probably hear from that in the morning," said Astrid. "I will look after those two in case they can track them. My enchantment may stop that." She scooped them up and dropped them in her pouch.

"What do we do with this one?" She pointed at the box. "I don't think that it is magic at all. I think it is a machine, and see...it is linked to the box up top. What if the top box is the seeing part... It is round like an eye, but it is flat, not round. Perhaps from the mountain it can see a long way and this part just shows what it sees."

Ayesha nodded. *I am no mage, but that sounds reasonable.* "But what do we do with it? If we cut the cord this part may not hear the other box, but someone who knows what it is may be able to fix it, and do we want that?"

"We will start by cutting them apart," said Astrid. She limped over to where the strange axe-weapon that had nearly killed her lay. "I am keeping this, and

I am going to learn to use it," she said as she picked it up and walked back. "It can thrust and defend and cut and, trust me on this, it is terrifying to face. I can tuck it into a loop on the saddle and still have a spear and bow with me."

She raised the axe thing and brought it down where the cord lay on the soft ground. It parted, but a series of bright white sparks spat out of the end coming from the box. *Just like a miniature lightning bolts grounding all around as the air takes on the smell left behind by lighting.*

Astrid...almost in reflex as a defence from the lightning...raised the axe-thing again and brought it down on the box and the screen. There was a shattering of glass and more spitting and hissing from inside the box as the lights went out on it. Astrid shrugged.

"I guess that this end won't work now," she said. "I am sure that it would be hard to fix something that looks like that," and she nudged the shattered remnants of the machine with little sparks still running around inside it with the axe thing. She looked up to the boulder. "What about that one? Do we break it as well?"

Ayesha shrugged "We should look at it first." She grabbed hold of the rope. "It is heavy. It must be made of metal." She pulled and kept pulling until there was a crash from up on the boulder, and then she pulled some more, as Astrid took another sip of healing potion.

She kept pulling until the box came crashing down onto the ground. She grinned. "It looks like both ends are broken now. Let us search the mage. You said that he had a wand the last time you saw him, and he used another one on me."

In the end we have found four wands. There is one where he dropped it after using it on me, another in a pouch of its own, and two more in an open pouch. We have three rings from him and an amulet of a spider in a pentangle with little red gems as eyes that was attached to the cloak. "He was supposed to be an earth mage—this will be something to help him cast then. Now it may help one of our mages."

Looking around, Astrid had an idea. She grabbed the wand that was on its own and started pointing it at things.

My spear causes it to make a quiet beep noise, as do the other wands and the rings, and even the amulet. She tried other things. *The axe-thing makes it go beep, and the mage's axe, and the sword of the first man I killed, and there is even a little stove-thing like the one that Rani made, and of course, the lights.*

They brought the saddles up, taking off their rings as they walked when invisibility returned to them as they left the lit area. They then loaded the things that were magic, and portable, onto their saddles and tied them down so that they would not lose them. Then, taking the rope up again and replacing their magic, they headed back to the *River Dragon*.

Astrid
a little later

A s they went, they detoured and flew over Skrice. *The village still seems to be quietly asleep in the night. Hopefully, the people there will not know that something is amiss until their watch point fails to report to them in the morning. They will then either have to head up the mountain to go and see what is wrong or else start looking for an attack.*

When they get to the top of the mountain, it may all be useless. Although they will know that the people up there were attacked and died, hopefully the device that sees through the hiding magic of the Mice and other attackers is now dead.

Of course, from up there, if it is daylight, they will be able to look out towards the ocean and see the ships that are coming against them, but perhaps it will be too late for them to do anything about it.

Chapter XL

Gamil

*A*nother *intervention that failed and I cannot help gloating at that. The Adversaries are growing desperate. Can they risk making yet another? This one is perhaps not as blatant as the other and fewer saw it, indeed it is almost disguised as if it were magic, but the technology that they have given to their people on Neron is at just as high a level and so is just as illegal.*

I now have another complaint to write out and lodge. What is more, I now know that, just as my own sensors are baffled, so are some of those of the Adversaries. That fact in itself is interesting. I wonder what else they have given to their minions.

Gamil fanned her wings as she sat back to start contemplating the words to use in the official complaint. *Surely, there can be nothing else to be revealed. At any rate, if there is anything else to be brought into play it will have to already be on the planet. There is that much consolation at least. Now, though, I must wonder if the ships are going into a trap, despite their element of surprise.*

Cast

Aaron Skynner: In his 30s, a tanner and widower from Glengate, comes to Mousehole seeking a wife. He marries Aine.

Adara ferch Glynis: Cousin of Bryony from Rising Mud and in love with her. She was rescued from the Master's servants in Pavitra Phāṭaka. She marries Stefan in an arrangement that allows her to share her co-wife with him. Her identical twin daughters are Finnabhair and Sinech.

Adrian Climacus: 10 year old older brother of Menas, added to the crew of the *River Dragon* at Southpoint as cabin boy and apprentice.

Aigiarn: Or Nogay Aigiarn, late of the Lion Clan, marries Hulagu, their daughter is Enq.

Aimee Tate: Mayor of Glengate and retired trader.

Aine ferch Liban: A former slave from Bloomact in The Swamp, she is now the brewer and distiller for Mousehole. She marries Aaron and their son is Abel.

Alaine: Or Boladtani Alaine, late of the Eagle clan, marries Hulagu, their daughter is Surtak.

Anahita of the Axe-beaks or **Vachir Anahita Ursud:** Khitan girl from Mousehole and Hulagu's köle, she is the mother of Būrān and Baul. She becomes one of the Clan of the Horse and marries Dobun along with Kāhina.

Anastasia: Insakharl sailor sent from Darkreach to help crew the *River Dragon*. She is married to Cyrus and their daughter is Leukothea.

Andronicus: Secretary to the Metropolitan of the North for Orthodox.

Anne: The new name of one of the prostitutes rescued from Warkworth. She is now a sailor on the *River Dragon*, one of the Saints and eventually wife of Marianus Gerontas.

Antonio Chino: Mage and confidante of the Count of Toppuddle. He is killed.

Antonio Scarlatti: Captain of the militia in Warkworth

Apinaya Sarin: Subadar (minor officer) of the River Patrol of Haven based at Garthang Keep

Archibald Neville: Baron of Toppuddle and servant of the Masters. He is killed.

Ariadne Nepina: An Insakharl (part Alat-kharl) from Antdrudge. She is partly trained as an engineer but wanted a quieter life as a brick and tile maker and layer after her parents are killed in an industrial accident. She moves to Mousehole and marries the Hob Krukurb. Their daughter is Nikê.

Arthur Garden: Farmer and youngest son (of four) from Evilhalt. He comes to Mousehole seeking land and a wife. He was talked into coming by Ulric. He ends up courting and marrying Make.

Asad ibn Sayf: Widower from Doro. He is a farmer and becomes the husband of Hagar and Rabi'ah. His daughter with Hagar is Alia and his son with Rabi'ah is Rāfi.

Asticus Tzimisces: One of three kataphractoi (heavy cavalry) from Darkreach who comes to join Mousehole and is sent straight into the fray against the Brothers.

Astrid Tostisdottir (the Cat): A part-Kharl girl from Wolfneck, in the far north of The Land. She is married to Basil. Her first children are Freya Astridsdottir, "the Kitten", and Georgiou Akritas and the second set are Anna and Thorstein. Her youngest brother is Thorstein, now a priest. The Sea Nomads call her Rongomaiwhenua (the earth mother).

Atã ibn Rāfi: A widower from Mistledross. He is a timber-feller. He becomes the husband of Umm and Zafirah. His son with Umm is Achmed and with Zafirah is Sughdī.

Athanasios Nichomachi: The Exarkhos ton Basilikon, or commander, of the Basilica Anthropoi.

Atli Runeson: A water mage from Wolfneck.

Ayesha: A ghazi (called assassins by other cultures) of the Caliphate who is assigned by a Princess to guard Theodora. She is the minor daughter of Hāritha, the Sheik of Yāqūsa. She eventually marries Hulagu as his senior wife and has Hāritha, his fifth child and her first.

Aziz (Azizsevgili or Brave Lover): A Hobgoblin captured during the attack on Mousehole. He falls in love with Verily and converts to the Orthodox faith and marries her. Their sons are Saglamruh (Strong Spirit) and Sunmak (Gift). Daughters Qvavili (Flower) and Fear. His former name is Saygaanzaamrat (Plundered Emerald).

Basil Akritas or Kutsulbalik (nickname from great-grandfather): Is a mostly human (one sixteenth Kharl) who appears as a youth just out of his apprenticeship (although he is ten years older). He is an experienced secret police officer of the Antikataskopeía of Darkreach. He comes from Southpoint from a military family and is now married to Astrid and living in Mousehole, assigned to guard

Theodora by Hrothnog. Their first children are Freya Astridsdottir, "the Kitten" and Georgiou Akritas and the second set are Anna and Thorstein.

Basil Phocas: Consiliarius or chief priest of the Basilica Anthropoi.

Basil Tornikes: Orthodox Metropolitan of the North at Greensin.

Bianca: A foundling from Ashvaria now living in Mousehole and married to Father Christopher. Their first children are Rosa and Francesco. Their second are Diogenes and Rhodē. She is also a member of the Khitan Clan of the Horse and Hulagu is her adopted brother.

Bilqîs: A tiny girl, from a trade background in the Caliphate, she now lives in Mousehole as an apprentice mage. She marries Tāriq as his senior wife. Their daughter is Zainab.

Bjarni Arildson: An apprentice mage in Wolfneck.

Bo'orchu: Tar-Khan of the Jijig Khushuu, the Axe-beaks.

Bridget: The new name of one of the prostitutes rescued from Warkworth. She is now a sailor on the *River Dragon*, one of the Saints and eventually a wife of Marianus Gerontas.

Bryony verch Cathan: A freckled redhead from Rising Mud in the Swamp. Her husband (Conan ap Reardon) and father (Dafydd ap Comyn) were killed at her wedding and she was brought to Mousehole as a slave. She is now married to Stefan and her sons are Aneurin ap Stefan and Trystan. She is cousin, lover and sister-wife to Adara.

Candidas: Animal handler for Carausius from his second trip on. He is also a member of the Antikataskopeía and marryies Theodora Lígo.

Carausius Holobolus: Darkreach trader in fabric, spices or anything else. His guards are Karas & Festus, his animal handler is Candidas, his wife is Theodora and his daughter is Theodora Lígo.

Cast Thy Bread Upon Waters Nile, Sister: She is the wife of Joachim Nile and so also Third Disciple of the Brotherhood of Believers (although subservient in this role to her husband) and a General in her own right. She is responsible for home defence and also a priest.

Catherine: The new name of one of the prostitutes rescued from Warkworth. She is now a sailor on the *River Dragon*, one of the Saints and eventually a wife of Marianus Gerontas.

Cecilia: The new name of one of the prostitutes rescued from Warkworth. She is now a sailor on the *River Dragon*, one of the Saints and eventually a wife of Marianus Gerontas.

Chinggiz Arghun: Tar-Khan of the Thunder Lizard clan and Kha-khan of the entire Kara-Khitan.

Christopher Palamas, Father: The chief Orthodox priest for Mousehole and husband of Bianca. Their first children are Rosa and Francesco. Their second are Diogenes and Rhodē. He becomes suffragan Bishop of the Mountains.

Cosmas: Orthodox Metropolitan for Erave town, Glengate (and, at least in theory) the Swamp and Haven.

Cyrus: Insakharl sailor sent from Darkreach to help crew the *River Dragon*. He is married to Anastacia and their daughter is Leukothea.

Danelis: A former slave originally from Warkworth, she now lives in Mousehole. She marries Father Simeon. Their children are Epanxer or Brave and a daughter Mehre, or Silver.

Demetrios: Orthodox Metropolitan responsible for the southern independent villages.

Denizkartal (Sea Eagle): Boyuk-kharl and Olympias's bosun on the *River Dragon* and her eventual husband. Their daughter is Thalassa.

Dharmal: Dwarf and leader of the brigands who attack Bianca's caravan. He ruled Mousehole and acted as the main servant of the Masters in The Land. He was questioned and executed after the Mice overturned him.

Dobun: Or Tömörbaatar Dobun, late of the Clan of the Axe-beaks, becomes shaman of the Clan of the Horse and marries Anahita and Kāhina.

Dulcie: A former slave from Bathmor in The Swamp. She is now the Mousehole carpenter and marries Jordan. Their daughter is Rebecca.

Eleanor Fournier: Caravan guard from Topwin in Freehold, then a slave, she now lives in Mousehole and works as a jeweller. She is married to Robin Fletcher and is one of the first in the village to fall pregnant. They have adopted Aelfgifu, Gemma and Repent and have a daughter Bianca and twins Michael and Sara.

Elizabeth: An orphan from Trekvarna in Freehold and former slave who now lives in Mousehole. She is married to Thomas and mother of Virginia.

Enoch Malachi, Brother: First Disciple of the Brotherhood of Believers, spiritual and temporal head of that religion. He is married to Will-of-the-Lord Malachi.

Eustace: A mage from Toppuddle and servant of the Masters. He is killed.

Fātima: A slave in Mousehole from an unknown background in the Caliphate. As Fātima bint al-Fa'r (Fatima, daughter of the Mouse), she is now married to Hrothnog as the Empress of Darkreach and Ambassador of the Mice. They have a son.

Fear the Lord Your God Thatcher: She is the adopted daughter of Rani and Theodora.

Festus: Part-Kharl & guard for Carausius, a Darkreach trader in spices etc.

Fortunata: A former slave from Ashvaria and now dressmaker and embroiderer for Mousehole. She is the first wife of Norbert, along with Sajāh, and her son is Valentine and younger twins are Bryan and Alice.

Gallas Narchina: Insakharl sailor and sailmaker/carpenter added to the crew of the *River Dragon* in Southpoint. She is married to Gundardasc.

Gamil: Chief Predestinator on the Vhast project and one of the Shing-zu. She set in motion the events described in these books.

Gerolt Mikelson: Weaponsmith in Wolfneck and a prominent person.

Giles Ploughman: Former slave and farmer at Mousehole. He is married to Naeve. His first daughter is Peggy Farmer and his second is Beth.

Goditha: Former slave from Jewvanda. She is sister to Robin Fletcher and married to Parminder. She is the mason of Mousehole and an earth mage. She is regarded as the father of Melissa and Daniel Mason.

Grim Lorenson: An air mage from Wolfneck.

Gudrid: A girl from Wolfneck, greenish skin, friend of Astrid. Her brother was caught up in Svein's plot.

Guiseppe Frangetti: A Freehold spy in Warkworth, he had a cover as the owner of a gambling hall. He dies under a compulsion from his masters while being questioned.

Gukludaashiyicisi (strong carrier): A Hobgoblin of the Cenubarkincilari and a carter around their tribe. He becomes their first trader to the Dwarves. He decides to call himself Guk outside Dhargev.

Gundardasc Narches: Kichic-kharl cook and sailor added to the *River Dragon* in Southpoint. His wife is Galla.

Guthorm Hennningson: A junior fire mage in Wolfneck. He was apprentice to Ketil, who died for following the "Old Gods".

Habib: Insakharl sailor sent from Darkreach to help crew the *River Dragon*. He is married to Thomaïs and their children are Delphinia and Isidore.

Hagar: Former slave from a farming family outside Dimashq in the Caliphate, she lives in Mousehole. She becomes senior wife to Asad along with Rabi'ah. Her daughter is Alia.

Harnermês (Har-ner-meess): Young man from Gil-Gand-Rask. He becomes Jennifer's lover and joins the *River Dragon*. They marry before the birth of their daughter Goditha.

Haytor (Pretty Bull): A Hob who joins the Mice for the campaign in the North. He goes on to work for Guk.

Hrolf Maurindson: A skald or bard of Wolfneck.

Hrolf Vidarson: A weaver in Wolfneck and a prominent person.

Hrolfr Strongarm: Dwarven Baron of Oldike in the South-West Mountains.

Hrothnog: The immortal God-King of Darkreach and great-great grandfather of Theodora. He is now married to Fātima. At the start of the books his race is unknown, but he is not human. He is, in fact, one of the Daveen.

Hulagu: A young Khitan tribesman. His tribe and totem is the Dire Wolf. He becomes a part of Mousehole. His children are Khātun & Yesugai (with Kāhina), Būrān & Baul (with Anahita) and Hāritha (with Ayesha). He marries Ayesha, Aigiarn (daughter Enq), and Alaine (daughter Surtak) and becomes Tar-Khan of the reborn Clan of the Horse.

Hulagu: Tar-Khan of the Arslan, the Clan of the Lion.

Irene: Insakharl sailor sent from Darkreach to help crew the *River Dragon*. She is married to Sabas and their daughter is Polymnia.

It Shall Come to Pass: A slave girl from the Brotherhood brought to Camel Island to be sacrificed to establish a master pattern. She is usually called Pass.

Iyād ibn Walīd: Muslim Imam of the main mosque in Ardlark.

Jaap Josefson: Notary and accountant in Wolfneck and a prominent person.

Janibeg: Tar-Khan of the Ünee Gürvel, the Clan of the Cow-lizard.

Jennifer Wagg: Young woman, guard and sailor, from Deeryas. She was rescued from the Master's servants in Pavitra Phāṭaka where she was brought as a sacrifice. She ends up as partner to Harnermeess. They marry before the birth of their daughter Goditha Atalante.

Joachim Caster: Mage and Mayor of Warkworth.

Joachim Nile, Elder Brother: Third Disciple of the Brotherhood of Believers, he is the General of their Army and a senior priest. His wife is Cast Thy Bread Upon Waters Nile.

Job, Brother: Second Disciple of the Brotherhood of Believers. He is responsible for doctrine and also in charge of the Flails of God when they are not active in the field as cavalry and scouts. When in the field he is subordinate to the Third Disciple.

Jochi: Tar-Khan of the Bürged, the Eagle clan.

Jonas Smith: His real name is "All these Curses Shall Come Upon You Smith", an Inquisitor priest and brothel keeper in Warkworth. He is the main conduit for information on the south. He is executed.

Jordan Croker: A journeyman potter from Greensin. No more potters are needed there and he came to Mousehole seeking a place to settle and a wife. He marries Dulcie. Their daughter is Rebecca.

Justin Speller: Mage of Bidvictor, nearly as powerful as Rani. He is a water mage.

Kãhina of the Pack Hunters or Bodonchar Kãhina Jugin: Hulagu's köle and mother of Khãtun & Yesugai. She becomes one of the Clan of the Horse and marries Dobun along with Anahita.

Karas: Part-Kharl & guard for Carausius, a Darkreach trader in spices etc.

Kebek: Tar-Khan of the Bagts Anchin, the Pack Hunters.

Krukurb (Strong Frog): One of the Hobs who join the Mice for the campaign in the North. He later marries Ariadne. Their daughter is Nikê.

Lãdi: Former slave from the Caliphate, she is the chief cook at Mousehole and very skilled. She marries Nathanael.

Lakshmi: Former Havenite, she has converted and is now Orthodox and married to Harald Pitt. Their eldest son is George and their second is Henry. She is the apothecary and midwife for Mousehole.

Lawrence Woolmonger: A rich farmer and Mayor of Bidvictor. He fought as a kataphractoi at One Tree Hill and as Stefan's lieutenant at Peace Tower.

Leif Galdrar: The second most important mage in Wolfneck. He is an earth mage.

Loukia Tzetzina: Cooper and cabinet maker from Mistledross. She lost her family in an earthquake and has moved to Mousehole.

Magnus Mikkelson: The oldest and strongest mage in Wolfneck. He is an air mage.

Make Me to Know My Transgressions: Young woman from the Brotherhood brought as a slave to restock Mousehole. She is usually called Make.

Malik or Sudhipala Malik Jugin: A hunter of the Pack Hunter clan who helps Bianca and Hulagu defeat the bird demons and then escorts them to Evilhalt. He is also Kãhina's cousin. They meet him again in Glengate where he acts as the messenger of the Mice to gather the clans.

Maria Beman: A kidnapped woman from Greensin, daughter of Johann Beman, brought to Mousehole by slavers after it was freed. She is now learning to be a fire mage.

Mary: The new name of one of the prostitutes rescued from Warkworth. She is now a sailor on the *River Dragon*, one of the Saints and eventually a wife of Marianus Gerontas.

Masters, the: Animated skeletons of the old Dwarven Druids with the ability to use magic as air-mages. They may no longer exist, or there may be more somewhere.

Melissa Mason: Daughter of Goditha and Parminder, elder sister to Daniel.

Menas Philokales: One of three kataphractoi (heavy cavalry) from Darkreach who comes to join Mousehole and is sent straight into the fray against the Brothers.

Mongka: Tar-Khan of the Bison. He is known as Mongka the Greedy.

Murgrątt: Insak-div killed by Astrid in the attack on East Zarah.

Nacibdamiir (Noble Iron): Young Hobgoblin and chief of the village of Dhargev and of the Cenubarkincilari, the southern hobgoblins.

Naeve Milker: Former Freehold dairymaid and former slave who now runs the herds of Mousehole. She becomes an apprentice mage and marries Giles. Her first daughter is Peggy Farmer and her second is Beth.

Neil: A bard in Glengate.

Neon Chrysoloras: One of three kataphractoi (heavy cavalry) from Darkreach who comes to join Mousehole and is sent straight into the fray against the Brothers.

Nikephorus Cheilas: A senior Palace servant from Ardlark, he is now married to Valeria and father to her children, Angelina and Eugenia.

Nikolai, Father: Senior Orthodox priest at Saint Irene's Church in Warkworth.

Nokaj: Or Qorhi Nokaj Jirgin, grandfather of Hulagu, senior shaman to his tuman, the Jirgin and his clan, the Khünd Chono (or Dire Wolves).

Norbert Black: He is skilled as a blacksmith, weapons smith and armourer and kept as a slave in Mousehole. When he gets free he marries both Fortunata and Sajāh. His sons are Valentine (with Fortunata) and Bishal (with Sajāh). He later has the twins Bryan and Alice with Fortunata and another son, Huma with Sajāh.

Olympias Akritina: Basil's sister, a junior officer in the navy in charge of a small, fast scout and messenger boat. She becomes Captain of the *River Dragon* and a Darkreach Epilarch (small-unit commander) in charge of all Darkreach vessels beyond the Great Range. She marries Denizkartal, and their daughter is Thalassa.

Orn: One of the watchers on top of Neron Island killed by Ayesha.

Parminder: Assistant cook and sometimes dressmaker at Mousehole, she marries Goditha and is sister to Gurinder. Her daughter is Melissa Mason and her son is Daniel Mason.

Procopia Ampelina: Praetor of the Antikataskopeía in Ardlark and former commander of Basil.

Rabi'ah: A poor spinner and weaver from Ardlark. Her drunken father sold her into slavery. She is sent by her Imam to Mousehole.

Rahki Johar: Harijan servant from Haven. She was rescued from the Master's servants in Pavitra Phāṭaka.

Rani Rai: A former Havenite Battle Mage and now co-Princess of Mousehole. She has broken caste and is married to Theodora and has adopted Fear and is regarded as the father of Aikaterine.

Robin Fletcher: Former slave, fletcher and bowyer for Mousehole. He is married to Eleanor and they have adopted Aelfgifu, Gemma and Repent and have a daughter Bianca and twins Michael and Sara. He is the brother of Goditha.

Ruth: Former Freehold merchant and now teacher of the village children in Mousehole. She is married to Father Theodule and their identical twin sons are Joshua and Jeremiah.

Sabas: Insakharl sailor sent from Darkreach to help crew the *River Dragon*. He is married to Irene and their daughter is Polymnia.

Sajãh: From the Caliphate, she is the Seneschal of Mousehole under the Princesses. She is second wife of Norbert Black, adopted mother of Roxanna and Ruhayma and mother of Bishal & Huma.

Shilpa Sodaagar: A former Havenite trader, then a slave and now in Mousehole working on the *River Dragon*. She takes Vishal as her partner. Their son is Abhaidev.

Siglunda the Wise: A mage and midwife, Captain (village leader) of Wolfneck.

Simeon Alvarez, Father: Catholic cleric and werewolf who is born in Xanthia in the Newfoundland. He flees from there and ends up in Mousehole through the offices of the Bear people. He converts to being Orthodox and marries Danelis.

Simon, Father: Senior Orthodox priest in Wolfneck.

Simon of Richfield: A traveller and chronicler from before The Burning and even from before the Schism of the Church. He wrote a book called "My Travels Over The Land and Beyond".

Siramon: Tar-Khan of the Elephant Clan

Solveig Dagnesdottir: A skald or bard of Wolfneck.

Stefan: A young soldier from Evilhalt. He is now in charge of the militia of Mousehole and is married to Bryony and her cousin Adara. His son with Bryony are Aneurin ap Stefan and Tristan. His identical twin daughters with Adara are Finnabhair and Sinech.

Styliane, Drungarius: A Drakreach naval officer and former commander of Olympias.

Svein: Man of Wolfneck and "suitor" to Astrid. He is an ugly (very Kharlish appearance), violent drunkard and around 40 years old. Owns a ship and is a rival of Astrid's father. He is the Northern agent for the Masters.

Tabitha: Born in a farming hamlet near Erave Town and a former slave, she now lives in Mousehole.

Tarasios: Othrodox Metropolitan of Ardlark and the east of Darkreach.

Tãriq ibn Kasĩla: A quarryman from Silentochre. He becomes husband of Bilqĩs (their daughter is Zainab) and Yumn.

The Vengeance of the Lord is Mine Quester (Vengeance): Brotherhood scout and Inquisitor from the Flails of God who comes to Mousehole to spy on it. He is executed.

Theodora do Hrothnog: Great-great-granddaughter of Hrothnog. She is not entirely human, a mage and, at 120 years, is far older than the late teens that she appears to have. She is now Princess of Mousehole with her husband, Rani, and their adopted daughter Fear and daughter Aikaterine.

Theodora Lígo: Daughter of Carausius and eventual wife of Candidas.

Theodule, Brother: A former monk and now assistant to Father Christopher at Mousehole. He marries Ruth and their identical twin sons are Joshua and Jeremiah.

There Shall Be Lamentations: A slave girl from the Brotherhood brought to Camel Island to be sacrificed to establish a master pattern. She is usually called Lamentations.

Thomaïs: Insakharl sailor sent from Darkreach to help crew the *River Dragon*. She is married to Habib and their children are Delphinia and Isidore.

Thomas Akkers: A younger son and farmer from near Bulga. He comes to Mousehole seeking land and a wife. He marries Elizabeth and they have a daughter Virginia.

Thor Thorsteinsson: Sergeant of the Rangers of Wolfneck.

Thord: A shorter and broad humanoid of the species locally known as a Dwarf. He comes from Kharlsbane in the Northern Mountains, but is now Mousehole's Ambassador to the Dwarves. He rides a sheep called Hillstrider. He is known as the Crown-finder to the Dwarves and is engaged to Ragnilde.

Thorgrim Baldursson: The new Mayor of Dwarvenholme. He is tall and broad with grey hair and beard.

Thorstein, Father: Priest in Wolfneck and youngest brother of Astrid. He moves to Wolfneck.

Toluy: Tar-Khan of the Khünd Chono, the Dire Wolves.

Turn Away My Eyes From Beholding Vanity: A slave girl from the Brotherhood brought to Camel Island to be sacrificed to establish a master pattern. She is usually called Turn.

Tzachaz: A hunter of the Pack Hunter clan who helps Bianca and Hulagu defeat the bird demons and then escorts them to Evilhalt. They meet him again in Glengate where he acts as the messenger of the Mice to gather the clans.

Ulric: One of Svein's crew. He poses as a suitor from Warkworth to gain access to the valley to spy for the Masters. He is executed.

Umm: A slave of the bandits from a poor farming family in the Caliphate, she is now in Mousehole. She is now the senior wife of Atã ibn Rãfi. Her son is Achmed.

Uzun: A hunter of the Pack Hunter clan who helps Bianca and Hulagu defeat the bird demons and then escorts them to Evilhalt. They meet him again in Glengate where he acts as the messenger of the Mice to gather the clans.

Valeria: A former slave from Deeryas, she is now the servant of Rani and Theodora and has married Nikephorus. Mother of Angelina and Eugenia Cheilas. Her brother, James, joins her in the valley.

Vera Frakkvinne: A furrier in Wolfneck and a prominent citizen.

Verily I Rejoice in the Lord Tiller (Verily): A former Brotherhood slave and slave in Mousehole. She has married Aziz. Their sons are Saglamruh (Strong Spirit) and Sunmak (Gift), and their daughters are Qvavili (Flower) and Fear.

Verina Gabala: An Orthodox miller from Mistledross. She leaves Darkreach after she loses her family in an earthquake and ends up in Mousehole married to Adrian Digge.

Vishal Kapur: A young armsman from Haven. In the pay of the Master's servants, he is captured and then joins the Mice. He is taken as a partner by Shilpa. Their son is Abhaidev.

Will of the Lord Malachi, Sister: First Disciple of the Brotherhood of Believers; although subject to her husband Enoch Malachi, she is in charge of many of the functions of government.

Winifred: The new name of one of the prostitutes rescued from Warkworth. She is now a sailor on the *River Dragon*, one of the Saints and eventually a wife of Marianus Gerontas.

Yegu: Tar-Khan of the Snake Clan.

Yumn: Orphan carpet maker from Ardlark who became a prostitute to raise a dowry or get enough for a loom. She is sent by her Imam to Mousehole. She becomes junior wife to Tãriq.

Zafirah: A poor spinner and weaver from Ardlark who sells herself into slavery to pay the family debts. She is sent by her Mullah to Mousehole. She becomes junior wife to Atã and their son is Sughdĩ.

Zampea Styliana: She was the Drungarius (Commodore) of Olympias Akritas' original flotilla.

Zeenat Koirala: A Harijan and former prostitute from Haven.

Zoë Anicia: An Orthodox baker from Mistledross. She loses her family in an earthquake and ends up in Mousehole.

Zạmratejedehar (Emerald Dragon): Known as Zạmrat. Hob and daughter of Guk, a student at the school in Mousehole. The 'ạ' is a long 'aa' sound.

Glossary

Abbey Green: a village of the Brotherhood

Aberbaldie: the most eastern village of the Brotherhood on Gumin Creek, east of the Amity Forest

Adversaries: a group of the more psychically active Daveen who are the major protagonists behind the evil that is infesting Vhast

Aissa River: called the Aisi Darya in Khitan, this is the main river of the west of The Land. It runs from a spring near Glengate to the ocean at Ashvaria

Alat-kharl: one of the Kharl tribes of Darkreach, they are most usually found working in the trades or mining

Allah akbar: an Arabic phrase, "God is Great"

Allāh wadhu: an Arabic phrase, literally "the one God"

Ambrose, Saint: a Christian Saint, Feast Day 4th Quattro, he is patron of doctrinal purity and also of beekeepers

Amitan: a Khitan clan, that of the Bison

Amity, the Forest of: a small forested area that is only a trifle smaller than the Brotherhood that it protects from the Khitan

Anne, Saint: a Christian Saint, Feast day 25th October, she is patron of those who slay the undead and protect against evil, she is also the patron of those who return from the dead

Antdrudge: a town in the north of Darkreach where molotails and other flammables are made

Ante Dvīpa: an island in Pavitra Phāṭaka mainly inhabited by the lowest castes and foreigners, its name means End Island

Antikataskopeía: Darkreach "secret police", an arm of the military who are concerned both with criminal investigation and treason

Ariun Süm Morin Tsereg: a Khitan term for the Basilica Anthropoi, literally "temple horsemen"

Ardlark: a major city and capital of Darkreach

Arslan: a Khitan clan, that of the Lion

Ashvaria: the capital city of Freehold

Ayanga Gürvel: a Khitan clan, that of the Thunder Lizard

Azrael: a gargoyle brought to Mousehole by Father Christopher; despite the name, she is female. Gargoyles eat evil spirit creatures

Baga khana: a Khitan term for the independent villages, it literally means "little walls"

Bagts Anchin: a Khitan clan, that of the Pack Hunters

Baloo: a village of the Brotherhood

Barbara, Saint: a Christian saint, Feast day is 14th Duodecimus and she is patron of engineers and ironworkers.

Basilica Anthropoi: a Holy Order of warrior monks of the Orthodox Church west of the mountains. They are heavily armed and ride as kataphractoi or kynigoi depending on their role. They will bear the Chi-Rho on their shields and the leader of a group will often have a painted icon there as well.

Baerami River: a tributary of the Aissa Flow; in Khitan it is the Bermi Darya

Bear-folk: a group of humanoids, living just north of the Swamp, who have a high number of bear-based lycanthropes among their number

Betterberries: a small, prickly shrub found throughout The Land. Its berries, when eaten either fresh or dried, heal tiny amounts of damage (say a minor cut from a thorn). People need several for even a small knife cut.

Bidvictor: an independent village of the north on the Yagobe Rivulet

Bird Demon: a flying spirit creature with four sets of claws and a beak

Bonaventura, Saint: a Christian Saint, Feast Day 14th Quinque and patron of negotiators

Böö: the Khitan name for a shamen

Brahmin: the highest caste of Haven society, it is made up of priests and money-lenders (often through intermediaries); they are forbidden any physical labour

Brickshield: a Freehold town on the Baerami River

Brinkhold: a town in the south of Darkreach

Brodir Lind: the Brother Shield, a tavern in Wolfneck

Brotherhood, The: The Brotherhood of All Believers are militant semi-Christians of an extreme Puritan type with a focus on literal truth and rigid obedience

Bulga: an independent village on the north coast of The Land

Bürged: a Khitan clan, that of the Eagle

Burning, the: a dread disease that causes people to go mad and destroy things; less than one person in twenty survived the years that it raged

Butsin River: a fast-flowing river in Darkreach near Antdrudge

Caliphate: a Muslim Kingdom nestled high in the south of the Great Range

Camel Island: an island near Camelback

Camelback: a village in the southwest of Freehold, it was once known as Khmel

Cangi Creek: one of the main watercourses draining the Amity Forest

Cenubarkincilari: a small Hobgoblin tribe in the Southern Mountains. The name means "Southern Raiders"

Choli: the blouse top worn by women under a sari; it usually has short sleeves and buttons at the front, leaving a bare midriff

Christopher, Saint: Christian Saint, Feast Day 25th September, patron of travellers and against water, tempest and sudden death

Curator Pyrkagión: title of the Darkreach official in charge of the Megas Fabrika, it literally means "Keeper of the Fires" in Greek

Cuthbert, Saint: Christian Saint, Feast Day 20th Tertius and patron of herdsmen, shepherds, and the town of Topwin in Freehold

Cyril and Methodius, Saints: Orthodox Christian Saints, Feast Day 11th Quinque, they are patrons of those who defend the faith and of translators

Dadanth: a jungle fungus that can be made into an unguent that repels insects

Dagh Ordu: Khitan name for a monolith in the Southern Plains; it has a ruined city on the top and a resident dragon inside

Darkreach: this is a multi-racial Empire that takes up the eastern third of The Land east of the Great Range; it is ruled (and has been since known time began) by Hrothnog

Darkreach money: the base unit of currency is the Nummus (N), a tin piece of 20g. Smaller coins are the Centi-follis (copper 2.5g, .01N), half-follis (copper, 12.5g, .05N), and Follis (copper, 25g, .1N). The larger coins are a Trachy (billion, a silver/copper alloy, 25g and 3,75N), a Numismata (silver, 2.5g and 15N), a Sesterces (silver, 25g, 150N), a Denarius (gold, 4.5g, 450N), and an Imperial (gold, 20g, 2,000N)

Dating: years run over a 48-year cycle; with the twelve zodiacal signs that are used on Vhast along with the elements of Earth, Air, Fire and Water. There are twelve months of equal length, each having six weeks of six days. The first parts of this story take part in the Year of the Water Monkey. A year thus has 432 days, so a year on Vhast is nearly a fifth longer than a Terran year. A person who is fifteen on Vhast will be eighteen on Earth

Daveen: one of the long-lived space-faring races contesting over the fate of Vhast; when they have visited Terra, they have given rise to legends of both vampires and demons

Devartetilcu Yamyam: the name that Ariadne's artillery group call themselves, the Hobgoblin phrase, "wall-striking monsters"

Dhargev: a Hobgoblin village in the Southern Mountains, it is the main settlement of the Cenubarkincilari tribe and the name means "Our Home"

Demaresque Creek: the stream, more a small river than a creek, that Southpoint lies on

Dimashq: capital of the Caliphate

Distance: common measures are a cubit of 6 hands (61cm), a fathom of 3 cubits (1.83m), a chain of 20m (or 100 links), a mile of 1,000 fathoms (1.83km) and a league of 3 miles (9,000 cubits). A pace is an informal measure and around 1m long

Dromond: the large warships of Darkreach that use a combination of sail and oar or, rarely, are propelled by their own magic. They are the most powerful warcraft around The Land

Drungarius: a Darkreach naval rank equivalent to a Commodore or a junior Admiral

Dwarvenholme: the legendary home of the Dwarves, it was lost a long time ago and then found and freed by the Mice

Dymphna, Saint: Christian Saint, Feast Day 15 Quinque, she is the patron of runaways, victims of incest, and nervous disorders

East Zarah: the tallest of the mountains on Neron Island and the most southerly and eastern of several peaks

Emeel amidarch baigaa khümüüs: a Khitan phrase describing themselves. It literally means "people who live in a saddle"

Epilarch: a Darkreach naval rank; there is no exact current Terran equivalent, but usually commands a flotilla or a small ad hoc group of vessels

Erave, Lake: almost a small sea, the lake lies on the Rhastaputra River to the west of the mountains

Erave Town: a town on the southern shore of Lake Erave

Ergüül: a Khitan word for the smallest "units" or patrols

Evilhalt: a town at the very northern tip of Lake Erave

Exarkhos ton Basilikon: the title of the Commander of the Basilica Anthropoi

False Sweetmary: this is a jungle herb, the roots of which make a fairly reliable abortifacient potion

Fenwick: a village of the Brotherhood

Flails of God: the Inquisitors and scouts of the Brotherhood of Believers, they are taken from among orphans and some selected children of slaves as infants and then raised as fanatic believers

Forest Watch: a Darkreach outpost on a large hill in the Great Forest, on a clear day it has a view of most of much of the central mountains area and, in particular, the approaches to the Darkreach Gap

Freehold: a kingdom that takes up much of the west of The Land, "sharing" some of the land uneasily with the Khitan. Its Queen is Daphne IV Acer, Baroness Goldentide. She is unmarried and has sat on the throne for ten years

Frosthill: this is more a fortress than a town. It has a village in the northeast of Freehold and is the usual first stop for caravans coming from Glengate

Ganesh: an elephant-headed Hindu god of wisdom and knowledge. He is often called "the remover of obstacles" and he rides a mouse

George, Saint: Christian Saint, Feast Day 23 Quattro, patron of cavalry and those who fight against demons and dragons

Giant's Drop: a very large mountain in the south of the Great Range

Gil-Gand-Rask: a large island in the Southern Seas

Glengate: a town to the west of Lake Erave on the path to Freehold

Great Range: the main mountain chain that runs from north to south across The Land

Greatkin: the capital of the Brotherhood, it lies on Cangi Creek

Greensin: a town north-west of Evilhalt. It is the home of the senior of the western Metropolitans of the Orthodox Church

Grono: a coastal settlement in the east of Darkreach

Hand: as a basic unit of measure it is made up of six fingers (1.7cm each) and so is 10.2cm long. Six make a cubit

Haven: a nation at the mouth of the Rhastaputra River

Healbush: this is a mountain herb that can be made into a curative potion with a spicy taste

Hippolytus, Saint: a Christian saint, his Feast day is 8 Tertius and he is the patron saint of horses

Hugron pir: a chemical mix that we would call Greek Fire or perhaps napalm

Iba Bay: a broad and deep bay formed to the east of the vast delta of the Swamp rivers

Insakharl: this is not a distinct race, but a name given to those who have part-Human and part-Kharl ancestry

Insak-div: the largest of the Darkreach races, and often referred to in the West as Dark Trolls, they are over twice as tall as a Human and a lot broader

Inshallah: an Arabic word that best translates as "if God wills it"

Irene, Saint: Christian Saint, Feast Day is 32nd Duodecimus, she is the patron of miners and quarrymen

Ironcone: a Dwarven town in the South-West Mountains with a large supply of iron

Isci-kharl: one of the Kharl tribes of Darkreach. They are large, strong and not overly bright

Jagganath: an aspect of Vishnu, Lord of the Universe who, with his brother Balabhadra and sister Subhadra, rides a chariot (Juggernaut). There is a major Festival, Rath Yatra, associated with him

Jijig Khushuu: a Khitan clan, that of the Axe-beaks

Jirgah: a Khitan word that best translate as 'conference', but could also be used to mean 'meeting' or even just 'decision making body'

Junia, Saint: Christian Saint, Feast Day 30th Secundus, she is the patron of prisoners

Kãfirũn: Arabic word 'Unbeliever'

Kapetánios: a Darkreach naval rank, 'Captain'

Kara-Khitan or Khitan: a group of mounted tribes who claim and occupy most of the plains

Kartikeya: Hindu God of War

Kataphract or Kataphractoi: a heavy cavalryman (or woman) from Darkreach, they ride on armoured horses and are themselves armoured, riding in close formation and employing a wide variety of weapons

Kessog, Saint: Christian Saint, Feast Day 10th Tertius, patron of those who fight monsters on land. Eventually taken as a Patron Saint by Astrid

Kha-Khan: The head of the Ayanga Gürvel, the Clan of the Thunder Lizard and leader of the Khitan, Chinggiz Arghun

Khanatai gazar khümüüs: a Khitan phrase that means 'town dwellers', literally 'people of the walled places'

Kharl: one of the Humanoid races of Vhast, they are the most common form of Humanoid after Humans. They vary greatly in appearance, but always have some animalistic features

Khristed itgegchid: Khitan name for Christians

Khün khanatai: a Khitan phrase used for all non-Khitan, literally 'walled in people'

Khünd Chono: a Khitan clan, that of the Dire Wolf

Khuyagt morin: a Khitan term for kataphracts

Kindjal: a parallel-bladed long dagger or short sword that is good for both stabbing and slashing

Köle: Khitan term that means something similar to captive or slave. It is for a term that is usually five years

Kshatya: an upper Havenite caste. It consists of warriors and rulers

Kynigoi: riders with any level of armour riding unarmoured horses. Their primary role is skirmishing and harassing as well as scouting. They mainly use bows in combat

Leatherwing: a furred flying lizard. They can be found in most areas, but particularly in the mountains and on the seacoast

Leat: the channel or viaduct that brings water from an upstream dam to the top of an overshoot mill wheel and provides a head of water

Living God, Church of the: a Darkreach religion, mainly practiced among the Kharl races, which directly worships Hrothnog as God-Emperor

Mary Magdalene, Saint: Christian Saint, her Feast Day is 4th Quinque and she is patron of sinners and those hoping for redemption

Maskirovka: a Darkspeech word peculiar to the Wolfneck dialect, it means a deception, usually a military one

Māta: Arabic for 'kill', we get the word 'mate' as in 'checkmate' from it

Mawmas: Arabic word for a drab, a whore or a slut

Megas Fabrika: the 'Great Factory' that is the heart of Antdrudge; it makes flammable and explosive ordinance, and fireworks

Menna, Saint: Christian Saint, Feast Day 15th November, patron of traders

Methul River: the river that comes out of the Darkreach Gap and heads north to reach the sea at Wolfneck

Mice: usually refers to an inhabitant of the village of Mousehole

Michael, Saint: Christian Saint, Feast day is 1st Undecim and he is patron of both graveyards and victory

Mogoi: a Khitan Clan, that of the Snake

Molotail: these are glass containers of hugron pir, a hypergolic liquid, we could call it Greek Fire, or napalm

Monteagle Creek: a tributary of Sundercud Creek

Mori: a Khitan word for the animal and clan of the Horse

Mousehole: a hidden village in the Southern Mountains that was freed from slavers, the inhabitants are now trying to destroy the beings that enslaved it

Mulwherry River: an ever-shifting river in Darkreach near Pain

Narjee: in full Qorchi Narjee Khadagin, a Khitan bard who brings the news of the Brotherhood to Nokaj, her tale is told in the short story *Rousing*.

Narwood: a village of the Brotherhood

Nekulturny: an insulting word in the Darkspeech of Wolfneck that means, literally, that a person is uncultured

Neron Island: an island to the north of The Land, the last inhabited island before the ice. The village of Skrice is there

Nicholas, Saint: Christian Saint, Feast Day 3rd Tertius, patron of perfumers and of children

Nithling: an insulting word in the Darkspeech of Wolfneck that means, roughly, that a person is nothing and beneath notice

Northern Waste: one of the names given in the north of The Land for the inhabited Artic regions

Oban Forest: the only major forest in Freehold; while it is called the Great Forest by Freehold, but is a tiny and tended fraction of the real Great Forest in size

Oban River: a river, largely in Freehold, that runs from the South-West Mountains to the ocean at Ashvaria

Oirmt Reach: a long and shallow stretch of water on the southern coast of Darkreach

Old Gods: a name for the Adversaries used in the north

Oldike: a Dwarven town in the South-West Mountains

Örnödiin: a Khitan word for Freehold, it literally means 'Westerners'

Orthros: the first Orthodox service of the morning, it usually starts before sunrise

Outville: an independent village of the north coast

Övs: the Khitan word for 'grass', it can also be used to describe the territory of a group

Owendale: the southernmost of the villages of the Brotherhood on the west coast

Pain: a town in Darkreach

Pancake Pali: this is a Festival the night before Lent, it is a party that uses up the last of the things that will not be used for the next month until Easter and that will not keep

Pandonia, Saint: Christian Saint, Feast day 26th Sixtus, she is the patron of goose girls and other female herders

Panic: the smaller moon of Vhast, it is less than half the size of Terror

Paradēśī: Hindi for an outsider, a foreigner

Pattern: a darkly-enchanted design used by the Masters to contact their minions

Pavitra Phāṭaka: also known as Sacred Gate. It is the capital of Haven

Peace Tower: a village and fortification of the Brotherhood

Pesh-kabz: a dagger with a t-shaped cross-section that goes in a curve from a needle point to being a couple of fingers-width. It is specifically designed to penetrate mail, but works well on finding a gap in most armour. It is ideal for killing from behind

Philip, Saint: Christian Saint, Feast Day 3rd Quinque, he is the patron of pastrychefs and hatters

Ploi_gós: a term used in Darkreach as the job title for a harbour pilot

Pulletop Creek: a watercourse that drains the west of the plains, it goes into the Western Ocean through the village of Warkworth with a waterfall

Rangers: what passes for a military in the village of Wolfneck, they are scouts and hunters more than anything else and fight from cover with bows if forced to fight

Rath Yatra: 13th Quinque, a Festival associated with Jagganath, an aspect of Vishnu, the Festival of Chariots

Rhastaputra River: the main river draining the mountains and area just to the west of them in the south

Rising Mud: a village in the Swamp built on islands of mud behind wooden walls

River Dragon: a brigantine owned by the Mice and Captained by Olympias

Sacred Gate: see Pavitra Phāṭaka

Samalaiṅgika: Hindi for a lesbian

Sanie eidan al-thaqab: Arabic for a matchmaker

Saraswati: Hindu Goddess and wife of Brahma, she is the Goddess of knowledge and the arts

Sari: a form of Havenite female dress which largely consists of a long wound length of cloth

Seardip: the most easterly town in Darkreach

Sebastian, Saint: Christian Saint, Feast Day 18th December, patron of archers

Shaitan: Arabic word for the devil

Shayk: an Arabic word that means, roughly, a wise man

Shear-legs: two long and strong lengths of timber that can have a block and tackle mounted to them, thus serving as a crane, particularly for putting masts in ships

Shepherd: not only normal shepherds, but also the only Dwarven cavalry. They are mounted on large sheep

Shing-zu: a very long-lived, and winged, space-faring race who built and populated Vhast, they are one of the races now contesting over its fate. When they have visited Terra they gave rise to legends of Angels

Shunakhai: a Khitan word that means 'greedy'

Silentochre: a town at the head of the Oirmt Reach

Simon, Saint: Orthodox Saint, Feast Day 15th Quinque, he is the patron of mages

Skrice: the only large village on Neron Island

Sleepwell: a forest tree that can be made into a potion that acts as if the drinker has had a night's sleep

Sluggard: one of Bianca's horses, a large pack animal

Sophia, Saint: Orthodox Saint, Feast Day32nd Secundus, patron of charity and sacrifice for others

South-West Mountains: the only real hills in the west of The Land and home to several Dwarven villages

Southpoint: the southernmost town in Darkreach

Sowonja: this is the language of the Brotherhood. It is derived from Latin and the "j" is pronounced as "h"

Spanker: the name of the rearmost mast and the sails on it on the *River Dragon*

Sparrow and Bull, The: a tavern in Glengate

Spilk: a tough and shimmering cloth woven from the web of a certain type of jungle spider and prized both by the wealthy and certain types of mages

Sundercud Creek: a stream that runs along the southern edge of the Amity Forest

Swamp, The: the common name for the Confederation of the Free

Tagma: a Darkreach Army unit, it is roughly equivalent to a battalion

Tangarag Khaalgach: a Khitan phrase, literally "oath keepers", a title of great honour among the Khitan.

Teló_ni_s: Aajob title in Darkreach for the person responsible for assessing and collecting customs fees and similar tolls and charges

Tenger Sünsnüüd: Khitan for "Spirits of the Sky". The central deities of Khitan religion, they are those who placed the Khitan down on the plains and who gave them The Land

Terror: the larger moon of Vhast, it provides over twice the light of Panic

Tar-Khan: the head of a Khitan Clan.

Teló_ni_s: a Darkreach official in charge of just customs and landing fees

Thomas: Saint: Christian Saint, Feast day 5th Quinque, he is the patron of those who seek answers

Toppuddle: a major town in Freehold near the South-West Mountains, it was once known as Topudle

Twelfth Night: a Christian Feast twelve days after Christmas

Umard Sünsnüüd: a Khitan phrase, literally "totem spirits", that means the personifications of the totem animals of the clans

Unasanid: a Khitan word, "riders"

Ünee Gürvel: a Khitan clan, that of the Cow-lizard

Ursula, Saint: Christian Saint and patron of virgins, Feast Day is the 6th of September. Bianca has taken her as her patron saint

Üstei akh düü: a Khitan phrase for their totem beasts of the Clan, it means "fur siblings"

Üzen yadalt ursgai: the Khitan name for Sundercud Creek, it means "Stream of hate"

Üzen yaddag düürsen: the Khitan phrase that refers to the Brotherhood, it means "hate-filled"

Varuna: Hindu god of water and oceans

Várvaros: a term in the Greek of Darkreach "foreigner" or "barbarian"

Vyāpārī Dvīpa: the Merchant's Island in Pavitra Phāṭaka

Warialda River: a river, largely in Freehold, that runs from Oldike to the Oban River

Warkworth: a free village in the west of The Land on Pulletop Creek, it lies on a sea-cliff between The Brotherhood and Freehold

Week: each week on Vhast has six days. Generally, across The Land, these are given the names: Firstday, Deutera, Pali, Tetarti, Dithlau and Krondag. Kron is the name given to the sun. The definitions and roots of some of these names are unknown

Wheel of chariots: a wheel is a term for a group of eight chariots, the smallest unit generally seen

Windin Cove: a wide bay more than a cove, at the head of which lies Pavitra Phāṭaka

Winifred, Saint: Christian Saint, Feast day 19th Primus, her patronage is of healing, particularly of those injured in combat

Wolfneck: a village of part-Kharls in the north of The Land. It is the original home to Astrid

Yagobe Rivulet: this is a small river on the north coast of The Land

Yavakh Bolomjgüi Gazar: Khitan name for the Swamp, "Land Where You Cannot Ride"

Yųmųkimşe: Hobgoblin word for Humans, it means "Soft One"

Zaan: a Khitan clan, that of the Elephant

Zim Island: an island in the south that is completely covered in an unnamed, ruined city and dense jungle

Zita, Saint: a Christian Saint, Feast Day 27th Tertius, she is the patron of house-wives and servants